LAURA TAYLOR NAMEY

The Library of Lost Things

Recycling programs for this product may not exist in your area.

ISBN-13: 978-1-335-90446-1

The Library of Lost Things

Copyright © 2019 by Laura Taylor Namey

This edition published by arrangement with Harlequin Books S.A.

For questions and comments about the quality of this book, please contact us at CustomerService@Harlequin.com.

Inkyard Press
22 Adelaide St. West, 40th Floor
Toronto, Ontario M5H 4E3, Canada
www.InkyardPress.com

Printed in U.S.A.

Not just for Edward.

But for that first, perfect look on his face when I said, "I've decided to write a book."

One

Unwelcome Mat

"'…let her cover the mark as she will,
the pang of it will be always in her heart.'"

—NATHANIEL HAWTHORNE, *THE SCARLET LETTER*

I'd read enough stories to know how they worked. You had your faraway settings and swoonworthy characters—extra points for tossing in a manic-pixie dream girl or stubbly faced bad boy. Great books give us spine-tingling plots or twists that reach right into your lungs and snatch your next breath. I knew about those; I knew about stories. Enough to realize I was sitting in the middle of one and already hated the ending.

"Why does San Diego insist on forgetting September's supposed to be chilly?" my best friend, Marisol, asked. "Fall means boots and scarves and sweaters, not tank tops. Ugh. Fix it."

"Just when I'm all out of weather wands and genie lamps." There was no weight in my words. I watched the painters taping and spraying my apartment building with new storm-gray paint.

"Darcy?"

I blinked myself back to her, smiling, turning worries into daydreams. And my friend was right—we were wilting with the sweltering afternoon. "Our" shaded courtyard table belonged to all of the tenants at 316 Hoover Avenue, but Marisol and I spent more time here than anyone else. Three benches curved like melon slices around a pedestal base. We hogged them all, scattering our lives across the chipped mosaic tile top. We rarely hung out inside my apartment, whether my mother was home, or not.

I grabbed another handful of popcorn just as Mrs. Newsome appeared in the doorway to unit 15B with her white poodle, Peaches. "Four o'clock," I told Marisol, and tipped my chin.

"On the dot and caftan-ready."

The entire complex could set their clocks by my neighbor and her floral print housedresses. As she locked the door, a bird swooped low across the landing. My eyes snapped to Peaches jerking away from her owner, dragging her leash toward the staircase.

"I'll get her, Mrs. Newsome!" I yelled, leaping up from the bench. I managed to swoop up Peaches from the bottom step.

"Thank you, Darcy!" my neighbor called. "I'll be right down!"

Dreamy-eyed, Marisol reached out and plunked the panting dog onto her lap.

Even a runaway pup didn't stop Mrs. Newsome from doing what she always did. Her feet crossed the landing and just as she reached my apartment, her steps slowed. She'd never want to be accused of snooping, but she still raised the brim of her straw hat to peer into my unit's front window. Maybe today the curtains wouldn't be so tightly drawn. Maybe this morning my mom had left a crack in the blinds.

Not today. Not ever.

I reached over and scratched Peaches behind one ear, knowing full well it wasn't just her owner who wondered about my apartment. About why we never propped open our door in the summer like the other tenants. Did they also wonder why our doorway looked different? Missing potted plants and a pretty welcome mat—but rarely brown shipping boxes?

Marisol sighed, flicking one fingernail under the poodle's white chin and snuggling her close. "I need another dog. One like this little boo."

"Right," I said on a short laugh, picturing her four siblings and two German shepherds. "Your house is just begging for one more thing with a heartbeat."

"Afternoon, girls." Mrs. Newsome flopped down next to us, helping herself to popcorn. I slid the bag closer. *Have at it, lady.*

"Oh, isn't it wonderful?" Mrs. Newsome gestured across the U-shaped courtyard to the units already covered with fresh, new gray. She grabbed Peaches from Marisol and set her on the ground. "You stay now." And to us, "Twenty-four years I've lived with that putrid green. Who knows how many more if it wasn't for Mr. Hodge finally selling the building. Only one month and new paint already. Have you and your mama met Thomas?"

"Not yet." I fanned myself with my English notebook.

"Well, he's awful nice. A go-getter, too. Not like that good-for-nothing nephew Mr. Hodge had managing for him. Barely showed his face around here." She munched on popcorn. "I'm sure Thomas will get around to your door soon. That's just the kind of man he is. Personable." She looked left, then right, leaning in like her next words were top secret. "He clued me in on some of the interior upgrades coming up. Besides the new railing after the paint, you know."

My face must've signaled I didn't know because Mrs. Newsome quirked a brow. "Didn't you read the flyer? Why, Thomas had them in the mailboxes early this morning. Like I said, a go-getter."

She waved goodbye, walking away with Peaches trotting after her, trapping me in a room where the air was slowly leaking out. Only I was outside, a planet's worth of oxygen around me.

I dabbed sweaty fingers on my black tee and nudged Marisol's binder. "Didn't you hear her?"

"What, that chatterbox? I usually tune her out." Marisol tossed popcorn between her fuchsia-colored lips and returned to her math homework. "I dunno. Blah, blah *Thomas*. Whatever, whatever *railing*."

During times like these, the differences between Marisol's life and mine showed the strongest. While my half-Cuban, half-Mexican friend spent time pondering treadmill versus spin bike, or what shade of denim best matched her coral top, I had to worry about the fact that now we had an on-site apartment manager who was actually doing his job. Maybe too well for my mother and me and our upstairs unit with no welcome mat.

Fingers tapped my shoulder. Marisol scooted all the way over to my bench. "Okay, spill. You went all white. And you're holding books again."

I glanced down, realizing my hands had crept into my black bag and reached for books. *David Copperfield* in my left, half resting on the tile. *The Scarlet Letter* in the curled fingers of my right hand.

I dropped the Dickens classic but kept *The Scarlet Letter*

close. "The paint is only the start. They're going to find out. Then where will we go?" *Mom and I. Her and me. Us.*

"The paint? What do you mean?"

But *I*, Darcy Jane Wells, could only watch as two workers appeared, draping drop cloths over bushes. All eyes pinned on to us from across the courtyard—we'd have to pack up soon. But not now. Not just yet. Besides, what did a few paint splatters matter to *this* table? Already timeworn and chipped, we'd also contributed to its demise with root beer stains and "oopsie" red nail polish blobs. A teeny black heart Marisol Sharpied years ago christened the edge. Next to it, you could still make out the five-pointed star I'd penned.

"Darcy. What is it?"

I scored my thumbnail over the brittle tile grout. "Only my real-life bedtime story."

"More like one of those sick and twisted fairy tales, by the looks of you," Marisol said.

"Yeah. It's the one where 316 Hoover gets a new owner and a new manager who now lives on-site," I said, then told her all the rest—how if the new manager could see everything, he'd want to know everything, too. After all the outdoor work was done, he'd want to make changes to the insides of the apartments. Thomas would have to inspect each unit. And workers would come.

"They'll have to go inside," Marisol whispered.

"Twelve years we've lived here. And Mr. Hodge always renewed our leases without doing anything. No inspections. Not even a phone call." I took a long sip from my water bottle, swept the cold plastic across my forehead. "Besides Mom and me, the only two people who have set foot inside that apartment in four years are you…and Marco."

Marisol braced my shoulders. "Don't start this again, okay? Marco's glad to help."

"He shouldn't have to *help*." My voice thickened but stayed low. "He shouldn't have to come all the way over here at night because my dishwasher's leaking."

"What, it's *maybe* twenty minutes from his dorm to your door."

"It's not about the drive." Other tenants called maintenance when their fixtures broke. *We* bought parts we couldn't afford and Marisol's engineering whiz/UCSD academic star brother did the work without anyone knowing. Sometimes, even without my mother knowing. "Even without the interior upgrades, our lease is still up in six months. And when this new Thomas guy comes to inspect our unit, or someone like Mrs. Newsome finally gets wind of what's behind our front door and blabs, there's no way they'll rent to us again. We won't get a decent reference to go somewhere else. And we can't go back to my grandmother's. Not ever."

"You'll find a way."

"Because you say so?" My life wasn't fabric my seamstress best friend could drape around my frame. Stitch into a perfect dress.

"*Yes*, because I say so," she said, like that was Bible enough.

The Scarlet Letter in my hand had a black cover with a red scripted *A* in the center. My mother wore an imaginary letter, too. One she'd branded herself with. "*She* has to want to find a way," I told Marisol.

My friend nodded. "She's gotten better, right? Even a little bit after you guys—"

"A little better is what you see now, behind that door. That's not enough to get our lease renewed. What am I missing with her? Like there's a huge piece, right in front of me, but I can't see it."

"Yeah, I know, D. I know." Marisol reached around me for her turquoise leather tote. She pulled out packs of gum, flinging them across the table. Two kinds of mint, cinnamon, strawberry, orange, classic bubble gum.

If there was anything Marisol loved more than fashion, it was gum. Maybe she thought her silly obsession would distract me. If so, it would be just like her—trying to cover my sticky pieces with bright wrapping and silver foil.

She jiggled the cinnamon pack and arched her brows, but I waved it away. "I'm good. Were you planning on serving gum to my whole building?"

"No-wuh," she mumbled. Chomped. Worked two sticks of the mint flavor around her mouth until they softened. "Just presenting options. Besides, it's a proven fact that chewing gum helps you think better." Her eyes flickered. "Speaking of thinking, Word of the Day. Go."

"Now? But—"

"Don't know why you're even protesting. You can't resist and probably already have one picked out."

"Fine." We'd played this game for years. It was my job to provide the words, the more obscure the better. The fact that Marisol never came up with the correct definitions never stopped her from asking. And asking. "Word of the Day is *muckspout*."

"Monkspout?" she questioned, snapping the gum with her tongue.

"No, muckspout."

Marisol put on her best scholar face and twirled her finger around her ear, like she was making parts move inside.

Yes, this was my life.

She straightened her posture. "Muckspout. Definition— someone who routinely drops small articles in the space between your driver's seat and the center console. Such as combs, water bottle caps, or hair ties."

"You're the poster child for that condition, but it's called 'doing too many things while driving.'"

She wrinkled her nose. "All right, what does it mean?"

I fanned myself with one of my books. "Someone who uses too much obscene language."

"No. Way."

"Truth."

"This one, I'll actually remember." Marisol tried out her best muckspout display, curse after glorious curse flowing out over cracked blue and green tiles.

I gave her a round of applause.

She bowed gracefully. "Well, that was fun. Now we need to see the flyer your popcorn-mooch neighbor was yammering about. Wherezit? You get the mail yet?"

I shook my head. Another thing my mother should have done.

"I'll go." She plunged one hand inside my bag. "I *swear*, if there's another book in here..." She missed my pointed glare as she fished out my keys. And when Marisol Robles and her designer denim cutoffs left for the mailboxes, she turned the courtyard into a fashion show, strutting like the models she dreamed of dressing one day. Walnut-brown hair, raked with sunny highlights, tumbled over her shoulders. Music played in all her movements, a samba in her steps.

Watching her, I couldn't help seeing my own body in the mirror of my oldest friend. Her curved, petite form made all five foot nine inches of my legs and torso seem even longer. Height did have its advantages—peering over crowds, reaching items on shelves, buying jeans off the rack with no hemming—but sometimes I had to work at arranging my limbs inside this world. While Marisol was shaped like a flame, I was built like a fire pole.

Mail in tow, Marisol returned to the bench, drawing bare

knees up to her chin. I separated the bills I'd worry about later and read the new manager's orange flyer. Just like Mrs. Newsome said, upgrades to the exterior and common areas would start first. Tenants were told to mind children and pets while workers installed a shiny new railing next week.

"You don't think they'll get rid of this table, do you? Our table?" Marisol asked.

I traced her little black heart and my tiny star on the edge in front of us. They'd faded over time, but we always knew where to find them. "Would majorly suck if they did."

She swept her gaze around, then removed the minty gum wad from her mouth and pressed it underneath the concrete top. "Something to remember me by."

Marisol giggled. I smiled. And then we laughed and laughed, so deeply it burned a tunnel down my throat and beat against my ribs.

We were swiping at tears when the jolting crash sounded. Our heads snapped upward, toward the only possible source. It could've been anything—glass, furniture, pottery—or even all three. But it hadn't come from just anywhere. We both knew it came from my apartment.

I frowned at Marisol, the small moment of laughter already a fading memory. I grabbed my keys. "Wait here," I said, swinging my legs over the bench.

She stood, too. "I'm coming."

"No."

"It doesn't bother me, Darcy. Just let me help."

"I need to go alone. Please?"

She exhaled a long sigh, her shoulders slumping. "Okay."

I shot up the stairs, without the use of the rickety railing. My key turned a lock, opening a door into a life only a handful of people could ever know about. A life with no welcome mat.

Two

Book-Shaped Heart

"'Well, I don't want to be anyone but myself, even if I go uncomforted by diamonds all my life,' declared Anne."

—L. M. MONTGOMERY, *ANNE OF GREEN GABLES*

Every day since my seventh birthday, that first shock of reality followed me into my apartment. Covered windows transformed the room into a black-and-white movie. The smells struck hard—cardboard and plastic, the tangy rubber of new sneakers. Throat-itching dust I could never clean fast enough. I smelled something new since this morning when I left for school. Dry dog food? A bag must've ripped open, one of maybe five stacked against the wall. They'd been on sale last week at a huge markdown, so naturally, she *had* to buy them.

Except...we didn't have a dog.

Somewhere, inside this den of unspeakable clutter, I would find a hoarder. My mother.

I flipped the lights, stepping around the newest pile of shipping boxes into what psychologists referred to as a goat tunnel. A few goat tunnels ran through our home—uncluttered passages chronic hoarders often left clear, where you could actually walk. This particular passage led from the front door through the living room, stopping at our tiny kitchen.

Mom owned dozens of baskets and vases for flowers she never picked. We hardly used tin cans, but we had eight can openers. Enough sheets and linens waited for twenty beds, when we only had two bedrooms. Cases of CDs and bargain bin movies lined the apartment. Dated VCR tapes and speakers, all in a silent home.

But wouldn't they make great gifts someday? One day, someone might need them.

I passed crates containing enough brushes, hair dryers, and curling irons to service the entire Miss America pageant. Bundles of unread magazines, with recipes she couldn't wait to make, if only she cooked. I inched by the blue tweed sofa, where she'd carved enough room for one, maybe two people. Mismatched pillows and knitted throws blanketed the rest of the space. We had one working TV you could watch, but only if you angled your head *just so* around the piles of piles. Six Bubble-Wrapped TVs stood like sentries along one wall. Shelves jumbled with cables and cords and boxes heaped with office supplies. Dozens of picture frames held no photos.

My stomach clenched when I finally found my mother— one Andrea Wells—bent over the kitchen counter, her elbows perched on the blue Formica. She rested her chin in both hands. A vodka bottle lay on its side, contents drip-dripping from its long neck onto the beige tiled floor. Near my mother's forearm, a glass was stained with red lipstick.

My eyes trailed to the cause of the crash and commotion: two dining room chairs had toppled over, and the mass of plates, stacked head-high on the counter this morning, lay in shattered pieces across the floor.

The loss of the plates was nothing, really. After all, Mom had collected at least thirty full sets of china, enough to service a grand dinner party for guests who would never come. Still, the loss would mean everything to her.

"Darcy. I… I'm sorry." Her voice wobbled and sloshed, like the alcohol she'd emptied from the glass. But how many times over? How much had she had to drink?

I couldn't bring myself to speak yet, so I focused on getting her settled. I pulled one of the fallen chairs to the counter through shards of broken china and folded her into it with some difficulty. She was long and thin like me, but moving her was akin to uprooting a statue. I stared into her brown, unfocused eyes; she'd drunk her expertly applied makeup into a clown face of raccoon eyeliner, feathered lipstick, and runny mascara.

Although my mother drank sometimes, she wasn't an alcoholic. Enough counseling and professional analysis had concluded that Mom didn't need the alcohol itself. She didn't need the routine oblivion of the drink. She overdosed on *things*. Our home was wasted with them.

"So sorry. Darcy, you know, baby."

"Yes, I know."

"Read to me," she said while I picked up the vodka bottle. "Just a little."

She always asked me to read aloud when she was drunk. *Only* when she was drunk. For years, she'd only tolerate books—the sight of them, the melody of their narrative—when her mind was clouded and delirious. This, from an English major who'd taught me to read at three years old.

There were no books nearby, none anywhere in this part of our house. She had her reasons for that. But I didn't need to hold a book to read to her. I had enough literature inside me to recite it by heart: a storehouse full of pages and passages.

"What do you want today?" I asked her.

"Something from *Emma*." Mom usually asked for Jane Austen until she woke the next day, hungover and remembering she hated books.

But I loved them. I could see the text.of *Emma* in my mind, clear as a photo. I closed my eyes and zoomed in on the novel like a lens, in a way no one has ever been able to explain. Least of all, me.

Since kindergarten, my mind has been a story bank. I read and read, and I remember.

After a deep sigh, I recited one of my favorite passages from *Emma*.

"While they talked, they were advancing towards the carriage; it was ready; and, before she could speak again, he had handed her in. He had misinterpreted the feelings which had kept her face averted, and her tongue motionless."

I stepped around my mother and picked up the other chair. "'They were combined only of anger against herself, mortification, and deep concern,'" I continued as I poured the remaining vodka into the sink, stopping before I threw the empty bottle away. She'd remember and ask for it, would freak out over its absence. Instead, I placed it under the sink, where twenty other liquor bottles stood, hearing her voice inside my head: *They'll make such nice vases one day.*

Where to even start with the broken plate disaster? I hauled out the trash can and began with the largest pieces. I recited;

"He had turned away, and the horses were in motion. She continued to look back, but in vain; and soon, with what appeared unusual speed, they were half way down the hill, and everything left far behind. She was vexed beyond what could have been expressed—almost beyond what she could conceal."

My mother's head lolled, eyelids sinking. I rushed to catch her before she hit the ground and cut herself. Unshed tears stung my eyes. "'Never had she felt so agitated, mortified, grieved, at any circumstance in her life.'"

I pushed damp strands of hair off her face. Not only the same body type, we also shared the same light pink undertoned skin and warm brown hair with a hint of mahogany. Not so much that you'd call us redheads, but enough that Marisol called it super special; she said only "straight-up colorist wizardry" could make just that shade. Mom wore hers grazing her chin, one length. Mine fell to my shoulders in long layers.

I never grasped for ways to be like this woman, but I was all she had. The only one to get her into bed, where she'd sleep until dawn.

I managed to lift her from the chair and hook my arm around one side. She felt so heavy, like I was supporting more than just a person.

I closed my eyes and whispered the rest. "'She was most forcibly struck. The truth of this representation there was no denying. She felt it at her heart.'"

As I spoke the final words, the load in my arms lightened. My eyes flew open, my chin crumpling at the sight and feel of Marisol supporting the other side of my mother.

"We should've taken off her makeup," Marisol said while we lounged, on my bed. Her breath smelled of watermelon gum. After tucking Mom in, we'd finished sweeping the kitchen and made the apartment as clean as any hoarder's home ever could be. "No one should overlook proper skin care," she added.

"She needs sleep more. And she'll live one night without her Clean and Restore Cleanser," I said.

Marisol opened her mouth, then let it fall closed.

"What?"

My friend hitched a shoulder. "It still surprises me. About her appearance. Her job."

"You mean how she shops our house into a junkyard but doesn't look like a slob herself?"

"Pretty much."

Marisol had a point. Some hoarders let themselves go, even ignoring basic hygiene. My mother did hoarding with style— no animal collecting or leaving rotting food on the counter. But constantly spending money required making some. So every day Andrea Wells left in current, clean clothes and went to her job at Macy's as the head sales rep for Elisa B. cosmetics. Hair conditioned, face perfectly enhanced with Peony Passion Blush and smoky eye shadow. Her work friends and freelance clients didn't know and would probably never guess her secret.

"At least she never forgets to bring makeup home for me," I said dryly.

"Having doesn't mean using." In Marisol's mind, my customary swipes of Elisa B. lip gloss and mascara were only the first thirty seconds of *makeup*. She slid halfway off the bed to the floor, digging into her tote. "We need chocolate. We needed it an hour ago." She found two chocolate, caramel, and nut snacks she called granola bars. But I gladly took one, tearing at the wrapper.

Before her first bite, Marisol removed her glob of watermelon gum and stuck it onto the fitted gold bangle around her wrist. She originally bought it because of some trend, never took it off, and often used it for this purpose. Which I loathed.

"You'd think by now I'd get used to...to..." I pointed to the pink lump on the bracelet. "That."

Marisol countered, "I unwrapped that gum *maybe* one minute before I decided we were hungry. Plenty of chew left."

I bit off some of the caramel goodness. "May I remind you of how your gum-conservation habit cost you one deliciously blond football star? Sophomore year?"

A slow-moving grin stretched across Marisol's face. She flopped backward onto my pillows, dreamy eyes to the heavens. "Brody Roberts. Oh, but he was a fine specimen, yeah?"

"Yeah."

Her voice smoothed into a purr, and I could almost see into her memory as she said, "Right before practice, behind the racquetball courts, where no one goes because—"

"No one plays racquetball anymore," we said in unison, then laughed.

"Anyway," she continued, "his eyes were icy blue and his hands were raking through my hair. It was stupid hot out, like today, and he was leaning in, and I was distracted. Dios mío. Can you blame me for forgetting I was chewing two pieces of that Cherry Slush flavor?"

"Which you quickly removed by pretending to push your bangs off your face, as I recall?" I laughed. "Talk about a first-class maneuver—one-handed hair swipe, stealth transfer of Cherry Slush from mouth to bracelet."

"One of my finer performances."

"Only, hon, you didn't do what 99 percent of other girls with hot guys trying to kiss them would've done. Like throw it on the *ground*?"

Sheepishly, Marisol said, "Habit. I wasn't thinking. A boy

that beautiful makes you forget stuff while he's trying to climb down your throat. Man, he was a good kisser. Your mind kinda goes to jelly, you know?" She guffawed and dragged one of my knitted throw pillows over her face.

Truthfully, I didn't know. About kissing, or throat climbing, or mind jelly, or any of it. Marisol knew I didn't know, and *I* knew she didn't mean to make me feel bad, but the words still pinched. My friend had kissed a fair number of guys; I'd heard about all of them. I'd also kissed dozens of guys—on paper. I'd fallen hopelessly in love, too—in books—with strong, flawed heroes. I had plenty of clock-striking paperback midnights.

But no real ones yet. Too many boxes blocked the view into my castle gates.

Brown eyes rimmed with winged liner emerged from behind the pillow. "Couldn't have been the gum."

"He never texted you again," I said.

"Which had more to do with Chloe Clark than my gum."

"It's like a beacon. You can't miss red gum where red gum doesn't belong. I love you, but he got weirded out."

"Fine, it *might* have been a factor." She bolted upright. "Time for some real food." Chocolate bar demolished, she popped the saved gum back into her mouth and grabbed her phone. "I can text Bryn to meet us at the Asian bowl place? It's her night off from practice. Math homework can wait."

I shrugged. We hung out with Bryn Humboldt, too, but never here. I considered the upside of going out and ending the day in any place but this one.

Marisol looked me over. "Now for your outfit."

I tugged my black tee and tan shorts. "I'm already wearing an outfit."

"No," Marisol said with a slow head shake. "There's a big difference between wearing clothes and wearing an *outfit*."

She pointed at my closet. "Get that denim shirt I made you buy and layer it on top, opened, sleeves rolled. Your tee has a little rip."

I glanced down. Grimaced.

"Then the necklace with the dangling blue stone that's hanging in your jewelry caddy, by your black jacket. And swap the flip-flops for sandals. The black ones with silver buckles."

"How in the—"

"After all this time, you're actually questioning it?"

I conceded with a hand flip and moved toward the closet Marisol freakishly knew by heart. One hand on the knob, I circled my eyes around my organized, tidy room. My mother's hoarding halted at my bedroom door. Despite the counselor's guidelines to define my own space in our apartment, I suspected there was another reason my room remained clutter-free.

Other than my bed and a white wooden desk, tall bookcases completely covered my walls. The ivory paint barely showed. And packed onto those shelves were countless volumes of my mother's old books. Books I rescued when I was eight years old, when my mom's hoarding worsened. After too many years of longing and waiting, she'd finally acknowledged that my father—avid reader and English teacher—was never coming back.

When Grandma Wells brought me home from school that day, and I saw my mother crating books, I begged to keep them, clutching my favorite copy of *Anne of Green Gables*. Mom relented with one condition: the books would remain in my room. Now she rarely entered my bedroom, where I slept in the middle of a thousand stories. I could trust the words in those books to remain the same, unlike the contents of our apartment.

I left the closet without the denim shirt or the blue stone

necklace. The books drew me close, a stronger pull than my clothes, a comfort softer than wool or cotton. I approached the nearest shelf and grabbed that same copy of *Anne of Green Gables* with its faded mint cover.

Marisol said, "You're not going out with me and Bryn, are you?"

"Marisol…" I sat on the edge of my bed. I thought of the gray paint outside and worried about how I was going to continue to hide my life and save my mother's. It wasn't like I could just run up to Mom and tell her to clean up and quit buying stuff. Her disorder didn't work that way. Even mentioning the hoard at the wrong time could drive her into buying more. When Mom felt threatened, she crammed and collected, then forgot to buy milk and bread. Neglected to pay the racked-up bills. Stress made my mother need more to soothe the shame of what she'd created—from shame.

The circle never broke. We lived in a home strung across tightropes.

I'd gotten used to my tightrope, but now a clock was ticking against my skull. The new apartment manager and our looming lease renewal meant I had to look deeper for new solutions. The month remaining before my eighteenth birthday was plenty of time for Mrs. Newsome or Thomas to see too much and call Child Protective Services. The story of Mom and me could not end that way. Investigated. Maybe separated.

Tonight, the books around me held all the clear endings my life could never promise. Some of them were even happy.

"Next time I'll go, I promise," I said. "But after today, I just…"

"I get it." Marisol crawled over next to me. She pulled her legs around, dangling them from my bed. "You need some Anne."

I sighed. "But I'll always love you best of all."

"*Always*, always." My friend smiled. "Darcy with a heart-shaped face." She tapped one finger on my chest. "And a book-shaped heart."

Three

The Beginning of the Middle

*"I cannot fix on the hour, or the spot, or the look or the
words, which laid the foundation. It is too long ago. I was
in the middle before I knew that I had begun."*

—JANE AUSTEN, *PRIDE AND PREJUDICE*

The next day after school, I stepped into work through the
metal alley door. Not like I was late, but when a parking space
opens up around the corner from Yellow Feather Books, you
pounce. Eerie quiet and a faint musty smell followed my steps
through the storage bay under thinning afternoon light. I
peeked into Mr. Winston's paneled office and found it empty.
No sounds of customers pacing the shop floor or children's
gleeful voices as they explored the picture book section. I
shoved my card into the time clock, ancient, like the owner
preferred most things. Mr. Winston only had one employee—
me—but still insisted I punch in every shift.

Whenever I hit the showroom at Yellow Feather Books, I felt like I was stepping back in time. Warm and familiar, it was a shop you'd expect to find on a cobblestoned Parisian street, rather than the urban San Diego neighborhood of North Park. A meticulously curated jumble of volumes packed with ink and words. A perfect opposite to the Dumpster chaos of my apartment.

My boss was the only splinter, but I knew how to handle his quirks and fastidious ways. He'd put on his favorite Tony Bennett album, keeping the volume soft through overhead speakers. A wooden cashier counter flanked the back, for transactions and homework, which I was free to work on between customers. Weathered oak floors carried mismatched Persian rugs. Italian glass chandeliers twinkled instead of fluorescent tube lighting. Chunky, claw-footed tables, scratched with years and use, showcased new releases. Two burgundy wingback chairs and a travel-trunk coffee table created a front sitting area, but I didn't know what for. Mr. Winston secretly preferred his customers to scram as quickly as possible after paying.

I glanced down at the computer, one of the few modern conveniences Mr. Winston allowed, though I was generally the only one who used it. He usually left a Darcy-Do list for me, like: (1) Print more flyers. (2) Organize YA section. (3) Order twenty copies of new fad diet book. (4) Find out the name of new fad diet book.

He'd left no list today. Nothing to separate my mind from *six months*. From the lease and my mother's morning hangover. I was at work, in a place I loved, but the memory of yesterday played and replayed like an earworm tune.

My phone dinged in my bag. Marisol texting, of course. Still no sign of Mr. Winston, so I fished it out.

Marisol: Mama invited you over Saturday. Small dinner

Me: Define small

Marisol: Just the family

Me: Define family

Marisol: The usual

Which could mean anything from her immediate seven, to a Robles extravaganza with the Mexican half of her family, requiring two extra folding tables set up on the lawn. Either way, I wasn't about to say no to Mama Robles's cooking.

Me: I'll be there

Marisol: Boom

Apparently, I had plans for Saturday. Laptop plugged in for homework, I crossed the shop to peer through the picture window and found my boss. He stood on the sidewalk with his ex-wife, arms crossed like they always were when he was talking to Tess. A striped oxford shirt and tweed cap teetered off his beanpole frame—also like always, even in eighty-degree weather.

The pair parted when they spotted me. "Hey there, Miss Darcy-Diva!" Tess called out, her brassy trumpet voice muffled through the window glass. She added a cheery wave, which I returned. Today, her hair frothed over her shoulders in platinum blond. Who knew what tomorrow's wig would be? I'd worked here for two years and had never seen her real hair.

An educated guess: Mr. Winston probably *had*, even though

they were only married for one tragic year and had been divorced for more than thirty. During the settlement, neither party wanted to surrender their co-owned, historic North Park building. The solution was to split 386 University Avenue into two shops: Yellow Feather Books on the right, Tops Wig Emporium on the left.

A bell chimed as Mr. Winston barreled through the front door. I made an effort to look busy—fluffing embroidered armchair pillows, turning the large potted plants to catch more window light.

"Hmmph," he muttered. Then a quick chin lift in my general direction. *Ooh, a good mood today.*

"Good afternoon, Mr. Winston." I tucked myself behind the counter.

He approached the archway leading to his office, pausing beneath the large antique oil painting of an eighteenth-century scribe armed with a bright yellow quill. "Well, it would be, if that woman next door would get her expenditure report in on time. Bookkeepers don't like to be kept waiting." He removed his cap, raking stubby fingers through sweaty gray-blond hair. It matched his mustache, forever dingy from years of smoking, even though he quit last spring. That April was a *fun* month around here.

"I'm sure they don't. The, um, bookkeepers."

He made a low, rumbly sound. "Don't grow up, Darcy. As if you're able to help *that*." Ratty sigh as he slammed his office door.

The words settled over me like a second skin. Dry and itchy. *Don't grow up?*

I clenched my hands around the lip of the worn counter. All day, my mind had flipped from stiff memory, to blank forgetting. Back and forth. It stopped now at the scene in my apartment at seven-thirty this morning, when I was just trying to be a senior at Thomas Jefferson High School. Just trying to start my college application for San Diego State University over breakfast. Even now, I could clearly picture my mother's bewildered stare as she stood by the kitchen counter.

"Something's different," she'd said, sipping the black coffee I'd made. "Wait, what happened to all the Williams Sonoma café plates?"

Peanut butter toast in hand, I sprang up from the table. Cursed her radar for *things*. "You mean the plates you shattered? The ones I cleaned up while you slept?"

Mom's puffy but fully made-up face paled baby powder white. I caught the exact moment she remembered. Maybe not all of it, but enough to say, "Oh. Darcy, I..."

I sighed heavily. "It's done. Over, okay?" I slid the stack of bills toward her. "These are from yesterday. Car insurance. Cell phone. One of your credit cards." No doubt maxed out.

"Yes, of course." Another sip of coffee as she stared at her phone.

"Mom."

"One second, hon. Crate and Barrel geode coasters are on clearance. Before they sell out, I need to—"

"Mom!" *Stop. Remember what the psychologist said. Stay calm. No emotion. Simple statements.* I took her phone and locked my eyes on to hers. "Please, just listen. Pay the bills first. You can't do without your phone or car insurance. And maybe pay down your card a little?"

"Yes. Today."

How many times had I heard this? But the lease renewal meant I had to start inching her forward. My mind abandoned the moment for books. Chapters and scenes fluttered across my brain like an old Rolodex, until I recalled a trick a secretary had used with her flighty private detective boss.

I breathed deeply, then said, "How about this? Can you

text me later to tell me you paid them? It might help you stay on track."

Mom flicked her eyes back to her phone, which I'd already cleared to the home screen. "Oh." Her brows furrowed. "Okay. I guess I could do that."

Now, with the bookstore empty and Mr. Winston in the back, I opened the search engine on my computer. Homework would have to wait. If I had any hope of protecting my home, I first had to educate myself in topics not covered in AP Government. I keyed in a few search terms and scanned the results.

When your apartment lease is up, what happens?
Your rights as a renter.
United States property law.

I heard the dusty echo of my boss's voice. *Don't grow up, Darcy.*

Too late, Mr. Winston. Too late.

"Darcy. Miss *Wells*!"

Jolted, I looked up. Mr. Winston was rapping his fingers on my counter.

"You must've been swimming in stories again. Goodness." He leveled a stiff glare at me. "I called your name three times."

"Oh. Sorry." I shook my head to clear it and shut my laptop. "Just preoccupied. Homework, err, problem." The small fib jiggled against my ribs, especially when I considered what my research had revealed.

The bad news: our landlord could deny our lease renewal for any reason.

The good news: he'd have to give us at least thirty days' notice to vacate.

I prayed our situation would literally clear up before it came to that. I set a mental date and would plug it into my calendar later. If nothing changed in three months, I would present this information to my mother. The psychologist had cautioned me against calling direct attention to the hoard, but the looming threat of losing our apartment left me with no choice. Until then, I'd try to explore some positive new strategies.

Mr. Winston tossed two envelopes in front of me. "Penny-pinching lawyer mailed *her* trust documents to my place. Couldn't be bothered to spring for extra postage to her house. Figures."

Inner eye roll as he left. He didn't have to tell me what to do with the papers. Apparently, five steps out Yellow Feather's front door to Tess's mailbox was miles too far.

But I did Tess and Tops Wig Emporium one better—hand delivery. I liked Tess, even spent most of my breaks out of Mr. Winston's earshot, chatting with her at Tops. She loved to fuss extensions or sparkly barrettes into my hair, always brewing green tea I didn't love but drank anyway.

As I pushed open the door to the wig shop, my ears were assaulted by the deafening whirr of a drill battling persistent drywall. I peered around, but found no Tess. Only Asher Fleet, a recent Jefferson High graduate.

I barely knew Asher. We were never friends and never had any classes together. But I knew *of* him, especially the notable and notorious points. Everyone at Jefferson did.

"Stupid piece of shit!" Asher roared, even louder than the drill racket. Furious hands yanked the metal drill bit off the tip. He cursed again richly, then tore through a nearby box, replaced the bit, and started up again. *Whoa.* But he still hadn't seen me.

And I hadn't seen him since May, when the entire school learned he'd survived a tragic car accident. Who would've guessed the only Jefferson student to hold a pilot's license would suffer a life-threatening accident—not flying solo in his dad's plane, but driving to meet a friend? All I knew of the rest of Asher's story was him finishing out his senior year in a hospital bed. He missed prom, Disneyland Grad Night, walking at graduation. Everything.

Blessedly, the noise ceased. Asher plunked the drill on Tess's counter and pushed two fingers into his temples. He looked different from how I remembered him. I studied his profile first, a full sweep of cheek ending in a rough, squarish jaw. But his cool-toned brown hair fell longer than ever, curling slightly above his collar. One section flopped over his forehead, partly concealing a jagged scar.

When he shifted around, I poked my head farther into the shop, eyes wide. He gazed right past me to a box of metal rivets. *Huh?* Fifteen feet away, and he didn't even notice me? "Hello?" I voiced, stepping closer.

His body jerked, but his mouth remained frozen in a turned-down scowl. "Oh. Thought you were just another head." No smile as he angled away from me.

What? I only recalled bits about Asher, but rudeness wasn't one of them. My eyes flitted around, hummingbird-like. It *was* true, though; heads were everywhere. Shelves of female and male mannequin busts lined the walls. A bit creepy, like standing in the middle of a stadium. By now I was used to the hundreds of forward-fixed eyes with no bodies. Just static heads and necks topped with wigs of all colors and styles.

But here I stood, and not made of plastic. Skin and flesh and bone, a beating heart. Each of my five foot nine inches being invisible to boys was nothing new. But a mannequin? *Just another head?* The words, the notion stung, and I had to push it back.

Asher raked one hand through his hair. The dark scowl remained—one I imagined coming from Mr. Darcy, of Jane Austen's *Pride and Prejudice*. I'd pictured the book version dozens of times. It used to be my mother's favorite, hence my name: *Darcy Jane Wells*.

Language master that I was, my own word game never clicked well with guys. I'd never quite mastered the art of the perfect response, either. But books held all the experiences I needed. If Asher Fleet was going to put on his best Fitzwilliam Darcy wig, I could reach into literature myself. *I* had no clue what to do with a boy with prickly words and a prideful, impenetrable stare. But what would Jane Austen's book heroine, Elizabeth Bennet, have done with him? I mentally scanned pages and donned her character, finding my next move.

I adjusted my body—spine long and lifted, eyes narrowed, straight mouth. I stomped three steps forward over his rudeness and stated, "Look. I need to get back to work, so is Tess around?"

Asher's stance softened a bit. He recognized me; I knew it. But no way would I let him know *I* recognized *him*.

"She went out. Something about a croissant from that new bakery down the street." Asher leaned forward on the counter, avenues of veins pushing through tanned arms.

Small victory. But heat still pooled beneath my cheeks. I dropped the envelopes near the register. "Well, you can tell her Darcy brought these by. And they're important, so don't forget or lose them." I halted just before the door and faced Asher with a dignified smile—because Elizabeth Bennet was polite and classy, if nothing else. "Thank you," I added before I launched into a dramatic pivot...

And crashed into the metal accessory rack near the entrance. *Ouch!* I'd definitely be sporting a nasty bruise by dinnertime, but that wasn't the height of my mortification. No, that honor went to the decidedly non-Austen shriek I'd made when my shoulder met metal. Not to mention the scatter of displaced statement necklaces, headbands, and gauzy scarves Tess recently started carrying.

And Asher had seen everything. Oh, now he'd seen *me* for sure.

I couldn't look. Didn't turn. I couldn't handle the disapproving twist that must've returned to his features.

As quickly as possible, I righted my blue sleeveless top and replaced the accessories. Then I scurried out the door.

Back at an empty Yellow Feather Books, my heart pounded. Sweat coated my palms. I rubbed my throbbing shoulder as a splotch of pink began to bloom.

My phone vibrated in my jeans pocket, but I took a few steadying breaths before I read the text. I'd hoped it was my mother, saying she'd paid the bills. But, no. And by now, didn't I know better than to hope?

Instead, Marisol had sent one of her SOS messages, and I welcomed the distraction as I kept drawing in air.

Marisol: Help! Being held hostage by a pair of juice box addicted short people

I had to chuckle; it helped slow my heart rate. Her four-year-old twin siblings were a unified force of nature. Even as I tried to purge my exit foul from my memory, I couldn't help being curious about Asher's presence at Tops.

Me: Sorry! Hey, I just saw Asher Fleet from school doing handyman stuff for Tess. Random stick up his ass, too

I'd save the gory details about our encounter for tomorrow.

Marisol: Asher? Really?

Me: Truth. Wonder how he ended up working over there? Can't ask Mr. Winston

Marisol: Duh. So ask Asher

Me: I repeat, stick. Ass

Marisol: Hold please. Back with details

I needed to put my hands somewhere, so I instinctively
gravitated toward the books. Nothing calmed me more than
paper and ink. As for the section, well—Asher Fleet hanging
shelves at a wig shop was a strange phenomenon, and my un-
dignified flub shot me light-years away from my comfortable
world. Ergo, I dragged the lingering effects of both to the sci-
fi shelves. Organizing, alphabetizing, waiting...
Ding, ding. Marisol already?

Marisol: Legal center across street

I bent around the bookshelf and looked out the big window, spying the brick building across University Avenue be-
longing to Mid-City Legal.

Me: What about it?

Marisol: Where Ash just started a temp. construction project.
His uncle's a lawyer there

Asher's uncle was Michael Fleet? One of Yellow Feather's
best customers? I guessed that Tess probably knew Michael, too.

Me: You found that out in 2 mins?

Marisol: You're funny, D. Twins being PITA gotta run

While Marisol dealt with Carlos and Camila, I moved from science fiction to the mystery section. First of all, I felt I had to honor the great Marisol Robles, proven ace detective. Secondly, I had a nagging hunch today wasn't the last time I'd run into Asher Fleet.

Four

All My World

*"All the world's a stage, and all the men and women
merely players; They have their exits and their entrances,
and one man in his time plays many parts..."*

—WILLIAM SHAKESPEARE, *AS YOU LIKE IT*

The slipup was my grandmother's fault. For two whole days,
I'd managed to avoid the new apartment manager. I feigned
being gone every time Thomas knocked, waiting anxiously
while he peered surreptitiously through the windows until he
gave up. After he left, I would scurry out my apartment door,
always quick to close it into darkness. Down the railingless
stairs and into my blue Honda Civic, where I could finally
breathe. That was my routine until the morning Grandma
properly utilized technology for the first time.

Grandma Wells owned a cell phone, but never texted. *Never,*
never. She said it was uncivilized, declaring all meaningful con-

versations required voices. But this morning, her name dinged across my home screen while I was heading to school. Shocked into carelessness, I halted in my wide open doorway, reading.

Grandma Wells: Could you come to my house for dinner?

My last visit with her was both too recent and too long ago. It had been the type of visit that made me wonder whether I *should* go to her house for dinner.

And that's when Thomas materialized, like he'd beamed himself from the Land of Nowhere. His pasty-faced, weasel— no, meerkat-like—form loomed in front of me.

"You're Darcy Wells, right? A moment, please?" Thank God right then for my towering height, because his pupils flicked around my left side. Then my right.

I slammed the door shut behind me so hard, the frame shook. "Er, good morning," I squeaked as the phone dinged again.

Grandma Wells: Why aren't you answering?

Seriously? She just started texting. How was she so fast?

Bushy brows lowered, Thomas crossed his arms. "I've been trying to get around to all of the tenants. I can never seem to locate your mother." Even though the door was closed, he stretched upward on clunky brown loafers, as if our tiny peep-hole worked both ways. "I realize it's early, but is she home?"

Sure, she's currently fussing over where to put the four sets of Crate and Barrel geode coasters that arrived yesterday. "She's asleep. She works long hours. Late shift," I said, hoping he couldn't peep into the truth I locked inside, every day. I'd gotten way too comfortable with this part—one of a liar.

"That's odd. Mrs. Newsome mentioned—just in passing— that your mother sells cosmetics at Macy's."

Of course she did. "She's a manager and works double shifts sometimes. She also does freelance work for weddings and photoshoots. So she rests a lot when she's home." *And orders more stuff and fiddles with things. Constantly. And forgets to pay bills.* *Ding* again.

Grandma Wells: Honestly, what could be taking so long? I need to speak with you. It's important. Dinner tonight or not?

I gave Thomas my best apologetic frown. "Hold on." I texted my grandmother a quick yes before facing the meerkat manager again. "I need to get to school, so—"

"I'd like your mother to be aware of some of the changes we're planning." Thomas impatiently tapped one foot on the landing.

"And we're so pleased," I told him, trying to sound convincing. "How about this—I'll tell her to pop over to your unit as soon as possible."

Big affronted sigh. "Well, it's only that I'd—"

I was already backing away. "Really have to run. Bell's gonna ring. Have a nice day!"

The lease. Six months. How was I going to watch my every move, day after day, and—even more important—find a way to ease my mom into some forward strides before I lost her completely? And then there was my grandmother. I had no idea what she wanted, or what had finally propelled her into texting mode, but I couldn't stress about it now. The day was already too cluttered by a full load of classes. By my own hoard of other worries.

After school, while sorting through my locker at Jefferson, a baritone voice behind me orated, "'Then soldier, full of strange oaths and bearded like the pard, jealous in honor, sudden and quick in quarrel, seeking the bubble reputation...'"

I grabbed my notebook and swiveled around. Ironically, the person who loved literature second-best out of everyone at Jefferson High wasn't a fellow AP English student, or even one of the English teachers. That honor went to Mr. Penn, head janitor. He waited for me to complete the quote, eyes wide with challenge.

"Come on, Mr. Penn," I teased. "If you're going to stump me, you'll have to do better than one of Shakespeare's most popular monologues."

He snorted. A solid, tank-sized man, tattooed arms bulging from the short sleeves of his olive coveralls. He kept his steel-gray hair military short, and wore a rasp of stubble over his ruddy, tanned face. "Miss Wells, all this trash talk about completing the quote without actually doing it?" He clucked his tongue, then kicked the maintenance closet door closed.

"Please." I smirked. "Let's see, 'Jealous in honor, sudden and quick in quarrel, seeking the bubble reputation...even in the *cannon's* mouth.'"

He wrinkled his nose and snapped his fingers. "Source?"

"*As You Like It.*"

"Gotta hand it to you. All these years, and you haven't missed once."

True, but I still said, "Plenty of time before graduation."

Mr. Penn winked, and his disappearing form claimed my vision for a half second before Bryn Humboldt's ballerina-turnout glide replaced it. She approached, all toned muscle and perfect posture.

"Can't you move your locker to senior hall like the rest of us? Then I wouldn't have to come all the way over here to ask you about Friday," Bryn said. "Even your twin moved hers over there."

Eye roll. Technically, Bryn and I were something between friends and frenemies. More technically, she was Marisol's friend, and *I* was Marisol's friend. Three years ago, that fact had forged some kind of occasional hangout link.

"Sorry." I patted my trusty locker door. "I've spent years breaking in this baby." Like Mom's old books, like the mosaic tile table in my apartment courtyard, sometimes you just wanted the things you knew best.

"So, Friday?" She dashed her arms out in exasperation. "My *Nutcracker* blowout bash? You didn't answer any of my texts."

Marisol suddenly appeared in a waft of cinnamon gum breath. She looped noisy, bracelet-filled arms around Bryn and me, pulling us into a group hug. "Of course my little book-opedia is going. Which means she has—*gasp!*—plans for both Friday and Saturday night." Big gum-cracking grin in my direction.

Somehow, when Marisol teased, it never felt like a dig. "What part are you trying for?" I asked Bryn, just now realizing I'd silenced my phone after my grandmother's earlier text invasion. I switched notifications back on.

Bryn's expression softened, almost dreamily. We'd gone to see her in the *Nutcracker* many times. Even my mom went when Bryn danced the part of Clara three years ago. "I want to dance in both the flower and snowflake waltzes. I mean, the costumes *alone*. Auditions start next week, so you know what that means!"

It meant Bryn, who already practiced at the ballet studio five days a week, would give up even more of her life to the annual ballet season. Every year she threw a big party before auditions, knowing she wouldn't have time for friends for months.

"Friday at six, South Mission Beach by the jetty." Bryn

backed away, adding, "Feel free to bring a date, Darcy. I mean an actual date, not some book boyfriend. See ya!"

Alone with Marisol, I swallowed hard, studying my sneakers until she flicked my chin up. "Ignore her, please. Bryn's brain is currently stuffed with pink tulle and satin." When I shrugged, adding a resigned smile, Marisol asked, "Hey, you're not heading to the Feather, right? Your day off?"

"Right, but I have to start on my college application essay for State." Her features sank; I knew her well enough to realize when she needed something. Needed me. I bumped her shoulder. "Which I can tackle tonight. What's up?"

She let out a relieved sigh. "You're coming with me. You'll see." She grabbed my elbow and pulled me through the hall.

"Coming with you, where?"

The *where* turned out to be the front row of the auditorium, right at the start of *Much Ado About Nothing* play practice. Cast and crew members buzzed around with scripts, some hovering near Mrs. Howard. The former stage actress, now Jefferson High director, stood skyscraper-tall and graceful, her dark Afro rising from a colorful head scarf.

"How am I helping?" I asked.

Marisol scoffed. "By keeping me focused. Like always. My design anxiety is at level five thousand." She took out a spiral notebook. "Designing costumes for both female leads is huge for me. I want to consider the whole ambience so I can capture the right looks for Hero and Beatrice. And no one knows Shakespeare like you."

Making her mark in the fashion world was Marisol's dream, but also the one thing that drove her to enough anxiety that she'd seek a moral support booster from the person who knew her best.

That's how we jibed. Marisol regularly—but gently—coaxed me from my library. But she also understood my book-

ish ways, and the magnetic pull of my alone time with stories.
Conversely, I was a calm figure in Marisol's big noisy life. A
low-drama constant. Her bustling world, and perpetually creative mind, needed the balance of my rational ways.

Though perfect opposites, Marisol was my champion. And
I was hers.

"My costumes have to do justice to the scenery." Marisol
pointed downstage with a hot-pink pen. "Look, the set's all
done, and it's fab."

Okay, it really was. Set in the garden of an Italian villa, a
stone courtyard was flanked on both sides by towering cy-
press trees. Builders had added three flower-covered arches for
mischievous characters to hide behind while eavesdropping
and scheming. The backdrop featured a gauzy scrim curtain
that could change hue from day to night.

"You're gonna nail this job. Costume glory," I said, and
we shared a smile. The cast began rehearsing a scene from the
play's opening act, voices echoing in the near-empty theater.

"Speaking of glory, look who's playing Benedick," Marisol
said. When Mrs. Howard sat in our row, Marisol lowered her
voice. "I could think of worse ways to spend my afternoon
than watching Jase shimmy around onstage."

I had to agree. Jase Donnelly was the obvious choice for
Benedick, the male lead. All signs pointed to him hauling his
talent and Hollywood good looks straight to film school or
the Broadway stage after graduation.

Mrs. Howard signaled the cast, her voice rising. "Jase,
Alyssa, give us more sass in your banter. Alyssa, you need to
sell the tension between Beatrice and Benedick." She glanced
down at her script. "We'll come back to this later. Let's work
on Act Two, Scene One again."

Alyssa, the willowy blonde playing Beatrice, nodded, studying her script and consulting with Jase. Mrs. Howard left to

join them, calling more actors over to switch scenes. Stage-hands pushed a faux stone fountain to the center.

Marisol rapped her pen on her notebook, staccato style. "The costume budget is tight, but I want Beatrice and Hero to have more than one look. Maybe I can make a base layer gown for each girl, but create different overlays with velvet jackets and lace toppers and…"

Marisol went on, but I was only half listening. The rest of my attention snapped to the tall male figure who'd just entered through the side door, and I recoiled when I realized who it was.

"I'm not here," I whispered, sinking down into my seat, zipping my black-and-white-striped hoodie. I shoved the hood up and over my head.

Marisol instinctively shielded my face with her big turquoise tote, but still asked, "What are you yapping about?"

"Asher Fleet. Stage left. Didn't he graduate?"

"Breathe, D."

"I am." But my cheeks flared hot as I remembered my "spectacular" exit from the wig shop. I still carried the painful bruise. Now Asher was suddenly showing up everywhere I went, too?

"Yeah, breathing like one of my dogs after a run." Marisol pretended to rummage through the tote, which was still shielding me. "What really happened at Tops the other day?"

"I told you at lunch. Yesterday."

"You told me pieces while you were eating hummus and crackers and also reading *Looking for Arizona*."

"*Looking for Alaska*. It's *Alaska*."

"Whatever. I may have missed crucial details. So tell me the real story again, without you reading another story."

"Oh, you mean the one about Darcy Wells going to take Tess some documents? Where Asher Fleet was playing handyman, and he was instantly rude and weird? And then Darcy was trying to execute this suave exit, but she crashed..."

I trailed off when Asher turned at the lip of the stage, boring his eyes right into mine. Just for a second. Obviously, my hoodie wasn't hooded enough. I averted my gaze until he spun around and traded waves with London Banks, who was currently playing the part of Beatrice's cousin Hero. Asher grabbed the railing and slowly climbed up to speak with a stagehand. I noticed his limp as he moved between the flowered arches.

"You done freaking out yet?" Marisol produced a pack of gum, offering me some.

"Maybe." I brushed away the disgusting grape flavor and whisked off my useless hood. "Can you explain why he hates me?"

"Hates you? He doesn't even know you. Plus, people run into fixed objects all the time. It happens."

The auditorium swelled with voices. Drama-filled conversations, on-and offstage. "Before that, he went all Mr. Darcy on me," I said. "What is he doing here?"

"Three reasons." Marisol pointed at the backdrop. "One—handy-dude Asher's been helping with the set. Two—he's still super tight with Jase. And the third—"

"Speak low if you speak love," I muttered.

"Huh?"

"Sorry." I shoved my hand forward. "Don Pedro—or, Connor, who's playing the part of Don Pedro—has messed up that line three times. It's not 'speak low if you speak *of* love.' It's just 'speak *love*.' The flub changes the whole meaning."

Marisol flopped backward, sinking down, arms to the heavens. "That's it. You're simply not of this planet we call Earth. For eight years, I've been friends with a Shakespeare-savant-with-no-script *alien*."

"Now *you're* being dramatic. The 'speak low' line is one of the most famous in this play."

Sure enough, Mrs. Howard finally caught Connor's mistake and corrected him. I lobbed a satisfied grin at Marisol.

"Still an alien."

"Fine. Tell the alien the third reason." Like it mattered.

"London, of course. And not the city." Marisol gestured, nails sparkling with glittery polish. "The senior."

I found the actress in question sitting on the prop fountain—London Banks. Aloof London with a well-tended, icy reputation. Not to mention the gorgeous long red waves clouding around her shoulders. She adorned the Jefferson stage like she was made for it, just like another performer I knew too well. London Banks and Bryn Humboldt: two best friends who loved to turn everyone's sunlight into their personal limelight.

"Asher and London have been on and off again for two years," Marisol told me. "You know that."

"I do?" Did I? Okay, something about that tickled my memory.

"You would if your head wasn't always hiding in print." She bopped her head sideways. "Exhibit A."

During this exchange—this comedy within a comedy—I'd reached into my bag again, mindlessly grabbing that copy of *Looking for Alaska*. Clutching it tightly. "Apparently, they're on again."

Marisol nodded. "She resurfaced after his accident. Helped him through rehab and stuff."

"And you know all this, how?"

"Oh, Darcy," she said on a low chuckle. "You kill me."

I shook my head and reached down to retrieve my persistently dinging phone. I read the text messages and shoved the screen into my friend's view.

Grandma Wells: Let's make it 6:30. My house

Grandma Wells: I've been wanting to use some new cookware

Grandma Wells: Leave home before 6. The traffic into La Jolla has been absolutely dreadful at that time

Marisol snorted with mirth. "G-Wells discovers the beauty of texting and—bang! Blows up her phone."

"And mine." I tapped a single response, covering all points.

"What do you think she wants?"

I shrugged. Grandma Wells had always supported me, faithfully sending money every month for bills. She also maintained a substantial college fund for me, so I could someday attend SDSU and pursue my beloved English degree without incurring debt. But we often disagreed over the way I coped with my mom's hoarding, and she rarely changed her opinion.

"If she starts up again about Mom, we won't make it to dessert," I said. "I just can't listen to it anymore. Especially after the couple of days I've had with more bills and more UPS boxes and that Thomas manager lurking around every corner."

Gaze locked on the stage again, Marisol nodded. "Plus Asher staring directly at you, and whatever *that* means."

"Huh? Where?"

She elbowed me both painfully and discreetly. "Don't look. Head down. I'll narrate."

"What do you mean *staring*?" I tried to obey, eyes fixed on the John Green novel on my lap. The left corner of my vision tracked Marisol lowering her costume notebook a bit.

"*Staring*, staring. I said stay down," she whispered, ventriloquist style. "Please locate your chill and trust me."

Ugh.

"You know how in *Much Ado*, the characters eavesdrop

from behind those arches and cause all kinds of trouble and misunderstandings?" she asked, then let out an amused huff. "What am I saying? Of course you know."

"Yeah, okay, but what does that have to do with Asher?"

"The cast is rehearsing, and Asher's hiding behind flower arch number three. But he's not looking at his buddy, Jase. Or Alyssa, or Mrs. Howard, or London. He's staring at you, and actually kind of...softly. Not in the way he'd glare at someone he hates, or snigger at someone he's pegged as a klutz. Well, he was for at least ten straight seconds. Now he's talking to a stagehand."

"Come on, Marisol," I scoffed.

She gasped. "Darcy Jane Wells, you don't believe me?"

I knew then that what she said and saw was real. Marisol Robles embellished herself—face and body—to all kinds of fashionable extremes. But since the day I met her, she'd never embellished her words. Her accounts were always straight and true.

Unlike me, Marisol never lied.

Five

The Collector

"Two things cannot be in one place."

—FRANCES HODGSON BURNETT, *THE SECRET GARDEN*

Thirty minutes into dinner, Grandma Wells still hadn't mentioned my mother. This simple truth kept me perched on the edge of my Queen Anne chair in her dining room, but I couldn't relax. Couldn't really enjoy the roasted chicken, green beans sautéed with bacon, and garlic mashed potatoes.

Grandma clapped her hands twice. "I made that wonderful flourless chocolate torte for dessert." She disappeared into the kitchen, her teal silk duster coat unfurling like peacock feathers. The torte was one of my favorite desserts. What was she up to?

While she fiddled, I studied rooms I hadn't seen in months. As a little girl, scampering around her La Jolla home was like navigating a flea market. Knickknacks were everywhere. Most flat surfaces buckled under miniature carousels, decorative clocks, and porcelain figurines. It wasn't hard to see where my mother's hoarding roots started, how she'd stretched the Wells collecting gene a thousand miles too far.

"Voilà!" Grandma Wells brought coffee and dressed the table with crystal plates, dessert forks, and a large knife. The torte in front of me was perfectly round, coated with chocolate ganache and dusted with powdered sugar.

I sipped water and breathed deep, hiding my thoughts inside her nesting dolls and glass vases. "Thanks, Grandma. You didn't have to do all this."

She scored the frosting with the knife, then swiftly ran the blade through. "Oh, it's no trouble. Besides, I haven't seen you for so long. And you're about to start a new life chapter. That's cause for a little celebration."

What about my life was worth celebrating?

She regarded my perplexed expression and slid over a hearty slice. "You'll be turning eighteen soon."

True. I was furiously counting the days until my birthday— the day CPS could no longer investigate my home, or take me away from a mother I couldn't bear to leave.

Grandma smiled fondly, her cranberry lips and rose-blushed cheeks framed by a cap of golden-brown hair she never allowed to gray. "You're starting college applications, too. You have so much going for you, dear. You're just brilliant, and the world is yours."

But…? I'd collected enough words to know where they belonged even when they weren't voiced. This one was so loud, I set down my next forkful of cake. "I guess so. I'm applying to SDSU for a start. Excellent English program."

"Naturally. But college presents unique challenges. Even greater than the substantial school load you're carrying now."

"I've heard." The first bites of torte spun inside my stomach. "I'll find a way to manage, same as I always have."

Grandma's hand curled around mine, soft and wrinkly like a crumpled paper bag, and smelling like gardenia hand cream. "What if I could help you find it?"

Ahh, here it is. "What do you mean?"

"You need to finally consider moving in here with me." She circled her hand. "La Jolla is one of the safest, most prestigious neighborhoods, and you'd have someone to cook for you and help with laundry while you go to class and study. You could quit that bookstore job, too. No worries about bills or money."

"But I like working at Yellow Feather."

Grandma sighed heavily.

"It's a generous offer," I said about the proposition she'd been making forever, packaging it differently each time. Tonight, it had "scary college" wrapping. "But Mom needs me. She doesn't have anyone else." *Not even you. Not you for years.*

Grandma gestured absently. "She's chosen her way. It's time to choose yours. It devastated me to take a hard line with her after therapy, but I had to protect my own sanity, even though she's my daughter."

"But—"

"Darcy, years ago, she made a few key choices of her own."

Every single day, I lived and breathed the lingering effects of those choices. A pregnancy for Andrea Wells during her sophomore year of college—me. A literature teacher fiancé with a lucrative opportunity to teach English for a year in Thailand—except one year turned into eighteen, and a brand-new life for him.

That loss eventually turned a collector into a hoarder.

"I'm not my mother," I told her.

"Definitely not. But you're growing up. Sometimes that means choosing the harder, but ultimately better, path. I understand why you've never wanted to move in here before. Young girls need…" Grandma's voice tripped, a certain emotion clouding her features that I couldn't read. "Well, they need their mothers. But now it's time to choose yourself and your future."

And leave Mom to rot? Or drown in a sea of things and never, ever get well? "Staying *is* choosing myself and her—us. It's choosing to be the one person who hasn't abandoned her. Even though it's hard."

"Yes, I'm confident it's more than hard. Grown-up choices typically come with consequences." Grandma sipped her decaf. "You're certainly free to continue taking care of your mother and enabling her behavior."

I puffed out a heated breath. "I'm not enabling her. I'm trying to help her work through it."

"Is she improving?"

"A little, yeah." But not enough. Not yet. Worry coursed through my limbs, dull and achy.

Grandma shook her head. "Even though I don't agree, I would respect your decision to remain with her. But you'll have to respect those consequences I spoke of. It's very simple. Live here, and you'll be comfortable and worry-free. Or stay with your mother, on your own, but completely self-sufficient, too. That means your allowance will cease when you turn eighteen." When my bottom lip dropped, she leaned in. "Don't misunderstand me. This is not a punishment, but my checks will no longer enable your mother's irresponsibility. Staying with her means you're choosing to become an adult."

An adult? Sure, the hoard had forced me to grow up and watch over my mom, but an adult was the last thing I felt like. I was still in high school!

"I'm sorry, Darcy, but adults pay their own bills. They find their own way. I wish your grandfather and I had taken this line more forcefully with your mother. We were too soft on her. Too liberal. Right here and now, you're more capable and sensible than she ever was." Her expression softened slightly. "But no matter where you live, you're still entitled to the college fund we arranged for you."

Even my grandparents' legacy gift couldn't stop the ache from honing cold and sharp, nicking my heart. How could she be so calm while she threatened to yank away one of the few things I could actually rely on?

While our apartment overflowed with things, Mom never seemed to buy the *right* things. Some days, even my most dire needs couldn't make her snap out of her random shopping whims. Grandma's money had helped provide my Honda and slick laptop. It bought sneakers and gasoline. Cold medicine and printer ink. The checks helped pay my insurance and cell phone bill, sometimes filling holes in my mom's income to buy groceries. And that was quickly becoming more often than sometimes.

If I stayed with Mom at 316 Hoover, the extra money would stop. In less than thirty days.

Grandma took her last bite of chocolate torte, while my piece sat half-eaten and unwanted. "Think about it. Picture yourself in my guest room. I've been saving it for you, and your book collection would look lovely on the built-in shelves in there."

I did think of that sunlit bedroom I once used as a playroom. The cushioned window box nook with its peekaboo Pacific Ocean view, jutting between rooftops and tree canopies. A quiet place to read and study. The distressed wood floors and white-paneled walls were just like the ones I imagined in the home from *Little Women*. And Grandma had recently added a modern walk-in closet Marisol would freak over.

Suddenly, the looming months and years grabbed tight,

squeezing. Would Mom's constant collecting plus the added stress of college be more than I could handle next year? For the first time ever, I wondered if maybe Grandma was right.

As I wearily turned my key in the lock, all I wanted to do was shut myself in my room and dump Grandma's ultimatum into one of my books, trading it for an inky promise where evil met its rightful end. Where heartbreak always bloomed into a final kiss, no matter how many times I'd read it.

Inside our apartment, the low-toned jabber of a male newscaster hummed from the TV. My nose itched, eyes watering before I sneezed. Time to clean again. When I looked up, I noticed one of the screws securing our door chain was coming loose—nothing I'd have to call Marisol's brother Marco to fix, fortunately. I could tighten a simple screw.

"How was dinner?" Classic Andrea Wells code for *how is your wealthy grandmother who refuses to speak to me?* Mom stood at the counter, her greeting card tub at her feet. She took one card from a dwindling pile and made a tally mark on a yellow legal pad.

"Grandma's looking good. The food was yummy," I told her. My code for *same uneventfully pleasant visit as usual.* Yet another lie. Sometimes I had to protect my mother from more than nosy managers and dust. I tossed my keys onto the counter and frowned at the stack of untouched mail. I ripped open the seal on the first envelope. Two words blared across the credit card statement, screaming in red ink.

I whipped around as my mother said, "I have everything here covered except Thanksgiving and Father's Day."

"What?"

She gestured to the virtual Hallmark store before her. "The cards. I have them for every holiday except those two."

This was her biggest problem? The entire scope of her evening? Who even sent Thanksgiving cards nowadays? No one I knew. And Father's Day? Of all the cards, that was the one we clearly needed. Sure. Because her father had been dead for seven years and mine was currently in Thailand with another wife and kids. A woman he'd married instead of abandoned. Babies he'd actually held when they were born.

Suddenly, I couldn't help it. My insides sputtered like I was inhaling rage instead of dusty oxygen. "This balance has almost doubled with interest because you haven't been paying it down." I shoved the notice into her vision. *Past Due.*

"Sometimes they get away from me." She placed another card into a pile. Jabbed a tally mark onto the pad. "I really am doing the best I can, okay?"

Your best? What about my best? When the psychologist counseled Grandma and me, did he know how much I'd despise having to act for Mom's benefit alone? Never for mine—all to keep a mother steady and functioning. His coping plan raked through my mind.

If you push too hard, she'll only hoard and shop more to cope. She doesn't have the tools to deal with stress. Redirect her instead of confronting her.

Tonight, the doctor's words were too faint against the roar of so much more than greeting cards. One nosy neighbor could start a CPS nightmare. The steady creep of the lease deadline. A grandmother's manipulation. This dusty, hideous home.

"Your best doesn't pay the bills!" I flung the notice across the counter. "Your cataloging..." I reached into the tub and grabbed the biggest pile I could hold, chucking them to the ground. "It doesn't do anything for anyone but you!"

"Oh," she said through a breath, absorbing a jolt like the clean shock of a gunshot wound. One...two...three seconds ticked as my heartbeat knocked against my ribs. Her hands flew over her mouth as she sank to the ground.

Trembling spread across my fingers, palms aching with heat. I'd finally said it: the perfect comeback that captured everything I'd been feeling for so long.

The aftermath felt anything but perfect.

Andrea Wells chose one of the scattered cards. It had a yellow bunny with a colorful straw basket. "Easter Sunday when Darcy was four." Her voice was almost unrecognizable—too high, too strained and wheezy. "She wore the prettiest mint-green dress with white polka dots." She laid it carefully in front of her.

"Mom."

She didn't answer, didn't even look at me. She grabbed a card with glowing votives and a holly wreath. "Christmas when there was a heat wave and Darcy was twelve. We walked barefoot at Mission Beach after she opened her gifts." She placed the card like a chess piece.

I could only watch as she attached old memories to the new cards, my eyes welling.

She spoke directly to a card with a pink-frosted cake and candy-striped packages. "Darcy's second birthday, when she got strawberry icing all over her jeans and her hair was long enough for spiral pigtails."

Salty tears rolled to my chin. It was like I wasn't even there, only snapshots of me. The chapter at my feet was too raw and overwritten, and I never wanted to read it again. But oh, I could make it stop. I could close this book, leave behind the stress, the clutter and frustration. When the clock struck eighteen, I could pack my life into the blue Honda and escape into the storybook room in Grandma Wells's house.

But the same me couldn't leave this scrap of carpet as my mother continued scrolling through holidays. Card after card arced into a rainbow of memory. I remembered, too—the streamers and banners that once flew over this growing hoard. Candles and dyed eggs and Halloween cat costumes.

I saw it then. On the floor wasn't only the perseverating motion of illness, the eerie panic over a bill, soaring out of reach like a loosed balloon.

I saw a person. A mother—*my* mother—whom I could not, would not abandon.

Six

Treasure and Thief

"We must go on, because we can't turn back."

—ROBERT LOUIS STEVENSON, *TREASURE ISLAND*

My decision meant I had to find a way to replace Grandma's checks. I'd previously approached Mr. Winston for a few more shifts or longer weekend hours, but "Mr. Cheaperson" said he was already extending himself with the time I currently worked.

However, I still had Plan B—Tops Wig Emporium. The next day, I shuffled over from Yellow Feather during my late-afternoon break, spotting one of Tess's favorite wigs before I all-the-way spotted her. She whirled around at the sound of my footsteps. Her long black locks mirrored the sinuous movements of her Pilates-toned body.

"Ah, right on time." Tess dragged over an extra stool and patted it. "Be right back with our goodies."

I sat wearily. Last night's greeting card incident still throbbed. Mom refused to return to therapy, but maybe she'd consider another tool if I brought it up carefully, at the perfect time. I pulled out my phone, tapping in a note to research support groups later on. Surely there had to be a group in San Diego for compulsive shoppers? For…hoarders?

Tess appeared with two teacups and saucers from her collection—hers, blue with an ivory lace design. Mine was white and trimmed with pink cherry blossoms. She went back for a plate of shortbread cookies.

"Thanks, Tess." I politely sipped her customary green tea, masking the strong earthy taste with a buttery cookie.

My companion lowered her cup and shot up again with twice the energy *I* could ever locate. "So, what will it be today?" she asked with a sly grin.

My insides cringed. Tess scooted to her small section of secondhand and discount wigs. We never played with the brand-new models on the wall, keeping them pristine for customers. She eyed me, holding up a shocking pink curly number.

God, please no.

"Thrilling, but we can do better," she decided. "This one clashes with your red top."

Yeah, that's exactly why it was all wrong.

Next, she brandished an electric-blue, shoulder-length monstrosity with straight bangs. "Perfection!"

"Oh, we really don't need to." *Really*, really.

Too late. The wig expert already had the itchy decoration arranged on my head. For kicks—hers, always hers—she added two rhinestone clips on one side.

"Much better. If you come through my door with tired eyes and a Darcy-frown, you get a silly wig." She sat across from me. "Now, tell me what's going on."

Where should I start? "Some…personal issues."

Tess sipped tea, then said, "I'm sorry to hear that. When I was younger, I used to journal about those things. Especially the matters I couldn't even tell my friends. It helped."

Didn't I already give my heartache to words and paper? "This is more of a money snag. I was wondering if you could take me on here for a few hours each week? Mr. Winston can't give me any more shifts."

At the mention of her ex, Tess's nose wrinkled. "Oh dear, I'm afraid I can't afford you either, honey. I can probably give you some temp hours around my busy time, though. Halloween's coming. Already bumping up inventory."

Well, it was something. But not enough to replace Grandma's checks. I'd file it away for later, but I'd need to keep looking for a more permanent option. "It's okay, Tess. I'll—"

"All set, Ms. Winston." Asher Fleet appeared in the archway leading to the rear storage rooms, the sleeves of his tan button-down shirt rolled up and a toolbox in one hand. Noticing me, his face ticked with... Disgust? Surprise? Simple recognition? I couldn't even decipher it. Not with me sitting there with tea and cookies, looking like three-quarters of an American flag. Red boatneck tee, asinine blue wig studded with sparkly "star" clips. Apparently, I was doomed to humiliation every time I saw him.

Tess wedged herself between us, one hip kicked out. "Have you two kids met?"

"Yes," Asher said, right when I said, "No."

"Well, not formally," Asher corrected at the exact time I squeaked, "Kind of."

Tess grunt-coughed and glared at Asher. Was she trying to imply that, as a gentleman, he needed to introduce himself, already? Too late for gentlemanly manners, Mr. Darcy.

But Asher set down the toolbox and stepped close. He held out his hand and beamed tourmaline brown eyes right into mine. Half of his mouth jerked upward. "Asher Fleet. You're still at Jefferson, right?"

He had to know the answer to that question, but maybe there *were* some manners buried under that nut-brown flop of hair, after all.

I accepted the hand; it wrapped around mine, warm and solid. A hint of sweat dampened the roots along his hairline. "Darcy Wells. And, yeah. I'm a senior." *With a ridiculous wig. Ugh, Tess.*

Asher turned to the shop owner. "If you need more hair models, I'm game." He smiled, cocking one brow at me. "Neon's fine, but it's a hard no on that rainbow clown model by the window. Oh, and you won't need a new exhaust fan. I gave it a little cleaning, and now it's working perfectly."

Tess clapped her hands triumphantly. "Excellent." She nudged her chin to the left wall of heads. "And the new shelves are fantastic. Thank you for pitching in."

Asher grabbed the toolbox. "Anytime." He nodded once at me. Then he moved toward the door, only half turning when Tess called after him.

"Heavens," she said. "I forgot to mention Darcy works next door at Yellow Feather."

Over his shoulder, he caught my eye again. "Ahh, cool."

Then he was gone, and I was trying to think of anything and everything but him, a boy with a girlfriend. A boy who hadn't been rude this time, but... Friendly. Like a fool, my thinking parts didn't tell my seeing parts not to notice his strong presence against the urban backdrop of University Avenue. He jaywalked with confidence, despite his slight limp. With a healing leg injury, plus a busy street, he didn't use the crosswalk?

Tess's oversize wall clock dragged me back to reality.

"Thanks for the snacks, but I need to get back, or Mr. Winston will—"

"Yes, he will." Tess cackled. "Hold up now, honey," she called when I grabbed the door handle. She came around the counter and scurried over to me. Swift hands plucked the blue wig from my head.

"Oh," I said with a nervous laugh. "How could I forget something like *that*?"

"I naturally come equipped with explanations for many phenomena." She smiled a tiny bit crookedly with jewel-bright eyes. "But I might save that answer for your next break."

I felt my cheeks blaze. Then a thought occurred to me. "Will you ever show me your real hair?"

"I might at some point." She tossed her head, wig flipping. "Or I might not, on account of every girl needing one secret. One thing she keeps hidden, just for herself."

Or more than one.

"No."

This, spoken by my stylish chauffeur while she waited at our courtyard table that evening. I halted halfway down the newly rerailed staircase. "What do you mean *no*? It's a beach party, not a fashion show."

Dramatic hand splayed over Marisol's heart. "Have I taught you nothing?"

I brandished my boyfriend jeans and navy blue sweatshirt. "Sand, bonfire and ashes...*sand*."

"Cute eligible guys, party of the season...*cute eligible guys*."

"But—"

"Don't make me come up there."

I surveyed Marisol's distressed denim and pale gray tee. Her leather jacket puddled on the table like black butter. Okay,

I was verging on basic, but still. "My outfit is perfectly acceptable."

Marisol grabbed her belongings and sprinted up. "You were warned." She dragged me into the apartment and, bless her—even though I was miffed—because she didn't throw the slightest glance left or right as she barreled through the goat tunnel into my bedroom.

Helpless, I stood like a Darcy-doll while Marisol played stylist. Not two whirlwind minutes later, she'd transformed my look to her satisfaction. The navy sweatshirt drooped on my bed, replaced by a black tee under a long, chunky black cardigan I'd forgotten I owned. She looped a baby blue infinity scarf around my neck. "It'll get chilly by the water." Speedy fingers raked styling cream through my layers. "There. And you can keep the sneakers."

How generous.

Marisol stood back, grinning. "My work here is done." She grabbed her tote. "I'll just touch up my face, and we're off."

I consulted the nearest bookshelf. "So I have time to read a couple chapters?"

"Hilarious." Marisol toted her polka-dot makeup bag to my mirror. "*Seriously*, Natalia?"

"Was sissy playing in your pretty-kit again?"

Marisol waved a rose-gold tube of what I recognized as a special edition Elisa B. lipstick. "I hope Natalia's enjoyed her thirteen years on the planet, because I'm going to...ugh! Look, I just bought this Raspberry Rose color yesterday. Right before I left, she begged for one swipe, and stupid me agreed." She shoved the tube into my vision. The stick had broken clean off, leaving only pink dregs inside the base.

I winced. "Bummer, hon. Those are thirty bucks a pop."

"Tell me. She probably pressed too hard and *snap*. Then

tried to hide the evidence. I bet she thought I'd blame little Camila, too."

I glanced through the open doorway, then back to Marisol. She eyed me suspiciously. "What does your scheming face have to do with my destroyed Raspberry Rose?"

It would be okay, right? Mom's at work, and it's just this once...
"Darcy!"

"Right. Err, follow me," I said, and Marisol did, until we reached the area most tenants called a dining nook. Andrea Wells had transformed ours into a mini cosmetics warehouse. Sadly, I knew exactly where to look. I unstacked four plastic tubs and opened one, to Marisol's stunned gasp.

"Dios mío, you think you know, but you really don't *know*, know," she said.

"Oh, I know." I knelt on the tile floor and dug two hands into the tub, netting brand-new lipsticks and glosses. "There has to be a Raspberry Rose in here somewhere."

Marisol joined the search. We found ten tubes of the newly released color. "Are all these from trade shows?"

I shrugged. "Mom gets the show swag at a huge discount, which only makes her bring home more. Then when Macy's has triple point days, well..."

"There's just...so much. I'll never understand how she's able to keep track of every item."

"And exactly where it goes." I shook off the tingling thought and held out the shiny pink-gold package. "You're going to take this tonight and hope she hasn't counted tubes of this particular color."

Marisol looked hesitant. "I shouldn't."

I pressed the lipstick into her palm. "You're going to, anyway, because you're my best friend and..." I trailed off and opened another tub, just to look. Hundreds of eye shadow pots, blushes, and makeup brushes piled inside. Elisa B. foundation tubes, concealers, mascara, and gift sets with specially curated colors. "There has to be thousands' worth of product in here."

Marisol sighed dreamily. "Oh, I dream in Livewire Purple Liquid Liner and Shady Pistachio Cream Shadow. And there are dozens and hundreds and so, so many. Welcome to my version of the *Cave of Wonders*."

"A real-life *Treasure Island*."

Marisol held up an eye shadow palette. "Just one of these retails for sixty-five dollars. The foundations go for fifty."

"Don't remind me. That's more than I make during one afternoon at Yellow Feather." I was saving Monday afternoon to visit the student job board in the Jefferson High front office. But any other work I found would mean even less time for studying, and zero free time. Or...

No. One replacement lipstick for Marisol is different.

Marisol studied my gaze. "Hey, that's your 'I'm about to do something questionable' face. Which, I might add, would do you some good to put on more often."

My throat pushed out a wordless sound. I began lining up random Elisa B. on the floor, heartbeat fluttering underneath the gauzy blue scarf. "Questionable and stupid, or brilliant and cunning? The money I'd make from selling one of these products replaces hours of work."

I watched Marisol's face shift from confusion to comprehension to concern in under five seconds. "Darcy, I know it's super tempting, but you can't."

"Or... I can."

"Doesn't this go against everything the counselor told you about? Not interfering with the hoard?"

My hands overflowed with product. "Every single thing."

"This makeup *is* all brand-new, though. Mint," Marisol

added wistfully. "Just sitting here in boxes, doing nothing. Unless you let it do something *for* you."

"Oh, so now you're in?"

"More like I'm cutting mental dress patterns. I haven't sewn any stitches, yet. Nothing permanent. We're just considering."

"Right. Considering," I mused. "A couple of lipsticks here, a blush and mascara there." My eyes lit on other items around the apartment, the relentless clutter. "And not just makeup. Those boxes are filled with expensive hair dryers and flat irons. I could sell just a few products, little by little, so she won't notice."

But after witnessing the heartbreak and panic of my mom, lost on the floor with greeting cards and memories... Could I knowingly betray the precarious boundaries of her illness even further? If Mom discovered my scheme, it could easily overwhelm her into a place I could never bring her back from.

Marisol scooted closer. "What about eBay? New cosmetics sell so fast. We'll just knock a few dollars off the retail price of each item, and there's no tax. Mama and I share an account where we buy and sell fabrics and vintage bits for sewing. You could list items under our profile until you turn eighteen and then get your own. We'll just separate your fees and pay you from our PayPal fund. Easy."

Relatively quick money, all without working more retail hours I didn't have to spare? I stared at the tubs again, knowing Mom had more upon more just like them. Pirates' chests filled with forbidden gold.

Wasn't it time *I* started taking back some control and progressing where I could?

"Okay. It's on," I told Marisol, with more confidence than I felt.

With a firm nod, Marisol opened the new Raspberry Rose and applied it flawlessly without a mirror.

"What changed your mind about the makeup, anyway?" I replaced the plastic tub lid. "You were all tripped up at first."

"Still am. I mean, *Darcy*," she warned. "It's like you're in the middle of a tug-of-war game. Protecting your mom on one end. Protecting yourself on the other. It's far from a perfect solution, but maybe it's the best one for now?"

I felt the desperate pull of all my limbs in opposite directions. "Yeah, but Mom can't find out. That's number one." I couldn't bear to imagine her reaction if she did.

"Then we'll make sure she doesn't. *We*'ll have to be smarter than she is careful," Marisol said. "But if you're about to do something questionable and stupid and brilliant and cunning, you're not doing it without me."

Seven

Just One Word

"I like strong words that mean something."

—LOUISA MAY ALCOTT, *LITTLE WOMEN*

Throwback jams pumped across Mission Beach while Bryn Humboldt entertained her friends with impressive jeté and pas de chat ballet leaps. I breathed in deep. The ocean air hung low and heavy with salt. I turned to watch slashes of sunlight flicker across the horizon and found myself strolling toward the water. Washed-up seaweed dotted the shore like tangled masses of mermaid hair. My mother had always woven that image into impromptu fables when I built sandcastles here.

"Hey." Marisol appeared behind me. "Let's check out the food poison."

I followed my friend to the buffet. Bryn's parents had arranged a spread on two folding tables parallel to the black rock jetty, then split, leaving her college-age brothers to manage the crowd. And, for once, not manage Bryn's caloric intake. Ballet demanded a strict diet of green juice and whole grains, minimally processed snacks and lean protein. But at her annual *Nutcracker* blowout, Bryn splurged.

"Oh no. Don't make a scene," I pleaded with Marisol, after a quick look at the second table.

"Huh?"

I pointed.

She glanced. Scoffed. Hooked one hand on her hip.

"Marisol."

"*Nachos?* You know—"

"Yes, that nachos are completely American-contrived. A hundred times over. You forget I'm totally schooled on your authentic Mexican food snobbery." Marisol loved waxing poetic about the link between cuisine and her native culture. "We'll just call it food. Not Mexican food, okay? Chips. Guacamole. Melted cheese and salsa. Sour cream. We *can* pile them together on one plate without emotional trauma. Not traditional, still highly edible."

Three steps forward. I swore I saw her nose twitch. "Tomorrow, we're having the real stuff at my house." Marisol grabbed a plate. "Don't you dare breathe a word about this to Mama."

No matter how expertly Marisol dressed me, I was basically a living party foul underneath the trendy sweater and scarf. It wasn't that I didn't enjoy the idea of parties. Food and drinks and music—all good. I didn't mind big groups of people, either. Unfortunately, what usually happened when I attended parties was happening now. I'd already eaten—two helpings of nachos and one giant chocolate chip cookie. I'd chatted up a few schoolmates, too.

But my hands wanted books.

I longed to curl up on one of the beach blankets with my portable reading light, letting the party around me settle into white noise fog. Allowing myself to temporarily forget I had to school myself on eBay listing strategy. Forget that I was about to risk my entire relationship with my mother.

There was just one problem: Marisol had confiscated the three novels I'd crammed into my purse when she parked her red Pathfinder.

So while my friend huddled with Bryn and a junior, Amy Hsu, I slinked around the firepit toward the water. I matched my breathing to the calming pull of the tide.

It was the small time between sunset and evening when the sky turned the color of crushed plums, bruised from the wounds of another day. I followed the shoreline toward the jetty, a wide peninsula of jagged stones poking into the Pacific like a giant stick of black rock candy. A lone figure perched atop the structure, one I thought I recognized. I stepped closer, looked again with focused eyes, and confirmed what I'd suspected.

Asher Fleet. His downturned face bent away, washed in the thin white light of outdoor lamps. He was using a flat stone as a makeshift bench.

Asher had never attended one of Bryn's *Nutcracker* blowouts before. Could he be *following* me? Right away, I dismissed the ridiculous notion. I wasn't the type of girl boys followed around a room, let alone the city of San Diego. It didn't take long to trace the connection, either. Asher was tight with Jase Donnelly, who was currently on another visit to the nacho buffet. Jase had dated Bryn briefly over the summer, but they'd remained friends when it fizzled. Plus, Bryn was one of London's faithful cohorts.

They were all good reasons for this brooding boy to be here, watching the sunset on a black rock, but none of them explained why I cared so much. Why I couldn't look away until a nearby movement caught my eye.

London was beelining toward the jetty and her on-again boyfriend. I watched the couple exchange words and whispers I couldn't hear. Asher shook his head and brushed away whatever London was offering from her purse. She didn't seem to take that well, briskly throwing her arms skyward before she stomped away toward the crowd.

Asher turned and saw me then. His mouth held tight for exactly one second before he swiveled back to the ocean. I wasn't delusional enough to think we were now besties, but we *had* officially "met" at Tops. Now he was back to freeze-out mode?

A blue pickup truck screeched onto the paved section of the jetty. Bryn's older brother Derek hopped from the cab and flipped the tailgate. "Bonfire! Come and get it, losers!" he shouted. "Let's make this happen, people."

Most of the guys in attendance, and more than a few girls, ran up to the truck. They tag-teamed, unloading wood planks and piling them into the firepit. I stood, camouflaged behind a group of cookie-eating juniors, curiosity piqued. Asher surveyed the action, but didn't help. Didn't even move. One hand cupped around his face, fingers digging into his forehead. Was he sick or something?

When the massive fire hissed and swelled to life, I dismissed Asher and his recurrent Mr. Darcy attitude from my mind and joined the crowd. Flames wove into darkness, curling orange tendrils into the blackened coastline. For a quick beat, I closed my eyes and heard the fire spit and pop, the music dip into softer tones.

Partygoers had pulled chairs and blankets close. Marisol lounged on her elbows at my left, debating something fashion-related with Alyssa. Even Asher abandoned the jetty for a fireside seat. He arranged himself on a shared blanket with London, his body lean, but tipped with a sharp, steely presence.

London turned away from some friends to smile at him, animated with laughter and trailing hair she could've robbed straight from the flames. Wild and coppery. Asher scooted closer to her side, pulled off his blue hoodie, and draped it over her shoulders.

I should've looked away when she stretched her arms around his back, kissing him slowly and deeply. But they could've been any one of the book couples in my bedroom library. I watched print come to life until they parted to chat with more friends. The image gradually waned until it was as small as a moonlike pearl, but I couldn't make it disappear. It lodged behind my tongue like a pill you can't seem to swallow.

Bryn's sudden laugh—loud and grating—startled me as it sliced through the night air. Along with firewood, the Humboldt brothers had provided gallons of cheap Chardonnay, cleverly disguised in chilled plastic water bottles. Being so slight, it hadn't taken Bryn long to jump past her tipsy point, and she'd probably gotten a head start on the rest of her friends.

One of the insulated coolers reached our blanket, another near Asher and London. The redhead took two bottles and slapped on a haughty glare that challenged anyone to have a problem with it. Asher waved off the bottle Bryn's brother Jon offered him. So, he wasn't drinking either?

Marisol was, though. She eyed me pointedly as she plunged her hands into the ice, fishing out a dripping bottle. "Treating myself. I've been working my ass off on those *Much Ado* costumes."

"Knock yourself out. But if you crawl too far down that thing, I'm driving us home and you get to spend the night at the Hoard Hilton," I whispered.

Marisol unscrewed the plastic top. "Don't get your book

bindings in a bunch. Just a few sips. Call it an early celebration, too. Our birthdays are coming up. Eighteen, baby."

"Eighteen," I said, trying out the word. Sampling the calm relief of the approaching day when no government agency could separate me from my mother.

My thoughts fizzled when Bryn jumped up suddenly. "Guys, guys," she bellowed, waving her arms. "I need a minute."

Marisol and I glanced at one another in horror. "Tell me someone's recording this, because good Lord," my friend whispered.

Bryn took a few steps, teetering like no ballerina ever should. "You are each here 'cause you're just so very..."

I gasped. "She's gonna end up in the pit." Luckily, I wasn't the only one who feared it. Soccer-mom-worthy arms readied, friends took turns gently guiding Bryn away from fiery peril as she wobbled on baby giraffe limbs around the crowd.

The reaction was mixed. Versions of, "Yeah, get it, Brynnie-boo," came from a group of fellow seniors. Some guests stared, mouths hung low, heads shaking. Cheers and laughs and flame-bright cackles rang as others rhythmically patted their denim-covered thighs, urging on our hostess.

Bryn bowed deeply. "*Soo*, I wanna first thank my Jon and Derek." She scanned the crowd until she spotted her brothers. She gestured broadly and said, "For all your work and the firewood and the good stuff you brought."

Marisol burrowed the base of her wine bottle into the sand. "Oh, the absolute humanity."

"Talk about theatrical," I said. "Forget *Nutcracker*, she needs to star in *Much Ado*."

Bryn planted herself onto a patch of sand. "I'm not gonna see you all for a long, long time because of dance and stuff. So much work."

Oh dear.

"I hope you'll all come see me this year, 'cause I'm very entertaining." Bryn held up one finger. "But now I think it's time *I* should be entertained. My party and I say so."

"If I wasn't watching this, I'd never believe it," Marisol murmured.

"You'd believe it."

Marisol's mouth twitched as Bryn continued, arm outstretched. "A few of you tried already." A half turn. "Robbie landed some back handsprings. Very impressive."

The crowd, including Robbie, snickered.

"Amy and Chelsea and a couple others were trying to ballet real good." Bryn pointed at no one and everyone. "And some of you think you can sing, but you really can't."

Well, based on the impromptu a cappella sing-off I'd heard earlier, that was probably accurate.

"But I'm looking for something...unique." Her eyes bounced from person to person. And what happened next, happened inside my body first. I knew before anyone else, feeling it rise the way animals sense earthquakes and storms.

It was too late to run, and there was nowhere to hide as Bryn crossed the sand, stopping in front of my blanket.

"Miss Darcy Wells has the most special of talents."

Helpless, I glanced at Marisol. She'd straightened up, her defiant chin poking out, smacking Bryn with a simmering glare that rivaled the heat of the bonfire.

Bryn ignored it and continued, "Darcy's a bona *fide* human dictionary."

Oh God. This was like being in the wig shop, but so much worse, because the eyes on me were *real*. The heads turning toward me were attached to bodies I had to go to school with on Monday. Then the comments started.

"Man, it's true, though. AP English test curve ruiner."

"Every time."

"Supersize brain."

Giggles. Snorts.

Bryn crossed her arms into a giant pretzel. "I'm betting Darcy here can stump any one of you. And I want to see her do it."

"I..." was all I pushed out.

The night wind snaked through the fire, flames bending and twisting, barreling over the hot coals of my cheeks. Was Bryn using me for cheap attention?

I gladly helped classmates analyze poetry or tricky literature themes. Group partners always chose me for AP English assignments. But all of that work was more private, and infinitely more comfortable. It was on my terms. Tonight, I was a party trick. A word freak.

"Oh, that *Nutcracker* ninny is gonna pay for this," Marisol whispered behind a grin as fake as Tess's hair.

"Darcy usually finds the weird words, and I never get them. But tonight, we're—" Bryn executed a sand pirouette "—turning it around. I did my tricks, and now it's Darcy's turn to do hers." She pulled out her phone, brandishing it high. "Time for some brain ballet."

I shrugged, my eyes cast low. "Fine."

Marisol leaned close. "Breathe, D. You got this."

"Who's found some good ones?" Bryn asked.

Bryn's circle of friends glanced at Google and dictionary apps, whispering to one another. But no one spoke. No one wanted the challenge?

Bryn threw one arm up. "Come on. They're just words! Can Wells beat *Webster*?" She giggled at her own antics.

Nothing but the harsh slap of the tide, the roll of waves and white foam as seconds ticked. Until...

"I have some words."

Bryn clapped her hands as I turned to the source. London Banks sprang up, waving her phone, flashing a satisfied grin. Of course. Bryn had offered a girl who always sought out stages a spotlight of firelight. She couldn't resist.

Asher shook his head, a hint of what looked like annoyance flashing across his face.

"I don't like this one bit," Marisol hissed into my ear.

London stepped off the blanket and squared her shoulders, front and center. "The first word is *couthy*."

"It means cozy or comfortable," I said immediately, but more to the sand than the crowd. I knew they were staring at me, and I'd never wanted to be more invisible.

"Speak up! We can't hear you," London called.

I glared at her, and caught Asher rolling his eyes before he trained them away toward the water. "Cozy or comfortable," I repeated with more force.

London nodded appreciatively. "She's right."

"Ha!" Bryn yelled. "Told ya she can't be beat."

I was rewarded with a few stray claps, but still felt ridiculous. A puppet on display.

"Maybe a lucky guess," London added. She scrolled her phone screen. "Try the word *draff*."

"Trash or refuse."

"*Deedy*."

"Industrious," I said.

"*Edacious*."

"Having to do with eating."

"Try *eremite*."

At this word, my head went entirely weightless, even as my body steeled like a pylon driven into the ground. *Eremite*. Since kindergarten, I'd heard that words have power. Sure, they wielded a different kind of power than guns or knives, but just one word could build or destroy. It could trick and wound and shame.

Tonight, this one did all three.

Eremite: Hermit. It was a rarely used term associated with scholars who worked in seclusion, or church workers under strict vows.

London had found a word I could easily define. But in doing so, I'd have to define myself out loud to everyone. Darcy Jane Wells: Alone. Recluse.

Any way you worded it, I was an almost eighteen-year-old who'd never had a date pick her up at her house or kiss her on a dance floor. A girl who'd never sat at a bonfire, curled under the arm of a boy who smelled of wood smoke and flannel. A girl who'd never had a sleepover birthday party.

No one could know why I'd waved an invisibility wand over my own body, my own heart. For years, I'd hidden my mess carefully from everyone but Marisol, keeping quiet, sticking to the shadows. I rooted for love in stories. I filled empty, invisible arms with storybook kisses and the happily-ever-afters authors gave to other heroines.

At night, I folded my truth between the pages. It was safe there. But speaking it was different. Speaking it made it real. It made it hurt.

"Darcy, do you know what on stupid Earth *eremite* means?" Marisol whispered.

"Yeah, I know."

"Shut her down, then."

"We're waiting," Bryn sing-songed, tapping her forearm. "Or do you admit defeat to London?"

The crowd grew restless. Shifting. I caught a few eye rolls and shoulder bumps, and more than a few bored faces.

"I...um." *Could the sand please swallow me whole?*

A male voice called out, "Hey, doesn't that word have to do

with monks or something?" It was Todd Blackthorn, senior class president. That broke the boredom. The crowd laughed, though a few curious eyes remained on me.

"London, why you picking monk words?" said another guy. More laughs. More of my insides churning.

London shrugged and flashed a demure smile before reclining again, leaning against Asher.

Just like one word, one singular moment could hold unspeakable power, too. And the next one did. Bryn's seagull-rivaling shriek hijacked her own game. Actually, Jase Donnelly and Derek Humboldt had hijacked it, sneaking up behind Bryn and hoisting her lithe form like a trophy.

"Sorry, but your games are over, Bryn," Jase said, arms tight around her shins. "We have a better idea for a show. It's called Bryn-Bryn takes a dip in the drink."

"Ugh!" She bucked and kicked. "You guys are gonna—"

"Don't worry, little sis." Derek backed toward the waves. "I brought plenty of towels. And we won't let you drown."

Suddenly, the bonfire and word games at my expense weren't half as interesting as two friends dragging a screeching ballerina into the Pacific, even if it was only for a token splash. The crowd, including London, scattered, most skipping toward the shoreline. A few brave souls abandoned their sweatshirts, rushing into the freezing water.

Others remained, preferring to lounge by the flames and drink cheap wine. Marisol and I were two of the nonswimmers. She leveled a weighty look at me and tucked the last five minutes into a simple, "Wow."

"You can say that again."

My friend thrust the sandy plastic bottle into my grasp. "Go on. After that last bit of what-the-hell, you deserve a couple sips."

I wasn't a big drinker, but I couldn't argue with Marisol's

logic. Not after a day of eBay schemes and pilfered lipsticks. Not after a night where I'd had to curl my toes around the edge of a towering sea cliff, an ocean of my secrets below.

So I raised the bottle to toast a cast-iron sky, spying the shadowed form of Asher Fleet. He stood alone on the hard-packed sand, halfway between fire and water.

Eight
Ink

*"This ought not to be written in ink
but in a golden splash."*

—J. M. BARRIE, *PETER PAN*

"Excuse me? Miss?"

I jolted, still sleepy after my late night at the bonfire. A middle-aged white woman was standing in front of Yellow Feather's cashier counter. Thanks to my mental sojourn into learning the eBay platform, plus devising a plan to best sneak the makeup from tub to auction, I'd missed the dinging doorbell.

"Sorry," I said, smacking my laptop screen closed. "Can I help you?"

The brunette pushed her glasses up and a paperback book forward. *Peter Pan*, by J. M. Barrie. "I need to return this. It's unreadable."

Unreadable? *Peter Pan* was a literary classic, and I'd read it countless times. I grabbed the copy and examined it—the cover was worn to faded emerald green, marred with scratches, and the front featured a silhouette of the main character, mid-flight, a cheeky feather in his cap. She must've found it in our used books section.

"Can I help you find a different book?" I asked.

The customer pulled the receipt from her purse. "It's not that. My daughter needs *Peter Pan* for her children's literature course at State. I was happy to find this one last week at a discount. But the previous owner ruined it, and it's too distracting for my daughter to read properly." She opened the book to a random page. "See for yourself."

I did, and gasped as I looked closer. Many of the hundred and fifty pages of text—so, so many—were swarming with blue and black ink. Passages circled or underlined. Corners dog-eared. Someone had penned countless notes and exclamation points and even hearts between lines, scenes, and paragraphs. Margins held lists, trailing from the tops of pages, down to footnote white space. Huge blocks of commentary and scribbled text flooded the story. I'd never seen anything like it.

I flipped pages, my eyes sticking to what looked like an original poem scrawled into the blank space after the Chapter Five break.

First, a daring leap into my scowling mouth,
bounding over a white-toothed fence,
tunneling down, down, down my throat.
He was in.
Proud of himself as he swung from vein to vein,
swimming through blood and life. Both, mine.
Until he felt it time to scale the bony rungs of my ribs,
slipping between to grasp the center thing that bucked and beat.
My heart.

The haunting poem snagged my own heart, like a sweater unraveling on a nail. Who had written this and all the rest? Why inside this particular book, which was technically a children's novel? I thumbed past a few more pages. More poems, more comments. More upon more.

"Miss?"

"Sorry, ma'am." Well, that was me. Lost in print again. But this was different, like a new story within one of the greatest tales ever written. I wanted to read it all. "Instead of a refund, I have another idea." I left the counter for the classics section Mr. Winston housed in rows of antique mahogany shelving. I shoved my hand into the *B* area, peeled off the price sticker, and handed the customer a new copy of *Peter Pan*.

She smiled. "This is why I shop here. You can't get this level of customer service from those big online retailers."

Customer service? Had she *met* my boss? I returned the smile and told her, "No problem. You're all set. Have a nice day."

When she left, I held the used *Peter Pan* and the barcode sticker. I'd made things right for the customer, but now I had to do the same for Yellow Feather. I rang up the new book, punched in my measly employee discount, then counted out bills from my wallet. I watched every single dollar my mother didn't, but even if I had to skip my weekly iced caramel latte, this book was mine. I could spend hours with these secret thoughts.

Mr. Winston's loafers slapped the floor behind me. I quickly dropped *Peter Pan* into my tote as he stacked catalogs on the storage shelf. "Thought I heard a customer."

"She just left." I headed toward the used books section, my favorite corner of the shop. L-shaped and tucked into the back, it made for a perfect hiding spot. Preowned titles rested on five vintage turquoise book carts. This cozy nook smelled like people's living rooms and leather messenger bags. Rose water and cigarette smoke. Potpourri and vacation sunscreen and binding glue, with a hint of wool and mildew. I preferred it to any of the Elisa B. perfumes my mother brought home.

"Well, did she buy anything?" My boss leaned across the counter, grimacing. Like it was my fault if she hadn't.

"Just browsing." Technically, it wasn't a lie. She'd browsed the counter. My laptop. My blunt fingernails Marisol glossed in pale pink the other day.

"*Hmmph.*"

I had to know. I rested my hand on one of the metal carts. "Do you keep records of the people you buy these used books from?" Maybe I could find the mysterious poet and scribbler. At least I'd know if it was a man or a woman.

Mr. Winston looked at me like I had a flower growing out of my head. "Never have. No reason to. You know that. I just take them by the box and quote a price for the whole load or offer store credit. Then price out each one for resale." Another *you know that, too* look.

"You check them out, though, before you purchase? To make sure they're sellable?"

His ashen face scrunched, his dry, yellowy mustache looking like it could shrivel up and fall off at any moment. "'Course I do. Why?"

"Just curious. No reason." Every reason. My new-old book should not have made it onto the shelves at Yellow Feather in that condition.

Mr. Winston reached the front door, keys jingling. "I need to run home. You can unbox and display that new shipment of bookmarks and those literary trinkets you're always making me order. I left it all in the back," he added before the door dinged shut.

It hit me as I walked to the storage bay: books could travel. A box of novels donated to charity could end up in ten different homes. Then shared, or kept in a library, or donated yet again. Or sold to an independent bookstore like Yellow Feather. That meant the author who'd written inside *Peter Pan* might not even be from around here. Maybe I'd find clues as I read the cryptic scratches, but now, one thought prickled across my skin: I should never have seen this book. It was even *sold* and still found its way back here. Not back to Mr. Winston while I was home or at school—back to *me*.

I couldn't shake the feeling that it was simply meant to be mine.

Twenty minutes later, I was convinced either Yellow Feather needed a new doorbell, or I needed new ears. I returned to the shop floor, arms full of new merchandise, which I quite inelegantly dropped onto the cashier desk when I saw Asher. Shallow gasp, too.

"Sorry. I didn't mean to startle you," he said. "I was just poking around and found this." He raised a preowned copy of a popular Stephen King novel.

My voice wasn't functioning yet. I just nodded and surveyed the situation. Asher had not only poked around, he was currently reclining—loitering, hanging out—in one of the burgundy wingback chairs, and *oh no*, he had both feet propped on Mr. Winston's prized travel trunk. Recipe for an instant blowup if my boss chose this moment to storm through the front door.

It got worse as I approached. A blue hoodie hung lopsided across the other chair, aviator sunglasses tossed on top of stacked travel magazines. And… Starbucks cup. In a flash, I grabbed one of our cork coasters and placed it under Asher's drink.

"Sorry," I mumbled. "The owner's a little uptight about his furniture."

Asher's feet hit the floor with a *smack*. "Gotcha. I came in last week to buy my mom a gift, and Mr. Winston helped me. He did seem a little...uptight. Knowledgeable guy, though."

Right. Yes. My head bobbed aimlessly while I tried to think around Asher being here, and *me* being here, the morning after Bryn's party.

"I mean, knowledgeable if you're after a coffee table book about pop art." He smiled—so warmly it tugged his entire face like marionette string, loosening his square jaw, springing his cheeks wide under brown tourmaline eyes.

I wrung my hands together. After plenty of practice, I knew what to do with his scowls, but felt clueless about his smile. While pleasant, I couldn't shake the fact that just last night, his girlfriend shoved me into my version of an introvert's nightmare in front of the better part of the senior class.

"No wigs required for employees in this half of the building?"

Tess's blue monstrosity. He remembered. I wanted to look anywhere but at him, trade his face for book pages, but that would be rude. "I spend my breaks next door, and Tess doesn't have any daughters...so..." More hand clenching. "She likes to feed me gourmet tea blends and play dress-up."

Asher tipped his chin at me, then toward the street. "Speaking of breaks, I think I found the perfect place to spend mine." He scooted back into the velvet chair. "This might be North Park's best-kept secret. Quiet, peaceful, old-world cool, comfortable chairs, and..." His gaze circled the room, ending with a fleeting grin.

And *what*? So many unwanted questions lined up behind me. Breaks? As in *plural*? He was planning on coming back to sprawl himself and his faded T-shirts that probably smelled like dryer sheets and sunlight, and his perfectly cut jeans, and black Converse all over the vintage furniture?

"You look weirded out. Does Mr. Winston frown upon people actually enjoying his fine establishment?"

"Err, no." *Yes.*

Asher rose and held up the book. "You have a good used section over there." He glanced at a page, then shut the cover. "Mental bookmark for my next break," he explained with a shrug. "Maybe I'll finish before someone else buys it. I got through five chapters before you came out."

This startled me back into complete sentences. "What do you mean, five chapters? I was in the back for maybe twenty minutes."

"I'm a trained speed-reader."

I nearly lost my footing. He might as well have said he was a puppy murderer or a chronic library book nonreturner.

"What, you don't approve?"

Speed-reader *and* mind reader. I shook my head, clearing it. "I just don't know too much about it. I enjoy regular reading too much to even consider reading for speed."

"Not surprising, after what Bryn was carrying on about last night."

Instant burn through my fingers, my skin; I felt the bloom of every red flower I could name under my cheeks.

Thankfully, Asher had already turned toward the preowned section. He shelved the King book. "Well, it helps with plowing through textbooks and those pesky required novels for lit classes."

I heard a weird, breathy noise, mingling with the low Sinatra anthem coming from the speakers. I realized it came from me.

"I learned the speed skills the last part of junior year." Quick shrug. "Figured I'd master it before…college." On the last word, the light left his eyes. I wondered why. "But I'm betting *you* still think it's a sacrilege."

I wound my way around the counter. "I've never considered any book, especially a novel or work of literature, something you should 'plow through.' The whole point of reading is savoring the story, immersing yourself in a whole new place. Maybe one that doesn't even exist." *Escaping, hiding, trading your life for another.* "How can you rush that?"

He followed, leaning his forearms on the wood top. "Assumption—you hate e-readers, too."

One step back, horrified hands over my heart.

He laughed. "I won't say the *K*-word, then."

I had to snicker. "Holding a real book is like holding something alive. There's the grit of the pages between your fingers as you turn them. The edges get soft and worn. With a real book, you feel the weight of the story more." My eyes unconsciously flitted to the copy of *Peter Pan* poking out from my tote. Then I looked up, met Asher's gaze. "Speed-reading just squashes the whole experience. You miss detail and pacing, and everything the author intended you to feel in the first place."

"Maybe I just like fast things," Asher said, and the words seemed to jump from every mystery novel on the shelves, inking between us. "You're wrong about one point, though. I don't miss any story details by speed-reading."

I raised a doubtful brow.

"Ask me anything from the first five chapters of that King novel."

"What's the famous menu item Al's Diner is known for?"

Asher immediately said, "The Fatburger."

"Impressive."

"What's more impressive is you didn't have to consult the book to find something."

I blushed again at the compliment. "Looks like we each have our special talents."

I expected another laugh from Asher, but got the opposite. His face dropped—not into the dour frown I first got from him. More a softening of his sharp features, tinged with a hint of sadness.

He cleared his throat. "I should probably get back to the center. Drywall won't hang itself."

"Since you're working for your uncle, hopefully he's more laid-back than my boss."

His brows jumped. "Um?"

"Tess filled me in," I said hurriedly. "She said you're doing some construction work for him?" More like Marisol's gossip train had done the filling.

Asher nodded. "Yeah, they needed a new conference room and break area. But I have two bosses, in a way. My other uncle's actually a contractor, and he's giving Uncle Mike a deal on the work. He hired out the foundation job, so I'm just tag-teaming with my cousin on framing and finish work. I'm hoping to finish up before I start classes at the *esteemed and prestigious* San Diego State campus next semester."

"You don't seem too excited. State's a good school. I'm applying there for the fall."

He frowned. Glanced at his shoelaces, then back at me. "It is a great school. It's just not Annapolis."

I knew next to nothing about the U.S. Naval Academy in Maryland, only that it was überhard to score an acceptance letter. "You wanted to go to Annapolis?"

"I *was* going to Annapolis," he corrected. "Always wanted to, since I was a kid. I got the final acceptance confirmation in April, just like my dad and my grandpa, years ago. I was all set, too—decent SAT scores, passed the interview, got a nomination letter from our local congressman. But now the family legacy ends with me." He rubbed his left leg, reading the silent question in my eyes. "Annapolis wants the most mentally, emotionally, and physically fit candidates they can find. Unfortunately, there are no slots for 'bionic knee boy.'"

Ahh... The limp. The measured movements. "Your accident?"

"Yeah. It happened in Del Mar and left me pretty banged up. My truck was totaled, and my left knee was shattered and completely rebuilt. Plenty of people and time to help rehab my leg, but there's no rehab for a shredded acceptance letter. State was all I could manage, but I had to wait a semester."

"I'm so sorry." What else could I say? He looked so forlorn, and any words I could add seemed too small to dignify his ordeal and the loss of his dream school.

"Thanks." He crossed the room to the trunk table and retrieved his Starbucks cup. A white string and paper tag trailed from the rim.

"Tea instead of coffee?" I teased. "Don't let Tess know, or you'll be drowning in herbal concoctions."

"Not by choice." Asher jiggled the cup. "Chamomile. Yum, right? I had to say goodbye to caffeine, chocolate, alcohol. Consider me the antivice poster boy." He sipped the tea. "I'm on a virtual cocktail of meds, and I don't mean the good kind. Also part of my PCS treatment plan."

"PCS?"

"Post-Concussive Syndrome. Which likes me so much it doesn't want to leave. Plus, it's working extra hard to keep me out of the cockpit until my healing progresses. PCS doesn't mess around. Let's just say, if you're considering a major auto accident for some Friday night excitement, stick to books."

"Gotcha," I said. Stick to books. I usually did, and usually wanted to. But not always. Most often, I poured the lonely ache of that right back into printed ink.

"Thanks for the quiet spot. It gets a little chaotic across the street sometimes, and chaos is something I'm supposed to be avoiding," Asher said. "The legal center attracts some major drama—maybe more than in that King novel. Curious to see if it's still here next time."

"You know, you could just buy it?"

Another sip. "You're thinking we're in a book*store* and not a library, yeah?"

Damn him and his bionic knee and his bionic superhero mind reading.

He must've caught the slight grimace I felt on my face, because he backed away, laughing. "I spent sixty-five bucks in here the other day on a shiny book filled with Lichtenstein and Warhol masterpieces. *And* dealt with Mr. Winston. I figure we're good for a bit, Darcy."

My mouth fell open, then snapped shut. Oh, we were good? Then why did the whole store suddenly feel tilted to one side, thousands of volumes sliding down helplessly as Asher walked out the door?

To steady myself, I dug out the copy of *Peter Pan*. It felt good in my hands. Solid and right. I flipped to that bit after Chapter Five again, running one finger over the handwritten poetry. This time, I noticed the title I'd blown right by at first glance: "Uninvited."

Uninvited. Like new daily coffee—no, tea—break mates? Maybe. But the thought of tea pricked another thought. I traded the novel for my laptop, searched "Post-Concussive Syndrome," and skimmed.

Medical sites described PCS as a disorder resulting from the lasting effects of a head injury, or concussion symptoms that wouldn't go away. Some people experienced these symptoms for months or even longer. Strong medication eased the discomfort, but it often worked inconsistently until doctors found the right dosage and the body adjusted. Diet sometimes helped, too—patients were told to avoid sugar, gluten, alcohol, and caffeine, just like Asher mentioned, which indicated he was sticking to his treatment plan.

The symptom list was long and daunting. A few leaped from my screen, eerily familiar. Impatience. Irritability. Confrontational attitude. Depression. Frequent mood swings. Dizziness. Headaches. Migraines.

I remembered the way Asher had snapped at me. His brooding behavior, and the way he was always rubbing his temples. I pictured him in that quiet spot on the black rock jetty. PCS explained why he could be friendly one minute, then aloof the next.

I'd gotten it all wrong—Asher wasn't rude or unpredictable. He was ill.

Nine

Mothers

*"It was the nest I have told you of, floating on the
lagoon, and the Never bird was sitting on it.
'See,' said Hook in answer to Smee's question, 'that is
a mother. What a lesson! The nest must have fallen into
the water, but would the mother desert her eggs? No.'"*
**Parenting, as explained by Hook. Even villains
know what a good mother is.**

—J. M. BARRIE, *PETER PAN*,
AND *PETER PAN* MYSTERY SCRIBBLER

I slammed the passenger door of Marisol's SUV and banged
my head against the headrest.

"Enraged much?" Marisol asked over the idling engine.

"Oh...oh...sometimes she is so—" I caught myself preswear,
spying the four-year-old twins, Carlos and Camila, in the
back seat. I let out a heavy sigh instead. "Thanks for the lift."

"Luckily you called while I was picking up los animales

from tumbling." Marisol's youngest siblings were blissfully sucking on juice boxes, dangling matching Adidas sneakers over their booster seats. Camila offered a quick flappy wave.

"You would have come for me, anyway." Big doe eyes.

"Possibly." She tapped her fingers on the wheel. "Can you repeat why you're currently without a car? You sounded like a banshee on the phone, so the most I got was—ridiculous, gas, pick up, dinner, pretty please, Marisol."

"That's most of it," I said wearily. "After the Feather, I shut myself in my room for a few hours to look at sample eBay listings, so my first attempt won't look like total newbie material. Also, homework."

"And your car was abducted by aliens?"

"There's mostly green aliens and purple aliens," Carlos voiced proudly.

Camila said, "There's pink ones and yellow, too. The books say that."

I laughed. "Know what? You monkeys are both right." Then to Marisol, "Mom's gas tank was on empty, and she forgot to stop last night. She just left a note saying she was taking my Honda to work."

"She didn't even ask first?"

The rumble in my chest started again. "She *assumed* I had no plans and was hibernating with books for the night."

"Here," Marisol said, popping open the minicooler she always kept on the back seat floor. When Mrs. Robles got a new car, she offered her eldest daughter the red Pathfinder on one condition: Marisol would help shuttle the twins around. Between various appointments, gym class, playdates, and park excursions, Marisol soon realized (1) Eva Robles was a genius. (2) Juice boxes created peaceful car rides.

I frowned. "Juice. Really?"

"Either that or gum, babe." She leveled an appraising look at me. "Juice, then." With one hand, she shifted gears, pulling away from the curb. The other felt around in the cooler and drew one out.

"Cran-Grape," I said. "Eww."

"How did I not *sense* that?"

"You got any *Cran-Irresponsible Mother* flavors in there? What about *Cran-Compulsive Shopper* with ten billion gallons of perfume, but not one in her gas tank?"

Marisol blazed through a yellow light and smacked a cold white box into my palm. Cran-Raspberry. Fine. I poked the straw into the little top hole and took a few sips. And found it oddly soothing.

With the twins unbuckled and rushing to the entryway, Marisol stopped along the flagstone path. "Okay, give," she said, like every time I came to dinner.

I whined, surrendering a paperback copy of *Everything, Everything* from my messenger purse.

A couple more steps, then, "Now the other one in the buckled pocket." She flashed an infuriating smile.

Damn her—my new-old copy of *Peter Pan.* "Mari, you know how your family gets. After a couple hours, your parents and siblings and innumerable tíos start speaking less English and more Spanish. Everyone gets all loud and...and... I could just move to the couch and re—"

"You could, but you won't. You'll socialize and have fun. Besides, you *are* family." I let Marisol snatch the book; I knew she'd never open it. She skipped up the porch and stashed both novels in the Robleses' mailbox. "You can bail these out before I drive you home."

I would've grumbled, but the *smell.* The front door of their two-story, Tuscan-style house hung open, and love wafted out in the form of garlic and roasted chilies. Of savory meats and citrus and sugar. I followed it and the sound of lively conversations chimed over chilled bottles of cerveza and iced colas with lime.

We stashed our jackets and purses in the foyer to the echo of laughter beaming around the rooms. I felt customary pats on my back, returned rosy-warm smiles. Brisk Motown music shook from the entertainment system, and children snaked through with hot, buttered tortillas and devilish cackles.

Eva Robles poked her head from the kitchen and waved us in. "There's my girl. Just in time." Marisol's mom kissed my cheek, chortling. And from this seemingly innocent exchange, I already knew my fate.

The vast kitchen, crowded with bodies—most of whom I recognized—fell suspiciously silent. Family members hovered in front of dark wood cabinets as Señora Robles sprinkled salt from scarlet-manicured fingers. Then one last lime squeeze over the huge bowl of homemade salsa. Marisol's sister Natalia handed me a tortilla chip and snickered as her mother presented her creation.

I tiptoed the chip into the red concoction. After one bite, *heat*, dragon-breath burn, and straight-up flame coated my tongue, my throat. I coughed. Gasped. Sputtered and sniffed with teary eyes and flailing arms.

The room erupted, boisterous and alive again.

"Bueno, it's perfect, no?" Mama Robles said, presenting the bowl to her other guests.

Unfazed, Marisol already had tissues and a glass of milk shoved into my watery vision while she chatted with a cousin. She discarded a purple gum wad onto her gold bracelet, then my fire-breather friend hit the salsa bowl.

I blew my nose and sucked down the cold, soothing milk. I knew from experience that water would only make it worse. "Whew," I told Mama, blinking.

"Pobrecita." She cupped satin-soft hands around my cheeks.

"I'm sorry, mija. But you're the best guinea pig!" She stepped back and held up one finger. "A ver…" Mama bent around to the granite island and grabbed a small container. "I made un poquito just for you. No seeds, and the other chilies you like better."

I accepted the bowl from the small-boned brunette. Mama Robles often prepared a milder version for me, but tonight, after empty gas tanks and emptier assumptions, her thoughtful gesture made my eyes fill. They burned with salt—and not the kind that gave the salsa life.

"Marisol." Another two steps. "I need an elevator. And thank God your dad's a doctor, because *ohmystomach*."

Ahead of me on the staircase, my friend chuckled. "Welcome to your penance for going back for seconds."

It was thirds, but Marisol didn't know that. And wouldn't have blamed me—the food was otherworldly. My usual dinners consisted of omelets or salads or grilled cheese and boxed tomato soup. But tonight, I lost all control when Eva Robles presented platters of grilled carne asada, vats of chunky guacamole, and shredded chicken stewed with tomato and onion. Plus Marisol's dad's favorite Cuban-style empanadas filled with spiced ground beef, and countless other sides. "Why do we have to go upstairs again?"

"Now you have beans in your brain. Remember? The *Much Ado* costumes? I've done enough for you to have a look."

Right, those. She'd been working all week on dresses for the female leads, Hero and Beatrice. After a few more painful strides, I followed her into the large sewing room she shared with her mother. Two steps across the threshold, I walked into a fairy tale. Yards of ivory fabric, expertly honed into one of the most beautiful wedding gowns I'd ever seen, hung from a ceiling hook like an elegant ghost. Eva Robles worked alone—except for her assistant, Marisol—and stylish brides waited months and paid small fortunes for one of her custom creations.

Marisol noticed my drool. "Yeah, this baby is beyond." She fingered the neckline. "Mama hand-sewed all these seed pearls, and there's a double row of them. I helped with the bodice. Gah! Those pleats."

I believed her. And like every time I stepped into this room, I wondered if it would ever be my turn, one day. Custom satin and someone to wear it for. But what would happen when I slipped a white gown shaped by Marisol's mom onto my own body? I could already picture the sweeping lace train, blackening with dust and straining under the clutter that always dragged behind me. So much for some happily in my ever after.

I sighed and left my worries with the silk; Marisol was waiting to show me her creations. The other side of the studio belonged to her. Two sewing machines, supply racks, and a wide cutting table filled the corner where she spent much of her time.

"I'm so stoked on how this one is shaping up. It's for Beatrice," Marisol said at the first mannequin. The robin's egg blue gown had cap sleeves and a high empire waist. "I decided on Regency-period styles, and Mrs. Howard loved the idea. Don't you think the color will look good with Alyssa's complexion?"

"For sure. I love it, too." I examined the neat stitching and fluid drape. Even a novice like me could recognize the expert workmanship. The extra details and artistic flourishes.

Marisol hauled over her sketch boards and some loose fabrics. She lifted the edge of a thick brocade with blue and pink flowers. "For look one, I'm going to make a short bolero jacket with this floral to fit tightly over Beatrice's gown. And she'll have a straw bonnet with blue ribbons and white gloves." She pulled out the second fabric, a pistachio-green background dappled with blue leaves. "Then for the big wedding scene, I'll use this for a long cutaway top layer with puffy sleeves and lace trim. And we'll swap out the accessories."

"Smart," I told her, then moved to the second manne-quin, which was pinned and fitted with a raw-edge bodice in ivory satin.

"Hero will wear this ivory gown with a similar pink bo-lero for Act One. For her wedding, I'm making a long lace overlay with a little sweep train."

Hero, played by London Banks. I tried to ignore the image of Asher's girlfriend in the romantic costumes and focused, in-stead, on their creator. I studied the full-color sketches Marisol must have shown Mrs. Howard. Hand-drawn pencil figures modeled all four looks, with fabric swatches taped to the sides. "This is brilliant." I smiled. "*You're* brilliant."

Marisol shrugged. "I'm just me." But a gleam flashed across her face, like a blingy jeweled button, fit for any one of her dresses.

"Well, you're going to be better than anyone else at FIDM."

Attending the Fashion Institute of Design and Merchandis-ing in Los Angeles had been Marisol's dream for years. Prac-tically born with a thimble on her thumb, plus an uncanny eye for style, she was destined to work with beautiful things. The same way I knew I had to work with beautiful words.

"It's always felt so far away, you know?" She returned the fabrics to their labeled shelf. "Until now, anyway. I'll start building my entrance portfolio after Christmas." She looked at me pointedly. "Los Angeles."

Los Angeles. We'd talked about the future countless times, hinged over our mosaic table with iced coffees and carb-loaded snacks. *Marisol's little black Sharpie heart. My tiny star.*

We'd never lived two hours apart before. Marisol was always going on about the amazing lit program at UCLA, trying to tempt me into applying. Just for the hell of it.

"You know why I can't think of bailing. At least not next fall. And I don't know what's going to happen with the lease," I whispered. School in LA was just another version of a new home in Grandma's bedroom. Both felt like abandoning my mom when she needed me most.

Two sticks of gum appeared in Marisol's hand. She unwrapped both and shoved them into her mouth. "Well, we'll still have our halfway pact. Once a week."

I smiled. Marisol would drive one hour south, and I'd head north. "Dinner or lunch and tons of trouble."

"That goes without saying." Marisol finished folding the two silver gum wrappers into one star and dropped it into my palm. I knew then, even in a twilight of unknown tomorrows, some things would still shine.

"Papi wants you guys down for dessert." Marisol's thirteen-year-old sister stood in the doorway. Natalia Robles jutted one hip forward in skinny jeans and ballet flats, dark ponytail swinging. "Warning, Tía Lucia just *had* to bring the caramel disaster."

Marisol groaned. "You'll take some anyway."

"But, Marisol—"

"*But*, you'll not only take some, you'll let her see you put it on your plate." Her voice dropped. "I won't tell if you sneak outside and feed it to Pepe and Carmen."

Natalia left with a dramatic huff.

"Catch me up," I said. "What did Tía Lucia make that's only fit for your dogs?"

"You know Mama's flan?"

Do I. Suddenly, my overstuffed tummy was feeling lighter.

Less encumbered. Practically empty, with plenty of room for the rich caramel custard dessert.

"Well," Marisol continued, "Mama's recipe is actually the Cuban version from my abuela Robles. But Lucia swears she's the flan queen. Different recipe or not, hers is always a rubbery, bland joke. And she bakes it in a rectangular pan, which makes Mama rant. They've been in a flan feud for years. She only brought her version because she heard Mama was making it tonight."

"Should I be afraid?" Of course, I'd have to be polite and eat a portion, too.

"Take small bites and chew thoroughly."

When we reached the dining room, Marisol's family was already gathered around the rustic wooden table. Eva Robles and her sister perched in front of their respective flan offerings, dueling serving knives ready, but my eyes lingered at the head of the table. Luis Robles was standing with Marco, the only other person here who'd stepped past my front door, who really knew how messy my life was. Both men were smiling, pride humming between them.

I moved closer; Marco saw me and instantly, his smile waned, his whole face captured in a fleeting look of regret I didn't comprehend. Too quickly, Marco's father swung his arm around him and signaled the crowd.

"We have wonderful news," Dr. Robles said over the hum of dessert eagerness and melodic *Spanglish*. The smoky-haired cardiologist was slight in frame, but unmistakably commanding. He eyed Marco, but his son motioned for him to continue. "Marco's going to be moving. He made such an impact during his internship, the engineering firm wants to start his training early at their main headquarters, near San Francisco."

Relatives cheered, but as the true impact of the words reg-

istered, all I wanted to do was flee and become invisible for
real. But that would bring questions I didn't want to answer.

"I'm transferring to UC Berkeley next term." Marco's voice
chimed bright. "I've been promised a job, too. Basically, my
dream position will be waiting for me when I graduate."

The extended family made a wall of hugs and swooping ges-
tures around Marco, and I elbowed Marisol. "Did you know
about this?" How could she have hidden this news while I
was inhaling tacos? Even while we'd swooned over wedding
gowns and floral fabric, vowing nothing, especially distance,
would change things between us?

"Come." Marisol dragged me into the empty kitchen. "I
swear, Mama and Papi have known for a couple weeks, but
they only told me and Natalia this morning."

I had to believe her. Marisol never lied.

"I just wanted you to have a nice dinner. Some fun. Marco
was gonna talk to you after dessert. I didn't know Papi was
going to announce—"

"I get it. You know what this means, though." My safety
net, my secret elf who fixed leaks and faulty lights, was leaving right after Christmas. *Six months. The lease.*

"Stop, Darcy. You're already writing the story, right, amiga?
You already have the bad ending planned."

"Sometimes those are the only endings I see."

"Well, you need better plots. Maybe Marco has a friend
from UCSD who can help. You'll be making eBay money
soon, too. You might be able to hire a handyman once in a
while."

I nodded over a flat smile, but those options required letting at least one more person through a front door that had
no welcome mat, into a life with no room left for hospitality.

I'd waited years for the psychologist's predictions to man-
ifest in my mom, my home, the way Rapunzel waited in a

locked tower. There were a few variations of hoarding, and my mother's behavior was typical of a category that was often provoked by a tragic incident. Hers turned a lifelong collector into a hoarder. According to the doctor, the need to compulsively shop and keep would improve once she acknowledged the issue behind it. Denial fed her illness, and she'd begin to heal once she declared her pain and faced it.

But the thing was... She already *had*.

Four years ago, Grandma and I sat in the counselor's office, listening to the whole of Mom's confession for the first time. Hurts even my grandma didn't know, sharp details of her devastating abandonment. It had emptied her, so much that she refused to attend any more sessions. We'd hoped the strides she'd made to finally voice her pain would be enough to push her forward.

But the motion was too slow and slight. Soon, Grandma Wells couldn't bear it anymore.

And I couldn't explain it anymore. Mom was regressing. Just this afternoon, three new shipping boxes were stacked at our door. The hoard was growing, and we were losing days.

Footsteps sounded; I turned to find Señora Robles holding two dessert plates. "Lucia watched me put her no-good comida on here with my flan." Mama handed a plate to Marisol and placed the second one into my hands. "But she was too busy with Marco to see me scrape it into the trash." She winked conspiratorially, and I found a short laugh.

As Mama leaned in, I caught whiffs of the Elisa B. Lilac Wish perfume my own mother had gifted her. For now, I had no new Mom ideas, but I had this family. And I had the best flan in the world. I tasted it. Vanilla and caramel slid down my throat, velvety sweet and cold.

"Always amazing," I told her.

She smiled and pointed to the granite island. "There. I made a package for you and tu mamá. The meat and beans and rice and some empanadas."

I'd known Marisol for eight years, but tonight, I realized something for the first time. Her house blossomed with cafecito and caramelized sugar, octave-spanning laughter sweetening each room. It embraced hip-hop dancing cousins and whining dogs at the screen door. Garlic and wedding lace. Floral brocade and sauce-splattered cooktops. It all rose and swelled like bread dough—pan dulce—pushing against windowpanes and straining walls. Love, and all the shapes it came in.

The Robles family hoarded, too.

Ten

Shadow

"All the world is made of faith, and trust, and pixie dust." **And the feeling of sneaking in your bedroom window after one kiss turned to ten, when you swore you were flying. And your feet didn't hit the ground until morning.**

—J. M. BARRIE, *PETER PAN*,
AND *PETER PAN* MYSTERY SCRIBBLER

After two weeks, I'd figured out enough about eBay to post my first listings and found enough courage to sneak out a few products. My mother had so much Elisa B. piled into the four plastic tubs, even she couldn't catalog it as carefully as some of her other items. Still, I had to act carefully, so Marisol and I established some guidelines:

(1) Choose items where Mom owned many duplicates.

(2) Only three or four items for every listing round.

(3) Take makeup when Mom was at work and store it in my bedroom, which she never entered.

During that same span of time, I'd become absolutely sure of three other things:

(1) My beloved *Peter Pan* mystery writer was female.

(2) The scribbled text was her version of a diary.

(3) Mr. Winston was clearly *over* Asher.

"Is Fleet's nephew going to drip tea all over my trunk table every damn day?" he whispered on day thirteen of Asher spending his breaks in our seating area.

I looked up from my book to the boy in question, who was currently racing through a used James Patterson thriller. Black sneakers rested primly on the floor. "Asher bought three picture books the other day for his cousins," I pointed out. "And last week, he got a poetry anthology for his grandma."

"I see," my boss said, then noticed a brunette, curly-wigged Tess waiting outside, one hand on her hip. "Cripes, what now?" he muttered, then blazed out the door.

Asher watched Tess and Mr. Winston's discussion with enough curiosity to pull him from the burgundy chair and over to my cashier counter.

"What's up with those two?" he asked, jerking his head backward. "I know they're divorced, but I've seen them out there a few times since I've been working at Mid-City. I mean, the hand motions alone. Lively." One dense but groomed brow jumped, and I stared a millisecond too long at the jagged scar just above it.

I cleared my throat. "They share the building, but that's all. If Tess needs to speak with Mr. Winston, she hovers out front until he notices, or until I alert him. He does the same in front of Tops."

"They won't text?"

"The esteemed Frederick Winston doesn't even know how to text. And you'll see farm animals flying outside before Tess ever sets her right toe in here. Same with him and Tops," I said, and watched his features dim right as I voiced the word *flying*. Sometimes I forgot he held an actual pilot's license.

"Do customers really use this?" He twirled one finger inside the Yellow Feather penny tray. The coins clinked as he read the little embellished sign. "'Need a penny, take a penny. Have a penny, leave a penny.'"

Now we were on to pennies? I wondered if short attention span was common to PCS sufferers, or if this was just Asher's attempt at small talk. At least his mood had seemed more even lately. "Sure," I said. "I top off people if they're short."

"Wouldn't the Mr. Winston I've come to know want you to hoard every coin you get?"

A billion words filled Yellow Feather, but this one pealed like a low-toned bell in the center of my chest. *Hoard.* "The tray was my idea. I doubt he's even noticed it."

Asher reached one finger out to tap my new-old copy of *Peter Pan.* "You're always reading this between customers."

Another subject change. I pulled the book toward me before he could open the cover. "One of my favorites. I keep going back to the story." Which technically wasn't a lie.

"But it's a kid's book, even though it's more than cool that he doesn't need a plane to fly. Still, I've been in here when you've discussed legit literature with customers. And eerily well. I guess I'm just surprised."

"Don't knock middle grade lit. Some of the most profound themes exist in short, simple packages." I picked up the copy, brandishing it. "I dare you to see for yourself. I mean, it's less than two hundred pages. You and your speed-reading could probably knock it out in thirty minutes."

"It's worth that much of my precious time?" Asher leaned forward so closely I detected a hint of mint leaf tea on his breath.

I realized the airy, wobbling sound in the room was coming from me, and it was my laugh. "Here's a preview. One of my favorite parts is when Peter finds his lost shadow and tries to reattach it," I said, hoping the familiar text about one boy would distract me from another. "Straight from Chapter Three. 'If he thought at all, but I don't believe he ever thought, it was that he and his shadow, when brought near each other, would join like drops of water, and when they did not he was appalled. He tried to stick it on with soap from the bathroom, but that also failed. A shudder passed through Peter and he sat on the floor and cried.'"

Asher smiled, shaking his head. "That little Pan dude is emo."

I had to laugh. "There's a new take, but I can't fault your analysis."

"I see why you like him," Asher said.

"I have a soft spot for Peter." I laid one hand over my heart. "Even though he spends a lot of the story acting kind of selfish and flighty—no pun intended."

I anticipated one of the broad, lopsided grins I'd come to expect after two weeks of him in my shop. Not even a hint of tease touched his face. "Speaking of selfish," he said under his breath. Then he straightened his posture. "Look, Darcy, something's been bugging me. I'm really sorry about what happened at the beach party. That was messed up, and I could tell you were pissed. London should've just ignored Bryn."

My next breath tripped. *Bryn. The beach. London. Eremite.*

Like Peter, I seemed to unhook from my body, the shadow-me on a beach blanket, tangled in mermaid hair and memory. Wine, so cold it hurt my teeth. The fire and smoke and shame.

"I should've said something earlier," Asher continued. His eyes pinched together in frustration. "Sometimes London forgets to leave the drama to her script. It's even worse when she's with Bryn. All that cheap wine wasn't helping, either. I should've tossed her phone into the drink cooler or something. You…you didn't deserve being singled out."

Oh.

The clean-edged focus of Asher's stare, plus the candor underneath the rest of him, grabbed me by the feet. Upending. Shaking. Parts of me—the shadow parts—were spilling out onto the floor and I couldn't stop them. I needed a story of another teen girl and how she handled another teen boy ripping into the middle of her.

Think.

After one, then two breaths, I got my story. Not one with a savvy book heroine, but something my *Peter Pan* mystery writer had scribbled in the margin, then underlined and decorated with exclamation points.

I realized it was all mine to keep, and to give away when I chose. Trust and sensitivity, and my vulnerable pieces, too. He couldn't take them! But see, here's what happened. When I got his heart and all his promises and gave him mine, he got all that other stuff along with it. I couldn't separate them!!!

Of course. This guy at my counter hadn't given me anything. No heart, no promises. And he certainly wasn't in the position to do so anytime soon. Any secret bits wanting to helplessly flee my body were mine to give and show—or mine to keep. Asher was simply speaking, and I was listening. *No big deal.*

I hid trembling hands under the counter and tucked my vulnerable pieces back inside, buttoning them up where they belonged. I lifted my neck and inched my shoulders back. "Right. There was more than a lot of that cheap wine," I told him. Then I smiled plainly. "And no worries. Thank you for mentioning it, though."

A fleeting smile touched his face. "Yeah."

From the counter, I saw the scowling, furiously approaching form of Frederick Winston before Asher heard the door ding. By the time he turned to witness the door nearly snap off its hinges, I was already on the move.

"One day," Mr. Winston said, strained and red faced. He feverishly plumped brocade pillows and set another coaster beneath the one already under Asher's tea.

At the thriller section, I grabbed the three closest Lee Child hardback books and smacked them onto the counter. "Asher, since you like the Patterson novel so much, I think you should try these next," I said with enough punch to carry over Ella Fitzgerald crooning through the speakers. Then a stealth wink.

"Oh, um, yes. Great idea," Asher said gravely. "You've always given such helpful recommendations to other *customers*." He lifted one, read the jacket blurb. "Ahh, Jack Reacher. Looks like an interesting character."

Mr. Winston slunk behind the counter. "Is one day too much to ask for? Just *one* without her…" He trailed off, surveying what looked like a hefty transaction.

I pretended to ring up the first book—opening the cover, double-checking the ISBN, making sure the dust jacket wasn't creased. Finally, Mr. Winston adjusted his tweed cap and fled into his office.

"He might be the best story in here," Asher said.

"A bestseller for sure." I grabbed the books and carefully replaced them.

Asher followed. "One question. Does Peter ever manage to become one with his shadow?"

I took six steps to the classics section and pulled out a new mint green and pale blue hardcover, displaying it proudly. "You'll have to read it for yourself."

The slow-moving, flat smile didn't quite reach his eyes. "I may just do that. Maybe emo Peter has some good advice." He leveled a wry look on a short huff. "You know, something literary and surprisingly profound."

"You lost a shadow?" I asked, thinking of the scene where Peter first sneaks into Wendy's bedroom window, searching for his missing half. And finds a girl to sew it back on.

"You could say that. Mine's lying somewhere on Del Mar Heights Road."

Oh. The accident. A shiver branched across my back.

But Asher already had his own Wendy Darling. London, with her sinuous body and hair like the shiny new pennies I gave to customers. If anyone was going to drag out a sewing kit and attach all his missing parts with needle and thread, it would be her.

Silly, silly, invulnerable me.

Not every girl gets to say she spent precisely twenty minutes as a platinum blonde. Tess's *wig du jour*, chosen to complement my ivory top and light-wash jeans, hit just above the small of my back. The bangs also hung a tad too long on me, so I had to weave my eyesight through silky strands to see anything. After two minutes of fun with head adornments, Tess hooked me up with tea she'd accidentally brewed too long, plus three homemade snickerdoodles, which made up for the tea's bitterness.

Good for her and Tops' cash register, she stayed busy for most of my break. October meant Halloween wigs and regular customers coming in for the specialty masks she stocked every fall. Mr. Winston could take lessons from that kind of marketing move.

While Tess helped a group of college girls with rainbow wigs, I took a selfie in my new bombshell 'do and texted it to Marisol.

Marisol: Ooh, I like. You should buy that one

Me: Bite your tongue

Marisol: Ha. You check eBay? Bravo!

Me: Call. T's working

Two seconds later, I answered Marisol's ringtone with, "What about eBay?"

"I checked those items you listed. Darcy, two sold today with *Buy It Now*, and you already have opening bids on the other two auctions."

"Seriously?" Currently, two Elisa B. pink lipsticks, one foundation set, and one eye shadow palette were for sale with Darcy-crafted descriptions and Marisol-snapped photos. I did the mental math and realized I might net close to a hundred dollars. And it was only my first week.

"I told you, new-in-box makeup moves fast. That means you need to pack up the *Buy It Now* stuff ASAP and ship it off. Info's all in your email."

Which I hadn't checked lately. I took another bite of cookie heaven. "Gotcha. There's a post office branch by the Feather. I can hide the shipment in my trunk."

Silence on the line, except for background noise. I detected strains of a preschool cartoon theme song and two German shepherds barking out their harmonies. "Mari?"

"Still here. Sorry," she said. "I was just thinking our plan might actually work."

Whenever *I* thought of it—beyond the bold lipstick and blush colors, beyond the promise of quick money—the deception filled me like smoke. And that was before the worry crept in. Then the questions and endless tragic scenarios. "I've been trying not to think of it."

"By just doing it?"

"Exactly."

"Your mom hasn't caught on, right?"

"Not yet," I said. "She's left those tubs alone, but it's only week one."

I heard Marisol's short sigh. "Week one and a hundred bucks, D."

After we hung up, I was still thinking. Feeling more of the dark, shadowed parts creep over the whole of me. Instinctively, I looked straight through the wigged mannequin heads along the side wall, visualizing the mass of books next door at the Feather. Weren't there countless stories of characters who did the hard thing to survive? Heroes who lied to save themselves or a loved one? Revolutionaries. Risk takers who were also "just doing it" because it was all they really could do?

Or was I just fooling myself—trying to craft a rightful heroine out of a sneaking thief?

"What's this, now?" Tess chirped. I hadn't even noticed her approach. She hopped onto a stool and tugged at my wig. "I dress you in these golden strands of fabulous, and you muck them up with another Darcy-frown. A supersized one, too, like that beehive Halloween wig I just sold."

I forced a smile. "Just a lot going on, but I'll be fine." Another cinnamon-dusted bite. "Your cookies help."

"Sugar and carbohydrates usually do, Darcy-Diva. I'll send you home with more." She sipped her tea, which had to have gone lukewarm. "A while back you were going on about financial difficulties. And even I know good snickerdoodles can't help you there, unless you're selling them."

I winked at her, nodding. "I think I've found a way to get through my snag." *By just doing it.*

"Of course you did."

But I barely heard her. I was paying more attention to the scene across University Avenue. A familiar white Volkswagen convertible pulled up in front of Mid-City Legal, top down. London Banks's sixteenth birthday present, or so I'd heard from Bryn when she'd whined to Marisol about it. London released her hair from a ponytail, shaking out waves like a lion's mane.

And then Asher emerged.

I was stealthy enough to sneak cosmetics from a hoarder, but not enough to fool Tess Winston. "She does that more often, lately. Picks him up," Tess said. "Pretty girl he has there."

"You've noticed?"

She shrugged, but her fuchsia-painted lips twitched a bit. "Flashy drop-top, flashy girl. Gets slow in here sometimes. I pay attention. Besides, I tend to notice good hair when I see it."

"London never comes to school without a magazine-ready style. And if anyone ever compliments her, she always mentions her luck of being 'just blessed with' her natural color," I said.

"Ha!" Tess snorted a laugh. "Natural? That's not what I meant."

"Huh?"

We watched Asher fold his long legs into the car and lean over to peck London's lips. But the pair didn't leave right away. What looked like a short, tense conversation ended with London shaking her head dramatically before putting up the convertible top.

"Darcy, London's red is no gift from the Almighty. No, ma'am. A red like hers takes the careful blending of many tones and top colorist skills. You can't get anywhere near that particular coppery auburn, which appears to be touched by unicorns and fairy dust, without help from a fancy-schmancy salon. Oh, she's a natural redhead, all right. She's just not *that* redhead."

I drummed my fingers on the glass countertop, considering.

"Trust me, if anyone knows hair, it's me." A customer entered the shop, and Tess scurried away to help.

After three more bites of cookie, Marisol texted again.

Marisol: Word of the Day. Go

Me: Lushburg

Marisol: Hmmm...

Marisol: Someone who drinks too many margaritas and plows a ship into an iceberg. Titanic style

Me: Laughs

Marisol: Darn. Wrong?

Me: Sorry yeah

Marisol: What is it then?

Me: A counterfeit coin

Eleven

One Story-Filled Head: An Inside View

*Things I hate: Grape soda. Endings. Beginnings. Peeling
nail polish. Beach sand. Grape-flavored anything.
Things I love: Flip-flops. Pretty stamps. Cardigan
sweaters. Sand dollars. Lemon drop candy.
The number 6.*

—*PETER PAN* MYSTERY SCRIBBLER

Besides poems and advice, my *Peter Pan* book was filled with
lists. Numbered or bulleted lists tucked into margins and
crowded into the space between chapters. The hate-love list
spun through my mind all day, drowning out my teachers and
even Marisol's cheery prattle. After school, I was still spinning
with it, wanting to question this writer over an iced caramel
latte. A girl who loved sand dollars, but hated sand? The laws
of nature required her to trudge through piles of one—feet
sinking, rough grains sticking in her flip-flops—to even have

a chance at discovering the other. Was she trying to tell me some shells were worth crossing acres of sand?

Boots shuffled across the Jefferson auditorium floor. I grinned at Mr. Penn, Shakespearean scholar/janitor extraordinaire, when he said, "'I had rather hear my dog bark at a crow…'"

"You get the source first. *Much Ado About Nothing.*" I pointed to the stage, where volunteers were hanging backdrop fabric from ladders. At his raised brows, I added, "'I had rather hear my dog bark at a crow…than a man swear he loves me.'"

Mr. Penn tapped the center of his chin. "Could be a lucky guess. Let's try, hmm…yes. 'When shall we three meet again in thunder, lightning, or in rain? When the hurly-burly's done…'"

"'When the hurly-burly's done…when the battle's won,'" I answered immediately.

"Source?"

"Since we're technically in a theater, I can't say the name of this particular play, because everyone knows that superstition. So, your quote is from The Scottish Play."

Mrs. Howard halted next to us, radio in one hand, script in the other. "Two questions. First, what was *that* business?" She looked pointedly at me. "And second, why aren't you in *my* play?"

Mr. Penn tipped his mop handle toward me. "I give you Miss Darcy Wells, once again besting my vast knowledge of The Bard."

I gave a hesitant smile.

Mrs. Howard frowned. "Here I am, trying to get my cast to convincingly orate an hour and thirty minutes' worth of Shakespearean language, while you appear to have an entire storehouse of it already in your head? With that kind of ability, you'd shine onstage."

"Been telling her that for three years," Mr. Penn said, and left with a short wave.

"Thank you, but no. I'll stick to reading the words." On the *Much Ado* set, the four leads had just entered to block out a scene. "As much as I love Shakespeare, I'm not comfortable with the spotlight or big crowds."

"Well. Our loss." Mrs. Howard sighed at the notion. "On the other hand, your friend Marisol's designs are going to add so much to the production."

I smiled. "That's actually why I'm here. She signed out early for the dentist, but said she left her sketches somewhere?"

"Jase found her notebook after rehearsal yesterday." She pointed. "We left it in the back for safekeeping."

I nodded my thanks and climbed the riser. After a quick look behind the side curtain, I found Marisol's book and sent her a quick text.

I needed to get to the post office for eBay, then over to Yellow Feather for my shift, but Jase and Alyssa were in the middle of a high-stakes scene between Benedick and Beatrice. I gave myself a few moments to watch the dialogue I loved come alive, feeling the tension and suppressed emotion. Mrs. Howard's words replayed in my mind, but I still reached the same conclusion.

No. My world was already too much of a stage, twenty-four hours a day. Enough of a real-life drama with an overstuffed set.

With the bliss of Mr. Winston away on errands, I locked up, hung a Be Right Back sign on the door, and toted three letters across University Avenue. The last two numbers in our address were the same as Mid-City Legal's, just reversed. Simple mistake by our mail carrier.

Today was my first time pushing through the center's dark green door. Dropped acoustic ceilings made the space seem more like a stuffy, cramped shoe box than a waiting room. Fake potted plants brushed against buttermilk-white walls. Rows of fluorescent light tubes jiggled and buzzed, shrinking me like a hamster in a too-bright cage. Sounds of hammering and classic rock music drifted through a temporary plastic construction barrier, echoing down the short, dim hallway.

I marched up to the reception counter, but found it unmanned. I was about to leave the letters when a female voice called from the rear, "Hold on, please. Be right with you."

They likely had a video camera. Wise. And I had a few moments to wait, so their mail would stay secure—also wise, from what Asher told me about this place. From my spot, I could still watch Yellow Feather's front door.

"Sorry about that." A curvy blonde with a deep tan and overgrown roots emerged, wearing a black floral wrap dress. Her name plate read *Hannah*. "It's never this quiet in here, so I was tidying up the supply closet. I don't recall any appointments—"

"Oh, no, I'm not a client," I said, and handed her the mail. "I work across the street and we got these by mistake."

"Thanks. At the bookstore? Asher likes visiting over there." Hannah wrinkled her nose and arced one hand. "I'm sure you can tell why."

The used books. The quiet. Mr. Winston's comfortable chairs. No other reason.

I cleared my throat. "Yeah, it's cozy." I turned to leave, but stopped, noticing a little girl just down the hallway. She sat alone on a narrow bench, holding a stuffed bear and a snack bag. Her skinny legs swung back and forth to the driving beat of the music. I looked back at Hannah, brows furrowed in a silent question.

"Her name's Olivia," Hannah explained. "She's only six and she's here a lot. Her mom is with an attorney, but I can't say anything other than it's a sensitive situation. I usually bring her paper and my highlighters."

My attention strayed back to the Feather, but my heart latched on to the child with golden, light brown skin and a tight ponytail trailing brown ringlets. She wore a cheery yellow sundress, but her features slumped with shadows. She looked as bored as this place felt.

"Would it be okay if I said hello?" I asked. "Just for a couple of minutes?"

Hannah considered, then said, "I don't see any harm."

I approached cautiously, but didn't sit. Olivia popped a cheese cracker into her mouth and eyed me warily.

I smiled down at her. "Hi, I'm Darcy. Hannah said your name's Olivia?"

Hearing the two familiar names, Olivia relaxed her shoulders. She nodded and hugged the fuzzy bear to her chest.

I leaned in. "I bet this place is really boring. If you want, I know a story you might like?"

The hammering in the back stopped. "But you don't have any books," Olivia said.

I sat on the bench, still eyeing the bookstore through the front window. "I have all kinds of books, right here." I tapped my head. "Have you ever heard the story of *Sylvester and the Magic Pebble*?"

Olivia shook her head.

"Well, it's one of my favorites. I work at that bookstore across the street, and we have a copy with pictures. But what you can do now is listen to the words and imagine the pictures in your mind."

She ate another cracker and nodded.

I recited the whole story for long minutes, watching Olivia imagine her way through the text, a smile tickling the corners of her bow-shaped mouth. When I reached the end, clapping filled the room, but not from Olivia. I turned; Asher stood behind us, midway down the hall. Warmth poured into my head, under my cheeks. How long had he been standing there?

I jumped up, nodding once at Asher. "I need to get back to the shop. It was nice to meet you, Olivia."

"Bye, Darcy," she said with a wave.

Asher caught up with me. "Hey, I was just heading your way for my break."

He guided us into late afternoon and a California-cloudless sky. Sunlight streamed, bouncing between metal window frames and car windows. I shielded my eyes and slowed my natural gait to match Asher's as we crossed University and entered the bookstore.

Today, the shop smelled less of paper and more like pungent molecules of lemon wood polish. And maybe so did *I*, since my earlier Darcy-Do list had included a solid hour of dusting and conditioning Mr. Winston's beloved antique credenzas and tables.

I expected Asher to take his usual break time seat on the burgundy club chair, but he didn't. He didn't hit the used books corner, either. When he followed me to the cashier counter, I noticed the other thing he wasn't doing.

"What about your tea?" I asked.

Asher clasped his hands and leaned the entire top half of his frame on my counter. My space. "I didn't feel like stopping today."

"Didn't the doctor suggest drinking herbal tea daily?"

"I'll drink some later."

"It's only a block. You could run over and..."

He shook his head. I tracked a swallow down the length of his neck. "Why are you talking about tea and ignoring the gigantic elephant you left back at Mid-City?"

"Huh?" is all I said, and even that came out half-voiced and fully squeaky.

"Darcy, what was that back there?"

"You mean with Olivia?"

"I *mean*, how you happen to possess an entire picture book inside your head?"

I shrugged. "I have a lot of books, or book *parts*, in my head."

"Not like most of humanity does. Now it all fits," he mused around a hint of smile. "What Bryn was talking about at the party. Way more than just a huge vocabulary."

It felt like he was looking right into me. Nerves fluttered like moth wings beneath my skin. I tried to exhale them away.

"So I can read words ten times faster than you can," he said. "But you never forget the words you read?"

"Not exactly. I mean, I don't have a true photographic memory. I've just...uh, spent a lot of time reading." *A lot*, a lot. "And my mind holds on to certain parts of text that affect me. Like, emotionally. My brain kind of takes pictures for me to look at later. I can't explain how. Also, if I have to memorize text, I can do that easily and quickly." I shifted my eyes toward the children's section. "My mom used to read me *Sylvester and the Magic Pebble* a lot." *Until she didn't.*

"My mom read that one, too. Olivia's in a rough situation. The details are confidential, but—just between you and me?" He waited until I nodded. "Her dad's a real piece of work.

Jealous, too, and the littlest things switch him into hothead ass mode. Her mom's been working with my uncle Mike to get sole custody of Olivia. She's always looking over her shoulder. I've walked them out to her car more than a few times after consultations."

A tiny corner of my heart cracked, falling soft. "She looked like a girl who needed a story."

"You made a good story fairy." He chuckled, then sobered. "We shared three years at Jefferson, but I never knew this about you."

You never knew me.

"See, now you have me wondering what else I don't know. What other superpowers you got going on?" Asher asked.

My chest tightened. "Just the one," I said. Was stealing from a hoard and running a secret eBay operation a superpower? If so, Marisol owed me a custom cape.

"Word gets around Jefferson, like most schools," he said. "If someone has a cool talent, people tend to find out. The almighty grapevine."

"I've kept the details of my little party trick to myself and a couple of friends. I suppose enough people who've been in my classes know, or they think they do. You heard the comments at the bonfire. But I'm usually not the girl at the other end of grapevines." *And never will be.* "Knowing a lot of obscure words and stories isn't like what *you* can do."

With the sudden courage of a sword-wielding fantasy heroine, I faced him—this boy in my store—leaning over my counter, not drinking his tea and asking about me. "It's nowhere as cool as being able to fly. Most of us feel lucky to end up with a driver's license on our sixteenth birthdays," I joked.

Asher sprang up, hands caged over his face. "Shit."

"What—"

"You said *birthdays*. I totally forgot. Today's London's birthday."

London. Of course. I'd conveniently forgotten about her, too.

He checked his watch. "She'll be here in a couple hours to pick me up. I already made reservations at this café she likes, but I was going to go out yesterday and get her a gift, and I…"

"Forgot?"

"She'll be bummed. Plus, my birthday was at the end of May and I was still in the hospital. She got permission to set up a surprise party in my room with our friends." Regret clouded his expression. "Showing up empty-handed feels even worse now."

I came around the counter. "It's okay. There's still time to find her a present."

He dug index fingers into his temples, grimacing. "No good stores around here, and I don't have my truck today."

"Asher, breathe. Aren't you supposed to be avoiding stress?" I swore I could hear the *thump, thump, boom* of his heart. Louder than any construction hammering.

"Yeah, but I can't avoid this. My fault."

"Have you forgotten something else? You're standing in the middle of a store."

He snorted a laugh. "No offense, but London's not much of a book fan."

"None taken." Truly. "You *have* been in here enough to know we have a gift section, though."

"I never… Really?"

I waved him over to a square table in the far corner. "We have all these pretty journals and stationery sets and mugs and decorative pens and…" Asher's face told me none of this stuff was fit to honor London Banks's eighteenth birthday.

Right then, I knew what *would* be fit. "We also have these."
I led him to one of the antique credenzas flanking the women's
fiction section. The newly polished cherrywood top held a
T-shaped rack filled with silver bangle bracelets. "About six
months ago, I begged Mr. Winston to start carrying some jewelry. Marisol said these are really hot right now, so he let me
test-market a small batch. They've done well." Each bracelet
expanded and contracted to fit snugly around the wrist and
featured a single dangling charm.

Asher brightened. "These are perfect." He ran his finger
along the hanging bracelets; they dinged like wind chimes.
"Not sure which one she'd like best, though."

"What does *she* like? Start there."

He muttered something under clouds of breath that sounded
like *complaining*, then laughed it off. "London doesn't have
many hobbies, and she's not into animals like the little cats or
birds you have." He looked at me like I was full of solutions
as much as words. "You're a girl."

Wow. Even *he* had a 50 percent chance of getting that one
right. I hiked a brow.

"I mean, girls know stuff about other girls, I suppose.
Which one would you want to get as a gift?"

The question wound around my chest like rope. No guy
had ever bought me a gift. I reached out and grabbed two
bangles. "I've always loved this one, with the arrow." I held
it up. The silver arrow wobbled back and forth. "The one I
would pick," I added softly.

Asher tilted his head on a contemplative nod.

Then I showed him one with a tiny rosebud. "We sell this
model most often. It's pretty, and most girls like roses. A safe
choice."

He took both, eyes volleying back and forth between the two charms. The arrow or the rose. "Could you demo them?"

When I held out my arm, he inched up the sleeve of my black top and slipped the bracelets over my hand. His fingers were warm and gentle as they slid along my skin. I forced myself to swallow. He took a step closer and lifted my arm, turning and pondering. "They both look good."

Asher glanced at me briefly before looping the arrow bracelet back onto the rack. He removed the rose and handed it over. "This one, I think. The rose is smaller and won't catch on her sweaters and stuff."

I released a breath. "True. We have boxes and gift wrap. I can make it look really pretty for her." The words left a bitter glaze on my tongue.

He looked at his sneakers, then up at me, smiling bright and wide. "Thank you. You're saving my ass here."

"I know. And did your ass also forget a birthday card?"

His mouth puckered like he was sucking on sour candy.

I pointed to another rack near the door. "Cards for all occasions. Go pick one while I wrap."

At the counter, I took my time dressing the square box in the turquoise-and-black-striped wrapping paper Marisol had also chosen during one of Mr. Winston's rare, generous moods. Asher scrawled out a message in a card covered with pink roses—the only prose in this room I had no desire to read.

He sealed the envelope and handed me his credit card.

"One birthday gift, ready for a fun night out," I said, nearly tripping on the words as I placed the box in his hands.

"I owe you big-time, Darcy," he said fervently. "I don't know what I would've done—"

I waved his thanks away, and he gave me one last smile before hurrying back across the street.

Mr. Winston returned a short time later, and I watched the world spinning by outside the window as I helped customers. Asher escorted Olivia and a petite black woman down the sidewalk. Later, he emerged again from Mid-City in charcoal pants and a button-down shirt. He traded the sidewalk for the passenger seat of London's convertible, the striped gift box I'd wrapped in his hands. Earlier, those hands had smelled of freshly cut wood when he held my arm. Sharp and clean. Mine still smelled of wood polish.

Twelve

Mash-Up

"The difference between ~~him~~ **her** *and the other* ~~boys~~ **girls** *at such a time was that they knew it was make-believe, while to* ~~him~~ **her** *make-believe and true were exactly the same thing."* **Sometimes you can't see where make-believe ends and true starts. And sometimes you can, and you cry.**

—J. M. BARRIE, *PETER PAN*, AND *PETER PAN* MYSTERY SCRIBBLER

Two knocks on my bedroom door. "Darcy?"

"Just a sec," I called, opening my desk drawer. I swiped the next batch of Elisa B. eBay products into the deep space before moving to the door.

My mother stood in the hall, still in her bathrobe.

I unwound my towel turban, raking back damp hair. "Don't you have to be there early for split shift today?"

"I…yes. But something's wrong. I was making breakfast and going through cabinets."

My insides flared. Today it was kitchen cabinets. The last thing I needed was Mom rummaging through her makeup tubs next. Tubs I'd tampered with. Stolen from.

I peered around her into the dining nook. The round table held a plate with a single piece of toast, a white coffee mug, and enough vases, figurines, and porcelain bowls to fill every remaining centimeter. "What's wrong?"

"The Elisa B. district manager is coming by our store today."

"Wait, back up. Your boss is the problem?"

Mom nodded distractedly. "I've been so nervous, I took out some of my favorite heirlooms and beautiful things from that curio shop in La Jolla. Just to look. But I can't find one of them."

I gripped the door frame. This was a bigger problem than one missing item. My mother only felt secure when her hoard was secure. Untouched. More nervousness meant more checking and maybe a keener eye for missing lipsticks and makeup brushes. I had to be even more careful. If I slipped up, and she discovered my scheme, what would I do?

I turned my head, dragged in a long gulp of air. *Think.* I had to do something. What usually happened in a novel when the main character was backed against a wall—sometimes, literally?

A twist. I needed a plot twist. A diversion. I had to shine the spotlight off the hoard and back onto her. "Why are you so nervous about the district manager?"

The question flared in the whites of her eyes, quick as static shock. "I haven't met her yet. She's coming down from LA, and a good first impression is everything."

"Didn't you tell me your Macy's has one of the highest Elisa B. sales volumes in the city?"

"Yes. By a big margin, too." A glint of pride sparked on her face and her posture lifted slightly.

"That's partly because of *your* leadership," I pointed out. "Doesn't she get sales reports?"

"Every month." She glanced toward the dining nook again, then back at me.

"Then you've already made a good impression. But you'd better get dressed and do your makeup really amazing today to seal the deal," I suggested. "Instead of spending so much time with kitchen stuff, maybe do something different and special with your hair? Like flat-ironing it and adding some of those jeweled bobby pins?"

She cracked a smile. "Yes. Thank you, honey. That's a wonderful idea. I don't know why I was so worried. I'm just…"

"I know." With her, there were always so many *justs*.

Mom tapped her lips three times. "That reminds me. I forgot to tell you that I saw the new apartment manager the other day, in my store. What's his name again? Oh yes, Thomas."

I fought to keep my expression even. It had to be a coincidence, right? I mean, people shopped. They needed clothes and shoes. But I still asked, "Did he come over? Say hi?"

"Yes, he passed by my counter. He was quite friendly, but it seemed strange that he was wandering the cosmetics section. I thought perhaps he was after a gift. I asked as much. He seemed a little jumpy and mentioned he got turned around and was looking for men's cologne. I pointed the way." She shrugged before turning toward her bedroom.

It's probably nothing, I told myself, before worry could completely overwhelm me.

"Oh, Darcy, about what I was saying before. I can't find my green crystal vase." Mom paused at her bedroom door, staring at violet-painted toenails. "You haven't seen it, have you?"

Why was I surprised? The hoard was always first in her

mind, no matter what else happened to drop into her day. I knew she'd roll that little scrap of colored glass inside her head until she found it. I possessed a new tool that could help; a website link and contact information about a hoarding support group waited inside my room. But I had to wait for a time when she'd be most receptive.

Now I faced her and nodded once. "Actually, that vase is on my desk." But a mother who never entered my room would never have known. "Tess gave me some garden roses." I darted inside and retrieved the small crystal container with two fat pink blooms poking out. "Keep them."

Mom took the vase, inhaling. "They're beautiful."

I smiled wistfully. "They just needed a home."

"Hey, Darcy, what do we like better? Frederess or Tesserick?" Asher asked.

I poked out from the Yellow Feather fantasy section with a feather duster. "Huh?"

Asher was sitting in one of the club chairs wearing paint-splattered jeans, an open novel across his lap. His usual cup of herbal tea cooled on the trunk table. He pointed out the window at my boss, his ex-wife, and today's sidewalk meeting. "Divorced or not, those two are worthy of a mash-up name. Tess plus Frederick. So, Frederess or Tesserick? Oh!" he added. "Tess did it now. Mr. Winston's pissed. I know the pattern. First the scowl, then the one-finger shake. Then, and only then, does he do that big shoulder shrug huff and puff maneuver."

I stepped closer, giggling. "And…he's stomping away for coffee, and she's just casually strolling back to Tops. Anyway, I think Tesserick has a nice ring to it."

"Then Tesserick it is. Every couple needs a mash-up name. Unwritten rule."

I wouldn't know.

Asher sipped tea, then said, "Even though they only lasted a few weeks, I dubbed Jase and Bryn as Brase last summer."

"Nice. Can you make a fake one for Marisol and someone?"

"Well, Marisol and Jase would be, um, Jarisol. Whereas, myself and Marisol would be Mashersol."

"Mashersol." I laughed. "She'd kill me if she knew I was doing this."

"Probably," Asher said. Crooked smile. "We can't leave you out. Now, you and Jase would be Jarcy."

"Which would last even less time than, er, Brase."

"Legendary, though. But that just leaves you and me," he said softly. "Has to be Dasher."

"Dasher," I whispered, toying with the feather duster.

"In which our mash-up name is also one of Santa's reindeer." His cheeks pinked. "I think it's a keeper. Clever. Has a nice ring to it."

My pulse pattered like raindrops on a tin roof. "Funny how that worked out, just like that."

"Pure chance, I swear." One hand over his heart. "Completely unplanned."

Before I all-the-way choked, the bell above the shop door chimed. The ensuing commotion of Marisol strolling into Yellow Feather wearing her new red leather jacket was exactly the distraction I needed to restore my normal breathing.

"What are you doing here?" I asked, my voice somewhat steadied.

Marisol exchanged waves with Asher. "I give you Darcy Jane Wells, pillar of extraordinary customer service."

I snorted and followed Marisol to the counter. "No twins, so you're not here for story time. What's up?"

"I might ask you the same thing," Marisol whispered. She discreetly jerked her head backward, in the direction of Asher's burgundy chair. Like a boy in a bookstore was a monumental deal. She already knew Asher had been coming in for his breaks.

I told her with my face it clearly *wasn't* a big deal, and to lay off, already. She innocently drew one palm to her chest, then smiled. "I come bearing gifts."

"Now you're talking."

"We're celebrating." Marisol drew an iced caramel latte from her tote. Despite transportation from Starbucks to the Feather in the base of a turquoise leather bag, the drink was perfectly intact.

I may have let out a tiny squeal. "Thanks, Mari." I took a long sip of my favorite coffee treat. "Celebrating what?"

She beamed and reached into her tote again, waving out a personal check. "Your first cut from PayPal. We did it, Darcy."

I took the check from her and studied it, a bittersweet flavor coating my tongue, and not from my latte.

Asher strolled up. "I need to get back in a minute, but just wanted to say thanks again for the gift idea, Darcy. It was a real hit."

Marisol swung her head right to left, Asher to me, a questioning look on her face—then did it again.

I told her, "If we hadn't convinced Mr. Winston to stock those silver charm bracelets, Asher would've been giftless in San Diego for London's birthday."

Marisol gave Asher a well-honed side-eye.

"Hey!" he protested. "It's complicated, okay? I mean, London's...yeah. She wore the bracelet today." Asher fiddled with the penny tray, coins clanging like the silver bangle charms. The arrow and the rose. "About London," he added, "she modeled the costume you made for *Much Ado* earlier. You're really talented, Marisol."

My friend brightened. "Thanks. She looked pretty in the

gown during the fitting. Just one more week of dress rehearsals."

London. I couldn't help thinking of one more mash-up
name: Lashdon?

"Are you two going for opening night?" Asher asked.

"It's our birthday weekend, so we might squeeze that into
the festivities," Marisol said.

"You were born on the same day?"

"One day apart," I said.

"Technically, twelve hours apart. Darcy first, then me."
Marisol lifted a shoulder. "It's how we became friends."

"Okay, I'll bite. What's the history of..." He drew an invisible line connecting Marisol and me. "This?"

I looked at my best friend, memory in my eyes, gaping
minutes of that day swallowing all of the now.

Marisol nudged her chin at me. "Tell it."

Tell *him.* Isn't that what she meant? Tell Asher Fleet, a boy
with adorable mash-up naming abilities and one hand in my
penny tray. Tell *him?*

No. I wanted to sweep my tenth birthday away like Yellow Feather dust. Bury the dead parts in books and say I had
to organize them or catalog them or sell them. Anything but
feel them again.

"Go on," she encouraged. "Our story has a happy ending."

"True," I conceded. One breath. Another. "Marisol and I
were in the fourth grade together. Mrs. Wood's class. We'd
played outside a few times, worked on group projects, but
nothing more." I sipped some coffee and turned to Asher.
"Did your mom ever bring treats to school on your birthday?"

He smiled, a hint of longing in his eyes. "She always
brought killer fudge brownies."

Brownies he couldn't even eat anymore, thanks to the accident. "You know how big of a deal it is, then," I said. "Well,

my birthday was on a Thursday, and my mom promised to drop off cupcakes for the class. I was so excited and told everyone. The weekend before, we picked out sprinkles and, well, she's not much of a cook, so she was going to use a boxed mix and store-bought frosting. But I didn't care."

Marisol's eyes held a watery glaze, cheeks flushed from everything but makeup. She nodded once at me. *Keep going.*

"On my birthday, morning recess came. Then lunch. Then afternoon recess. But no cupcakes. No mother." I clenched my hands, biting off the next words from a storm cloud. "She forgot."

Asher's face dropped. "Wow. Intense."

"You remember being ten? Trying to fit in?" He nodded. "I wanted to hide under my desk, and all the kids were asking where the cupcakes were. Our teacher always called birthday kids up front for the 'Happy Birthday' song, and she made construction paper crowns with stickers. My crown sat on her desk all day. I knew Mrs. Wood felt bad, trying to wait until the last possible moment."

"The moment never came, huh?" he asked softly.

I shook my head. "But Marisol came through." I laughed. "Ten minutes before the final bell, my girl here stands up. She announces that we were doing something big that year, because we were both turning ten. Like a surprise. And since her birthday was the next day, her mom was going to bring stuff for both of us. I remember her looking at me, and me looking back right into her eyes, finally smiling."

"I couldn't leave her hanging," Marisol said.

"After lunch the next day, Marisol's mom brought an entire party. Bigger than anything anyone else's parents did all year." I smiled at her. "Remember?"

"Of course! Mama came with balloons and cute plates and

juice boxes and popcorn in little striped boxes. And…" Marisol gestured my way.

I nudged my friend's shoulder. "She brought the most beautiful cupcakes I'd ever seen. Huge bakery cupcakes with mounds of swirled frosting and confetti sprinkles. And the best part—two of the cupcakes had plastic picks stuck on top. One had a pink heart, the other had a yellow star. Just for the birthday girls."

A flash across my mind. *The mosaic table. Marisol's little black Sharpie heart. My tiny star.*

"I still have my plastic heart," Marisol mused.

"I kept my pick, too. After school, I thanked her, but we never really talked about it. Never said, 'Hey, you're my best friend now.' From that moment, the two of us just *were*."

"And still are," Asher noted.

With the tale done and told, the shop fell silent. I lost the hum of traffic along University, couldn't detect a strain of Sinatra or muffled jazz horns. Until my friend let out a big, sweeping breath and broke the hush. She glanced at her watch. "Almost time for the twins' gym class, but first we need a Word of the Day because, well, we just *do*." She explained the game to Asher.

"I'm better with a drill than a dictionary, but I'll give it a go," he said.

I finished the rest of my coffee, thinking. "Okay, I've got one. Today's word is *funambulist*."

"A funambulist is a rare books collector," Asher said.

Marisol wrinkled her nose. "Asher, you have no idea what that word means, huh?"

"Not a clue."

"Thought so. Neither do I. So, when you don't know, you're supposed to make up the most absurd definition you can think of, which always makes Darcy laugh. That's the whole point."

Asher eyed me carefully, his gaze perching on the edge of my face before finally sinking deep. As my stomach jolted, his smile bent, revealing just a hint of teeth. "All right. I can do that."

"'Kay," I thought I said. I was still pinned under his stare, and that alone made me not want to laugh. It made me want to duck behind my cashier counter and read.

"Watch and learn, Ash." Marisol held up a finger. "Funambulist. Someone who writes entirely in bulleted lists. Their lives are documented in fragments after little black dots."

Asher's chin trembled before he broke into a reluctant laugh. I had to follow. This time, we shared an easy look topped with headshakes and eye rolls.

"Okay, Asher, you're up," I said.

He crossed his arms. "Funambulists are obsessed with rescue vehicles. They can't get anything done because they follow them around town, taking pictures of them. Selfies with paramedics are the gold standard. And they make siren noises all day for fun."

"That is just wrong," Marisol told the ceiling.

Asher shrugged. "But you're laughing, right?"

She was. We all were. It felt good and true, and for a few seconds, even better than reading.

"Worthy and creative efforts," I said. "But a funambulist is a tightrope walker."

As twilight fell, friends and others who still didn't fit into any definable *who I am to Darcy* category had long gone. Customers spent enough money to make Mr. Winston not grumpy. My boss flipped the lights off and locked the door to Yellow Feather, sending me down University Avenue. That was when I saw her and the silver Mercedes parked behind my Honda.

Grandma Wells straightened the lapels of her black blazer. "Hello, dear. I thought about meeting you at the bookstore, but traffic was awful, and I pulled up right at closing."

The words *what on earth are you doing here* sounded too rude in my head, so I kept them there. "This is a surprise." I shifted my school bag to my other shoulder.

"I have important news." She looked at her gray ballet flats for a beat. "I felt you might not be ready to come for dinner again after our last conversation. Actually, about that…" She shook her head. "I'm getting ahead of myself. Is there a café nearby? You must have homework, but—"

"Finished it at work." I shrugged. "Starbucks is down the block."

"I suppose that will do. Although I've never understood the appeal of all those fancy, sugary drinks."

"They do have regular coffee, Grandma."

A short walk later, we entered the half-empty coffee shop. Grandma Wells ordered her simple decaf while I stared blankly at the menu board. Since Marisol had already brought me the iced latte, I was happily full of both sugar and caffeine.

The barista leaned in. "And for you?"

"Just a large chamomile tea," slipped out before I could catch up to it.

Grandma Wells sat across from me at the nearest two-top. "How long have you been a chamomile drinker? Your mother could never stand the stuff."

"Not long, Grandma."

She plucked a blue envelope from her purse, pinching it with tense fingers. "I won't patronize you with small talk." She exhaled roughly. "I received this in the mail a few days ago." She spied our drinks on the bar and went to fetch them, while I stared at the mysterious rectangle. The contents had been enough to drag my grandma out of La Jolla during rush hour traffic.

I accepted the chamomile tea from her, shaping my hands around the cup the way I usually did with novels. The little paper tag hung like a charm.

"Darcy, the letter is from Thailand. From your father."

Thirteen

Paper Dad

*"'It is only make-believe, isn't it,
that I am ~~their~~ her father.'"*

—J. M. BARRIE, *PETER PAN*, AND DARCY JANE WELLS

The weird part was, I didn't—couldn't—even cry. Not back at Starbucks, when Grandma Wells had unfolded the pale blue stationery paper. Not now, while I reread the same letter, over and over, on my living room couch. My mother was working, and for the first time in a long time, I didn't want to hide in the clean comfort of my room with my favorite books. I was tangled, and it only seemed right to sit in the most chaotic place I knew.

I trailed fingertips over the blue-inked stationery, one of the few things in my possession my father had also touched. Foolish, yeah, but I still lifted the paper to my nose, trying to smell the faraway land it came from. I followed his slanted scrawl, noting that he formed the letter *L* just like I did. What else did I have of him?

Dear Darcy,

If you've gotten this far, maybe you'll have the grace, and if not that, possibly the curiosity to read the rest. There hasn't been a day in all these years that I wish I hadn't made different choices. I knew better, but still kept making them. I stayed in Thailand for selfish reasons, which I justified because you were safe, loved, and provided for. At the time, I feared that coming back would have made life worse for you. It was a comfortable lie I told myself. But recent news from your grandmother tells me you're a brilliant young woman, and I often find myself regretting that I haven't been there to see you grow up.

I've started this letter a thousand times and left it unfinished a thousand more. I don't deserve to be your father, and you never deserved the kind of father I was and still am. But it's been long enough, and I am done with cowardly choices. Even though I don't have the right, I'm going to ask anyway. I'm finally traveling back to California next year, and I would love to meet you. I have too many years' worth of apologies stored up, and I would like to say them in person. The choice is yours. And if you decide that it's too much, too painful, or even too late, then I will accept your decision. But after too many years, I had to ask the question.
Your father,
David Elliot

I folded the letter, weighing the words one by one, trying to make the sum of them add up to a real person. But I couldn't. And I also couldn't begin to make the choice he was asking. Right then, *father* was the one word beyond even my forever vocabulary.

Two hours ago, Grandma Wells pushed this envelope across the Starbucks table and said I should take it home to ponder, alone. But when had I done anything my grandmother suggested lately?

She'd watched as I read; my eyes stayed as dry as deserts, my expression cool and considering. Finally, Grandma sighed deeply. "When I saw it was addressed to you, I almost fainted."

"I'll bet," I whispered.

"Truthfully, I've been waiting for this moment, even though you were convinced he would never reach out." She ran one finger along the paper. "Even if he hadn't sent this, it's time you knew a few things. You're ready."

I couldn't help the glare. I guessed in her view, if I was ready to pay my own bills, I was ready for tough words.

"Darcy, don't forget about my guest room. This new revelation will likely make things extremely difficult and confusing, and you'll need someone stable to help you through it."

"I found a solution for the money. Your guest room is perfect, but I don't know what would happen to Mom if I left. Right now, she can't lose me, too. And my father showing up is…" I shook my head. "All I *do* is deal with family members who make bad choices. What's one more?"

Her mouth flinched like her coffee was too hot, but she wasn't drinking. "I see." She fiddled absently with one pearl earring. "Dear, there's something about your father even your mother doesn't know. Something I've kept to myself all these years, thinking it was the best thing for her."

My eyes popped open over my next sip of chamomile.

"You must understand—your mother's relationship with

David was unusually intense," she explained. "Even uncomfortably passionate, right from the beginning."

I winced. This was getting way too close to the *TMI* zone.

"It was also volatile." Grandma dashed slim fingers across the space between us. "Your grandfather and I thought David was certainly a smart enough boy, but we always hoped things would fizzle out between them. They fought constantly. Many times, we heard them yelling in the driveway, doors slamming. They had trust and jealousy issues, constantly pushing and pulling at each other. Your mother often cried herself to sleep. I've always felt she lost a lot of herself after she met David."

"How?"

"Before he came along, she was always a strong girl. Studious and focused, with so much promise. A lot like you."

Was I strong and focused? Maybe. But none of that seemed to matter here, with her, with the six-by-eight-inch piece of paper sitting next to my tea.

Grandma drank, then said, "She'd had other boyfriends, but David was another situation entirely. He became part of her identity, like an addiction. She was no longer living like a freethinking, capable young woman. As she spent more time with him, she began to ignore her friends, until most of them gave up. Eventually she saw herself as just one part of a duo."

"And then he left."

She sighed. "Darcy, your father was young and obviously immature and flighty. But when he left, and spent some time away from your mother, he began to see how unfit they were for one another. How toxic. He realized he never wanted to see Andrea again, for his own well-being. That's what he's referring to in his note—the selfish reasons." She laid one coffee-warmed hand briefly on my forearm. "But when he learned about you, he was very conflicted and torn. He contacted your grandpa and me, right away, asking what he could do."

I stared in disbelief.

"He was determined to stay in Thailand. That point wasn't negotiable. He'd found true happiness and peace there, and he was somewhat estranged from his own family. Bangkok was a new start. But he was also determined to support you financially. He assumed we'd fight him for that, anyway."

"Wait. You didn't?"

"We did not. We made other arrangements. Grandpa told David we would take care of your mother and you, and that his paternal support wasn't needed. As a result, you were given our last name, not Elliot. However, we agreed to send periodic updates about you. Pictures a few times a year. He's aware of your gift with literature, too."

The news tussled around my body like a tornado. Pieces of everything I'd believed my whole life, netted into the spin. "Mom thinks my father completely peaced out from our lives this whole time. No contact or...care for me at all. So you're saying that's not true?"

"No."

"Why didn't you tell her?" I demanded. "Why didn't you tell *me*?"

"Honey, this is going to sound all wrong, but at the time we thought we were doing the right thing. We did tell your mother about his offer of financial support, but she refused to accept that David was never coming back." Grandma inched her hand forward again, but didn't touch me this time. "We decided to hold back the fact that your father had requested updates, and that I've been sending them faithfully. Back then, your grandpa and I believed the separation would eventually affect her in the same way it had David. That she would realize what a terrible match they were, and move on with a fresh start, with her child. We felt if she knew he'd requested updates, it would make moving on that much harder. We feared she'd obsess about it and want to control the interactions. That it would only hurt her more in the long run. In our minds, we were giving her a better chance to rise up."

"That turned out well." Mom never rose; there were no ups. Instead, she sank, buried under a hoard. She'd obsessed anyway.

"Grandpa and I never predicted your mother would spiral into that level of grief and denial. Many people eventually learn to thrive after adversity. Your mother declined, and we misjudged her. We should have done more for her during that time." Grandma's head dipped. Her breathing turned ragged, and her forehead gleamed with a sweaty sheen. "For that, for… so much more, I've always been terribly guilty, Darcy. I'm guilty of keeping this from you, too. It was out of fear. How could you, as a child, handle information your own mother couldn't support you through? In hindsight, that was wrong, and we should have found a way. We inadvertently lumped you and your mother together when we should have trusted you to be strong."

Was this how it was always going to be? My mother's issues, my issues? My mother's weakness, my weakness? Her hoard, my hoard?

But I didn't ask. I wasn't sure I wanted to know the answer.

Later, on my couch, I pressed my mental stop button on the Starbucks replay. Pieces of Grandma Wells's revelation clanged and cluttered around me, along with frying pans and clothes no one here fit into. So loud—deafening—like the information was waiting for me to act against it. To do something, to *feel* something. But I had no idea what that something was. Or even what it should be.

My phone dinged.

Marisol: Hey, I left my red jacket at Tops

Me: Tops?

Marisol: I stopped after bookstore. Saw some new fringe scarves in the window... Tess showed me a lime green one

Me: Which you bought

Marisol: Duh? But it clashed with the red so I took the jacket off when I tried on the scarf. Idiot me left it

Me: Tess will keep it safe but you know she tried it on

Marisol: Of course she did

Me: I'll fetch it next shift

Marisol: Thanks, D. Anything new?

Anything new? God. I opened the letter again and found a man I didn't know *how* to know. A father who made the letter *L* like I did, but had never made his way into my life. A prickly chill rooted in my feet, winding through my limbs.

Saying it makes it real.

And so I, Darcy Jane Wells, texted five words to the girl I'd always, *always* told every single thing to for eight years.

Me: Nothing major. See you tomorrow

I was staring at the blue text bubble on my phone when keys jiggled in the lock. Mom was home early? I moved as quickly as anyone could through the goat tunnel maze to my room. I stepped in, dropping the letter on top of the book spines housed in the nearest shelf. Then I ducked back out and closed my door, leaning against it, panting.

"Darcy?" Mom called.

I met her halfway, springing off the door toward the kitchen. I poured a glass of water I probably needed anyway.

Mom pushed at her temples in a move that reminded me of Asher. "Terrible headache after all that worry about the district manager. Caroline took over my second shift post so I could call it a night."

I nodded. My hand trembled around the glass.

She searched the cabinet where she usually kept alcohol. The shelves overflowed, but not with vodka, gin, or whiskey. She'd come home empty-handed, too. Her wallet was likely as empty as her stash. Instead, she sighed over a water glass. After swallowing two aspirin, I thought she'd escape to her room to sleep off the headache. I wouldn't have to look at her then, or try to do human things, like eating and talking.

But Mom didn't budge. She eyed me curiously as I planted my sneakers onto the floor tile, grounding myself when she framed my cheeks with clammy hands. So close, I could see tiny gray hairs sprouting along her center part. When was the last time she'd touched me like this?

Cold thumbs grazed over my eyebrows. "I've been neglecting these. Let me shape them."

"You should get some rest. Your head." *My life and the lease and the letter.*

"I'll be fine. These need help." She pulled me into the bathroom and quickly transformed the tiny, product-heavy space into our own personal Elisa B. brow bar. She sat me down on the toilet seat while wax heated in one of our six electric facial wax pots. "Close your eyes."

Wisps of her kohl pencil drew guidelines around each

brow. Wax smeared off the wooden brow stick, always too hot when it first met my skin. The kind of pain that disappears the instant you feel it. She pressed with clean cotton strips. Expert strokes ripped them off, and I flinched a little each time.

"Relax your shoulders, honey. You're so tense."

A hot breath staggered out. *I'm lying to you. And the apartment manager might evict us.*

She trimmed with scissors and shaped with tweezers. "School's okay? Your forehead is all creases."

"It's fine." *Grandma's news. And no one can come inside this house. And you won't stop buying things.*

Her movements slowed. I knew she was almost done when she rubbed tingly Elisa B. brow gel over the newly plucked skin. She took the time to massage my temples before her hands netted my hair, kneading into my scalp. Comfort, the only way she could give it, I guessed. Eyes closed, I smelled her herbal shampoo and tuberose perfume as she dabbed creamy lotion over my eyelids.

"There. Beautiful." She unplugged the wax and set her tools on the counter. "Now I need to sleep. 'Night, sweetie." She patted my cheek again.

I rose only when I heard her bedroom door against the frame. Behind a closed white panel, stolen makeup hid inside my desk drawer. Atop the books, a father waited—a fantasy world, a make-believe life, a man I never knew encased inside a small blue rectangle. I swallowed and faced the room that held all of my risk as much as my comfort. I didn't know what to do with the father, but I knew what to do with the letter.

Which one would it be? Steinbeck or Rowling? Lewis or Atwood or Fitzgerald or Austen? Then it clicked—Charles Dickens. I had just the book, too. I found my hardback copy of *Great Expectations*. The prose was perfect, notes of poverty and theft and orphans. A woman starred in the story, too, forever dressed in a tattered wedding gown, waiting and dying for everything and nothing.

I slid the blue stationery into the center section, closed the book, and shelved it in its usual place. *Take him*, I thought. *Do what you always do.*

Fourteen

Mirror, Mirror

Remember it was me who grabbed Time
by its fine-boned neck?
Black cloaked, I cut the pulse,
stopped the red pulsing heart of the universe.
You saw me then,
staring for long minutes that no longer were.
Until I released my hold.
Time doubled over under coughing spurts, bruised,
staggering backward too far
into the breath of yesterday.

—*PETER PAN* MYSTERY SCRIBBLER

Tess, wearing a long, russet brown bob not unlike my real hair, petted Marisol's gorgeous leather jacket before handing it over. "Why didn't you come over for your break earlier? I got this new tea. Cinnamon Chai Maté." She glanced at a large silver wall clock. Just after six-thirty. "Too late for it now. Stuff has more caffeine than coffee."

"You know the shipment from the new distributor that was supposed to come in little by little over the next two weeks?" I matched her grunt with an eye roll. "Instead, the boxes came in one big load, and Mr. Winston got all…"

"*Winstonish?*"

"Exactly. So I stuck around and tried to get the new merchandise sorted quickly for everyone's well-being." I draped the red jacket over the counter, where I'd already placed my tote and a new book Asher's uncle Mike had been anxiously waiting for. Yellow Feather had received its copies one day before the official release date, but the deliveryman had barely caught Mr. Winston and me before we closed up, lights already off and keys in the lock. According to my boss, Yellow Feather's personal brand of customer service—more like *my* personal brand—meant I would hand-deliver the preorder before going home for the day.

Tess tapped one corner of her mouth. "Now I'm certain you need a boost." She dashed to the used section and came back with a wig I'd never seen before. "This is a guaranteed mood lifter."

For once—and after last night—I felt like believing her. I let Tess give me the full treatment. Instead of just shoving the wig on me, she grabbed a nylon skullcap and fed my real hair underneath the stretchy fabric. Then she molded the new wig over the cap. Made from real, black hair—but not an overdyed, fake black—it was like wearing a night sky. The wig fit tightly to my head, sweeping back and upward into a sleek, long ponytail.

"Look at you, Darcy-Diva!" Tess beamed.

Oh, I *was* looking, mouth parted. This time, she'd *gotten* me and seemed to know just what I needed, even though I hadn't said anything about the letter.

I stepped tentatively. Right, then left. Back just a bit, then a twirl in the mirror, the long tail swooshing over my gray sleeveless top.

Tess approached. She braced gentle hands on my shoulders. "I swear, this one was made for you. But we're not done yet."

"We're not?"

She grabbed the leather biker jacket from the counter and pushed my arms through the sleeves. "Your Marisol won't mind."

Marisol's body was the opposite of mine in every way, but the red jacket fit my frame like it had appeared with the flick of a magic wand. I suddenly had curves. The waist nipped and corseted. The flap collar spread across my chest like wings. "I, uh—"

"Where's your lipstick?"

"I don't think I have any with me. Maybe some nude gloss I put on this morning."

"Hmm. That won't do." She reached under the counter for her pink makeup bag.

"Tess, it's okay."

"Nonsense. Humor me. I've been wanting to do this for weeks." She chose a tube, checked the shade against my skin tone.

"Dooerrr wut?" I asked while Tess applied the lipstick.

"Hold still." Another swipe, a quick fix with her thumbnail. "Voilà." She turned me toward the mirror again. My glossy lips looked fuller, bee-stung and tinted strawberry red.

"I've been wanting to bring your sassy side out to play. This, right here, is my Darcy-Diva. Strong and fabulous. She's ready to take on all the boys at Jefferson with her flirty self."

"I do *not* flirt. I don't even know how to flirt. What to even do with my uh…self," I added softly.

"Bah!" She clucked her tongue. "Flirting isn't about *doing*. Flirting is something you *are*. The confidence of a girl who knows what she wants—or who. Knows she's worth it." Tess pressed her palm down the long line of my back. I straightened. "Now walk. Strut your stuff, Miss Superstar Hair and Jacket of My Dreams."

I frowned. "Tess…"

She grabbed my hand, led me down the center of Tops like we were taking Fifth Avenue for a late-night strut. Back and forth, the wigged mannequin heads our only audience. "That's it, honey."

At first, I felt like the definition of *ridiculous*, cat-walking to Tess's high-pitched cues to lift my chin, purse my painted lips. Lead with my hip, but subtly. Just a touch, nothing overdone. But after a few minutes, I started to have fun.

Tess stood back, clapping her hands. "I knew you had it in you. Stunning. The whole package!"

I skidded one black ballet flat to a stop on the tile. *Package.* "Oh no! It's almost closing time, and I totally forgot." I glanced out the window to Mid-City Legal. Good, the lights were still on. "I'll be right back." Grabbing Michael Fleet's book, I ran out into the dusk.

"Darcy! You're still…"

Tess's words vanished into the crisp October air as I sprinted off. At the crosswalk, I patted my head and I realized I was still wearing Tess's black ponytail wig and cap. But I couldn't go back and risk the center closing; admitting to Mr. Winston I'd missed a delivery because I was playing dress-up with his ex-wife was not an option.

When the green walk signal appeared, I forced my legs into brisk strides, wondering—not for the first time that day—why Asher hadn't come by Yellow Feather for his break. I hated that I'd noticed. Hated that I'd come to associate him and his tea and his speed-reading with part of my daily routine.

I couldn't help associating Mid-City's brick building and

dark green door with Asher, too. I rolled my eyes at myself, and at the business hours sign on the way in. Tonight they were staying open an hour later for walk-ins. I'd rushed over in the black wig for nothing.

Voices boomed and bodies crowded, unlike the last time I was here and found little Olivia alone on a bench. Waiting clients chatted in groups or jammed to tunes through earbuds. Hannah looked overwhelmed trying to help a family of four at her reception desk while fielding a stream of incoming calls.

The crowd shifted enough for me to squeeze through toward the office hallway. I slipped the book into the clear plastic door caddy hanging on Mr. Fleet's closed office door. Rock music pumped from the taped-off construction zone, along with whirring power tools.

The entrance door suddenly smacked open, a sunburned, dirty-blond giant swallowing up the threshold. "Where's he at?" The man staggered in and I instinctively stepped back.

Hannah stood from behind the counter, grimacing. "Mr. Andrews—Jeffrey. They're not here. You need to leave. Now."

Jeffrey Andrews roughly pushed through the crowd, prompting a litany of complaints.

"Watch it, dude."

"Chill, bro."

Mothers tucked children between their bodies and the wall. Others retreated onto the sidewalk or pulled out cell phones.

Jeffrey approached the counter, scowling. "Not Olivia and that cheating slut mother of hers." He looked left, then right, even into the supply closet behind Hannah. "That Fleet kid."

Hannah flinched, drawing back. "He's not here—"

"You're lying. I need to have a private conversation with him, now. Fleet!" he barked.

I froze. *Olivia. Fleet kid.* Jeffrey Andrews was Olivia's father and currently spreading his explosive reputation all over the center. My feet were already moving before my brain caught all the way up. I slunk down the hall, almost bumping into a suited man—likely an attorney—as he dashed from his office toward the waiting room scuffle. But I kept moving, reaching the plastic construction barrier as chaos exploded behind me.

Jeff shoved the approaching lawyer away, and the man lost his footing, careening to the ground. Jeff forced his tank-sized body into bystanders like a battering ram, eyes hunting. Voices rose. Clients swarmed the felled lawyer and tried to subdue the assailant while Olivia's father openly yelled Asher's name.

I didn't know why Jeffrey was looking for Asher—I only knew that I had to warn him.

Past the barrier, I peered into a tumble of dust, chalky plaster, and scattered debris, all backed by an Aerosmith guitar riff. Asher was facing away from me, drilling through studs, oblivious.

I yelled his name and ran to cup his shoulder.

Flinching, he turned. "Darcy?" He stepped back, slack-jawed, maybe trying to reconcile this black-haired, red-lipped stranger with the ordinary Yellow Feather shop clerk. He cut the power and shoved plastic goggles above his head. His lips closed and he eyed me so intensely, I swore I could feel his stare tunneling up and down my body.

Me. He was looking at me—*more* than looking. The dreaming part of me wanted it to last forever, but we didn't even have minutes. "No time." Then I, Darcy Jane Wells, queen of words, lost all of mine. Even the small ones. "Have to go. You…we." I couldn't make them work, adrenaline fizzing through my body.

Brows furrowed, he set down the drill.

Click. Finally. "We have to hurry." I locked on to Asher's face. "Trust me." I tossed off his goggles and grabbed his forearm. This room had a rear alley exit; the door was already propped open, twilight edging in.

At the threshold, Asher locked into the moment, too. He fought against my pull. "Slow down. My knee. What's going on?"

I sought the wide expanse of safety at the end of the alley as shouts echoed from the waiting room. But we couldn't run, not with Asher's leg the way it was. Years of book scenes buzzed around me, needling in. Pages of heart-stopping thrillers and clever authors told me what to do.

I knew what would work.

Grabbing on to a strength I didn't know I had, to a life I'd never lived, I jerked Asher fifteen feet into the narrow space between two brick buildings.

One nudge, and he was against the wall. One more, and I was against him, the full length of me. "Please, just trust me," I told him again.

Marisol's jacket was too distinctive, too *red*. I ripped it off and pinned it between Asher's back and the faded brick wall. *Sorry, Marisol.* Autumn wind blew scents of grease and cigarette smoke, of jasmine mixed with days-old trash, over my bare shoulders. Reckless and stupid and goose-fleshed, I swung my arms around Asher and whispered into his ear. "Olivia's dad is after you."

He shivered. His breath wafted across my skin in uneven spurts. "Jeff?"

Our pursuer must've reached the hallway. Office doors creaked and slammed as he shouted Asher's name amid a string of curses. "He's lost it. Play along." I placed my cheek against Asher's. "Pretend you're…with me." *Not real. Just make-believe. A back-alley fairy tale.*

I logged the passing of one clean second before Asher proved he was every bit as good an actor as his girlfriend. He trapped my waist in the tight circle of his arms, angling his face so close to mine, I doubted even a sheet of paper could fit between us. He licked his lips; I felt the warm heat against my own mouth. His eyes seemed twice their normal size. Wild and unblinking, as if he was trying to see beneath all my surfaces. When he inhaled sharply and fixed the rounded collar on my top, his feathery touch shot straight to my knees. He shifted along the wall, and my foot slid on the filthy concrete.

"Sorry," he whispered as he caught me. Asher sloped his chin into the cleft of my neck, arranging my body until I was pressed against the solid plank of his right leg. One hand splayed across my back, traveling up and down my spine as Jeff entered the construction zone. Metal and wood crashed as I held on tighter to this flying boy, and lost the part of me who cared he wasn't mine. That he belonged to someone else.

Tess, I don't even know how to flirt. Just acting. I left that behind, too, abandoning myself to a dizzying kiss that wasn't even happening. I bounced aimlessly between sensations I'd never felt before. The rapid gunfire of my heart, of his. The heady scent of his skin, corded muscle laced with sweat and soap. He keened deep inside his throat as my hands looped into the dusky brown curls grazing his neck. Soft—I knew they would be.

"Your truck's still here, and so are you!" Jeff Andrews bellowed as his bouldering footfalls reached the alley.

"Shhh," I whispered, more to our bodies than our mouths. We burrowed even closer, folding into one another, chests pattering with the breath of hummingbirds, trying to blend into the urban cityscape. Asher's fingers dug into my back as Jeff sprinted past what hopefully looked like two love-struck teens hooking up in a shadowed hideout.

We stayed still and quiet until Mid-City's rear door flung open again. This time, I peeked as two men ran out and ap-

proaching sirens cut through the distant rumble of traffic.
Finally.

"Down there!" a man called out, and ran off. His hair was
the same color as Asher's, his work clothes similarly paint-
splattered. His older companion hurried behind on brown
work boots.

"That's James, my cousin. And my uncle Brian," Asher
murmured.

I nodded. The commotion shifted to the intersection of the
alley and Twenty-eighth Street. Even Jeff wasn't a match for
Asher's uncle and cousin. Speed, agility, and brawn had him
pinned, bucking against a Dumpster in vain until two police
cars skidded into the alley entrance.

I let out a sigh of relief. Asher's attention shifted from the
scene to me, his eyes darkening to onyx as he slowly unhooked
himself from my arms. From all of me. He grabbed Marisol's
jacket and tried to help me back into the sleeves, but our fairy-
tale scene was over.

I shook my head. "It's not mine."

A single nod. "Well, thank you. That was genius."

Make-believe. Just pretend. "You're welcome."

Asher glanced down at his knee. "I'm not exactly fit for
fighting, lately."

"That's not what I was thinking when I brought you out
here. I just wanted you to be safe."

His mouth slackened. "I know."

We righted our clothes, and I draped the red leather over
my forearm. I even smoothed the fake fall of black on top of
my head. Lingering adrenaline ignited aftershocks through
my bones. The threat was over, but I couldn't outthink the
last few minutes. I couldn't escape them. They beat inside me
like a second heart.

Here, I wasn't the storybook maiden of my bedroom library, graced with glass slippers, true love kisses, and midnight clocks. For the first time in seventeen years, I was the villain in a black wig, body painted with deceit and red leather. Not a castle, a dirty alley shrouded in plummy-dark night. A stealthy thief, pressed against another girl's boy.

No, not the princess. The evil queen.

Fifteen

The Other Boy Who Could Fly

"'Come,' he cried imperiously,
and soared out at once into the night..."

—J. M. BARRIE, *PETER PAN*

I was glad to have something to hold on to, even if it was only a taco.

After the police questioned witnesses at the center and hauled Jeff Andrews away, Asher had insisted on showing his appreciation. Plus, it was dinnertime, and Roberto's Taco Shop was just a few short blocks from Mid-City Legal.

Asher plucked fallen carne asada from his paper plate and tossed it in his mouth. "Was I right about the grub here?"

"Best I've had next to Marisol's mom's." I took a bird-sized bite of corn tortilla, snaring only a few chunks of cheese and carnitas. The food at Roberto's was better than decent. But my stomach still buzzed with nerves, like it was more beehive than digestive organ. Puking all over the brown table was not in the plan, so I was playing it safe, coaxing my body back into food.

"Glad you approve." Asher swallowed another mouthful, then said, "A diversion like you pulled off deserves a better reward than Starbucks."

Not real. Just pretend. A diversion.

Canned Mariachi music underscored my thoughts as I tried to reason with myself. Just like the *Peter Pan* mystery writer inside my tote, I could make lists. My mind titled the one I was currently composing: *Things Our Dinner Is Not.*

(1) A date

(2) A major life event

(3) Anything to puke over

"Now that we have something in our stomachs, I'll tell you why I think Jeff wigged." Asher motioned toward the window, North Park bustling outside. He arched one eyebrow. "And you can tell me about *your* wig."

I let out a wobbly laugh. Marisol's red jacket hung over my seat back, and the vampy lipstick had faded, but I was still black-ponytail girl. "Extreme dress-up time at Tops." Then I told him all the rest—how I'd forgotten the time and run out in the silly getup, his uncle's book, and my escape into the construction zone after Jeff stormed the Mid-City waiting room.

Asher shook his head. "Talk about timing."

"Do you think Jeff's episode was about you walking Olivia's mom to her car sometimes?"

Asher sipped lemon water, then nodded. "For a start. He's super possessive, so he spies on her. Goes ballistic when stuff doesn't add up for him."

I attempted a bite of rice. So far, so good. "I got that part pretty clearly."

"Olivia asked me about you yesterday. She was wondering when the tall story girl was coming back."

I grinned. "Maybe she'll visit me at the bookstore."

"Poor kid's had it rough. Those picture books I bought for my cousins were still on Hannah's desk. You said Olivia looked like a girl who needed a story, so I decided to give her one. I thought she'd like the book about the dog who goes to camp to learn to be a wolf."

Right then, in a stuffy taco shop, with Tess's wig on my head, and London's boyfriend across from me, my heart squeezed. So tight, I had to turn from the image. From him. I followed streams of headlights out the window.

"Darcy?"

"Sorry. Right." I forced a smile. "We sell a lot of copies of that dog book. Really cute."

"She loved it. And when I walked them to their car last night, her mom hugged me, just in thanks for the gift. Olivia did, too."

"And her dad must've seen and figured you're more to them than just a guy working at the center."

Asher was down to one taco. He picked it up and tipped it at me. "Bingo. Uncle Brian was on-site yesterday and James has been working with me almost every day. Before you came in, they'd gone to the truck for supplies."

Now it made sense, how the two men had appeared to help wrangle Jeff before the cops arrived. "Good thing they showed up, or..."

Our eyes met. "I'm trying not to think about the *or* part," he said.

That made two of us. Only, I was trying not to think of what we'd done in the alley to avoid that *or* part.

"Before last May, I would've gone after Andrews myself." His mouth quirked in a quick sigh of frustration.

"You'll get back, right?" I instinctively reached out to touch his hand, but caught myself. I grabbed my cup instead. "You're still recovering."

"Strength and mobility, yeah." He shrugged. "But other things, I'll never get back."

"Annapolis?"

His face dimmed, like he'd swallowed a bit of autumn night sky from beyond the window glass. "My Marine pilot dad reminds me of that every chance he gets."

I lobbed a quizzical look at him.

"The accident wasn't my fault on the road." He tapped his forehead scar, his leg. "But the injuries are still my fault. Everything I've lost is really because of one person. Me."

"That can't be true."

"I wish it wasn't." He finished the last bites of his taco, then gulped icy lemon water. "You sure you want the gory details?"

I nodded without even thinking. Wasn't my own life just another kind of gory?

"That night, my grandma was driving from Los Angeles to visit, and my parents went to a military ball. Dad told me to stay home and wait for Grandma. But about an hour before she was supposed to arrive, Jase called about this huge event in Del Mar. Like an album release party. Food, music, beach house."

"So you went," I said quietly, knowing he never made it to the party.

"I figured, what the hell? It was Friday night. I called Grandma from the road and told her I had to run out and left a key under the mat. She was cool."

"Do you remember the accident itself?"

He pushed his plate aside, clasping both hands on the tabletop. "Pieces. My last clear memory is exiting I-5 onto Del Mar Heights Road. The rest I only know because of witnesses. Police reports, paramedics."

God.

"The man who hit me wasn't drunk or anything. Sixty-three years old. He had a seizure while driving down one of the hilly roads crossing Del Mar Heights."

I gasped.

"He ran the red, straight through at what they figured was about sixty miles per hour. His minivan hit my truck, driver's side. He survived with minor injuries." Asher gestured toward his left knee again. "I flipped and rolled three times. The air bag deployed, but my head struck the window on the rollover. Hence the concussion and the scars."

And the Post-Concussive Syndrome he still suffered.

Asher's phone lit up with a text message. He glanced at the screen, then typed a series of responses. "London. She just finished play rehearsal."

Clearly my exit cue. I scooted my chair back, but stopped when he held out his palm.

"I told her I'm not going over. She has a poetry paper to finish for Monday. She hasn't even started, and I'd just get in the way."

I hid my smile behind my napkin. A tiny part of me wanted to analyze why he was really choosing to stay at Roberto's, but thoughts like that often led to more vulnerability than I could afford. I cleared my throat. "London and I have the same English teacher. The paper's on T. S. Eliot's 'The Love Song of J. Alfred Prufrock.'"

Asher ran one finger around the rim of his plastic cup. "I remember from last year. I'm guessing you've made a good start on yours, or you wouldn't have let Tess take the time to wig out your hair." His chin tilted. "And you wouldn't still be sitting here with me and grease bomb tacos and accident sob stories."

Wouldn't I? I hooked my wandering mind on to something I knew. Something I could always count on. "I finished my paper at Yellow Feather between customers." When he nod-

ded appreciatively, I said softly, "Asher, your story is just…
awful. But…at least you're *alive*."

"I tell myself that every morning when I'm forced to swim
instead of run, or when I'm popping tablets like popcorn."
Eyes flitted outside, then right at me. "And trying not to notice every plane flying over my house. Or every officer in
Marine green I run into."

I looked down at my plate, realizing I'd actually been eating. Only a few scraps remained. "Even though Annapolis is
out, you can still enter the military another way, can't you?
Or fly for an airline one day?"

"Not with all the hardware in my body. Plus one of the
drugs I'm on is a serious narcotic and banned for commercial
pilots. At least my doctor finally got the combo and dosage
right, the balance. So I've been feeling more like *Me Before
May*," he added in a radio announcer voice.

I considered that information for a moment. Maybe that's
why he'd seemed less moody lately. Less Mr. Darcy from
Pride and Prejudice. "But what about when you can get off the
medication?"

"I get migraines. The PCS will hopefully go away, and
then I can ditch most of the drugs, but the migraines might be
mine for life. Basically, it's unlikely I'll be fit to fly for money
or carry passengers for a living. Ever."

"You'll never fly again?" The words stung rising from my
throat.

"I can fly for recreation. But aviation guidelines want me to
be migraine-free for one week before I hit the runway again.
No dizzy spells, either. Seven days straight. So far, my record
is only five without either one of them."

"I'm so sorry."

Roberto's was rapidly filling up with short-order diners,
and there weren't enough tables, so we traded ours for the

sidewalk. I followed Asher's measured pace as we headed to-ward my car.

Asher crossed his arms. "My earliest memories are of me in my dad's old Piper Warrior single prop. He took me up as soon as I could sit in the seat by myself." He looked over at me. "Dad was deployed a lot when I was little. Flying was something we did together when he was home. He let me first hold the stick at six years old, just for a few moments. He used to fly fighter jets and now works in a command position at Miramar. There was no question whether or not I would fly, too. It's always been part of me, like I was born with wings as much as arms. Reminds me of you and your books."

I smiled. "That bad, huh?"

He laughed, a smooth baritone sound. "Inbred. Dad taught me himself. I did my flight hours, passed all the tests, got my license, and was flying Jase and my other friends around be-fore I could vote."

Before I thought better, I was asking, "Does London like flying with you?"

"You mean *did* she like it. I haven't flown since May, re-member. But no, it wasn't really her deal. She always joked that she'd fly with me if she was sitting in first class and I was up in front wearing gold wings and shoulder stripes." We stopped at a crosswalk. "So I guess she never will."

"You must miss it so much."

"More than anything. A couple years ago, my parents used some inheritance money from my grandmother and bought a preowned Piper Meridian. Amazing turboprop." Asher dug out his phone and flipped to his photos. He slowed even more to show me a picture of a white aircraft with a black base, black wings, and matte silver propeller. "I took this baby up every chance I got."

"It's beautiful. Your dad let you fly whenever?"

Asher nodded. "For Dad and me, flying is kind of our *thing*. There are three brothers on his side, but only my dad took after my grandfather and got the aviation gene. Dad's teaching James to fly right now. But my uncles made sure to leave their mark, too. All the Fleet cousins know how to shoot a gun in self-defense, land a single prop plane in an emergency, work a few power tools, and debate ourselves out of any mess."

I laughed, but the sound quickly flew away under my own thoughts. What skills had my mother taught me? How to fall apart, but still look presentable? How to pretend and lie to survive, or shop your bank account dry? I'd learned more about life from books than my own mom. Even the poems and scribblings in my new-old *Peter Pan* had gotten me through more emotional tight spots than her words ever had.

And then there was my newly resurrected dad. Instead of asking myself about him, I questioned Asher about his own father as my blue Honda loomed a few yards away.

"Dad blames me for that night," he answered quietly. "For the way I am now."

I halted at my car door, staring at him in shock. "But you almost died!"

"And he thanks God every day that I didn't," Asher acknowledged. "But he curses the part of me who should've been home waiting for my grandmother instead of out on the road at all." His expression darkened. "I lived, but my future died on Del Mar Heights Road."

Sixteen

Winged

"Fairies have to be one thing or the other, because being so small they unfortunately have room for one feeling only at a time." I wish this could be me. To have only one thing to feel for the whole day. And that the one thing would be anything but him.

—J. M. BARRIE, *PETER PAN*,
AND *PETER PAN* MYSTERY SCRIBBLER

I may have broken Marisol. Two minutes into my run-through of last night's events, I thought she was going to topple off our mosaic table bench. By the time I'd gotten to street tacos and Asher's accident story, I'd shocked her completely into Spanish.

"¿Mientras que yo estaba a la escuela, tú estabas besando a Asher?" She fanned herself. I'd conveniently left out the part about her jacket being lodged against Asher's back and a brick wall. Besides, she was too preoccupied with *me* lodged against Asher lodged against a brick wall.

"For the tenth time, I was not kissing him. I was pretending to kiss him. Big difference. Like, all the differences." *Not real. Make-believe.*

She sipped the blueberry smoothie she'd brought, our Saturday morning tradition when I didn't have work. "You've changed everything, though. Won't it be weird now?" Marisol said, back to English.

I pressed my fingers against both temples. "There was nothing between us to change in the first place. Our alley antics were just me, remembering stuff I'd read and thinking fast. No big deal."

Every big deal. His mouth resting against my neck. His—

"He probably thought about it all night, Darcy."

"He didn't, and I didn't, either." *Only from midnight to four-thirty.*

"He bought you dinner."

"Because I saved his ass. And…*and*, he has a girlfriend. Whom you dressed in finery and just watched prance around the Jefferson stage."

Marisol grinned *that grin*, and I knew it was gonna get bad. "You mentioned he has a girlfriend like it matters."

"Look, he's just a Jefferson graduate who happens to speed-read his way through his breaks at my workplace. Nothing more in my world." I drank my mango smoothie, stopping just short of brain freeze.

Except it won't stop feeling like something more.

But I couldn't, *couldn't* tell anyone—not even her, my shorter, curvier other half. My North Park fairy tale could never have any language of its own, whether Spanish or English, or anything out loud.

Behind us, a door slammed; a trio of tiny black birds fluttered from one of the courtyard olive trees, zooming past our heads. We both turned to see Thomas, manager of the year, cross the patio toward the staircase.

"Where does he buy his jeans? SaggyFrump.com?" Marisol whispered.

I closed my quivering lips around my straw as he stopped short of the stairs and turned to us.

"Ahh, Darcy. I was just heading up to see your mother about the bathroom fixtures."

I tensed. "Sorry, what fixtures?"

"You didn't get my flyer? About the rising cost of water in San Diego?" He tapped his chin. "They were in all the mailboxes a few days ago."

"We must've missed that one." Or I'd been too preoccupied with surprise letters and wigs and boys who didn't matter.

Thomas pushed a wave of overgelled black hair away from his face. "I thought so. Your mother didn't make her finish choice or confirm an installation date, so I figured I'd pay her a visit." He held up a checklist.

"Installation date?" I asked. *As in, someone going inside.*

"All of this information was in the flyer, but…well." Then a shrug. "We're replacing all bathroom showerheads with low-flow options and installing low-flow aerators on sink faucets over the next month. The owner wanted to let each tenant choose a finish to match their existing bathroom fixtures. We've contracted with a handyman service for the installations. I promise we won't take too much of your time."

A shiver crept up my back. "Um, I…my mother's still sleeping."

"I need to place the order with West Coast Hardware by Monday."

"Let me see that brochure, please." This from Marisol, who'd jumped up and swung around the table, coming nose-to-nose with Thomas.

The manager reluctantly handed Marisol the glossy tri-fold booklet.

Marisol grinned, tracking pictures with one bloodred fin-gernail. "Darcy and her mother would like the antique pew-ter finish, please."

Thomas snatched the brochure back. "I'm afraid I'll have to hear from Ms. Wells herself."

"That won't be necessary. I'm their designer."

I gaped in her direction as Thomas laughed. "Their *de-signer*?"

Marisol nodded once. "I'm going to design school in the fall. And I've made plenty of selections for Ms. Wells already. Her entire bathroom suite—towel bars and drawer pulls—are antique pewter."

I managed to collect myself before Thomas turned to glare at me. "She's right," I said. "We'll go with the pewter."

But Marisol wasn't done. "We'll also be handling the instal-lation ourselves, since it's a simple change-out. This way, Ms. Wells doesn't have to adjust her work schedule. And Darcy doesn't have to worry about being home during school or her work shifts, either." She glanced from me to Thomas and grinned again.

He pointed a shaky finger right back at her. "*You're* going to install a showerhead and aerator? You do realize it's noth-ing like picking out sofa swatches or even painting. It requires tools. Wrenches and pliers—"

Marisol straightened her neck. "My father makes it a point to teach me practical skills. So I can take care of my own home one day without relying on others so much." One step forward on camel gladiator sandals. "That includes big, scary tools like wrenches and pliers."

"Oh." Blood flooded Thomas's cheeks; his fingers clenched

the brochure, wrinkling the edges. "I'm sure it does. I just meant—"

"It's settled then." My friend sat again, crossing her legs. "You place the order. We'll handle the installation and even deliver the old showerhead to your door."

After an audible huff, he was gone. I whipped around to face Marisol, hands flailing. "That... I mean...you..."

Marisol patted my arm and pulled over my smoothie. She patted that, too, urging me into mango. "Easy, babe. What's got your tacos in a tangle?"

"You never lie. And you just...the faucet..."

Marisol sipped her own smoothie. "Nothing I said was a lie."

"*We'll* handle the installation?"

"I said we'll *handle* it. The situation. Not necessarily the work."

"Fine. Then, design school?"

She shrugged. "FIDM *is* design school. I never mentioned what kind of design." Marisol leaned in. "Come on, word girl. You can recite Shakespeare till you're purple, so you'll have no problem remembering every syllable that just came out of my mouth. Go on. Press Rewind on the last minute, and if you can show me even one lie, I'll buy all the smooth-ies till summer."

I did, and I couldn't. She was a genius—I told her so.

And scary. I told her that, too.

"Still, about the install—and not just this one—I can't ask Marco anymore," I whispered. My new-old *Peter Pan* novel rested by my smoothie cup on a chipped tile. I toyed with the soft, timeworn edges.

"I know but, Darcy, you're the smartest person I know. And you're missing the most obvious solution of all time."

My brows narrowed.

"Babe, every time you go to work, your solution parks his paint-splattered denim on your boss's furniture and plows through book pages like 'The Very Hungry Caterpillar.'"

I shook my head rapidly. Marisol had been around my house and hoard so long, sometimes she forgot how much I needed our *un*welcome mat. "No way. Absolutely not."

"Give me one good reason why not."

Dozens of reasons shook my insides. "He's still recovering from the accident."

"Please. If he can hang drywall at the center, he can install a showerhead and probably tackle most issues in your apartment."

"Marisol, he works all day building and…installing. Another fix-it project is the last thing he'll want to take on during his off-hours."

"Excuse me, but didn't you just save his ass big-time last night? I know he'd help as a thank-you."

"What if London found out? And started gossiping? Because we both know that's the one thing she does better than acting."

"Do you hear yourself?" she asked incredulously. "He wouldn't say a word if you asked him not to. Just tell him. I know it's scary. But you felt the same way when you asked Marco for help three years ago."

"I can't."

Marisol sighed. "In less than a week, you'll be eighteen. You're going to have to stop hiding your life from your friends. Darcy, no one cares."

"*I* care!" I protested, tears pricking my lashes. "I live it every day. Right now our home is too disgusting, too cluttered, too…everything."

She traced our black Sharpie heart and star, nodded. "I didn't mean it like that. I know you're doing your best to push her forward without shoving too far."

It was barely ten o'clock in the morning, and I was already exhausted. I glanced up at my unit, then back to Marisol, whispering, "Aren't weekends supposed to be fun—shocking, I know—or at least somewhat weekend-ish? I've got a manager up in my business and even creeping Mom's work. Besides that, I need to choose my next eBay items when she leaves. *And* ship off the stuff from last week."

"You're right." Marisol bobbed up again, piling her jacket, my book, and my keys into her bag. One expert toss, and both our foam cups swished into the trash can. "I'm gonna fix that right now. Fix our Saturday. Come on, I have a surprise."

She grabbed my forearm and dragged me out to the street, then folded me and my endless legs into the passenger seat of her SUV before running around to the driver's side and buckling up.

"I swear, if you try to give me gum or another juice box…"

"Not today, babe. I have another plan."

"This is your plan?" I peered into the large closet in the Robleses' sewing studio. Inside, two wedding dresses hung on the rack, white satin puddling onto the carpet. "My surprise is looking at used gowns?"

Marisol grabbed one. "Oh, we're not going to look. We're going to put them on and then do something deliciously amusing."

"First of all, why? And secondly, they're your mom's." The last thing I needed on an already-sucky Saturday was the wrath of Eva Robles.

"Correction, they *were* hers. Mama ordered these gowns from eBay for nothing. Cheap, cheap, cheap." She pinched the white satin. "And so is this grade of fabric and the iridescent sequins. Shameful. She'd never make something this tacky."

"Then why—"

"See, on Mama's cutting table? Gowns from this designer and series used a particular embroidered lace trim that she loves. She's going to rework it onto a mermaid-style gown for a new client." Marisol lifted the dress to reveal the raw edges along the neckline and cuffs. "The missing trim doesn't affect the fit, and she has no use for the rest of these gowns. So we get to play." She eyed me. "Why are you wrinkling your nose?"

"It's weird. Wearing someone else's wedding dress." Wearing someone else's fairy tale.

"Whatever, we're doing it anyway." Marisol thrust the gown into my arms and grabbed the other one for herself. "Now bride up."

I did, reluctantly, then walked over to the full-length mirror. My eBay bride must've been shorter than me, because the satin skirt hung right above my ankles. But the embellished bodice fit perfectly, cinching my waist like Marisol's leather jacket.

My friend appeared, wearing the other, similar gown. We bowed. Twirled. And we laughed and laughed at our frosted cupcake reflections in the mirror. "Now for part two, my perfect cure for a sad-faced, mopey Darcy."

Five minutes later, I found myself staring at Carlos and Camila's backyard trampoline. Wearing a wedding gown.

"You've got to be kidding me."

"C'mon, this is going to be epic. Ever since the gowns came in—well, ever since forever—I've wanted to do this." Marisol hoisted herself onto the gigantic round trampoline. "Watch and learn." She started tentatively, just gentle baby bounces. Her caramel-streaked hair waved as she gained momentum, higher and higher. "Darcy...get...up...here." She giggled and squealed.

Marisol certainly seemed to be enjoying it. And I was already zipped into the silly gown. What the hell? I hopped up onto my rear and swung my legs around. Marisol was there with a hand. I began as she had, the black, springy surface warm under my bare feet. I grabbed fistfuls of satin and jumped.

Wind and motion grabbed my hair; tulle layers floated, soft and billowy around my legs. Then my smile took flight, stretching its wingspan across my cheeks.

"Yes! Look at you go, D!" Marisol yelled and spun.

After a few moments, I was able to jump the world away. A world that always wanted to tether me down with the gravity of responsibility. I leaped away the unbearable secrets and shame. I soared feet above a foolish family, a father's Thailand letter. My body shed the worry I knew would return tonight. It always did. But for now, life coursed through my limbs.

It felt something like freedom.

After long minutes, we couldn't manage another jump. We collapsed, our bridal bodies stretched out side by side on the trampoline. Lacy chests heaved. Sweat glistened across my forehead, misting underneath the itchy white bodice. Flush-cheeked, I stared at the sky, pretending the earth had flipped us upside down. The wide-bowled sky lapped like an ocean, white clouds cutting across the blue like boats to faraway kingdoms.

My fantasy cracked when the screen door smacked open. High-pitched screeches trailed along the yard. Carlos and Camila rushed the trampoline, springing up to us like tiny gazelles.

"Mama! Darcy and Marisol have the big dresses!" Camila laughed and jumped by my legs. "The white wedding ones like you make."

Carlos ran the perimeter in sock-covered feet until Marisol tackled him, dragging the kicking, giggling boy on top of her. "You guys are home early."

"We didn't get to go to the park or Target to get toys. 'Cause we didn't do good at the food store," Carlos said, panting.

"Carlos y Camila, vengan, por favor." Eva Robles stood in the kitchen doorway.

The twins obeyed. They hopped off and ran to their mother. She bent low to speak between their bright faces, then moved so they could run back inside.

I cringed at Marisol as Mama Robles crossed the patio onto the lawn, one hand on her hip. She looked me over, then her daughter. "Por Dios." Her chin quivered, soundless laughter rippling her chest. "I'm going to make you the chilaquiles now."

Alone again, we snickered. My mouth watered, already tasting the steaming dish made from salsa-dredged chips, eggs, and beans, topped with cheese. "Okay, time to change. No way I'm spilling food on this satin snow castle. But this was actually...fun."

"Never doubt me again." Marisol grinned when I turned my head.

"Lesson learned."

She raised up onto one elbow. "Good, then you can also not doubt the next part I'm about to say."

"Which is?"

"That you could try more than being goofy with tacky wedding gowns. Part of taking care of yourself is letting some people in once in a while."

My breath skipped, knowing exactly which *people* she meant. But how could I? I sat up and looked through the doorway into the Robleses' warm and vibrant home. I thought of my own home. How could I open that door and let him see the messiest part of me?

"I get it, but I can't tell Asher. Not yet." And I couldn't

tell her why. I had to remember I was invisible. Most of all, I needed to abandon a story that could only have a tragic ending.

Marisol flopped down. "Okay, okay. Will you at least promise to think it over? You know, consider him?"

I faced my sweet friend and spoke my clearest piece of truth that day. "I will."

Some things, I couldn't jump away.

Seventeen

Much Ado About Something

*"There was a star danced,
and under that I was born."*

—WILLIAM SHAKESPEARE, *MUCH ADO ABOUT NOTHING*

As we rounded the corner toward the Jefferson High auditorium for opening night, I realized Marisol wasn't the only designer contracted for *Much Ado About Nothing*. "It's beautiful," I told my friend, spinning a slow circle. Thousands of white fairy lights twinkled from tree branches, and a musical trio, decked in Elizabethan garb, played brisk tunes on lute and piccolo.

Marisol pointed toward a short row of booths offering crafts, meat pies, and mulled cider. "So cute!" More costumed hosts and hostesses sold tickets and passed out programs. "We can pretend all this pomp and swag is for our birthdays."

I guffawed, shaking my head. Technically, her birthday wasn't for a few more hours, but we were well into mine.

We heard them before we saw them—the brass-tipped laughter and animated speech usually accompanying the Robles family. Marisol's parents and Natalia bounded up to us.

"Feliz cumpleaños, cariño." Eva Robles drew me close for a floral-scented embrace. Her husband kissed my cheek.

"I didn't know you guys were coming," I said.

"¡Claro!" Mama Robles waved one hand. "We want to see Marisol's designs on the stage. And..." She motioned toward her younger daughter. Natalia produced two identical pink boxes topped with curly sprigs of white ribbon.

Marisol's father continued, "Since it's your big birthday, we wanted to do something special for you two."

I accepted my box and turned to Marisol. "Did you know about this?"

She took hers and shook it. "Not a clue."

We unraveled the ribbons and lifted the box lids together, a lively jig sounding from the musicians. Tears pricked the corners of my eyelids as I pulled out the daintiest gold necklace I'd ever seen. A tiny gold star hung from the chain.

"Oh!" Marisol held an identical necklace with a heart pendant. "Look, Darcy. There's an *M* engraved on one side." She flipped the charm. "And a *D* on the other."

"On mine, too," I said before my best friend and I enveloped her parents in a shower of thanks and hugs.

While her family explored the craft booths, Marisol and I took turns fastening our gifts. Then we entered the buzzing auditorium and found seats near the stage. I glanced down, lifting the gold star. "I can't believe they did this."

"Even more, that they managed to hide them from me." Marisol grabbed my wrist. "Speaking of accessories, your mom did good this year." She flicked one of the silver charms on my new bracelet.

"I hate saying I'm still shocked." My thoughts rewound to

my first waking minutes of *eighteen*. Mom had gotten up early, thrown on sweats, and cleared off just enough of our dining room table. A cinnamon bagel with cream cheese from my favorite shop was waiting for me when I woke up. And even though a black gift box sat next to the plate, my greatest gift needed no wrapping paper and pretty bows: CPS could no longer investigate my mother, or take me away from her.

"Happy birthday, honey." Mom enveloped me in a strong hug.

"Thanks, Mom." I rubbed sleep from my eyes.

She pulled away, splaying both hands over my cheeks. "Amazing girl." Mom stepped back and reached for the black box, nodding for me to open the lid.

Inside was a thick silver link bracelet with a handful of beach-themed charms. I fingered a seashell, a crested wave, and a sand dollar. Then a detailed sandcastle and a wavy-haired mermaid. The final one, a sun with spiky rays. "It's so pretty. Thank you."

"I didn't know what to get you." She glanced down for a beat, then up at my eyes. "I thought you'd enjoy something to remind you of your childhood."

Memories flashed—skipping along the surf and digging with shovels, bunches of mermaid-hair seaweed. I wanted to tell her that what I *really* wanted, more than beautiful jewelry, were all the beautiful parts of her again. I knew they were still there, buried under useless items. I knew *she* was still there.

"Room for one more?"

My eyes snapped sideways, cursing my insides for instinctively jumping when I saw Asher beside our row. "Sure," I squeaked.

Marisol waved, scooting one seat to her left and pulling me to do the same.

Asher took my place at the end. He stared briefly at the

small bouquet of roses he'd brought before resting them on his lap. The colors popped against his dark jeans. Pink, red, and ivory petals. "Hey, happy birthday, by the way."

"Um, thank you." He remembered? I'd told him about my birthday sharing the same day as opening night more than a week ago.

Asher leaned behind my head to Marisol. "And you, too. Eighteen, huh? Big time." He split his gaze between us. "You guys have to spill your birthday bucket lists. What does one pack for a Darcy-Marisol eighteenth birthday extravaganza, anyway? Night-vision goggles and rappelling rope? Or passports, wigs from Tops, and knives hidden in lipstick tubes, James Bond style?"

My smiles always came too easily around him. "Hardly."

"We had school today, so the mountain-scaling and highway robbery is gonna have to wait," Marisol said.

"We did treat ourselves to our favorite Asian bowls before showing up at this joint." I held up both hands, wiggled my fingers. "Whew! Epic, huh? Alert the paparazzi."

Marisol shrugged. "I dunno, mostly it feels like just another day. We were talking about this at dinner. How we've been thinking about turning eighteen for months, and that everything would magically change." She flipped through her play program.

"Maybe you built it up too much?" Asher said. "Few experiences live up to their hype."

"Is flying one of them?" *Flying.* I frowned instantly, wishing I could reel it back in. What was wrong with me? "I'm sorry. I didn't mean—"

"It's fine. Really," he said, then warmed the entire theater with a smile. "And yes, flying is definitely one. Among other notable things."

I swallowed hard as a lanky figure swept down the aisle.

"Marco!" Marisol called, waving the program like a flag.

Marisol's brother halted and spun a one-eighty. He looked sharp in a black dress shirt tucked into gray jeans. His dark hair was slicked back, still damp. "Ahh. I ran into Papi outside." My eyes widened at the two identical bouquets of colorful roses he was holding.

"I was hoping you'd make it." Marisol scooted left again. Marco gave a quick nod to Asher and crab-walked into the empty space.

"'Course I made it. And feliz cumpleaños." Marco kissed Marisol's cheek, then both of mine, handing us bouquets of six roses. Each bloom was a different color. "Family plan had you getting these along with the necklaces, but I got held up on campus."

"Thank you—they're beautiful." I sniffed my roses.

Marco leaned close. "Hey, sorry again about the dinner surprise. I feel really bad about leaving you without a handyman."

I gave a quick, dismissive nod. My eyes flitted left and right to make sure no one else had heard.

"Everything okay there?" he added.

This wasn't the place to get into my fix-it woes, and my eighteenth birthday wasn't the time. "All good, thanks. I'll take care of it," I said, because it had to be true. "And congrats again on the new job."

I glanced at Asher. He'd slouched down in his seat, right elbow plunked on the armrest, index finger propping up his chin. His body angled toward me. Watching. A half smile dressed his face as he glanced from his flowers to mine. He rested his bunch in front of his feet.

"Asher, you haven't met Marco, right?" I asked. "Marisol's older brother?"

Marco reached across me, tipping his chin. "Hey." Asher returned the greeting.

"Marco must've been a senior your first year here," Marisol told Asher. "Knowing my snob brother, he didn't mingle with lowerclassmen and never knew of your existence."

"I bring you flowers and all I get is shade?" Marco said.

Asher snorted. "Nah, it's all good. I was back here for a couple weeks building the set, and it felt super weird. Sitting here must be even more surreal for you after all these years."

"Oh, that was you?" Marco pointed at the stage. "Marisol mentioned some alumni pitching in to help. She said it looks really good."

"It looks better than good. It looks real," I said.

Asher nodded at Marco, but landed soft eyes on me. "Well, you're the best the judge of that, Miss Newly Eighteen Lit Expert. I hope people who really know Shakespeare appreciate the mood I was…"

The houselights lowered over Asher's words and the lingering gaze between us. My next breath fell heavy as *Much Ado*'s melodic prelude streamed into the theater. The curtain parted, and Asher's set *did* look real—more magical and authentic than during rehearsals. Stage lights and shadow work framed the foliage, stone walls, and scenic garden features, creating the illusion of height and mass.

I soon forgot about Asher. After all, it was the Shakespeare I loved, right in front of me. For all the plays I'd read, I hadn't seen many performed live, the language real and present. My mind couldn't help tracking along with some of the more famous passages. The cast translated the funny and poignant story well, and I only caught a couple of flubs. Marisol's costumes worked beautifully, adding a touch of refined elegance to the story. Asher's Italian garden sets did, too.

We stood, enthusiastically applauding when the actors linked hands for final bows. As the lights came up, Asher grabbed his flowers. I thought he'd bolt, searching out London, but he matched my lazy pace and escorted me to the stage door while the Robles siblings barreled ahead. A small crowd hovered; cast members were trickling out, greeting guests and posing for pictures.

Marisol and Marco left to chat with Alyssa as Jase crossed the courtyard in jeans and a sweatshirt. After a short wave in my direction, he high-fived Asher and tugged the cellophane paper. "Major fail, dude. You know yellow roses are my first love."

Asher snapped his fingers. "Nice job on Benedick," he told Jase. "Gonna kill UCLA theater."

"Thanks, man." Jase backed away, saying, "Now I'm gonna kill one of those meat pies."

"Aww," I said, glancing down at my own bouquet. During the play, one of the stems had snapped. I flicked the dangling pink rosebud. "Oh well."

Asher stepped closer. "Nope, that can't happen. No broken birthday flowers for Darcy Wells tonight. Turns out, this handyman works outside of University Avenue, too." I watched, wide-eyed, as he plucked out my broken pink flower and tossed it into a nearby planter. He dislodged one of the red—not pink—roses from his bouquet and held it out.

I was so busy trying not to lose both my cool and my footing, I missed a costumed London Banks striding up to us. "Ooh, for me?" she said, grabbing the bouquet and snatching my fix-it flower right from Asher's hand. I shifted uncomfortably when she pecked him on the lips. "Thanks, babe. My favorites, and a spare to keep backstage on the makeup table. Sweet. Makes my bitch of a headache not so bitchy." She smirked at me. "Quick, my mom wants pictures before I change."

"Right," Asher mumbled, following on her arm. He turned back for a quick, apologetic frown.

I shrugged, forcing a smile. Asher's bittersweet gesture lodged inside my chest.

Jase returned with a meat pie, watching his friend pose for a series of shots. "London did pretty well as Hero. Between you and me, she would've made a better Beatrice."

I didn't want to say what was in my head, but my mouth opened anyway. "Based solely on snark and attitude?"

"'Tis truth you speaketh, milady," Jase orated. "But Alyssa really shone in her audition. Nailed Beatrice's sharp tongue and sass. Mrs. Howard had to give her the part."

"You nailed it, too. Tonight, I mean." I fiddled with my bouquet. "So you're going to UCLA?"

He crossed his fingers. "Let's hope. And thanks."

"Marisol's going to design school in LA, too."

A wide smile cracked his face. He leaned in, dark eyebrows wagging under his bangs. "If I catch her out and about and up to no good, I'll report back to her keeper."

I couldn't help grinning back. "Deal."

Marisol left Mrs. Howard's side and came up to nudge me. "Time to bust this joint and find us some more birthday."

"Whose birthday?" Jase pointed at me. "Yours?"

I nodded. "And Marisol's, in a few hours."

"You know, I'm as big a theater nut as anyone, but *this* was the evening highlight of your celebration?"

I lifted one shoulder. His rich, stage-honed voice made it sound even more pathetic than it was. "Well—"

"That's what they think." This from Asher, who'd crept up behind us. Bionic knee, stealth motion. "We're only getting started with birthday antics."

We are? Marisol leveled a curious look at him. And where was London?

"I'm feeling pretty good tonight. I can round up a few more

partygoers? I mean, unless you have some other gig brewing?" he asked.

We didn't, and our faces must've told Asher, because he leaned into Jase's ear, whispering.

Jase considered, then bobbed his head. "Interesting, and a little out-there. I like it. Clever."

"So, you're in?" Asher asked his friend.

Marisol draped her crossbody purse over her shoulder. "In for *what*, exactly?"

"Your milestone eighteenth birthday is missing one key component," Asher declared. "A unique activity you've never done before."

When he looked at me, challenge splashed across his face, I almost choked on my own tongue. Something I'd never done before? My mind reeled.

Marisol gave me her best *sure, why not, it might be fun* expression.

"All right, I'm game," I said. Of course, London would be included in our group, which I'd have to accept along with Asher's secret plans. Tonight, I didn't want to miss out, and my curiosity was climbing by the second. And London or not, I was still touched that he wanted to celebrate with me and Marisol.

Asher grinned. "You'll need the address." He looked around and settled for the play program he was already holding. Marisol handed him a pen. "Give us maybe thirty minutes for, um, preparations."

"My mom is probably looking for us anyway," Marisol said, glancing at me and rolling her eyes. "You know how she is about birthday pictures. They could take twice that long."

I laughed and accepted the program. I recognized the street name, but couldn't remember driving it.

Asher stepped back. "Put that into your nav and turn into

the main drive. Take the first left and park in any of the spaces until we get there." Then he was off, with his partner in crime trailing behind.

Marisol snatched the program, squinting. "What's at the end of this goose chase? A rave hall?"

"Or a secret club where you need a whack-a-doodle password for the door to swing open?"

When we finally left campus to follow Asher's directions, we realized our guesses were way off. Marisol exited the freeway when the navigation voice commanded, and I started to get suspicious. "He can't be serious."

Marisol stopped at a red light, eyes narrowing out the passenger side window at the endless, blocks-long complex running parallel to the road. "Maybe there's a restaurant along here we don't know about."

But there wasn't. Marisol took a right turn and followed the access road, straight through the main gate of Montgomery-Gibbs Executive Airport.

Eighteen

Piper

"'It was then that I rushed in like a tornado, wasn't it?'"
**Again. You'd think I'd learn to just stay
under safe cover for once.**

—J. M. BARRIE, *PETER PAN*,
AND *PETER PAN* MYSTERY SCRIBBLER

Marisol set the parking brake and looked at me, dumbfounded.

I thrust out both arms aimlessly and laughed. It came out half breathy, half hysterical. Even though it was late, the airport lot felt too deserted. Only a handful of other cars surrounded Marisol's SUV.

"Well, I guess we wait." Marisol unwrapped two pieces of strawberry gum and stuffed them in her mouth. She flipped down her visor and checked her lipstick in the mirror.

"Hopefully Asher isn't punking us, and sending us to Montgomery-Gibbs for no reason is his idea of 'something new we haven't done,'" I said.

"Ugh, bite your tongue. If that's true, I'm going full force on Donnelly and Fleet."

I believed her. I rummaged through my tote for a novel, but let go when another set of headlights streamed into the lot. Asher's black Ford pulled up beside us. "Looks like you're gonna have to find something else to sic your Robles on."

Marisol blew a bubble and unlocked our doors. "Don't tempt me, babe."

Asher gingerly hopped out of the imposing truck. Jase followed and Alyssa jumped from the rear cab, holding a stack of blankets.

"Welcome to my happy place," Asher said.

"You'd better let them off the hook before they think we're actually going flying," Alyssa said.

"Yeah, not this time." Asher eyed me quickly, a hesitant smile tugging his mouth. "But tonight, you guys are getting more than just cake. How many people can say they've had their eighteenth birthday party in an airport hangar?"

Then I understood. Asher was trying to give two best friends new memories. My heart caught again, a snare hooking behind my ribs.

I could only manage a grateful smile. But Marisol, always equipped with whatever I seemed to be lacking, said, "This is more than decent of you guys. Once my mom finds out, she's going to bury you in tacos."

Jase wagged his brows. "No better way to go. We're perpetually hungry, so your birthdays are giving us license to pig out." He started unloading bags from the truck. "We tried to round up a couple more people, but Bryn has early *Nutcracker* rehearsal and London went home with a nasty headache."

I glanced over at Asher. He nodded. "Yeah, it was only getting worse. She's got the matinee tomorrow and needs a bottle of aspirin and one of those glitter bath bombs she spends ten dollars apiece on."

This tidbit was better than any rose. Considering what had gone down the last time London and I were at a party, I wasn't entirely comfortable around her. I slid into a faded denim jacket and followed our small group from the access road onto the taxiway. A silent prayer of thanks fell from my lips when Marisol tossed her chewed gum wad in the nearest trash bin rather than saving it for later. As we reached a section of stowed private aircraft, the setting—unique, like Asher had promised—reminded me of a graveyard. Unlike gravestones, the white planes rested with inert life. The promise of movement and power seeped from wings and propellers, even though they sat tethered and still.

We walked on until Asher stopped at a small hangar, with its opening directly facing the runway. He swung the wide door upward and flicked on lights. There it was, the beautiful turboprop I'd seen on his phone. "Our family jewel," Asher announced as we entered.

The Fleets' Piper Meridian was larger and sleeker than many of the other planes we'd passed. The nose stretched long and narrow, like the snout of a powerful animal. Black and speckled gold swept around and underneath the front of the plane, then dipped one side of the tail in solid color. Marisol strolled the perimeter, her designer's eye skimming over the carefully crafted details.

Alyssa spread beach blankets outside, right in front of the entrance, and unpacked the snacks. Jase keyed up music on his iPad and portable speakers as the rest of us joined them.

"As for party fare," Jase said, "I'm afraid Ash being Ash limits our beverage options." A deep bow, even though he was sitting. "Apologies, ladies, your party has been designated squeaky clean by Mr. Anti-Vice over there."

Asher pulled glass bottles from a cooler bag. "What's wrong

with this? It's the best brand of cream soda and root beer out there."

Jase's expression soured. "Doesn't make it real beer."

"Seriously?" Alyssa smacked Jase on the shoulder. "Like Ash would actually drink on a tarmac, flying or not."

Post-Concussive Syndrome or not, I thought.

Alyssa pulled out chips, napkins, and dessert plates with green and blue stripes. She handed them to me to unwrap. "I tried to find some cuter birthday ones, but Food King didn't have much in the paper goods aisle. Plus, Asher was rushing me out. We *had* to go to a special place for the cupcakes."

"What?" Too much surprise pitched my voice as my fingernail slit through plastic wrapping.

"He insisted on a real bakery. Heavenly Cupcake." When my eyebrows flicked up, she asked, "You've never been there? It's right by school. We were late because we couldn't decide on flavors."

Asher produced a white bakery box with a gold halo logo and hinged open the lid. I spotted Marisol, one hand dropped over her chest as she gazed at me with soft eyes and a parted mouth. She realized what Asher had done, and why. But after what Alyssa just said, I also knew he hadn't told the others *why* he had to bring artisan cupcakes with mounds of pillowed frosting.

"Asher, you really went all out," Marisol said. "Thanks. These look amazing."

He ducked his head. "I'm breaking my no-sugar, no-gluten rules tonight, so we need the good stuff." He glanced up at me, smiling. "Your fault, birthday girls."

My throat closed for a beat. I knew I had to stop trying to make these details and this night more than it was. Cupcakes and celebratory sugar, just a kind gesture for two friends. That was the beginning and end of it.

"Marisol and Darcy get to pick first. We have salted caramel, lemon cream, and chocolate marshmallow," Jase said.

Marisol's eyes grew wider. "Chocolate? Ooh, my magic word."

Alyssa grinned and handed her the large treat with toasted marshmallow icing. I chose salted caramel and so did Asher. He might risk a few bites of sugar and flour, but never prime migraine-enemy chocolate.

Jase shook out a grocery store bag. "We forgot candles. How could we forget candles?"

"Instead of candle flames, you guys get runway lights," Asher said. "But we still have to sing. Triple-threat Jase can lead us in a Broadway version of 'Happy Birthday.'"

And he did, with Asher and Alyssa joining in. We ate the delicious cupcakes, along with salt-and-vinegar potato chips, washing it all down with chilled bottles of frothy cream soda and root beer. I reclined on the blanket and drank in the extraordinary view, too. Yellow slashes of flood lighting grayed the night sky.

Minutes turned to an hour, then nearly three. Asher took us on a tour around the hangars and rows of tied-down planes. Alyssa taught us silly dance moves, and Jase, amateur comedian, entertained us with impressions and stupid jokes. He even challenged Marisol to a foreign accent duel and conceded my Mexi-Cuban masterpiece of a friend made a better Australian than he did.

I couldn't help remembering another party, not so long ago. Only this time, I stretched my legs over blanketed asphalt instead of beach sand. Airport warning lights twinkled instead of stars. A few late-night aircraft landed, the whoosh of engines pulling another kind of tide. Back then, I'd felt uncomfortable and shamed—alone, even though I'd sat in the middle of a huge crowd of classmates. But *alone* wasn't any part of now.

I checked my watch. Grinning, I sat up and pulled Marisol away from her conversation with Jase. "It's happening! It's officially been your birthday for five minutes."

She draped her arm around me, squeezing me tight. The group sang again, just because. And when Jase and Asher went inside to fiddle with the plane, Marisol said, "I have an idea." She removed her heart necklace. "Take yours off."

She handed me the heart and took my unhooked chain with the golden, dangling star. "I've been thinking about this since Mama gave these to us. I'm going away next year, and…"

I filled in the rest myself, emotion glazing my eyes. "Let's do it." I fastened my star around her neck. Marisol's smile gleamed, wide and lopsided, as she clasped her gift around mine. It felt good wearing a little piece of her. The biggest heart I knew.

What would happen when Marisol eventually packed her SUV with her trendy clothes and shoes—with all of *her*—and I had to watch the red Pathfinder drive away?

I shook away that lonely thought and returned to the others. Jase and Alyssa were complaining about their early call time for tomorrow's matinee.

Marisol stretched and sprang up onto her knees, addressing the two actors. "Hey, since I live right by school, I should drop you guys off at the lot to get your cars. It's only a few blocks to my house from there."

Then, to my surprise, she signaled Asher. "Could you give Darcy a ride, since she's on the other side of Adams, like you are? Then neither of us will have to double back."

How does Marisol even— I cut myself off. Marisol usually knew whatever needed to be known.

"Sure, no problem," Asher said. He looked at me. "Maybe we can clean up, so they can get some sleep?"

"Um…sure. Of course."

The next few moments flew by at sound-like speed. I counted only a handful of blinks between everyone agreeing and saying goodbye. Then it was just me, alone with Asher and the remains of the best party ever.

He was filling a trash bag with empty bottles, so I found another and stuffed in plates and napkins. I rolled the tops of a couple of chip bags and put them aside.

"Before we go, do you want to see the inside of the Piper?" Asher asked as we worked together to fold blankets.

"I'll admit I'm curious. Can't say I've ever been in a private plane."

"Give me a sec." He unlatched the large door on the right side of the aircraft, then disappeared inside. The cockpit and the remainder of the interior lit up through the windows before he stuck his head out. "Come on up."

I entered the hangar and climbed three riser steps into the center of the cabin. Four passenger seats, trimmed in smooth, honey-colored leather, faced each other. Asher was already seated in the left captain's chair. I inched my way to the front seat at his right. "It's incredible. Bigger than I thought, too."

"One of the reasons my dad splurged on the Meridian. We use it a lot for family vacations. My sister, Avery, is away at Emerson College—Boston. When she's home we usually take trips together."

"Does Avery fly, too?"

He cocked his head. "All Fleets can fly. My dad wouldn't have it any other way. My mom and Avery don't care about being licensed, but either of them can land this baby in a storm with no control tower."

"That's so amazing," I marveled.

The cockpit wrapped around us in an overwhelming array of lights and buttons and levers. Three illuminated monitors spread across the front, as big as laptop screens. I glanced across and down; my side also had a smaller control wheel and a set of wide foot pedals, just like Asher's. "You can fly the plane from my seat?"

"Sure can. First time I took the stick, I was in your seat in our old Piper Warrior." He pointed to the floor. "Those are rudders for steering on the ground when you taxi. And there's the brake. Very important." He touched the center section, tapping his hand over a set of levers. "Here, we have the throttle."

I pointed to the endless dials and switches on the dash and overhead. "How do you keep all of these gadgets and gizmos straight?"

He laughed out a breath. "These *gizmos* keep you alive. You learn them until you start seeing them in your cereal bowl. After a while, it's second nature." One shoulder popped up. "Like all those stories and words in your head. If I saw all that inside, it might look just as scary and complicated."

Now I laughed until a thought sobered me. "Is it hard being here? Now?"

"Is it difficult for me, sitting here with a license to take this baby up, but without the health to keep it up?"

"Yeah." Why was he so easy to talk to?

"At first, I couldn't handle even coming to the airport for maintenance. But as I healed, I missed the planes too much. I missed *this* plane. Just after sunset is my favorite time, when it slows way down and the tower closes." He traced the edge of the gray control wheel. "My dreams are here. I don't want to be afraid of those anymore. My big plans changed, but I know I'll get back some form of flight. And right now, this seat is as close as I can get."

His words soared with the nimble freedom of hope, touching down on the surface of my skin with a gentle *bump, bump, glide.* But they hurt—stung—because of what I still wouldn't...

couldn't admit to myself. Me, spending midnight in a copilot's chair, put me so close to a reality I was too afraid to even call a dream.

It wasn't that I never longed for a repaired family and future, or someone to love. But I spent so much time battling the clutter scaffolding my life, so much time hiding. Dreams came, settling inside me. When they did, I lived in a new house, clean and free. I kissed the prince and danced with the hero, maybe even one like Asher Fleet. But I had to move those dreams out, every time. Evicted.

How could I hold real love inside an invisible heart?

Asher, though—he was nearly there. He only needed a string of seven healthy days to fly again. In the same leather chair, with the same controls at my hands and feet, I felt eternities away from takeoff.

Not real. Just make-believe. Breathe it away.

I changed the subject, something safe and dangerous all the same. "Thank you again for the party. The cupcakes." I risked a look at him. "You made it really nice for us."

A soft, flat smile. "Good friends are hard to find and worth celebrating. Your birthday story with Marisol was so..." I watched him struggle for the right word. He tapped his chin, eyes circling the cockpit, peering out the angled windows built for flight.

I had enough words for both of us, but just said, "I know. It was, and still is."

"Ever since that day, I've wanted to ask you one thing."

"What?"

"When you guys told me the school party story, you never said what happened when you went home. You know, with your mom?"

I felt my eyes close over the memory. "Mom remembered right before she came to pick me up. She was in tears when

I got into the car. She brought a grocery store cupcake she'd grabbed on the way." My hands itched for a steadying book to hold. "She tried her best to make it up to me, taking me to dinner and the mall."

The only way she knew how to fix anything—shopping.

"Wow," Asher said, forehead creasing.

"She's never forgotten since. Today—or yesterday, I guess— she gave me this." I showed him the silver charm bracelet.

"Nice," he said. "What about your dad?"

My whole body tensed, like someone had zipped up the skin from my feet to my face.

Asher must've noticed, because he leaned in, wincing. "Sorry, is he a touchy subject? Nasty divorce or something?"

I shook my head. "My parents never married. Kind of a volatile relationship. My dad left for Thailand for work before learning my mom was pregnant, and he never came home." I spoke to the orderly rows of dials in front of me. "He knows about me, but has never seen me."

I swore I could hear Marisol in my ear, urging me to tell Asher about my mom. About the hoarding. But I—

Asher sighed so loudly my thoughts backed away. "Last week," he said, "I was going on and on about my dad and his grudge about the accident. His disappointment and 'what-ifs.' And here you've never even met *your* dad."

"Nah, you didn't know. And this will probably sound weird and maybe cold, but the idea of him is kind of a numb spot with me because I've never known anything different."

"Would you ever want to meet him? If you could?"

"I...can," I said, two words of pure truth I hadn't told another soul. Not even Marisol. Immediately, my hand pressed over my ribs, trying to hold in all the rest. But my mouth kept moving, the words fleeing my body without my permission. "After all these years, he finally sent a letter to my grandmother for me."

Asher's eyes waxed bright and wide as moons. "That's huge, Darcy. What did he say?"

I felt the words flow stronger, clearer. I couldn't have stopped them now. "Basically, how guilty he's felt. That he's spent the last eighteen years being a coward, and he's planning a trip back to California next year. And maybe we could meet. But no pressure, and it's my choice."

"What *is* your choice?"

"I haven't made one yet." More truth. More upon more— a hoard of truth. Then a jolt of panic. "Could you keep that information quiet? It's kind of on a need-to-know basis."

"Of course." Asher held up one palm, placed the other on the throttle. I imagined it was the most sacred thing he knew. "Piper swear."

Nineteen

This, Too?

"Thus with a kiss I die."

—WILLIAM SHAKESPEARE, *ROMEO AND JULIET*

I shut both my locker and my eyes, leaning against the metal door. Most of my classes were honors level, which made for a difficult enough Monday. But trying to survive calculus and AP Government while I was the living definition of the word *distraction* had been too close to impossible. I exhaled, long and steady. Classmates scurried past me as I replayed the two-minute loop my brain refused to forget.

Me, telling Asher Fleet about my father.

I still hadn't told Marisol—*couldn't*, until I figured out what to do about the letter in my bookshelf and the man who'd written it. Marisol was the most important person in my life, but Asher was all kinds of never-be. He was neutral, an impossibility, and I'd come to realize that was exactly why I'd spilled my secret to him in that midnight cockpit.

I knew my way around words. And I understood, more than anyone, that sometimes they just needed a safe place to go.

My phone dinged. I retrieved it from my pocket.

Marisol: Still on campus?

Me: Yup

Marisol: Come to auditorium. Emergency

I didn't reply, just swung my leather tote over one shoulder and bolted through the hallway and across the grassy quad. No police officers or yellow caution tape met me in the auditorium foyer, only the smells of mildew and lemon-pine floor cleaner. I pushed through one of the old wooden doors. Stage lights flooded over the set; the rest of the hall felt dim and too quiet for an emergency. I spotted Marisol speaking with Mrs. Howard while the Shakespeare cast members sat on the lip of the stage, feet dangling.

Halfway down the aisle, I felt everyone's eyes clinging to my approaching form. Marisol turned and waved me over. "Alyssa had an accident."

A jolt buzzed through my body. Lately, the word *accident* held more meaning than ever before. "When? What happened?"

"This morning. Alyssa was wearing socks on her wooden staircase," Mrs. Howard said. "She slipped and broke her arm in two places. She's having surgery tomorrow and can't perform in closing night on Friday."

Jase and London hopped down from the stage, edging closer. I thought of Alyssa, a girl I'd hardly known before the weekend. She'd tagged along to my impromptu airport birthday and helped make it special. "I should send her a card. I can help with some class notes, too."

Marisol shook her head and cracked a wad of peppermint gum. "That's really nice, D, but not why I called you here."

A static jolt again, stronger this time. I volleyed from my friend to the director.

"Darcy, I was short actors this year," Mrs. Howard explained. "We had one understudy, but I already used Lily to fill in for Megan's part of Margaret, Hero's maid. Megan's down with a terrible sinus infection. No voice. So we thought…"

"Wait, *me?*" I sputtered. "I may know Shakespeare, but I'm not an actress!"

Mrs. Howard's expression was full of understanding. "That's the magic of Shakespeare. The words do much of the work. Get them right and feel them, and they guide you through the role and straight into the character." She eyed me knowingly. "And Marisol tells me your language skills are far greater than you let on before."

I shot Marisol a look full of needles, which she returned with an innocent smile.

"No one else at Jefferson can do what you do. Actually, I've never met anyone who can do what you do." Mrs. Howard motioned toward Jase. "The theater director at UCLA will be in town this weekend, and Jase applied for a seminar scholarship program there. She's coming to see him act out the Benedick role."

Jase stepped up, wincing. "All true."

"But…" I looked around. Even London Banks was eyeing me with something resembling hope.

I took the script from Mrs. Howard with shaking hands. Beatrice's parts were already highlighted. So many yellowed passages. "The performance is only four days away. And I work after school."

"We'll hold extra rehearsals, all around your schedule. You'll be able to practice plenty with Jase," Mrs. Howard assured me.

"I'm going to need a few minutes." I dragged Marisol far up the aisle and into two seats.

"How can I make time for a play when I've already got so much going on at home?" I asked. "Remember the manager and the lease? Trying to push my mom forward?"

"Darcy, breathe. I understand about your mom, but in the big scheme of things, it's only a few days. You can do this."

Marisol was probably right, but still, my nose wrinkled. "I'll have to act with London, though. *London!*"

"Yeah, but London's spotlight goes *poof* unless you're there to play her vibrant cousin, Beatrice. Trust me, she'll be thankful."

Could I even look at London without picturing her boyfriend against a rough alley wall and my body against his? Guilty thoughts pelted me from every direction until my insides stumbled into a muddy haze. I needed *something*. Books— no, not even books this time.

My eyes locked on to Marisol's purse. "Gum. I need gum."

"What kind?"

"All the kinds."

Marisol's eyes widened. She methodically opened her bag and pulled out packs, one by one, fanning them out on her palm.

I opened a stick of cinnamon, shoved it in, and started chewing. "Tell me, how can I even pretend to be Alyssa?" I took a stick of orange, popping it into my mouth. "She's tiny. Nothing like my shape."

"You don't have to be Alyssa. You only have to be your version of Beatrice. And Mama and I can alter the costumes. Easy. I still have all the fabric, so don't worry about that."

I took two peppermint sticks, stuffing them in. More chewing. Angry, frustrated chewing.

Marisol examined me with great trepidation. "What the hell is wrong with you? You're scaring me."

"Well, *I'm* scared. Terrified."

"You, my alien friend of planet Book, can memorize those lines in your sleep."

True. But that wasn't the whole of it. The entire cast was milling around, waiting on my answer, and I owed them one. I could keep some secrets to myself and boys who didn't matter, but I had to tell my friend the real reason I was silently freaking out. "Marisol, you read the play."

"'Course I did. Hello? The costumes?"

"Marisol. You *saw* the play."

"I sat right next to you and watched it on your birthday. What are you on about?"

Two more watermelon sticks. "For *goss sake*, Add Five." Of course, now I couldn't talk at all with the gigantic gum wad. I removed half and wrapped the multicolored ball in a tissue. "Act Five," I said again. "The huge scene near the end of Act Five."

Marisol nodded. "Okay…that's the part right before Hero and Claudio's wedding, right? Where Beatrice and Benedick are squabbling and denying they love each other and there's all this sexual tension? Great scene. You'll do fine. I'll help you with the sass."

I groaned and chewed, pressing fingers into my temples. "Not the sass. I can fake the attitude. Probably," I added.

"Then what is the problem?"

"The kiss." There, I said it, pushing it out through too much gum and even more anguish. "Benedick kisses Beatrice right before the ending. And not a peck on the cheek."

"No, he grabs her face all dramatic-like. And, yeah, last week Jase landed a good one on Alyssa. Hot."

"But now *I* will be Beatrice," I reminded her emphatically. "*Me*, not Alyssa. Me, kissing Jase."

Marisol pursed her lips. "You could do worse, D. He's really—"

"I know, I know, he's stellar. But that's still not the problem." I spit out all the gum now, my throat itchy with emotion. "You've kissed plenty of guys. Alyssa probably has, too. Jase has kissed at least a few girls. But I haven't," I whispered. "I've never kissed anyone."

She knew this. But now her bit bottom lip and flushed cheeks told me she was beginning to feel everything it would mean for *me*.

I opened the script to the final act. "If I play the Beatrice part, the first kiss of my life will be on that stage. If not in the show itself, then for sure in one of the extra rehearsals. That's not how anyone's first kiss should be. Besides, everyone will be watching." I sank into the wooden seat.

Marisol softened. "But it wouldn't really be your first kiss."

"Real or not, it's technically still a kiss. A boy's lips against mine. And to make it worse, Benedick even speaks a line about silencing Beatrice's mouth before he lays one on her. They can't replace the stage notes with 'Benedick gives Beatrice a warm hug.'"

Marisol curled her fingers around my arm. "I hear you, babe. I get it. Only you can decide what you can and can't take." She pointed toward the stage. "But they need you. The whole school does. And—" Her phone buzzed with a text. She read it quickly, then slung her purse across her body. "Of course Mama has a last-minute dress fitting and I have to take the twins to tumbling." Her face wilted. "Lo siento, amiga. I don't want to leave you here like this."

My head rattled. "S'okay, you go. I'll figure it out."

"Darcy," she warned.

"Later. Go."

When she disappeared up the aisle, I studied the script again.
Benedick: Peace! I will stop your mouth.

I lifted my eyes and searched out Jase, found him chatting
with London and Mrs. Howard. Jase was every definition
of *hot* I could come up with. Tall and lean and black-haired,
with deep green eyes and a voice like the soft velvet of his
costume waistcoat. He was genuinely nice, too. But now the
world was asking—begging—me to kiss him onstage, trapping
one more piece of my life into ink. Anytime I'd drifted into
dreams about my first kiss, I always pictured some heart-stopping version of me, alone with a boy, and a stomach swarming with butterflies.

Instead, I'd live out just another costumed act, flooded by
artificial light and make-believe.

Twenty
Forbidden

"'Who are you?'
No answer."

—J. M. BARRIE, *PETER PAN*

Before bed, I'd made my choice and told an ecstatic Marisol: I would help my school and play Beatrice, accepting all that meant.

It also meant my new-old *Peter Pan* book was banished to my tote for a few days. I had other words to read—and memorize.

The next afternoon at Tops, I sipped green tea from a butterfly print teacup before trying the Beatrice monologue again, Marisol and Tess my only audience.

"What fire is in mine ears? Can this be true? Stand I condemn'd for pride and scorn so much? Contempt, farewell! And maiden pride, adieu! No glory lives behind the back of such. And, Benedick, love on…"

I scrunched my face, willing the rest of the line into my head. Marisol nodded toward me. "C'mon, you know it. 'I will re——'"

"'I will requite thee,'" I orated, the text materializing, "'taming my wild heart to thy loving hand: If thou dost love, my kindness shall incite thee to bind our loves up in a holy band.'"

Marisol set down the script and clapped. "I won't ask how late you stayed up last night."

"Wise." I yelped when my friend whipped off my blond ringlet curl wig.

"Lines, solid. Lead actress look, not quite there." Marisol held up the bouncy springs of yellowy blond, which could double as a mop. "This one screams *Little House on the Prairie*, I can't even make a proper Regency updo with it."

I checked my watch. "Whatever it screams, we have ten more minutes before I have to get back. Mr. Winston's already been side-eyeing me for mouthing lines over his precious Sinatra tunes."

Tess zipped over to us like a flighty sparrow, her black shoulder-length wig tipped with retro-glam curls. "Marisol, that one you just vetoed is the best I could find from my used stock. I thought I had one with longer waves and a softer tone, but I must've sold it."

Marisol was already poking around the other side of the shop. She pointed at the faceless heads. "The wigs in this section are synthetic, right?"

"Yes, but those are all new." Tess frowned. "I can't lend them out."

Marisol grabbed a long, golden blond number. "We're not borrowing this time. We're buying."

I envisioned the price, which was sure to be high, even on one of Tess's cheaper synthetic models. "I don't have extra money for a wig. I can wear the Nellie Olsen special and——"

Marisol's pick was already on my head. Romantic and airy, with a center part and subtle layers framing my face. Then she tweaked the rolled-up sleeves of my chambray shirt, because she never could help herself.

"You're not buying anything. I am. Stop," she added when I opened my mouth. Marisol fluffed the waves. "You have no say in the matter. You're wearing my designs onstage, and you will not pair them with mediocre."

My sigh, cluttered with exhaustion and stress and pages of lines and kisses, nearly shook the walls. "It's expensive."

"Not really, and we could use a good wig around my house after the play. Halloween, or dress-up fun for Camila."

Tess handed Marisol two peanut butter cookies and watched her decorate her gold bangle with chewed pink gum. "Why, isn't that resourceful? And you're a good friend, honey. Everyone could use a Marisol."

I smiled gratefully and reached out to touch my friend's forearm for a moment. "Thank you, lady."

Tess swiped Marisol's debit card. "Darcy, I'm closing early on Friday. Going to Jefferson High to see my best girl onstage." She handed me the blue Tops shopping bag. "What's your strategy for getting through the week and all the material and details?"

"We're not speaking of it. We're trying not to even think of it. We are just doing it," Marisol said, and bit into a cookie.

My head throbbed, but I flashed Tess a thumbs-up. My new "strategy" was focusing on the part, the stage, and the language. If I stopped my mind on the image of my lips getting way too close to Jase's, Beatrice's lines would smudge into an inky blur.

Tess chuckled, then handed me two more cookies. "Take these. You'll need them. And I'm sure Frederick gave you the rest of the week off to prepare for the show, so I won't see you until curtain time."

"Actually, no," I told her. "He said he needs me for inventory this week, but it's all right. We're holding rehearsals after my shift until ten."

"What about your homework?"

"I'll manage."

Tess walked around the counter. "Sometimes you need to do more for yourself than just manage."

When would that sometime ever come?

"If you had the rest of the week off, would that work financially for you right now?" Tess asked.

Marisol discreetly ran one finger over her coral lips. A couple extra Elisa B. products on eBay, this week only, would make up the lost time on my paycheck.

"I could make it work," I said grudgingly. "But Mr. Winston won't change his mind."

"Hmm," Tess said, a villainous glint in her eyes. "We'll see about that."

"We will?"

She nodded once, firmly. She peered through Tops' picture window. Then she marched out the door, hung a sharp left, and strutted into Yellow Feather Books for the first time in who knew how many years. Marisol and I followed, trading stupefied looks.

The bookstore was empty, but bits of Mr. Winston's muffled phone conversation sounded from his back office. Tess spun in a lazy circle, smiling. "I must say, this is a lovely space." She ran her hand across the walnut display table. "Oh! Look how cozy the children's section is." She drifted into the nook to ogle picture books and stuffed character toys.

While Tess explored, Marisol bumped my side, whispering, "How is this happening? *Is* it even happening?"

I glanced out the window just before the door dinged. "Whatever's happening is now gonna keep happening with Asher as witness, too."

Three steps in, the newest Yellow Feather guest swung his gaze from us, to Tess, then back to us. His mouth hung open. His black jeans hitched low across his hips, barely meeting the hem of his charcoal gray tee.

I swallowed forcefully, clenching my fingers around the Tops bag as Asher wedged between us. "I swear, I saw no flying farm animals between Starbucks and here," he said.

I snorted a laugh. "Before you ask, we don't know—"

"Yes, we do," Marisol said. "Darcy's worth violating sacred laws of nature."

"Apparently she is," Asher said. I shouldn't have looked, but I did, feeling my stomach flutter at the sight of his mouth quirked sideways, his eyes flashing with good humor. "You're the Helen of Troy who's gonna inspire a war as soon as Mr. Winston gets out here," he whispered, and snagged my runaway smile.

Were his looks starting to "look" longer recently, or had I been reading too many *Much Ado* romance scenes? "I already have to play one character I didn't plan on," I said, forcing myself back to reality. "That's enough for one week."

"Yeah, Jase filled me in on Alyssa and your surprise gig."

My reply and most of my oxygen cut off when Frederick Winston strode onto the shop floor. He peered from underneath his houndstooth cap at our furtive little huddle. "What the devil is going on here?" He pointed one finger at his ex-wife. "And you! Since when do you grace my walls with your presence?"

"Since now." Tess marched up to the counter. "Here's how it's going to be. Our Darcy has always been a loyal employee, and this week she needs some time off. She'll finish her shift today, take the time she needs to get ready for her play, and then she'll be here bright and early Saturday morning."

"Saturday? But it's inventory time." Mr. Winston's words shook. He cleared his throat. "I already *told* her I can't spare her."

Tess smiled sweetly, teeth gleaming. "Of course you can't. That's why I'm going to help you."

Who was this Tess, and what alternate reality had I stumbled into? Mystified and a little unnerved, I leaned a bit closer to Asher, who was just casually sipping tea and nodding appreciatively.

Mr. Winston's brows crept downward. "Have you lost your mind?"

"Probably. But I'll still come in an hour early and sort out your inventory woes. Then if you're short-staffed, you can just—" she pounded their adjoining wall three times "—do that, and I'll hang my Be Right Back sign and come fill in."

Marisol munched peanut butter cookie pieces like popcorn kernels, chew-smiling the entire time.

"Even if I did agree to your ridiculous notion, you don't know my system," Mr. Winston challenged.

Tess guffawed and beelined around the counter. "Do, too." She chose a bookmark from the mini display rack. "Ms. Random Customer, you'd like to purchase this fine bookmark adorned with rainbows and unicorns? Let me just ring that up for you, dear," she sing-songed. Tess scanned the item, making the computer beep just like it did for me. "Oh, and all of you would like to go in on a *card* for that poor girl who broke her arm?" Tess poked her chin at us, then toward the spinning rack of greeting cards.

Marisol caught on immediately, grabbing the closest Get Well Soon card and placing it on the counter. Another beep. "That will be six dollars and thirty-seven cents, please," Tess said.

I hated the thought of Marisol spending more money today, but my friend seemed to be enjoying this way too much. With a grand flourish and a grander smile, she dug into her wallet and presented Tess with a ten-dollar bill.

"Why, thank you. However will I make change?" She fanned herself in mock distress as the cash drawer shot open.

Marisol pocketed her bills and dropped three coins into the penny tray. I swore I heard Asher say, "Nice touch," under his breath.

Mr. Winston had been surveying this entire exchange with a scowl and crossed arms. "Hmmph."

Tess faced him squarely. "Are we settled, then? Darcy's off until Saturday?"

He thrust his arms up and released another breathy huff. "Well, since everyone around here is so *capable*, I'm going out. PO Box and office supply and an espresso. Lord knows I need a triple today." He spun toward the back door.

"That's more like it," Tess murmured with satisfaction, then turned to me. "Better now, sweetheart?"

Touched, I nodded. "Thank you, Tess."

She left, blowing me a kiss before the door shut. It flew straight between my ribs.

Marisol was next. She hugged me goodbye and went home to finish the re-work on my costume.

"What is it with you and wigs?" Asher flicked the Tops bag still clutched in my hand.

"This time it's Marisol's fault." I opened the bag so he could see the new blond number. "Say hi to Beatrice."

"Ooh, a blonde Darcy this time." He smiled. "So far I've witnessed electric-blue rave queen and black-ponytail girl. Must be fun getting to play all these new characters."

My chest tightened, and I pushed out a rough laugh. I was

currently having enough trouble playing my true self, living my true life, without the extra roles I'd encountered lately.

Asher went on. "All kidding aside, I gotta give you props for filling in last minute. I'll be cheering you on from the front row."

My stomach rose into my throat. "You're going Friday?"

"Wouldn't miss it."

I escaped the beam of his stare by winding around to my metal stool. I felt my face blush a shade Elisa B. probably didn't even make. Wasn't it bad enough I was going to have to kiss Jase onstage? Now I had to do it in front of his best friend, a boy who...

Stop.

Thinking about Act Five again wouldn't get me to Friday, let alone through tonight's rehearsal.

Asher perched one elbow near the penny tray. "Tell me, memorizing all those Shakespeare lines so quickly, is that your version of speed-reading?"

I shrugged. "I don't even know how speed-reading works."

Turboprop airplanes. Soaring through text. Maybe I just like fast things, he'd said.

"Short version, I was taught to combine two techniques. Chunking, and reducing subvocalization. Chunking means learning to see groups of words as a whole unit instead of individually. Your peripheral vision kicks in and helps you absorb more text that way. Speed-readers learn to minimize eye jumps, so your eyes spend less time skipping back and forth."

"Interesting. I know subvocalization means saying the words in your head as you read."

He grinned. "'Course you do."

I ducked my head over a barely there smile.

"We still subvocalize because all readers need to for comprehension. But I guess we manage it differently." Asher drank a long sip of chamomile and nudged my script. "So how does your brain turn all this print into memorized lines in less than four days?"

"I guess I do the opposite of speed-reading," I mused. "I read words, and they become a part of me, especially when I really focus on them. So, I do more than subvocalize. I... internalize. My mind grabs on to the language and holds on to it, like something important." My voice got smaller and smaller. "Like you would something you really care about."

"This might come out weird, but I'll say it anyway." Asher blinked, eyes flecked with bits of earth and sun. "It sounds like you fall in love with the words. And that's how they stay with you."

"If falling in love means you can't stop thinking about... them, then yes."

"I've always felt that's the first clue you get when you're falling in love." He seemed to lose himself for a moment, a pilot caught between compass points. His face went slack—jaw and cheeks and barely parted mouth. Then he straightened, clearing his throat. "That's a big part of love. I mean, the thinking about someone a lot. For people who are *actually* in love, I guess."

Was he a person *actually* in love? God, I didn't dare ask. But I knew the question would join the other words I was cramming inside my head—the Beatrice lines I was pining over—losing my heart to them until my mind learned them for good.

"However you do it, I'm here for the Darcy show. It's not every day you get to see a literary savant in action. You're downright extraordinary."

Oh. A perfect, beautiful word. I wanted to wear it around my wrist, the first gift a boy had ever given me. Still, I wasn't that hopeful. Asher was a friend, but that was all he could be. "Thanks. But what you call extraordinary in here usually comes out as super nerd at school."

"Then they're wrong. And probably just jealous."

"I...you're not reading," I blurted stupidly. "I mean, in your usual break spot." I licked my lips, tasting vanilla from the lip gloss Marisol tested on me earlier. Instinctively, I reached for books. I had to. *Peter Pan* was tucked inside my bag, so I grabbed my script, curled my hands around it, and breathed.

"Yesterday, I finished the last interesting novel from your used section." He backed up and gestured toward the burgundy club chairs. "Now I have to drink my tea without reading material. And, tempting as it sounds, I can't bother *you* the whole time."

My eyes skipped, locking on to his for a quick beat. I inched around the counter to the thriller shelves. I picked up a hardback that had just hit the *New York Times* Bestseller List and handed it over.

He scanned the book jacket. One brow rose.

"You break it, or spill tea, or get construction stuff on it, or crease the cover, you're the new owner. And every day until you're done, which will probably be day three or four, you shelve it right here." I tapped the empty shelf spot. "Then you can pick another."

His smile, a firecracker. "Even *Peter Pan*?"

"Actually, that's forbidden. All others are fair game but Peter." On the last word, I realized I was joking and bantering. With a boy. Who *was I* today?

"See, now you've just made me want to read it more. But rules are rules. And thanks," he added, drifting toward the club chairs. He opened the book, plunked one sneaker on the coffee table, and "forgot" a coaster for his tea. He smirked dramatically. "Let me guess, Mr. Winston makes a stink if you sit over here."

"I only loiter in that spot to clean."

"Since he's out, he'd have no clue if you sat here between customers, right?" Asher patted the second chair. "No idea at all if you took a load off while learning your lines. Way more comfortable than your counter stool. I won't say a word."

No. A terrible idea. Positively forbidden. "Sure," I said.

Twenty-One
Paper Doll

At daybreak,
unfold me like a chain of paper dolls.
Thin and flat.
The part of me who's much too loud.
The quiet her who slips into a hidden corner.
The silly girl who giggles in the library.
The she who watches from the second story window.
We hold hands—me and her and her and me,
until nighttime when we fall together,
pressed, body to body,
thin and white and flat enough
to fit between
the yellowed pages of a
great, wide book.

—*PETER PAN* MYSTERY SCRIBBLER, IN THE BLANK SPACE
BETWEEN CHAPTERS EIGHT AND NINE

Mrs. Howard should've hooked puppet strings on to my sweater. *Move downstage, now stage right. Step up, but not too close. Hit your mark, but angle your body toward Jase, not the audience.*

On a much-needed break, I flopped offstage into the left wing and drank half a bottle of water. Sufficiently hydrated, I considered the good things: with my work schedule cleared, Mrs. Howard had moved the extra practices to right after the afternoon bell. And another "good," the cast was treating me like some kind of porcelain doll. If I broke, their curtain would not rise on Friday. Who knew I only had to attempt the impossible to make my "super nerd" parts acceptable and maybe even favorable? At least for a few days.

Jase ducked around the curtain and clinked his water bottle against mine. "Cheers. You're mind-blowing."

"Thanks. But I'm just, you know, trying to get it done." I felt myself flush, and not from the spotlights. The last "good thing" was the language itself. The Shakespearean lines were the only part of my new role that made sense, giving me something to hold. I knew my part. Words had never failed me, but now they showed themselves stronger than ever. And I needed all the strength I could get. Sooner or later, I'd have to close my eyes and surrender my first kiss to the guy in front of me.

Jase swiped his forehead. "Marisol's out front with Mrs. Howard, but she was looking for you."

"Yay, I get to be her Beatrice *Barbie*. She loves this stuff."

"Well, after we block and run Act Five for you, that's it. The whole enchilada." He winked and fanned the script like a deck of cards. "It's a good one. Alyssa and I had fun with the wedding scene. Big emotions and drama. Funny, too."

Oh, downright knock-you-over hilarious. And yeah, big drama, complete with big, long, dramatic kisses. Was today the day? Shivers pricked my arms.

"Did someone say enchiladas?" Marisol buzzed over, waving Beatrice's pink-and-blue bolero and nodding for me to remove my cardigan. "This piece has been a major bitch to redo, so I gotta see if I'm on track. Only one more day."

Oh, my sweet friend. "You know you're amazing and incredible, right? And please tell Mama thanks again when you get home."

Huge grin, framed in burgundy. "I know, and I will." She helped fit the floral jacket over my thin black tee. One eye squinted as she tucked and arranged. "Jase, grab the silver pin container from my sewing kit, yeah?"

He obeyed, finding the item and thrusting it into Marisol's outstretched hand. "I'll check when Mrs. Howard wants to start up again."

Marisol rolled the cuffs to my wrists and pinned. "If you don't hold still, you're gonna bleed."

I tried, but still felt myself trembling a bit. "I can't help it. Today we're running *that scene*."

"Maybe I should just grab Jase and tell him to lay one on you right here to get it over with."

Horror. Blood rushed to my head. "Don't you d—"

"Relax, babe. Kidding." She sighed heavily. "Mrs. Howard said you're brilliant with the lines and the role. Focus on that, okay? The good you're doing."

"Sure. Easy."

London came up with a box of granola bars, her mass of apparently enhanced red hair wound into a topknot. "Fuel? We've got a couple more hours left." She shook her head in wonder. "I don't know how you memorized all those lines so fast. Amazing. Maybe you can give me some pointers."

An unlikely scenario, but I still said, "Okay. And thanks." She held out the box again, but I shook my head. "I'm good." I couldn't even think about food.

London asked Marisol, "Could you fix a tear in the hem

of my white gown? It's on that rack in the green room. My fault. I snagged it on a set piece coming off stage last week. It barely shows, but since you're here..."

Marisol shrugged. "Sure thing."

London cracked a sideways smile and fled.

"She's actually been sort of...nice," I told Marisol. Acting with London on set wasn't nearly as awkward as I'd feared.

Pin in her mouth, she made a low grunt. After one tuck, the sharp point pierced the elegant fabric. "For her, that translates to basket of fluffy kittens."

Despite my impending kissing doom, I snorted a laugh.

The London working with Mrs. Howard and the *Much Ado* cast seemed more patient and helpful than I usually found her to be in class or at school events. She kept everyone motivated, and truly cared about the show and presenting our best to the audience. London and I would never be friends, but I had to admire that level of dedication.

Marisol stepped back. "Done and ready to sew. Mama's finishing up the blue gown right now. Then we have to try the bonnet over your new wig. Should be fine."

Fine or not, before I could answer, Mrs. Howard called everyone to the stage again. "Act Five," I mouthed.

"Do you want me to stay?"

"Nah, might be worse." I shoved out my hand. "I mean, not that I—" What did I mean? I heaved a weighted breath.

She rested the jacket on a table and braced my shoulders. "I get it. Quick, let's be you for just one second. Not Beatrice, only Darcy. Word of the Day—go."

Instantly I said, "*Bobsy-die.*"

Marisol tapped one finger on her chin, a cheery grin splitting her round face. "Bobsy-die sounds all fussy, like ruffled collars and bridal trains that are way too long. Hmm, a real diva of a word. I think it must mean a huge, stupid deal of trouble. What?" she added when my jaw dropped open.

"You…the definition. You got it right." For the first time, ever.

My limbs had steadied by the time I set my parking brake hours later, half a block from my apartment complex. But my insides still quivered, mainly and especially from Act Five.

As promised, I grabbed my bag and called Marisol as I walked the rest of the way home.

She picked up immediately. "Tell me everything."

"I don't even know where to start."

"Just go."

I wound around a group of neighborhood kids shooting hoops. "After you left, Mrs. Howard dismissed everyone who wasn't in Act Five, so it was a small group."

"And?"

I halted at the entrance to 316 Hoover. "You have got to be *kidding* me." I'd smelled it first. The scent of razed, exposed earth and pulled roots and concrete dust.

"Darcy, what? It was that bad? I knew I should have stayed."

"N-not the play," I stammered.

"What's going on?"

I narrated the scene to Marisol. The complex courtyard was half-demoed, sections of weathered pavers ripped from the ground and replaced with temporary plywood walkways. Flowers and hedges were uprooted, leaving empty dirt rectangles and scattered leaves. And then, the worst part of all.

"Marisol, our table. They took our table away."

Her gasp strangled the connection.

I hovered over the empty spot—sacred to both of us. Tears welled, scratching the back of my throat with dry salt. God, it was just a *table*. An old piece of furniture. I knew why they'd removed it, of course. Thomas probably ordered a new, sleek model to go with the refurbished railings, the snazzy gray paint. But I didn't want new and modern. I wanted those mosaic tiles. The faded chips and broken pieces. I'd gotten used to them and made them mine. A tiny black heart, a little black star, drawn in permanent ink.

My hand flew to the golden pendant around my neck. Was Marisol doing the same a few miles away?

Finally, she said, "It's okay, D. We'll find a new spot, right?"

"Yeah. We will."

"And they can have their table. Yup, they can totally take their shitty, ugly-ass tiled monstrosity and shove it where... wherever you shove the nastiest, tackiest stuff of all time," she said. But her voice had dropped with raspy emotion, though I'd never call her on it.

I laughed despite my own emotions—ill fitting and mismatched, like my friend's designs would never be.

"All right." I heard Marisol's cleansing breath. "Okay, then. Back to the play. I'm dying here."

My vision circled, lost and aimless. I didn't know where to go. Finally, I folded my impossibly long legs over a low staircase step. "When we got to the Benedick and Beatrice kissing part, it didn't happen after all."

"How come?"

"Jase was all up in my personal space while we were doing the bantering scene. That part was fun, even though I thought I was going to puke from nerves about the end. But right after Jase delivered his stop your mouth line, Mrs. Howard yelled *cut*."

"No! Did you run out of time?"

I told Marisol the rest as I remembered the Jefferson stage, how it had looked and felt an hour ago. Asher's romantic Italian garden set with yellow jeweled lights like stars. Jase's Act

Five lines—his mouth so close, I'd smelled chocolate and oats from London's granola bars on his breath. Then…

Cut. That's a wrap. Darcy, amazing. You're going to be spectacular tomorrow night.

The next scene was all real. It opened with my eyes stuck wide, Mrs. Howard's cues ringing in my ears, and my lips arranged like I thought they should be if I was about to be kissed. However that was.

"Oh," Jase muttered softly. "Sorry. Someone should've told you. We save the real kisses for the shows. Alyssa and I, um, pretended until last Friday."

"Of course." I hoped my smile looked like I couldn't care less.

Jase stepped back. "So, after I do the stop your mouth line, I'm going to throw both arms around you and tilt you back a little." A short laugh. "I promise you won't fall. And I'll, um…press a little hard, so it looks passionate. But no tongue or anything."

Oh my God.

Marisol screeched in my ear. "He said that? He actually said that? No tongue?"

"Down to the letter."

We hung up after a few or ten more freak-outs and heart attack moments. And when I finally entered my apartment, I found my mother leaning over the kitchen counter, eating a bowl of cereal.

I dropped my things at the doorway and cut my eyes to the dining nook. Disturbed plastic tubs circled around the table. Items filled the top, not a centimeter of clear space left. My stomach cramped, and my throat parched.

The makeup. She was obsessing over Elisa B. product.

I gathered clever excuses and desperate rationales with each step, but they snapped away when I realized her sorted objects *du jour* were only office supplies. She'd grouped pen boxes, staplers, paper clips, and rolls of tape, probably counting and fussing over them. One look underneath the nook window told me her Elisa B. tubs—the ones I'd carefully pinched from—were still stacked.

"Darcy, you're not ill, are you?" Mom rested her spoon in the bowl and laid her palm across my forehead.

I panted away the last thirty seconds. Could she feel the guilt, the lies underneath my heated skin? "I'm..." My heartbeat caught up to my sweet relief. *Slow down. Breathe. It's fine.*

Mom poured me a glass of water, handed it over.

I gulped, almost too fast, and had to right myself again. "I'm okay. It's...it's just the play. I'm beat."

Mom nodded on a sympathetic smile. "Rehearsal went well?"

London and the almost kiss and Asher was coming to see me. "It...went," I said, feeling myself come all the way back to my body. Another breath. "I guess I'm all set for tomorrow."

"They're lucky to have you."

But I was staring at the office supply overflow on our table, the opened tubs. Behind me, I heard, "Stressful workday. Quarterly reports are coming, and I just..."

I whirled around. A risk, but I said the next words anyway—not only for a sick mother, but for a daughter who had to steal to survive. I had to get her to curb the need to rummage through boxes. To count and catalog. "I found a place nearby." I bit the inside of my cheek, waiting for her attention. "A place you could go to talk about..." *Don't say* hoarding. *Not now.* "Um, to talk to other people who...shop a lot. I read it's really positive and nonthreatening."

"I can't," she said after a pause.

"But maybe you—"

"No one will understand me. I'm not like them."

Why had I expected any other answer? I'd found a place to help with her issues, but I didn't know how to reach through her sense of denial. Not yet. I abandoned my wish to the layer of dust she'd disturbed, and spoke no more lines from the script of our messy life. I said nothing more about my real play, either. She probably wouldn't come; Shakespeare had been a favorite of my father's, and watching might dredge up bad memories.

For the next few hours, I did my normal things. I made a ham sandwich, and scrubbed off the day in an extra-long, hot shower. I even managed to throw two focused hours at my homework.

But then I did one totally abnormal thing. I put down *Anne of Green Gables*, resting it on my comforter next to my new-old *Peter Pan* copy. Then I rose and opened the Dickens hardback, drawing out my father's letter. I scanned each word carefully. I hadn't read it since that first night.

Of course, I had to be the one to decide. Should I tear him to shreds and forget his existence forever? Or should I try to be someone I'd never really been before—a girl who had a father? One call or letter, and I'd transform him from legend into flesh and blood, a towering cage of bones. But when I did, who would I end up turning myself into?

For years, I'd been a happy granddaughter to Grandpa Wells. But nothing I'd ever read, nothing in the books lining my walls, had ever shown me how to be David Elliot's daughter.

My eyes caught the glossy blond of my new Beatrice wig—plumped and brushed for my new role tomorrow—along with an idea.

A role. A character. Not real, just pretend.

For now, I could play a second character: Darcy Jane Elliot. I left the wig on my dresser but imagined myself in another story. Me, as another me, and my bedroom as another kind of setting. I crafted my scripted response:

"Dear David Elliot," the actress-me said out loud. The lines rang clear and smooth. "I'm your daughter, Darcy. I just turned eighteen. You've never met me, and I've never met you. But did you know your letter *L* looks just like mine in print? I know you love books. It's why my mother hates them so much. I just wonder if you love them half as much as I do."

I stopped when I felt the character begin to fade into the real me. I wasn't ready for that, not yet. Maybe I would be soon—or maybe never.

I folded the letter again. I slipped it into its Dickens home and pushed the volume back onto my shelf. Then I tucked myself between my own clean ivory sheets.

Twenty-Two
Act Five

"'It's like this.' ~~She~~ He kissed ~~him~~ her."

—J. M. BARRIE, *PETER PAN,*
AND *PETER PAN* MYSTERY SCRIBBLER

Robin's egg blue fabric swished over my ankles, the fanciest dress I'd ever worn. Marisol tugged the thick brocade around me until it draped like a dream. Underneath the elegant folds, nerves and adrenaline teemed through my blood.

"You did eat, right? Actual food?" Marisol asked as we entered the cast makeup area.

"Yes, Mom. An entire cinnamon bagel and cream cheese." Which was currently rolling like a disaster in the pit of my stomach.

"Yay for carbs." She helped me into the reconstructed floral bolero for Act One and fastened the ivory buttons. Then she tucked my hair under a nylon cap and slipped the Beatrice wig, arranged into an elegant twist, onto my head. "You're a precious angel flower, babe." Stepping back, she grinned. "The prettiest girl I know."

My lips turned up in a shaky smile. Those words in that particular combination rarely seemed to follow me. But my friend never lied.

"Now it's time for…" Marisol peered over my shoulder.

I turned, not to something, but someone. "Mom?"

Andrea Wells stepped in from the green room doorway, wearing a navy blue dress and tall, chocolate-brown boots. "I'd like to help with your makeup." She held up a portable kit. "I'm sure Marisol has everything figured out, but I do know stage application."

Marisol glanced at me, and I nodded. She directed my mother to a spot on the vanity table. "Awesome. You can set up right there, and my work here is done."

While Mom unpacked her kit, I pulled Marisol aside. "I couldn't have gotten through this week without you."

She winked. "I know. Wait, is your grandma coming?" she asked, and mouthed the word *awkward*.

"Thankfully me, onstage, is all the awkward I'm facing tonight. She's in Cancun with her book club friends. I told her I'd get a video of the play for her to watch."

Marisol nodded, then exhaled a barely there sigh, eyes boring into mine.

"Don't," I whispered, holding out my palm. "Not right now."

Leave the kissing scene on the page. Saying it makes it real.

"Okay. Well, the fam's saving me a seat." Marisol wound her arms around me. "Oh, Darcy, I won't tell you to break a leg. That's not good enough. Break an entire body."

But hopefully not my heart.

★ ★ ★

My only job was to sit absolutely still at the vanity table. Mom finished a dramatic cheek contour, then filled in my brows with a golden tan pencil. "This is fun," she said, more brightly than I'd heard her speak in months. "Remember when you were little and you liked painting my nails all different colors?"

I had to keep my face frozen, but made a tiny sound of acknowledgment. When she pulled the brush away, I said, "And you always kept the messy rainbow polish on even when you left for work."

Mom smiled into the mirror. "I redid my manicures at the Elisa B. counter before opening time so you wouldn't see."

My chest throbbed, heart warming. It was so different here, outside of our apartment. It felt normal, just a mom and daughter playing with makeup. I ached for the day when we could be this way inside our own house. Would Mom ever find enough freedom to make our space clean and free, too? I hoped so. But after so many years, I knew what to do with hope. I held it an arm's length away.

Running line after line in my head helped, too. The language steadied me.

With my eyes done, lipstick was the final touch. Mom swiped on a nude-pink color. "Do you like this one? I think it accentuates your skin tone without interfering with the period look."

"Perfect," I said.

"I rarely miss when choosing lip shades for customers." She placed the tube on the counter. "Keep it for touch-ups."

I didn't mention I'd sold two of those on eBay in the past month. I felt hollow from it. *I'm sorry, Mom.* More lines and monologues filled the gaps. More Shakespeare.

At last, Mom framed my face. "You're a star, sweetheart." A weighted sigh. "I guess I should find a seat."

Did she know she would be watching my first kiss, tonight? I never talked to her about such things. Only to books, and sometimes Marisol.

"Thank you," I said, making the space between us so much simpler than it really was.

She finished packing her kit and blew me a final kiss.

Alone, I visited the full-length mirror. I topped the wig with my bonnet and tied the blue satin ribbons. Then a final tuck, a shift of pressed fabric and lace trim.

Jase breezed by in his Benedick finery, whistling. "The whole week, you sounded like Beatrice. Now you look like her."

True to what usually happened on epic, monumental life days, I forgot a few details, even misplaced entire chunks of time. But other moments rang so vividly, I knew, years later, I'd still be able to press Play on the memory of them like movie clips.

That Friday night, I threw myself into Beatrice. The actress-me floated on her lines, going where she was supposed to go, reacting, teasing, laughing—whatever Alyssa would've done. Acts One through Four fused together in one clouded rush, the way time sometimes moves in dreams. The way we move in them. One dreamy blink, and you could be in another place. Even watching yourself from the eyes of another person. Some classmates on the Jefferson stage rippled into shadow, while others blazed, the heat of them real upon my skin.

Jase blazed like a comet. Lovesick characters Hero and Claudio were finally reunited and preparing to wed. But on their way to the chapel, they confronted Benedick and Beatrice for pretending to be only friends and denying their love. Jase was showcasing his best Benedick for the visiting UCLA director. Acting opposite him, I played off his skill and polish.

Because this play was all about trickery, London and I were veiled when we entered the set for Scene Four. For long moments, I watched my fellow cast mates, hidden behind the gauzy tulle Marisol had made for our bonnets. But then, it happened. As Jase revealed my face to the audience, I felt the veil begin to slip from my heart, too. Panic beaded, warm and steamy across my forehead, and I had to stop it. I had to halt this *now*, because I was running out of lines—and time.

Beatrice. The audience could only be allowed to see Beatrice. Darcy Jane Wells needed to stay hidden. So, as I spoke my penultimate lines, I reached for the only tool I had—the only tool I'd ever had since that day my mother packed up all her books: words. I veiled myself with language and bricked a story wall around the real me before facing Jase, head-on. Isn't that what I'd been doing for years, anyway?

Oh, just a half second to breathe, before...

"'Peace! I will stop your mouth.'" And he did. The arms of an excellent actor braced my back and pulled me toward him like a wanted thing.

It's not real. Make-believe.

Jase set my body at a pronounced angle I knew would look sexy and fierce from the audience.

And now he's going to...

His mouth pressed over mine.

So *this*...this was a kiss.

The pressure and warmth were the same as real, if I had to make a guess. But if I'd expected to feel anything beyond biology and moving lips, I was wrong. An actor kissing an actress—that was the beginning and ending of us. Still, I closed my eyes, and the kiss stretched one more beat as the crowd laughed and whistled. Then Jase pulled away, grinning. The director's notes said Beatrice had to grin, too, but hidden-Darcy's lips remained still and closed as the scene played out to the bows.

Burgundy velvet curtains closed behind us. Clapping roared in my ears and a stagehand filled my arms with flowers.

My life as a girl who'd never been kissed had just been erased by Shakespeare's pen—technically, anyway.

I tucked myself into a dark, quiet corner of the wings, the scent of wood and sweat and metal masked by the roses in my arms. I pressed two fingers against my lips and shut my eyes. Still costumed and technically still onstage, I let myself replay the kiss. Just once, and then I'd have to let it go. Just once, before I hid the invisible want of a book-shaped heart inside another book.

This time, my Benedick was not a boy who could act, but a boy who could fly.

Later that night, music shook the Donnelly house, an over-boosted bassline weighting down the classic Spanish home with deafening gravity. Jase's pad was a good choice for the *Much Ado* cast party—with an emphasis on *party*, since only a handful of the guests were actually in the cast.

After final bows and changing into my favorite jeans and black sweater, I'd spent a short time outside the auditorium. I'd accepted warm hugs from Mrs. Howard, Tess, and Marisol's family. My mother, too—she'd beamed with pride and surprised me with a bouquet of daisies. But after all the sweet accolades, I left the stage, and everything that had happened on it, behind.

Not five minutes after we'd arrived at Jase's, Marisol smacked a red plastic cup into my hands. I sniffed.

"Relax. It's soda. *Only* soda," she said.

"Thanks."

She pulled me aside, her voice close to my ear. "Are you ready to throw a few words at it yet?"

I knew exactly the *it* she was referring to. I tucked my bottom lip under my teeth, still tasting remnants of the pinky-nude shade. "Not even a few. But soon, yeah?"

Marisol nodded once, cracking minty gum.

"One thing, though. From the audience, did it... I mean, did I...?"

"You mean did the *action that shall not be named* look real enough?"

"Basically."

"You had me convinced." She bumped my shoulder. "I'm going after whatever eats I can scrounge up. If I know you, you're not quite ready to throw any food at your mouth yet, either."

"You do know me." I wiggled my hand. "Go forage. I'll just find a seat and, um, sit."

"Right. Sit." Her mouth twitched, eyes twinkling. "You did notice this was the first time I didn't confiscate your books at the porch, right?"

I shook my head at her exiting form.

Alone with *Peter Pan* already in my grip, I entered the foyer leading to the Donnellys' formal living room. The music was a bit less headache-inducing in this space.

Bryn appeared as I passed under a curved Spanish archway. "Darcy, wait up."

I'd barely said anything to her after her drunken bonfire game night, and I'd gladly continue my freeze-out streak as long as possible, but I couldn't exactly ignore her outright.

"Look, I was there tonight," she said. "You nailed the part. Pretty much the equivalent of me having to dance *Swan Lake* with four days to learn the moves. So, right on."

"Thanks," I said sincerely, but warily.

"Oh, have you seen Asher?" Bryn pulled a white phone charger from her purse. "He left this in my car." She rolled her eyes. "If he was desperate enough to hijack my USB port from his house to Jefferson, he'll freak trying to survive the whole night without this."

Wait. My posture snapped straight. *Asher's house to...* "You took Asher to the play? Why didn't he drive himself?"

Bryn nodded. "Poor guy had a migraine most of the day. But an hour before curtain, he asked if I could give him a ride. Jase and London had already left for makeup. He was drowsy from the meds and couldn't drive." She shrugged. "He said it was important and didn't want to miss."

My next breath hitched. "Oh." He still came after a migraine?

She handed me the phone cord. "Can you find him? I know he's here somewhere, but I need to bolt. Rehearsal at seven tomorrow morning, and I have a date with a foam roller."

Instead of cocooning myself in the living room, I changed course for the one remaining place I could find Asher, owner of the charger in my hands. And a boy who was arguably too sick to be at a party he'd attended anyway.

Jase's backyard looked straight out of a resort, even shadowed with nightfall. A tropical-themed pool with rock slide and grotto was lit into deep turquoise. Some classmates huddled around a blazing firepit table. Other groups leaned against walls with salty snacks and drinks likely spiked from more than a few hidden flasks.

The space bent around the white plaster home. I bent myself, too, into a large side yard complete with more seating areas and a jungle gym play area. And there was Asher, sitting on a swing, alone.

"Hey there." He smiled as I approached, grabbing the thick chain of the second swing. "Take a seat."

The smart, typically prudent Darcy Jane Wells would've tossed Asher the phone cord, thanked him for coming to the show, then spun on sand-filled flats back to the living room. Back to books.

Turns out I wasn't that smart, after all. I breathed out an assenting noise and perched on the black rubber swing. "Bryn," I said, offering the cord to him.

"Thanks. Decent of her. My phone's on fumes." He wound the cord and stowed it in the pocket of his olive bomber jacket.

I pushed back into slight motion. "Come here often?"

"Just wanted a little nostalgia. Avery and I had a swing set when we were little. I used to close my eyes and get up as high as I could."

I smiled at his memory, pictured him in my mind.

He glanced at the house for a beat. "I should've known Jase would pump the bass. Not exactly postmigraine friendly. And today would've been day six of no migraines or dizzy spells. So close."

Seven healthy days to fly again. "I'm sorry, Asher. The pain sounds horrid."

"I've had so many, I feel them coming on like thunderstorms. I try to get right on the meds and head back to bed. Then I can usually get some of my day back. If it's mellow." Asher waved his arm around. "The quiet and fresh air help."

"But you came to the show anyway? Stuck inside with bright lights and cheering?"

He smiled, but it was only a flicker of movement. "You know you were amazing up there, right?"

Lifting, floating, I could easily drift into a place I could visit, but never call home. My personal Neverland. I slowed and anchored the ball of my foot onto the ground, clenching the chains. "Thanks. I was just trying to get through each act. You know, survive."

He searched my eyes. "That was more than survival. I've been watching Jase's shows for years, and I've seen my share of plays. Have you thought of acting for real? You could learn the scripts like nothing."

I blessed the night for its dependable darkness, knowing my cheeks were flaming pink. "Nah, I mean, I enjoyed some parts of the stage tonight, but that's not me."

"Okay, fair. Who are you then?"

I went for safe. "I want to do what I do best—work with words. State's probably a shoo-in for me, and they have a good English program. I've read so many books, and I think I'd like to work with the people who write them."

"Like an editor?" When I nodded, he chuckled. "I see where this is going. You'll get too good, and you'll be editing *me* without even thinking."

I shivered. Could I edit him and me and... Us? Could I strike a pen through a messy manuscript? Deleting London, searching for lifelong crutch words: *hoard, illness, invisible, fatherless.* Replacing them with opposites and antonyms: *clarity, freedom, lovable, daughter.* Opened before me, it seemed like an insurmountable task.

"Darcy?"

"Sorry. I'm here."

"Good. But still—who are you, really?"

I'm a liar. A secret keeper. A thief. "Who am I, really?" I repeated, so softly, even the distant bass pulsed right over it.

"Well, you're not all those books you read. You're not even your mad skills. What's under all the words?"

Each syllable scratched across my heart, marks from end to end. "I'm..."

He tipped his chin encouragingly.

I couldn't say. I just couldn't. But I didn't run. I stayed on that swing.

Asher pursed his mouth tight. "You know, I don't tell many people everything about the accident. What I've lost. Plenty of friends know the big picture, but not the real cost. How it feels."

"Why did you tell me?"

"Because you..." He paused, shrugging. "I dunno, when you told me about your tenth birthday, I sensed that you're a person who understands disappointment. Loss, too. More than most people our age. Then I proved myself right when you told me the secret about your dad."

I wanted to look away, but his quick stare caught my movement.

"There's more going on than just your dad, though. The deal with your mom is more than cupcakes, right?"

My mouth opened, but not to breathe in anxious gulps— no, not even to ask why he was prying. I didn't ask Asher why he was digging so deep when he had another girl to drive him home. When he had his own life that might never align with mine, no matter what universe we'd flown into on black rubber seats, with questions and truth and trust swinging back and forth.

And trust. Just tell him, Marisol had said.

"The problem is way more than cupcakes," I told a boy who couldn't, *shouldn't* matter. But one whom I knew could listen.

"I figured, Darcy," he said gently.

There was only one word large enough to describe the weight behind my walls. For so long, I'd barely been able to say it out loud, but tonight, this cluttered word felt closer and clearer than ever. If I was really going to trust him, I had to grab it. I had to voice it.

I took a deep breath and said, "My mother is a hoarder."

Twenty-Three
Constant

"Friendship is constant in all other things,
Save in the office and affairs of love."

——WILLIAM SHAKESPEARE, *MUCH ADO ABOUT NOTHING*

Some things remained the same. The large takeaway cup, square chamomile tea tag dancing off one side. Sneakers planted on the rug while he read, because Mr. Winston was there. His work clothes, washed into shabby softness. The place, too, my first afternoon shift at Yellow Feather Books the following week.

But *I* was different. Today I wasn't just Darcy, friend and bookstore clerk. I was the Darcy who'd revealed the truth behind her apartment door. *We* were different—the girl who'd told her most guarded secret, and the boy who'd held every word like glass, because he'd known it was.

Did I look different to him today? A "hoardier" version of

myself? Even though I'd proven I could reach into my soul to speak to Asher Fleet, there were some questions I was still afraid to ask.

He waited until I rang up two picture books for a young mother pushing a baby stroller. Then he made a big show of shelving a new thriller exactly the way he'd found it.

I snorted. "How's the story?"

Cockeyed, he said, "Thrilling."

I shook my head on a dramatic eye roll. *So far, okay.*

Asher grinned, then sipped hesitantly from his cup. "Olivia's mom just shared a little tidbit with me. I have to tell you, even though it's..."

He locked on to my eyes, and I pantomimed zipping my lips shut.

"Jeff Andrews's incident at the center sealed his fate with Olivia's custody battle."

"Oh?" I restacked bills and shut the register drawer. "I guess making a drunken scene in a waiting room, assaulting a lawyer, and hunting you down an alley didn't paint him as father of the year?"

"Guess not. And this wasn't the only episode Olivia's mom had documented. But the judge took special notice, and she has sole custody now, plus a restraining order."

I sighed in relief. "I feel so much better for them now."

"Me, too." Asher glanced sideways toward the fiction section. "Without the center incident, she would've had a longer and harder fight. Sounds weird, but I'm glad it happened."

For a beat, I lost myself inside the memory of red leather and a black ponytail. "I...then I'm glad it happened, too."

"I'm also glad it happened without me becoming one with alley road dust, and that's because of your quick thinking."

"That's me," I said, and cleared my throat. "Darcy Wells,

actress extraordinaire. At your service for alley shenanigans and last-minute Shakespearean roles. I should hang a sign."

"Do you also do corporate events and birthday parties?"

"Sure, but never bar mitzvahs or weddings."

He clucked his tongue. "You gotta draw the line somewhere."

"Some are definitely better left uncrossed."

"Some," he said quietly, his eyes never loosening their hold on mine.

The sound of the doorbell halted the rush between my ears, slowed the blood juddering into my arteries. Marisol was here, along with a grin and the stylish ripped jeans and navy sweater she'd worn at school.

She brandished two Starbucks cups, then tipped one to Asher in greeting. "I realized we needed coffee."

I accepted my favorite ice-cold treat with a grateful sigh. "Bless."

"What's up around here?" Marisol's eyebrows dived into a wide V. "When I walked in, you guys looked like you were discussing politics or religion or some steamy gossip I should know about."

"Nothing quite that scandalous. Just Darcy's boss acting ability," Asher said.

My friend squealed in true Marisol fashion. "Didn't she kill it up there?"

"Absolutely." Asher nodded at me. "The one actual death in the play."

Even I had to laugh. "Thanks. I think."

Marisol softened. "I'm a proud bestie. She's the only person I know who could've pulled off that feat. Most people aren't dealing with half the stuff she is on top of learning all those lines."

In a quick flash, I watched Asher beeline his stare onto Marisol. "You're right. And I do, um…know," he told her.

I was standing behind Asher; he couldn't see me nod at Marisol.

Just tell him, Marisol had said.

But she saw it all. Her lips parted in awe, then snapped shut like a clamshell.

I shrugged. "Come on, it wasn't that monumental. Not like I know anything different."

Asher swung around, smiling at me hesitantly. "Right. But all you've got going on at home is already more than enough. Then add in your father's letter."

Asher's words landed like a punch to my gut as Marisol stepped forward. "Your father? What's he talking about?"

Oh God.

Helpless, I looked at Marisol, caught the hurt souring her features. I'd seen the way it clouded her face a dozen times before. But it was usually after a stupid boy or family drama, never from me.

Asher paled. "I'm so sorry. I thought she knew."

"What letter?" Marisol demanded. "When?"

"Before our birthdays. My father contacted Grandma with a letter for me."

"You…" Marisol paused, studying her ankle boots.

"I was gonna—"

"All that time. All your *words*, and not one to me about this." She looked from my face to Asher, back to me again. In a swoosh, she picked up her coffee and hitched her bag onto her shoulder.

"Marisol—"

"Later. I need to go."

"Marisol, wait."

She didn't. I watched her stride away, then covered my mouth with both hands, flinching when the doorbell clanged.

Asher touched me for the first time since the alley. The wide span of his hands braced my arms. "I'm so, so sorry. When you said not to tell anyone, I had *no* idea that included Marisol. You said it was need-to-know, but I never thought for a second she hadn't made the cut. I mean, you guys are... she's..."

I let out a shaky breath. "We are, and she is. You had every right to assume I would've told her."

"You didn't, though." Oh, I heard the rest, even though it stayed hidden behind his lips. *But you told me.*

"It's complicated. She's the closest person in the world to me, but it's my father, and I still..."

His eyes were filled with a rumbling warmth. "Hey, stop." His grip tightened over my shoulder bones. "You don't have to explain. Not now."

My fingers toyed with the gold heart around my neck.

"I feel horrible," he said. "You trusted me, and I screwed it up."

"No, Asher," I insisted. "*I* screwed it up."

He scrubbed one hand over his face, then shot a quick glance at his watch and swore. "I need to get back to the center." Then right into my eyes, again. "I'm really sorry, Darcy. And I won't insult you by saying it's okay."

"No, it's not okay."

After he left, I called Marisol three times. No answer. Finally, I sent a simple text message.

Me: Word of the Day: Sorry

My world already felt bruised when I returned home after my shift. But I pushed through my front door to a sight that rubbed a bruise into a burn. "Mom?" I asked, spying her pacing the goat tunnel, hands gripping a small tub. All wrong. Totally wrong. She was supposed to be at work.

Makeup streaked down her face, hair in tangles. She wasn't opening and sorting through boxes tonight. She was rearranging them. "Difficult morning. Easier to tell work I was sick."

No—she'd missed her shift. This could *not* become a new habit. My eyes welled, heart twisting. Everything just *hurt*. Coming from Marisol and Yellow Feather, I barely had the energy to speak, let alone deal with her or the hoard right now.

I fled to my bedroom and the comfort of my books. I didn't register the item sitting on the floor at first—only the faint image of something tan in color and large in shape whisked across my peripheral vision. I dropped my belongings on my bed and turned.

And there it was.

Maybe I already knew.

My skin iced over. I set my jaw, spearing my vision, and went to face the cardboard shipping box.

To: Andrea Wells. From: Pottery Barn.

To Andrea Wells from Pottery Barn and dropped, placed— *hoarded*—inside the one-and-only safe haven I had ever known. Even my book fortress hadn't stopped her this time. Nothing could stop her.

Tonight, it was me who sank to the ground. At once, I was thousands of pages of rage and fight. Every one I'd ever read. *How dare she?*

Pottery Barn? She'd bought yet another item from a home decor store. But this disgusting place wasn't a home; it was a warehouse, an overgrown shrine to past hurts.

The psychologist made her promise. "Darcy needs her own space."

Oxygen fled my lungs. I was chapters teeming with legions of warriors, the blood of Crusades staining hot and red over

my bookshelves. I wanted to open all the windows. I wanted
to take these boxes, these…*things*, and cast them out into the
street. Could our big city even absorb it all?

*"You have to establish clear boundaries and respect this one area,
Andrea."*

My fingers dug into worn carpet fibers, and I must have
cried out some unknown noise, because my mother came to
my doorway. Her face was blank, and I wondered how much
of her was truly there.

I pointed to the box. "Why?"

She nodded. And nodded again, like all the nods were
tracking and cataloging syllables this time. "I was reposition-
ing things. I'm running out of space." She moved to grab the
box. "I'll just—"

"Stop," I said.

She flinched.

"I give up." I shook and shrugged. "I give up, Mom. You
know what?" I held out my arms and knew that I had lost—
and not because she'd violated my space with one box. It was
because she'd ever thought she could.

I surrender.

"You win." I swept my hand around. "Take it. Take the
space you need, floor to ceiling. Have it all." *Have the rest of
me. You already do.*

I quit counting seconds. I didn't know how long it was before my mother finally moved, but not to my side. She walked,
almost trancelike, wrapped her wool-covered arms around
the box, and lifted it. "I shouldn't have. I'll just find another
place," she said, and left.

I cupped my face, hanging my head low as tears leaked
through my fingers. Marisol would know exactly what to say.
Exactly what to do. She would come and bring me a smoothie
and offer me colorful gum and hugs. She would tell stupid

jokes or razz on my clothes or make up ridiculous word definitions. She would *listen*. I wanted—*needed*—my best friend, but I'd hurt her. Marisol needed time away from me to think after what I'd done.

I stood and brushed sweaty palms on the jeans she'd picked out for me. I surveyed my whole room, wall to wall, shelf to shelf. All I had tonight was a bedroom full of books. One of them held my father.

They had never looked so powerless.

Natalia letting me in the front door the next evening was a good sign. Natalia telling me where Marisol had fled with her sketchbook thirty minutes ago was a better one. After a quick stop at home, I was off.

All day at school, I'd left my friend alone. Morning passed with no texts or locker visits. I ate lunch by myself under a tree by the quad, rehashing my mother's shipping box and my gnawing guilt over Marisol and Asher in the bookstore. Asher—the thought of him clung to all the others, even though he'd missed his afternoon break at Yellow Feather. I didn't see him my entire shift.

Now, when Marisol looked up from her table at our usual Starbucks, I led with what I thought was the most effective word right then. *Silence*. I edged close enough to place the folded sheet of light blue stationery before her, taking a mental snapshot of my friend: messy topknot and Jefferson High sweatshirt. Lipstick-streaked coffee cup and the bird crumb remains of a chocolate muffin. Spiral-bound sketch of a faceless figure with angled arms and the penciled beginnings of a tank bodice.

I let a paper father talk to her first.

While she read my letter, I ordered hot ginger tea, remembering something I'd seen online about the wonders of this root for upset stomachs. Mine had turned all of yesterday and today into the digestive version of a full bout of teary despair. Swirling and churning.

"Darcy."

I dropped my honey packet and whirled around from the condiment station. Steamy remedy in hand, I approached her more slowly than I ever had in eight years. She clutched the letter, her eyes red and puffy with tears. "This is unreal."

"More than you know."

Marisol glanced left, then right. A group of college students had pooled at least four tables and were doing more laughing than studying. She quickly packed her belongings and nodded toward the door. "Come on."

The scene outside was no quieter, but my secrets melded into the bustling anonymity of University Avenue. Here, a hundred people could pass by, and maybe even look at two teens strolling with drinks and totes, but not see us at all.

"What are you going to do?" Marisol asked after a few strides.

"I haven't gotten that far," I admitted. "I'm still waiting for the day I wake up and see the spot where I've been hiding the letter and don't think I'm in some fantasy world."

"Why?" Marisol breathed out a sigh. "Why not tell *me*?"

"I had to let it sink in."

"No, that's not why."

I sipped the spicy-sweet tea and barely avoided a loose chunk of concrete. "It's too overwhelming."

"For sure, but that's not why, either."

Damn. The only word I could think of. "Marisol, I—"

She halted in front of a mattress shop. "Haven't I been there for you, in every major life moment, for years?"

"Every one."

"Since fourth grade, right? Since cupcakes?"

"Every day."

"Haven't I seen it all with you? Stuff no one should have to see or go through?" Her face and neck bloomed with blotchy red. "Haven't I cleaned up dust and broken plates in your apartment, and stopped you from buying ugly shoes, and helped you pull off the makeup resale scheme of your life, and snapped eBay photos, and *eleven-billion* other things?"

"More," I breathed. "Yes, Marisol, you've—"

"Then *why*?"

I spat it out like rotten food. "Because I couldn't say it out loud. I couldn't put it into words or give it any language. Saying it makes it real." I plucked the letter from my bag, waving it around. "Keeping him in ink and paper makes him just another story."

Marisol's posture wilted a bit. She trained her eyes onto the stream of traffic.

I dashed the first tear from my cheek and sucked back the rest. "All I know are books. I read them over and over and dream and lose myself in them. But even I know they're not... real."

"So you're trapping him inside a story because it's safer? And you can shelve him away like the rest of your books, and not deal with him or acknowledge him?"

Of course she understood. "Yeah."

"But, Darcy, you *did* give your father words. Out loud. You told Asher."

"He's not real, either," I whispered.

Make-believe. Just pretend.

"He asked, and the words just slipped out," I said. "They felt safe. But Asher's only part of a legend in my world. He's not really inside my story. My life."

Impossible boy, invisible girl.

"But *you* are," I told her. "The minute I tell you anything, it becomes part of my truth. I don't know if I want my father there, too. Not yet." I scrubbed my face. "Look, I know it's dumb. I can't hide from the letter or him forever. I have to make a choice."

"But you don't have to rush it. Just don't shelve him away anymore. Then you can decide how you really feel. What you really want to do. And talk to me, okay?"

Marisol was right. She usually was. "I can do that. Promise." I shivered audibly as a fall gust trailed us through an intersection.

"Yeah, you can, but apparently you can't remember the rule of November plus nighttime equals lightweight outerwear. It's a good rule."

I felt myself smile for the first time in hours. "Your favorite kind of equation. And I left my hoodie at the bookstore." We'd just reached the block where Yellow Feather lived. I gestured across the street at the historic building; lights were still on at Tops. "We're going in. Mr. Winston's gone, but Tess keeps an emergency key."

Less than five minutes later, we flicked on half the shop lights. Although I'd worked alone here many times, it was oddly thrilling to sneak in, promising Tess we'd leave no trace.

Marisol swooned into one of the club chairs, arms and legs akimbo. "Never ever do I get to sit here." She stretched and wiggled and then added, "Chunky gooey leather and supreme vintage style." She exhaled *ahhh* and pulled an Asher by going coaster-less on the trunk table with her decaf cappuccino.

I sat, too, even decadently folding my long limbs up onto the seat. "About that talking to you promise…"

And then I did. I told her about my mom's Pottery Barn box and what it meant, how that first sight of cardboard packaging had felt. Afterward, Marisol leaned across her chair and gave me a big sandwich hug. Like she had with one half of my drunk mother in my kitchen, she helped carry the weight of this, too.

I remembered, then, why we were actually trespassing and sprang to my cubby behind the counter. I grabbed my hoodie and slipped on the black-and-white-striped cotton. But my eyes slipped across something else.

Need a penny, take a penny.

Have a penny, leave a penny.

The little penny tray I saw every single shift held more than copper tonight. Metallic silver glinted from the top of the tarnished coins. I reached for an object that was definitely not there earlier when I'd traded books for bills and credit cards, over and over.

My breath caught as I cupped the tiny silver acorn in the center of my palm.

Twenty-Four

Acorn

*"'Now,' said he, 'shall I give you a kiss?' And she replied
with a slight primness, 'If you please.' She made herself
rather cheap by inclining her face toward him, but he merely
dropped an acorn button into her hand..."*

—J. M. BARRIE, *PETER PAN*

A charm. The stem of the acorn was a small, silver loop meant
for a chain necklace or bracelet. My mind went everywhere,
leaping into stories. Just one story, really. But it couldn't be.

Marisol was already at my side. "Why all the shaking?
Something fishy in your tea?"

"More like in the penny tray." I held out the silver bauble
hammered with intricately carved ridges and details.

Marisol smiled. "That's super cute. But what was it doing
in there?"

"I'm almost positive someone left it on purpose. But the

only two people who work here are Mr. Winston and…me."
My legs quit, and I sank lower and lower until I was cross-
legged on my boss's prized area rug.

Me. The acorn charm had to be for me. But that meant the
kind of fairy tale that crashed into every reality I could name.
Before I sorted that out, it was time to make something else
all the way real.

Marisol huffed. "And I guess we're sitting now. Nope, no
germs and grimy street goop to worry about. Everything's normal." She followed me down and snagged my gaze. "You're
giving me the jeebs, babe. Catch me up."

"I know," I said through a tangled breath. "But first, I need
to show you a book." I stretched long and reached for my tote.

"What's new about books? Aren't you always showing me
some novel? Aren't I always confiscating some novel?"

I fished out the new-old *Peter Pan* and placed it into her
hands.

"I've seen you toting around *Peter Pan* a hundred times. Especially lately," Marisol said.

"You've only seen the outside. Open it."

She did and went slack-jawed, just as I had when I'd first
lifted the worn, dark green cover at the counter, so many
weeks ago. "Whoa." She turned the book every which way,
pausing to read quotes and lists. Poems and crossed-out text.

There, on the thick Persian carpet, I told her the whole
story—beginning until now—of how closely I'd cherished
the book and how the advice had guided me through awkward moments. The mysterious scribbler experienced so many
emotions. She knew about the heart, too—how much it could
love, fiercely and completely. And with one word, how it could
shrivel into the smallest version of itself.

Marisol read the "Paper Doll" poem. She smiled. "Oh, the
feels. I can't believe this book just *found* you." She closed the

cover and handed it back. "But what does it have to do with the acorn charm?"

My own heart leaped. *Shhh, easy now.* "Besides you, only one other person knows I've been reading *Peter Pan*. Asher. We've discussed the story a few times, but never the acorn from Chapter Three."

"Asher? Wait, the acorn is from *Peter Pan*?"

"Peter gives an acorn button to Wendy." I lifted my face to meet hers. "After he asks if he can give her...a kiss."

It took Marisol a moment before realization bubbled around her in manic silence. She was all motion. Her skin flashed bright coral, hands gesturing wildly, waving and shaking my shoulders like I was a rag doll. She bounced up and down on the floor, silent movie screams splitting her face. She mouthed every expletive I knew.

Finally, she dragged out her voice. "Asher Fleet is dropping major signals? Asher! See, I knew something was up." She rattled her head. "But wait, I mean, do you even like—"

"Stop," I said, holding up both hands. "Don't, Marisol. Not yet. I mean, what about London? As far as I know, she's still in the picture, and it's weird, and I have to find out more first."

She nodded, and I placed one palm over my heart, holding back the wild beating.

Real beating shook the front of the store. We turned to see Tess yelling into the window glass. "Ladies!" She bent closer, spying us on the floor and shaking her head. "I don't even want to know, but *Wheel of Fortune* is on in twenty minutes!"

We laughed and I waved her key high. "Coming!"

I unfolded my legs, but Marisol stopped me. "The penny tray, though." She pouted. "Adorable."

My heart thumped to the rhythm of my footsteps jaywalking across University Avenue the next afternoon. I waved to

Hannah, then marched down the corridor at Mid-City Legal, clutching the acorn charm so hard the edges dug into my skin. A newly hung door led into the addition, propped half-open. I inched through. One brown-haired handyman in blue and denim worked alone, touching up baseboards.

"Asher?"

He turned and stood, his intake of breath so deep the wrinkled folds of his shirt swelled. "Hey." One thumb to the propped rear door. "Can we?"

"Yeah." I followed. The alley again, familiar sharp smells and litter scraps tumbling around us. This time, there were no wigs and red leather to hide behind. I came as Darcy Jane Wells, bare and exposed—a hundred times more frightening than fairy-tale forests and sinister queens with magic mirrors.

Asher stopped two feet from me, or maybe three. "Hi, again."

"Hi." I opened my fist and let the silver acorn catch the light.

Now his smile was brighter—too bright—like flinging up the shades to glaring sunrays, when I was so used to the dark. "Glad you found it before Mr. Winston, er, *Winstoned* it."

"What does this mean?"

"What do you think it means, Darcy?"

"It means you read *Peter Pan*."

"For a start." When I couldn't speak, burying my vision into alley cracks, he said, "I read it last week. Bought a copy on one of your days off."

I grabbed on to the book buoy inside my head. Any book, all the books. Paper and ink keeping me afloat again. "Probably took you twenty minutes," I said through a teetering laugh.

"I didn't speed-read it. I went slowly."

My head snapped up. "Why?"

"A few reasons." He glanced at our shoes, then up again. "For one, I knew the story was important to you."

"The acorn, though," I said.

"Because *you're* important." One step forward. "I'm, uh… not with London anymore. Since right after the cast party."

After our time on the swing set. Well, that was progress, but… "That was—what, five days ago?"

"I know it seems fast." Another step, so close now. But he didn't touch me. "I bought the charm after I finished the book, but I didn't see London the whole week before closing night, because of all your extra rehearsals. Please, let me explain…all of it?"

I nodded tentatively.

"London and I should've ended months ago." He raked one hand through his hair. "Really, we should never have gotten back together in the first place. After my accident, she showed up at the hospital and helped a lot when I was released. She really tried to be there for me this time, and she was so positive about my recovery."

"So she was just some obligation to fulfill? For her standing by you?"

I noted a quick wince. "More like, last May, my world was upended, and I was in a ton of pain. I guess I just fell back into something comfortable. But no matter how hard either of us tried, London isn't right for me, and I'm not right for her. Both of us knew the truth for too long and wouldn't face it. I hate to admit a lot of it was me, trying not to be lonely. I already felt alone enough after losing flight."

"I get that." Lonely. Alone. Still, images flashed of London Banks coiled around him like bonfire smoke. The pair sharing whispers and driving off in her white convertible. I didn't want her here, the third person in this alley. "But it's still less than a week." I held up the acorn. "And you'd already bought this for me."

His eyelids closed for a beat. "You're afraid that's my typical flight plan with girls."

"You told me yourself you like fast things," I said. "You fly through the air, you fly through books. And now you're flying fast from Friday to Wednesday. London to me?"

"Darcy." He swallowed hard, his Adam's apple slipping behind his neck. "I know how it looks. But listen, am I wrong, here? Can you tell me to my face that there's nothing between us, and we're just meant to be friends who chat over tea and books?"

Never. A boy had never said anything like this to me. "I can't tell you that. And this acorn means a lot. Especially since it was from you." I turned the little charm over in my fingers.

He smiled, but the tiny, lightweight acorn became an anvil. Truth was, it stood for a kiss, my first real kiss—not a costumed, scripted theater move—with the first boy I'd ever really wanted to kiss. I was suddenly too aware of my body in this space. I had to look like a fool, my knees trembling and fingers twitching and fiddling. God, why was I blinking so much?

This time, though, I didn't want another love interest's how-to manual. But what did I have? I carried the legacy of a toxic love affair. And for years, the only real playbook I'd lived with was lost inside the strained walls of my house.

Asher moved closer still. "You look panicked. Spooking you definitely wasn't part of my plan."

"Any spooking is not from you, and it's not about London, either." I tapped my head. "That's all manufactured right here. What's going on at home, and then my father, and…"

"I get it." He offered one hand and I stared at the calloused palm curved between us before I reached out, too. Warm and solid and slightly damp with nerves—that's how I'd re-member it.

"If you can stand not rolling your eyes at another pilot analogy, I've got one. Before takeoff, we have to complete a preflight check. One faulty charge or unresponsive sys-tem component could mean tragedy. So, no air until every-thing clears. It's nothing less than Bible to us. But with you, I skipped the list and stormed the runway, rushing to get where I wanted to go." He let out a soft sigh. "I didn't stop to think enough about where I'd been or how that would look. My bad."

I wanted to believe him, even though his revelation was still rattling around inside me, trying to fit. "Okay," I told him. "And if you can stand one from me, I remember sitting in your plane. How you can easily see what's ahead from the cockpit, but not what's in back of you without…"

"Without those gadgets and gizmos?"

"Yeah, those."

"Right. But you should know, I didn't take off one day and fly at jet speed from London to you." Asher pointed toward my feet. "I was already here."

A sound pushed up and out from my chest, maybe a whim-per. Had I ever whimpered before? I felt my mouth widen before it closed again around all these new questions and feelings gathering into yet another chaotic space, this time my heart.

I didn't even let people inside my home. And here, accept-ing this little symbol meant letting Asher Fleet inside my *life*. What would he find there? What stung, what dulled the shiny silver in my palm: *I* didn't even know. I simply did not know who I was, stripped from the clutter of my life and the books lining my walls.

But Asher being Asher meant I wanted to try. "I'm here,

too," I said. "Despite all the stuff I told you at Jase's, and what that means. I'm...here."

A ghost of a smile touched his face. "Good. More than good. How about this—let's rewind a little and take some time before anything...more?" He nodded in the direction of Yellow Feather. "Get to know me, and let me get to know you, without your grumpy boss looking over our shoulders?"

He really did get it. The top half of my body eased. "I'd like that."

"I've heard you can actually *go* places for coffee or tea and sit. In real chairs." His brow rose. "If you're lucky, you can get these nifty baked goods on actual plates, too."

"You don't eat sugary baked goods."

"Only on birthdays, but they do have fruit cups." When I laughed, he squeezed my hand. "I'm stuck here late, but how about tomorrow? We can check out that new poke bowl place on Thirtieth, and just...."

And just.

I could *just*. I could do that.

My eyes drifted fifteen feet away to the brick wall we'd leaned against weeks ago, folding into each other.

Asher took the acorn from my fingers. "About this." He gestured toward the same brick wall. "None of the times I've thought about kissing you included a replay in an alley surrounded by questionable substances. Or where we get to leave smelling like Cassie's Chicken grease without even sampling Cassie's Chicken."

My stomach dropped to my sneakers, and I had no clue how I found coherent language. "You mean the memory of outsmarting restraining-order candidates wasn't in the...mix?" God, there was a mix. I was the other half of a mix.

He chuckled. "Definitely not." He met my eyes. "I mean, I'd be willing to overlook setting, but...no. Not yet." He closed my palm over the acorn, words playing around his mouth. "You keep this. Hold on to it, and whenever you're ready, you can make good on that trade."

Twenty-Five
Heirloom

"…she would wear his kiss on the chain around her neck."

—J. M. BARRIE, *PETER PAN*

I lived in a house containing seven toasters, but couldn't find one simple chain for the charm tucked inside my pocket. My phone buzzed from the counter, and I set down my turkey sandwich, dinner edition.

Marisol: I have decided

I thumbed my response on the way to my bedroom. I couldn't help it—my chest pulled tight every time I entered this space, ever since my mother had violated it. I half-expected more brown cardboard, but the floor was as clear as it had been this morning. I exhaled and pressed Send.

Me: Do your worst

Marisol: White jeans not the old ones the new ones

Me: White? I have to remain grime and stain free through school and then my whole shift!

Marisol: So remain grime and stain free and don't argue

Me: FINE. What else?

Marisol: Red pointy flats and that black Swiss dot top we bought last summer

I read her instructions three more times, scanning my closet. Total blank on what shirt she was talking about.

Me: What the hell is Swiss dot?

Marisol: Hold please

Sooner than not, a photo came through my messages. Marisol had not only snapped a T.J. Maxx dressing room shot of me modeling the ruffled cotton blouse, she'd kept this picture and knew exactly where it was.

Me: Awestruck and terrified

Marisol: Grins

With photo reference, I sifted through, finally locating the short-sleeve top wedged between a pink turtleneck I hated and a bad concert tee Marisol and I had scored for free from a worse indie show. I fluffed the airy cotton.

Me: I'll have to iron but done

Marisol: Also, no hoodie. Wear a hoodie and I will find out

Me: FINE but it's just a casual thing. Poke café not princess castle. Not even exactly a date

Marisol: It's not NOT a date either

Mom was beginning her own sandwich assembly when I returned to the kitchen nook. After greetings and basic pleasantries and *yes, I'm fine, and you're fine, too*—fine, fine, everything was fine—I nibbled the rest of my dinner and tried to sound… Fine.

"Do you have an extra chain necklace you're not using?" My cheeks heated. "One I could borrow? Or keep?" I kept my head ducked and stared at whole wheat crusts and my ocean-themed charm bracelet.

"Hmm." Mom shuffled into her bedroom and reappeared after a few minutes. "This is perfect to layer with Marisol's heart charm." She held out a thin gold necklace, letting the delicate links fall from her fingers. "The jewelry counter at work is selling loads of these chains lately. For a while it was all about those big, bright statement necklaces. Now dainty layering is key."

I silently thanked Macy's for this bit of mental diversion, then thanked my mom out loud. "It *is* perfect," I added, accepting the necklace. Instantly, I knew it was real gold, not plated or filled, or something that would turn my neck green. "I've never seen you wear this."

Mom shrugged but kept her face even. "It's been in my jewelry box for years."

I curled the gold into my palm, one single thought spiraling around me. It couldn't be. This couldn't be an old gift from my father. She'd gotten rid of a library full of books because of him. Would she keep a piece of jewelry—

"It's from Grandpa Wells," Mom said quietly.

My heart caught on to his sweet memory.

"He gave it to me with a gold daisy when I was sixteen or seventeen. Stupid me lost the charm. Anyway, now you get to keep it. Seems right."

Rarely was anything right between us, but these few minutes of my mom sharing a tiny part of her past were the most right we'd been in days. I smiled from the necklace to her, and she smiled back.

My phone dinged again. "That would be Marisol for the twentieth time."

Mom reached for the mayo and a knife. "Tell her hi from me."

I fled into my room, fishing out the phone and expelling a short gasp. Marisol's name did not start with the letter *A*.

Asher: Just getting home. I didn't think to ask if you even like raw fish. Also, hi

I fell into trancelike motion, backward, walking until my legs bumped the bed.

Me: Hi, yourself. Sushi, poke, ceviche, all good

We were now people who texted. I'd texted Marisol a thousand times. I could text a guy, too—sure.

Asher: Cool. I need to know these things. Had a hunch after you and M mentioned Asian bowls

Me: I generally like stuff in bowls

Me: I eat most foods

Me: You have a good memory

Asher: For some things. But not genius level like yours

Me: Thanks 😊 How's the addition going?

Asher: Should wrap up this week. We'll need an official inspection but no biggie

We volleyed back and forth. Topics ranged from his latest Netflix obsession, to my classes, to the pool at his YMCA being closed for two weeks and how he planned to crash Jase's pool at six in the morning. Between texts, I took the time to learn every centimeter of the acorn charm, the dents and nicks and ridges. Then I fed it on to the gold chain and hooked it around my neck. I typed and erased and keyed again until:

Asher: Hey, my mom just yelled my favorite word...pizza. She does a mean GF crust

Me: Yum

Me: Sounds awesome

Asher: Wait...question

Me: ?

Asher: Do YOU have a favorite word?

Asher: Wait, better. A favorite book?

Me: Hmm...

Asher: All those stories you've read and you don't have a favorite?

Did I have an all-time favorite story? No one had ever asked. I'd never even asked myself.

Me: Have to ponder and get back to you

Asher. Counting on it. So, tomorrow?

Me: ~~Can't wait~~

Me: ~~Sure~~

Me: Tomorrow

Asher: Counting on it

My phone battery dipped into the red zone. I stretched across my bed for my charger and gave it life. With the initial shock of Asher's first text, I'd left my door open. I turned my view to the threshold, to the waiflike sight and muffled sounds of my mother padding from box to tub to box. I watched, hyperaware of the new chain around my neck. Mom had given me a bona fide heirloom—a ritual many moms did for their daughters.

Here's something of mine. Now it's yours.

I pulled Asher's acorn from underneath my tee. Imagining a real kiss, not a make-believe one found in the *Peter Pan* book on my desk or the thousands of stories lining my walls. Beyond them, my mother moved in dusty light and shadows.

Like I'd urged her countless times, I had to move forward, too, out from my own bookish hideouts. Out from shadows that kept me pale and made me slow in alleys with boys I really liked, second-guessing every move.

Here's something of mine. Now it's yours.

No matter what I wanted, this was the legacy I wore. My future kiss moment dangled from a thousand past-lived moments. My first real kiss and all the ridges, the dents, and the intricate details of it hung from an old heirloom chain my mother used to wear.

Twenty-Six
Everland

"Of course the Neverland had been make-believe in those days, but it was real now, and there were no night-lights..."

—J. M. BARRIE, *PETER PAN*

And just like that, red miso sauce dripped from the end of a cucumber chunk, outwitting my napkin and splattering into an oily blob on my white jeans.

"Ooh, bull's-eye," Asher said, wincing.

I attacked the stain with ice water. "Don't tell Marisol." My dabbing was only making things worse. "This is her top definition of tragedy. She'd call it Sartorial Murder at North Park Poke Shop."

He leaned over with another sympathetic cringe. "Right when I was about to compliment your stellar chopsticks skills." I laughed, then he promised, "And not a word to Marisol."

"Thanks. She kind of manages my wardrobe."

"She knows what looks good on you," Asher said, and when I looked up from checking my Swiss dot top for more stains, I found him definitely not eating and softly tapping his chopsticks against the rim of his spicy tuna bowl. And gazing, too—not staring, *gazing*—from my face to the silver acorn hanging from my neck. With his free hand, he reached out and gently tapped the little charm, smiling.

I smiled, too, praying I didn't have seaweed salad lodged between my teeth. "How was pizza night?"

"Extra good because I didn't have to fight off my dad for my second—or, um, third—helping." He tipped his water glass at me. "Work trip."

I tripped on another word. *Dad.*

"Hey." Asher nudged my hand. "Sometimes I forget about the deal with your dad." That my father was on an eighteen-year work trip.

"It's not *that*—you saying it. Talk about your dad whenever you want. I'm not usually this sensitive." I attempted another bite, thankfully dribble-free. "A couple of days ago, Marisol challenged me to start letting in the idea of having a father. Not even worrying about meeting him yet, or anything." I popped up one shoulder. "She's right. Still, it's different."

He nodded. "Like having to imagine the life you know while adding in this other person who's never been there before."

"Exactly," I said. The newness of acorns and London being gone and promised kisses didn't change one thing about us: Asher was so easy to talk to. I felt myself blush at how much I'd already said tonight—admitting I basically needed Marisol to dress myself properly and that trying to show the real Darcy Wells meant having to start thinking about the man who half created her.

Saying it makes it real. And I was.

I trapped a clump of sticky rice between my chopsticks. "My

mom and I—like I said, our home isn't…right. But it's all I've ever known and she has a job she likes and I've been able to slay school and prepare myself for some kind of future. What I'm trying to say is, she…*we've* gotten through, despite…"

The hoard. Asher's brisk nod completed my thought before I dragged it out myself.

I went on. "My father wasn't there for my first Disney trip or my first day of kindergarten. Mom and I and sometimes my grandparents clocked all my milestones alone. But now, there's this figure in the mix who *was* there all the time, even while he was on the other side of the world. He's real, even though I pretended he wasn't. Like make-believe."

"And now it's almost like trying to Photoshop in a person's face who missed the shot," Asher said.

"Or an entire childhood of shots. What would it have been like to have a father drive me to get my wisdom teeth out? Or to have someone around who fixed stuff, so I wouldn't have to rely on Marisol's brother to cover for maintenance?"

"Wait, what?"

Oh. Fix. Maintenance.

Now I'd done it and couldn't hit Rewind. I'd gone too far, and the reason was currently adjusting the collar of his black polo. It was stupid to peg all the blame on to him, but really, Asher was simply too *Asher.* Too kind, his eyes too focused and accepting, his heart too warm and patient.

Then there was the soft fullness of his mouth and his tightly strung back, swallowing up the metal café chair. From across the table, he'd drawn me miles ahead into saying words I used to protect with all my life.

Okay. It was okay. Asher already knew about the hoard; he could know about the side effects. I breathed in deeply. Then I began with how we'd kept managers and workers out for years and ended with, "So now that Marco's moving, I want to handle this latest fix-it issue myself. So if you know some good tutorials for installing low-flow faucet aerators, send them my way." The parts had arrived on our doorstep.

"YouTube has tons, but that sounds like a fifteen-minute fix for me."

Which sounded like hell on earth for me. Felt like all the fish I'd eaten were schooling through my stomach walls. "We're fine, but I appreciate it. I can learn to do a few handy things for myself." I couldn't meet his eyes. I poked through raw veggies and saucy rice.

"Darcy, why do all that when—"

I waved it off. Waved him off. "I should actually make good on Marisol's overselling of our skills."

Could I? I'd have to. There were too many steps between Asher knowing about my mother and our life, and Asher seeing the hoarded grit of my apartment. I was still getting used to *him*. I inched my face up and found him studying the few remaining chunks of ahi poke in his bowl.

"About your father," he said after a minute of silence. He cracked a smile, righting the awkward tilt of my universe after the last five minutes. "I mean, you said he's always been make-believe. So maybe, in the spirit of obeying the Oracle of Marisol, you could start by talking about him as real. You could even imagine him and think about what he'd be like. Out loud." He opened his palm over the table, inviting me to close the space. I did, and he threaded our fingers and squeezed. "Do you have any idea what he looks like?"

"Not now. Only a guess from twenty-year-old pictures. But this is all good. Me, getting used to the idea of him."

He tipped his chin. Winked. "My mom is into this power of declaration technique. Especially when I was early in my recovery. She urged me to say stuff like, 'I'm Asher Fleet and

I will get through PT and walk normally again.' Or, 'I will get off all these meds one day.'"

"'I will fly again'?" I offered softly.

His upturned mouth landed in a flat line. "I say that one every single morning."

This time, I did the hand-squeezing. "I already believe in flying for you, but how do I believe in a father for me? What would I even lead with in some hypothetical letter or phone call? 'So...how's Thailand been for the last eighteen years?' Or, 'Is the pad thai really that much better there?'" I possessed enough words to start a hundred conversations, but I didn't know the right words for this one. Not without actress-me scripting them out in costumes and blond wigs. "I can't seem to get there. Not yet."

"You don't have to get or be anywhere yet. Try talking more about him with Marisol." He leaned in. "And me."

And him.

Asher continued with, "Start adding him to your declarations, like, 'I'm Darcy Wells, and I have a father, and I'm going to crush that comparative poetry essay in AP English.'"

I laughed, then tried, "Um, I'm Darcy Wells, and David Elliot is my father, and I'm also going to crush San Diego State in the fall." And, wow. The declaration didn't feel ridiculous. It felt true.

"Even better," Asher said.

"I'm Darcy Wells, and David Elliot is my father, and I will keep these jeans clean next time."

A chuckle rumbled in Asher's throat and a twinkle spun from his eye just before he said, "What about, 'I'm Darcy Wells, and David Elliot is my father, and I'm having coffee with Asher Fleet at that cool Italian coffee shop around the corner on Saturday night'?"

★ ★ ★

Every December when I was little, Grandma Wells gave me
an advent calendar—the kind shaped like a thin cardboard box
with a snowy Christmas scene on the front. December mornings, I'd wake up and break open one tiny, perforated door to
reveal a surprise, a little something. There could be truffles or
hard candies. Sometimes I found stickers or miniature baubles
or plastic toys. Behind the door for December 24 was always
the biggest treat: a miniature ornament or foil-wrapped chocolate Santa Claus.

The past week of getting to know Asher had taken this
same shape. Not red-coated and white-bearded, but advent
calendar–shaped. Each day gifted a little something of him.
Saturday, it was coffee—yes, at the adorable Italian place in
North Park.

Another day we shared a phone call where I stared at a ceiling blackened with nearly midnight, and he said he was lying
faceup on his bed, too.

Where, at least a full hour in, I said, "Okay, you're so, so
exhausted. Your words are slurring."

"My name is Asher Fleet and I am exhausted, and these
meds don't help, but I will know the answer to my question."

"Too hard to choose." I yawned. "Not fair."

"Sometimes we have to make the hard choices. So which
is it? Only one forever—flan or cupcakes?"

Another yawn. "Ugh, fine. Flan."

"Understandable. Sweet dreams, Darcy."

"Good night—wait. No. Cupcakes. It's for sure cupcakes."

"Yeah?" The word was sleepy-soft.

"Yeah."

Then yesterday, a picture sneaking through my messages
during calculus brought a tear to my eye. No caption was

needed for the Piper-eyed view through the cockpit window of a tropical drink sky. "You will fly again," I declared in my head and hoped in my heart, typing the words back to him.

Now my phone dinged from Tops' counter while I munched break-time ginger snaps and Tess filled a special order for a theater troupe.

Asher: Hi from doctor's waiting room. Check-up. Do a crossword puzzle with me?

Today was Friday. Asher asking me to partner on a crossword puzzle moved *Friday* to my list of all-time favorite words. For a few minutes, Asher fed me clues and I did my thing.

Asher: Opera anthem, four letters

Me: Aria

Asher: Fits! Stuck here. Clue is threw a party for, five letters, starts with F

Asher: I thought feast but doesn't work

Me: Feted

Asher: That's a word?

Asher: Shit it works with the other clues

Me: Told ya

Asher: Squirrel food, five letters ending with N

My breath hitched. I twirled the silver charm around my neck.

Me: Really

Asher: That's six letters. Fail. Try again. Oak tree nut, five letters

Me: A-S-H-E-R (who is every kind of nut)

Asher: Winks. Hey, nurse calling me back

Asher: Last minute thing at Jase's tomorrow night. You in?

Me: I'm in

I traded my phone for my teacup, doing another heartbeat check. I did focused breathing until the thumping slowed from racehorse to my normal book-reading rate. Lukewarm green tea slid down my throat as I pondered a calendar week where Asher proved he wasn't impossible anymore. And I was learning, little by little, how not to be invisible.

"Well now, I wouldn't call that a Darcy-frown," Tess said, snatching a cookie from the plate. "But something's knocked that beautiful mind of yours real good."

"Right. Real." I conjured a hint of smile. "I would like to know what's real. I want that." The real me. A clear, uncluttered view into what drove my mother to compulsively shop. How a flesh-and-blood father might fit into my life.

Two hands over her heart, Tess wound around the counter and faced me. "Miss Darcy Wells, you do make a noble request of the world." Her eyes homed in on the acorn around my neck. "Well, isn't that an interesting little bauble. I've never seen you wear it before."

Instinctively I grabbed the charm I'd worn all week but kept hidden under necklines until today. "It's new."

Her smile opened like a rosebud. "Today calls for something new, too. Different."

"Can we nix the wig dress-up? Just for now?" More than any other time, I didn't want make-believe coverings, even for a few minutes, not over the girl who'd text-flirted with Asher and agreed to attend a party without consulting Marisol first—who honestly had to know by now, anyway.

"No, none of that today. I said *different*. A while ago you asked, and now it's time." Slowly, Tess raised her arms to the wavy fall of deep chestnut she was wearing. She tugged, pulled, and lifted to reveal a flesh-colored skullcap. My eyes grew wider as she peeled off the cap and tossed it behind her. Tess Winston's natural hair was beautiful—not quite blond, but not truly light brown, either. The shade reminded me of brown sugar, or the way beach sand looks just before sunset.

She reached for a brush and combed out the strands until they fell softly, barely grazing her shoulders. The layered cut was current and modern. "Real," she said.

My mouth still gaped. "Your hair is so thick and shiny. So pretty. Why all the wigs?"

"When I opened the shop, I wore them for advertisement. But then it became a treat to play with all the different colors and styles. Eventually it morphed into my trademark. Not the wigs as much as the mystery. Yes, I enjoy the mystery the most. Now it's better self-care than a spa day or a diary. And it's fun."

"Why didn't you show me before? The real you?"

"The real *me*?" Her soft, lavender-scented hand around my cheek. "Honey, you met the real me ages ago."

Twenty-Seven
As the Stars

"'Then tell her,' Wendy begged, 'to put out her light.'
'She can't put it out. That is about the only thing
fairies can't do. It just goes out of itself when she
*falls ~~asleep~~ **apart**, same as the stars.'"*

—J. M. BARRIE, *PETER PAN*,
AND *PETER PAN* MYSTERY SCRIBBLER

The Saturday night scene at Casa Donnelly reminded me of
the series of vintage Choose Your Own Adventure books I
read over two weeks in the first grade. Did I board the unknown spacecraft or stay to explore the mysterious planet?
Should I sneak into the cave, through the submarine hatch,
or into the castle armory? I alone could decide my fate.

With his parents in Cabo, Jase's house offered many such
choices to what felt like at least a quarter of the Jefferson High
senior class. While Marisol hit the bathroom, I slunk around.

Each room held a different vibe, but Jase had tacked up the same sign inside every one: Respect the property. Don't break it, spill on it, puke on it.

I hovered in the kitchen doorway, which featured some game involving Fireball whiskey, pitching mini cheese crackers into people's mouths, and rules that were unclear from my view. The participants seemed way too amused.

The family room morphed into social media central. Phones were out and Instagram was cued up. Voices hushed. The custom lighting system was set to washed-golden-somber, so selfies came out prefiltered. Girls lounged and posed on the oversize velvet furniture like big cat zoo animals in halter tops and bodycon dresses, ankle boots dangling over armrests.

Marisol found me in there. "I poked my head outside," she said and cracked her gum. Cinnamon. "Robbie and his debate club boys are jumping into the deep end from the top of the pool house overhang."

My nose crinkled as a distant splash plus cheering rang out over the moody jam piping through the entire property. "Brrr," I said, thoughts of chilly November in my head.

"You forget we're at Jase's. Home of portable backyard heaters, a Jacuzzi grotto, and a pool temp set to just south of volcanic. They're fine. Unless someone cracks a skull or something."

I let out a brief snort as my phone buzzed from the black mini crossbody purse I'd borrowed from Marisol. The WOC—or wallet on chain, as she called it—held my license and a few bills, keys, a lip gloss, and the phone. Not even a folded book cover would fit. Tonight was one of the first times I'd ever left my apartment without at least one novel.

Marisol grinned. "He's already here, right?"

I flipped open the bag and scanned. "Out back." A terrifying thought suddenly occurred to me. "Do you think London will show?" Even though we'd found a bit of common ground during the play, facing a postbreakup London while I was hanging publicly with Asher was a different matter altogether.

She drew me out of "overhear and repeat" range. "I haven't seen her yet. But London's not going to shade a party and her entire friend group just because the host is in a perpetual bromance with her ex." Marisol leaned in. "Look, from what I've heard, she's already moved on, so she's probably not home decoupaging his old love letters onto jars to collect her tears."

I surveyed the room again. "Still awkward. Really, especially awkward. I'm kind of new at this, remember?"

She fake-pouted. "My baby is all grown-up." She smoothed the off-the-shoulder neckline of my fitted cream sweater. "And how incredible does this masterpiece make your boobs look?"

Now even more conscious of my strapless bra, I ignored that and whispered, "New. At this. I haven't even kissed him yet."

Marisol snorted. "I'd know if you had, and you will, once you get yourself all figured out." She fluffed the beach waves she'd created in my hair, then spun my rigid form toward the patio doors. "I'm gonna mingle around here. Now get outside and forget about London."

I went.

Asher's text navigated me to the firepit. I followed the pool perimeter, where the jumping crowd had switched to floating around on huge blow-up mats, turtles, and swans. I shivered just looking at them until I saw Asher. He sat behind the orange row of flames curling up from the concrete table. He angled forward, eyes widening at me along with a star-touched smile. Another kind of shiver waved through, forehead to foot.

I settled beside him. Todd Blackthorn was entertaining the fire-seekers with a story and bonus hand motions.

Asher leaned in and whispered, "Todd's giving us his Glamis trip highlights."

"The desert sand dunes place?" I asked.

He nodded. "Says there was some kind of paranormal event out there, and he still has the jeebs. Also, you look really nice."

My mouth fell open, ready with—*Thanks, Marisol did my hair and makeup and remembered I had these black tall boots and the sweater was on clearance. And you look incredible, too, and smell like citrus and mint and a hot shower.*

Just in time, I enabled strikethrough, editing myself. "Thanks. You, too."

Asher slid his left arm halfway across my back, then answered my smile by drawing me closer. We'd hugged a lot lately, after dinners or coffee. Still, this felt different. Everyone could see us, which amped the reality factor. The gray flannel he wore was close to the one he'd worn at Bryn's party. Tonight it grazed the bare skin above my neckline instead of my imagination.

"Todd, it was your brother," Alyssa said, brandishing her purple cast. "No ghost arranged all your gear into a pattern outside your tent."

"Swear," Todd emphasized, and showed the evidence on his phone, which I could barely decipher from my spot. "Kade was out the whole night. He pounded all this *NyQuil* before we crashed."

Alyssa grabbed the device. "The stuff's all zigzagged. Zigzagged! This was Kade, meds or not." Handing it back, she caught my position inside Asher's arm. She lobbed a half smile across the fire. I shrugged like it was the smallest of deals, and attempted to embody the classic definition of *demure.*

As time ticked through the party, one thing was clear: I was Asher's date. He never left my side as we munched salty snacks and wandered in and out of rooms, drinking nonalcoholic fruit spritzers. I stopped wondering where the heck Marisol was and if London was going to pop out from one of the Donnellys' manicured hedgerows.

After three spritz drinks, my need to pee had gone from subtle signal to SOS. I excused myself, almost crying when I saw the lines in front of both downstairs bathrooms. I was shifting my weight back and forth when Alyssa sidled up and whispered, "Just pretend you missed the notice on the staircase and save yourself."

"Good idea." I shimmied recklessly past the Keep Out. Yes, That Means You sign and up toward bladder freedom.

Freedom found—along with some cute ideas for bathroom decor—I bolted back out into the hall with the kind of thoughtless movement people make when they expect an empty space and no company. But I was wrong. There was company—the female kind—and I smacked right into her with an, "*Unf.* Sorry."

My bowed head crept upward from platform heels and bare legs to black knitwear that hung an inch too long for a sweater but a few too short for a dress. She'd gone with dress anyway. Lifting more, I saw the red curled strands that shoved my next breath down into all the wrong places.

"Darcy," London said, not smiling, but not frowning, either. "I was hoping to run into you."

I'd prayed the opposite, but still said, "Okay."

"FYI, Asher and I are cool." She tipped her beer at me. "So don't think you're stepping on my toes or anything."

I blew out every scrap of awkward I could fit into one exhale. Didn't even make a dent. "We're just hanging out." For now, this was true. "And I promise, I didn't do anything to get in the middle of you two."

She raised her chin. "You didn't have to. You being yourself was enough."

My mouth dropped.

"I'm not stupid," she said mildly. "Asher didn't show up to

closing night because of me. I know what he does and doesn't do after a migraine day."

"London, he—"

"I saw you guys at the cast party, okay? On the swings." She motioned toward Jase's sister's room.

Oh God, oh God. I fought to steady my face. Through the partially opened door, I spotted Maren Donnelly, Bryn, and a couple of other girls lounging around.

"I watched the whole show from Maren's window. The way he was looking at you—wow. In two years, Asher never looked at me like that. So when he came to me later with his little spiel, I was already done."

I closed my eyes. This could still go either way. "I don't know what to say."

London smirked. "That's cool, but here's the thing. Even though I was halfway to boredom with him since the summer, you have to understand my natural sense of curiosity."

"Okay," I repeated slowly, because it seemed best.

She stepped forward. "I've been at Jefferson for four years. But until this fall, you barely made a blip on my radar as anything more than some reclusive brainiac."

The barb stung, but I supposed that was what years of playing invisible had gotten me.

"But *then*, you fill in for Alyssa and totally nail Beatrice to, like, spiritual levels. Props." She toasted me, then sipped. "And then the swings happened, and you can't blame me for wanting to know where my past was heading, if you get my drift."

Drift gotten, I just nodded.

"So I tried to find out," London said. "See, I'm the type of girl who knows everything, down to what soap brand people prefer. But when I asked around about you, I got the same answer—nothing. The only person who's even been to your house is Marisol." There was a pause, then she leaned close.

"Either you're cleaner than Bryn's lavender SoftSoap, or you're hiding something filthy, my friend. But I'm done caring now. Enjoy your prize." She smiled, a little menacingly, then fled into Maren's room.

The door slammed. I slumped against the wall, pulse on fire, wishing I could shove all of London's revelations and accusations into the room along with her red lips and velvet heels.

"Darcy?" Asher said from behind.

I turned on a quickened breath. "Long line. I—"

"I know. I ran into Alyssa." He laid warm hands on my forearms. "Listen, my head's starting up. Not a migraine, but I got a couple dizzy flashes. I'm okay to drive, but I should bolt." He eyed me carefully. "You okay?"

I wanted to tell him about London, but with his head bugging and those dizzy spells spoiling his return to flight yet again, it could definitely wait. "I'm fine. Let's go downstairs." And far away.

He grabbed my hand, but as we moved through the end of the hallway, two figures tumbled into the loft at the top of the staircase, giggling. I caught enough turquoise floral print to know it belonged to a minidress attached to one Marisol Robles. Who was attached to some guy.

Asher and I glanced furtively at one another before peeking around the wall. The couple landed on a stuffed chair in the corner of the loft, arms and lips and legs entwined into some new polygon math didn't know about yet.

I spoke into his ear. "But that's…"

"I know," Asher whispered as we swept past the oblivious pair to the first floor.

"But she's with…"

"I know."

Marisol Robles and Jase Donnelly.

We stopped by the front door. "I need a minute to process that."

Asher laughed. I looked. Our eyes locked. My red, hot cheeks played traitor to my imagination. Was he picturing another couple and a list of possibilities?

He tucked his mouth into one corner, brows hiked, and I would've bet my books he was.

"Um," I said. The silver charm scored a fiery brand into my chest.

"Right." A forever pause, then, "I think your ride home is gonna be occupied for a while. I'll take you, if you don't mind bailing early?"

I cast one last look through Jase's house. "I've had plenty of party," I said, and followed him out to the black Ford.

After helping me in, Asher shut his door. "Shocked? Awed?"

I breathed out a laugh. Marisol and Jase? The *Jarisol* mashup was real. "Aren't you? I did not see that coming."

"I did."

My head whipped around.

"She's been on Jase's scope for a while. But last summer it was Bryn, and then he was a chickenshit. And now..." He drummed his hands over the steering wheel before calling the engine to life. "Apparently they went for it." He smiled and pulled away from the curb. "No doubt she'll fill you in."

No doubt, and soon. I buckled my seat belt, remembering the night Asher drove me home after our airport party. How the webbed strap of fabric across my chest had teased London's perfume. Her candy-sweet scent had faded now, but I couldn't shake the cloud of London's words.

I'd been trying to be a better Darcy to myself. Growing into a visible girl, who wanted a boy who was so much more than a prize. I tried to tell myself the good words, declaring the true ones. *My name is Darcy Wells, and I'm wearing a promise around my neck that's all mine to make real.*

But London wasn't wrong about what she'd said back at Jase's house. *Hiding. Reclusive. Blip. Filthy.*

These four were also mine.

In my little black purse, I had no books that could swallow those ugly syllables into smallness. From two blocks away, my bedroom library called with old remedies, but my stomach clenched as Asher turned onto Hoover Avenue. "There." I pointed to the large curbside parking space far enough, but not too far away from my building. "This is good."

"Okay." Asher stretched the word and pulled in.

I undid my seat belt and rubbed his shoulder. "I'm sorry about your head. Sleep it off, yeah?" I wedged open the door, my body angling to be gone.

"Darcy." He cut the engine.

"Call me tomorrow. And thank you."

"For chrissake." Healing knee or not, Asher moved with furious speed from the driver's side to the sidewalk. "What's going on? I'll walk you up."

"It's fine. Your head."

His entire body tensed, hardening into a shape I'd never seen before. "Not my style, no matter how shitty I'm feeling. I don't drop girls I'm dating on the street with a 'see ya later, babe.'"

I exhaled, then conceded after a long pause. "I know you don't." *And it's what I wanted. A guy who didn't honk or text for me to come down. But that meant...*

"You know, there's been this common denominator each time we've hung out. You *met* me at the coffee place or for tacos or Asian bowls. Marisol took you to Jase's tonight. I didn't pick you up. You didn't want me to."

"I'm trying, I promise."

"I know. God, I know, Darcy. But you're sidestepping me."
My eyes snapped wide.

"The work your place needs." He turned, scrubbing his chin. "If I thought for a second that you really wanted to take up home improvement as a hobby, I'd bring over my whole tool kit and get you started. Cheer you on. But you only want to do the work so I won't have to. So I won't have to see the space."

I studied the clumped grass of the parking strip, browning with drought. The oxidized metal of the streetlamp pole on the corner of Hoover and Anderson. And knew he was right. But the mess that made my home had never felt bigger. Filthier.

"You won't even let me stand in front of your apartment on the off chance that I might catch a glimpse inside."

Tears pooled, trapped in the corners of my vision. "My mom could be home or pulling in, and she doesn't know anything yet. The questions..."

"I know I'm pushing the issue. My head's in a vise grip, and I'm not as level as I should be. But I can't do pretense anymore. I don't have the energy or health for it." He pressed three fingers into his forehead. "My whole deal with London was all flash—at least on her part. What looked good, being seen at trendy joints, dressed out like the perfect couple. A sham." He gestured toward my building. "I need simple. Straightforward. After the alley, I thought we were moving toward something real, slow or not." He swallowed forcefully. "I thought you put that acorn on a chain because you eventually wanted what it stands for, too."

Goddammit, I had real thoughts for him. Powerful words that could explain where the fear and shame really fell. I tried to shake them loose from my head. "I do. I really do," is all I managed. Worthless.

"I believe you. But I don't want to start anything on half-truths."

Half-truths: lies wearing wigs and makeup, dressed up pretty in borrowed leather.

"I don't care if the entire Fashion Valley Macy's is in your living room." Asher leaned close, his voice barely above a whisper. "Don't you know? You've got me, Wells. But what stings isn't you not being ready to show me your house or let me meet your mom. That's up to you." His head bent low. "It's that you're keeping me out but *pretending* you're not. And that really…"

Oh, his face. Where I thought all the light, all the stars had brushed his smile, beamed the silvery glint into his eyes, I found nothing but a flyboy missing another kind of shadow. Tonight, I was the thief, not a car accident. I had taken this one. So many times, I'd read about hurt, but now it stood at my feet with a heartbeat.

I reached out, but he stood back, paled and hollow. He shook his head, then rubbed his temples. "I'm not rushing you or pressuring you, and I never will. Deal with your mom and cope on your terms. You need me to cover for you? I'm down. But all I ask—the next time you have to put up a wall, just let me be on your side of the bricks." Another step toward his truck. "Think about it. Take some time. Be sure about me."

"Asher."

"Be sure about you, too."

Twenty-Eight
Heart-Shaped Heart

"..."

—DARCY JANE WELLS

Elisa B. Raspberry Rose Lipstick, item number 8898, was what Marisol referred to as a chameleon cosmetic. The slightly iridescent tone was just pink enough not to be called red, and red enough not to be called pink. The first time I saw the limited-edition shade, I thought if a kiss could be any color in the world, it would be Elisa B. Raspberry Rose.

Coming home from Jase's party with a sore heart and Asher's charm still around my neck, I shouldn't have been surprised when a kiss foiled me once again. This time it wasn't a Jefferson High stage, but a hoarder's apartment. When I'd shut the front door behind me, my mom said nothing about my puffy eyes and tearstained cheeks. I got only a quick greeting before she returned to her task. The scene around her fell over me like one of the poems in my new-old *Peter Pan*:

After Asher

A mother on the floor, counting.
The makeup tub I'd gone through with Marisol.
Nine tubes of Raspberry Rose
dressed in their pink-gold boxes.
A simple question.
The truth.

So easy to answer the question I knew was coming with, *Yeah, you're right, Mom. You did give me one of your ten tubes of Raspberry Rose and forgot.*

Only minutes old, the memory of Asher walking away still pulled like no story ever had. I'd told myself I wanted what was real, but Asher was right: I was still clinging to half-truths with him, like the ones I'd made years ago to protect my family and home. I'd practiced them until they felt so close to real truth, I forgot the difference.

I wasn't only doing it with Asher, either. I hung on to lies with my mother, all my make-believe festering inside. It rotted soul-deep and would only spread and consume if I didn't stop. And stop, now. Right now. Tonight, it was time for my own *The End*.

I pinched my eyelids closed. "Mom. I need to tell you something."

She glanced from side to side, hand gripping the top of her tub. "Look, I just had to—"

"Not that." Not the hoarding. Not the array of rose gold Elisa B. packages in front of her. "More like, I have to show you something."

The room suddenly felt like we'd set the thermostat too high. My pulse raced as I logged into eBay on my laptop and pulled up my listings page. "I've been selling Elisa B., just like you do."

"What do you mean?"

"Read the titles."

She cased the screen. "English Wisteria Lipstick, Duo-Base Concealer, Peony Passion Blush." Mom's lip quivered. "Where? Where did you get these?"

"I'm living in them. Swimming in them. We both are."

"Peony Passion..." She attacked the dining nook, tearing into the rest of the plastic tubs, lids flying.

"Mom!" I hurried to her side.

She knelt, pulling out product after product. "You took them? Why?"

"I had to! I need to pay bills, too. Grandma has been helping me with money for years, but she stopped when I turned eighteen."

The words smacked against her. "But you have a job."

I shook my arms: *Look at me! See me! Hear me!* Couldn't she see outside of herself for once? "It's not enough! And I can't go to school and get all my work done plus work enough hours to make it be enough right now. That's why Grandma helped and never told you. You would've spent my extra money, too. You would've shopped it all away."

"Darcy." Hands crossed over her heart.

"My bookstore check doesn't cover my car insurance and cell phone. And what about the ninety-nine times out of a hundred that I have to buy groceries instead of you? What about clothes that actually fit me?" I picked up a random folded sweatshirt, waved it high. "We even have boxes of ridiculous stuff that wouldn't fit Marisol's little sister."

The mass of ugly black truth I'd exposed wanted somewhere to go. I didn't know how, but even this maxed-out den found space to absorb it. The light eclipsed, dull and watery gray. My mother absorbed it, too, shaking her head, trapped in steady motion. Her mouth formed word after word that never came out.

"I'm sorry, Mom." My voice thinned, and I turned toward my bedroom. Only a fraction of my books showed through the doorway. So many. I did more than read novels and then pass them on or donate them. I *used* books. I *had* to keep them and read them, over and over. Other people who didn't understand might call my collection an obsession. Maybe a compulsion. Some might even call it...a hoard?

Oh...*oh.*

I grabbed this thought before it doubled, shelving it with all the other volumes for now. But when I faced my mom again, the whole room looked different. Through all the clutter, I finally saw *her.* "I don't understand why you have to shop so much. But now I really get that something inside *you* knows why you need to."

My mom froze, then let out a single, heated breath.

"And if you need to keep buying, you go ahead," I added. "But there is so much money sitting in these tubs. And for now, I have to keep selling to replace Grandma's checks. Just what I need to cover bills and groceries. No more. So I can keep living here with you."

Control. She needs to feel some sense of control, the doctor said.

I owed her this. "I'll tell you exactly what I post. No surprises. I'll write down every item for you so you don't have to check." Dashing away tears, I grabbed a notepad and listed the three products currently on eBay auction.

She took my offering with an unsteady grasp. "The money you need—yes. I do understand. I want you to stay, baby. So much." She shook the notepad. "But can just keeping this list...be enough?"

We had to try. For both of us.

Word of the Day: *Enough*.

I stepped away, facing our galaxy of things—my eyes pinned to boxes and tubs, to makeup, plates, and pillows. I pictured *Anne of Green Gables* and *Great Expectations* and a thousand other stories walling my room. I ran through years of lies and pretending.

Enough, I thought, and knew all that simple word could really mean.

"Wait, wait," Marisol said from the opposite end of the table. She set down her portfolio.

I lifted my foot from the sewing machine pedal and looked up at her.

"Plant your guide hand a little more firmly. Pull more. No slack in the fabric."

I tried again. The machine whirred, the needle tapping stiches into cotton. Three days had passed since Jase's party. That next morning, Marisol had opened her door, and I'd all but fallen in. Cross-legged on her studio floor, I'd told her everything about my confrontation with Asher. Then I spilled about eBay and my mother after she prodded Natalia to bring up steaming bowls of sopa de tortilla, topped with avocado and crunchy tortilla strips.

Self-care—according to her, I'd been doing a tacky, knock-off job of it. She hijacked my phone, reminding me that Asher's wish for me to take some time didn't include stalking my messages. I needed to unplug from more than technology.

She'd thrown me into the shower with fancy soaps and lotions her aunt had brought from Paris, then tucked me into her bedroom with a satin eye mask. When I woke hours later, my overnight bag was perched at the foot of her bed, along with my toiletry case and a perfectly styled outfit for school.

I did my Monday shift at the Feather and my usual in classes, only briefly popping home. For three days, my mother and I were figures who sometimes met in goat tunnels. She hadn't tried to store another piece of her hoard inside my room. She didn't speak of the eBay cosmetics, either. But I still sensed the faint outlines of that box on my carpet. I saw the yellow notepad on the counter, and though my confession was the right choice, the products haunted me. Peaches and pinks, swipes of lipstick and pearly eye shadows, threw their pigments around my house. Too bright. Too new.

My self-care required more space than my apartment could give. I had to think about Asher. I had to think about my father. I had to think about me.

Marisol didn't prod. She worked, too, drifting over text messages between sketching and creating. I knew who was on the other end of her loopy smile.

Sunday evening, I'd paused over all that thinking and asked something of Marisol I knew she'd waited years to hear. She'd nearly given up, too. We were in her bedroom when I sat up from her gleaming white comforter and said, "Teach me to sew."

She made me declare it two more times before she dressed herself in a bedazzled grin. Marisol taught me the basics first—hours learning the machine, sewing fabric squares, and hand stitching buttons. We cocooned alone. And while I learned the most basic scraps of my best friend's passion, her mother filled me from her kitchen.

I almost drowned in bowls of garlicky Cuban black beans and rice. Yesterday, Carlos and Camila stormed in with sticky fingers and freshly baked pan dulce, crowned with cinnamon and butter. And this afternoon, after I was ready to try a simple dress pattern, Eva Robles brought tacos heaped with chorizo con papas. The mix of fried potatoes, onions, and spicy chorizo spilled from corn tortillas. On top, she'd sprinkled queso panela and crema and chopped cilantro.

We halted our sewing to eat on the studio floor until Marisol stopped eating long enough to say, "I haven't told Mama anything. But now I'm sure she's figured out why you've been hibernating."

"What?" I set my own plate aside.

"Chorizo con papas is our ultimate comfort food and her heartbreak specialty. Unwritten family rule. Can't believe I never told you that."

I stared at the taupe carpet fibers.

"Darcy."

"You and Jase," I said.

"Yeah?"

"Even Asher knew, but I had no idea." I lifted my eyes. "I should've known." Of course, I could assemble the clues now. How she was always the first to notice him, the little gibes and sidelong looks. "I've been so wrapped up in my problems that I missed your happy. You *are* happy, right?"

"The happiest. We're just seeing where it goes. But you and me," she added, cocking her head, "our friendship's lucky as hell you didn't feel any earth movement during that stage kiss."

We shared a laugh before she grayed it out. "Speaking of happy, or happy places, I haven't seen you open a novel in days. Not even your *Peter Pan*. One boy isn't worth giving up your books. Not like your mom did. You love them so much."

"I...my..." Yes. Okay. The simple words worked. My mouth was finally ready to try a few more—infinitely more complicated ones. "I'm not giving up books for good, and it's not because of one boy. Not at all because of Asher, or what I told my mom, either."

"Then why?"

"I can't use characters and what they've done anymore. The paths they chose, or what they did to survive. I can't do what Elizabeth Bennet or Jane Eyre did. I have to do what *I* do."

My friend nodded. "Why now?"

"Because I saw what years of lying and hiding has done.

And I *really* saw what's on the other side of all those book covers. I felt it, too. For the first time, I felt what I've been reading about for years," I whispered.

Her big, round eyes on mine.

"I'm tired of pretending." My chin quivered. "Tired of hiding and keeping secrets. Tired of chasing perfect stories and using them."

She scooted forward, rested her hand on my knee.

I dug my nails into the carpet. Quivers turned into sobs. I'd teared and sniffled before, but the paper forest in me sagged under the sudden downpour, raindrops streaming over leaves. "I hate that I have to tiptoe around my own mother. We both walk on eggshells in our own home."

Black streaks marred Marisol's perfect makeup job. She trembled and grabbed my hand. "I know."

"The hoarding and how we deal is just another fairy tale. A dark one. And I'm done. That's one thing I *can* do. I can be done." My body worked itself loose, bones igniting like matchsticks. The blood in my veins roared in wild, tumbling rapids. "I thought giving up was the answer, but it's not. It's being honest about what and who we are."

Marisol caged her hands around her face, tears streaming through.

I stilled, quieting. And right then, I faced the last piece of my invisibility. The one that hid my heart from myself and everyone else. The one that kept Asher on the curb and half-truths on my tongue. "I'm a hoarder, Marisol. Like her."

"God, Darcy."

I declared my truth again. "I'm Darcy, and I'm a hoarder of words. Words in dictionaries and in stories and books. I'm going to read them—forever—but I'm not going to hoard them anymore. I'm not going to hide in them anymore, either." I looked at my precious friend. "I want to live out my own story. The autobiography of Darcy Jane Wells. A real story."

Marisol nodded, again and again. "Start right now. With Asher."

The flood again, leaking from cracks and crevices. "Before, I pretended Asher didn't matter, but that was a lie. And when I found out I mattered to him, I forgot to stop pretending."

"So get real now," she said. "You did your thinking. What did it tell you?"

Saying it makes it real. "That... I love him."

"Oh," Marisol said through a sob.

"But these last few days...it *hurts.*" I pressed shaking hands over my chest. "When I think of him buying this acorn, it's so sweet I want to explode. But London was right there. Her words hit too close, and she wasn't wrong. Then Asher's face Saturday night—I'll never forget it. I hurt him for real, too. And I got a glimpse of what it would be like if I pushed him away for good. I know he hasn't texted to give me time, but I miss that, and everything. I miss *him.* So all these feelings keep fighting each other, and I don't know what's happening to me."

Marisol did the last thing I expected. There, on her studio floor, next to half-eaten plates of comfort tacos, she giggled and grinned. Hands outstretched, she reached out and placed them over mine. "Darcy, welcome to your heart. You can put your feet up and make yourself at home."

"What?"

"Don't you see? This, what you're feeling—all the wild-ride emotion—it's not your book-shaped heart." The smile turned soft. "It's your heart-shaped heart."

"Oh," I squeaked. "This is what love really feels like?"

"This is what love really feels like," she said.

"It's awful."

She cackled again. "So awful. But it's also *not* awful, in the most not awful of ways."

For the first time in days, I truly laughed. Wet, teary waves of laughter.

I slowed, then stilled when Marisol unhooked my mother's necklace and dropped the acorn into my palm. "Asher drives a black truck, not a white horse. Even the best guys aren't storybook princes. They're messed up and flawed. I mean, he did rush from London to you, and that made you doubt yourself. And you hurt him, Darcy. You didn't trust him and lied around it. You both kinda fumbled. But that's how real love stories go."

"No knights storming castles, no damsels in distress."

"Right, and that's super boring anyway," she said. "Real hearts love for real. But they also hurt each other for real, sometimes. It's what's inside that tells you whether to work it out or run. So, after all the time you've spent with Asher, who does your heart—your heart-shaped heart—tell you he is?"

I thought of the boy who drank tea in my bookstore. The intelligent and brave soul who could build and fly, who was thoughtful enough to help a little girl and her mother. He thought my nerdy book brain was cool—extraordinary, even—and not boring and lame. He'd listened and listened and... "He's the kind of guy I don't have to pretend around."

She nodded. "And he must know what's really inside you, too. He's still got you on his radar, waiting for you to figure it out. So figure it out. You don't need another book character."

"No, I don't. And this time I'm going to do what Darcy from *The True Story of Darcy Jane Wells* would do."

"What's that?"

I breathed truth into the real me, not the invisible me. "Ransack your sewing room for a thimble."

Twenty-Nine
Thimble

"'Surely you know what a kiss is?' she asked, aghast.
'I shall know when you give it to me,' he replied stiffly,
and not to hurt his feeling she gave him a thimble."

—J. M. BARRIE, *PETER PAN*

Even without Marisol's cellular wizardry and powers of information, I could've guessed where to find Asher. Dusk touched down onto Montgomery-Gibbs Executive Airport as I eased into the lot and spotted his truck. I parked next to it, under a sky tinted purple-gray and bloated with steel wool clouds. An orange wind sock followed my motion. Today it pointed toward the rows of tethered airplanes, the breeze heralding my arrival like breathy trumpets.

Nothing royal about me, though. I came in black jeans and a floaty white top with eyelet panels. Marisol had insisted on five minutes with me and a brush, face wash, and a dab of soft blush and rose-pink gloss. Then she sent me out with two silver baubles in my palm.

I approached the hangar bay where the Fleets kept their Piper. The entrance was open, and the cabin lights glowed in the distance. The riser was lowered. My palms glazed with damp and my belly rolled with marbles.

I approached the plane from the front, straight toward the nose. Asher would see me from the captain's chair. And when I finally spotted him, one paralyzing thought came: maybe I was too late.

Asher pressed his face toward the large cockpit window. His expression was muddied behind the glass, but he stood quickly and appeared on the riser seconds later.

I tried to hold my head high, waiting.

Asher exited the hangar and stopped a few feet away from me, worrying the cuffs of his gray pullover the way people do when they don't know where to put their hands. "Lesson learned. Never tell Jase your hiding spot."

Enough play rang in his tone to keep me from spinning on the ball of my foot. Still, I spoke from the middle of a wire stretched across canyons. "You didn't want to be found?"

"Only by some people. I think you'll find the list surprisingly short."

"Did you think I wouldn't come?"

He lowered his head briefly. "There was this one moment at coffee last week. You looked up at me from your latte, and I thought you were gonna reach across the table and just kiss me right there. So, no. I hoped whatever was behind that look hadn't changed, and you'd find me. Somewhere."

I stepped forward, already feeling my own atmosphere change—calmer, the edges brushed soft with want. "I never lost you. But I had to take my time. I had to find me first."

"Did you?" His eyes honed to steel, like they'd robbed a bit of sky.

"You were right, on the curb," I said gently. "I was pretending, and you deserved better. I'm sorry. And, yeah—it's all me, here. And these." My left hand uncurled, revealing his little acorn charm. Then I flattened my right hand, the worn thimble dotting my palm. I placed it into his waiting hands.

"What does this mean?" he asked, his smile widening around the same words I'd said days ago in the alley.

"It means I want you to know I'm here for more than making good on your promise. I want to give you one of my own. And I'm glad J. M. Barrie was clever enough to plot the thimble, so I'd have something to come here with. But I still don't have a clue how to do the part that's supposed to happen next," I said.

"How would you write it if you could?"

My face crinkled, and I wondered if I'd heard him correctly. "Write it?"

"You've read thousands of stories. How do you want the rest of yours to go?"

"I—"

Asher took my free hand, the one not holding the silver charm, and squeezed our laced fingers. "You didn't choose a mother who forgets birthdays and shops so much you can barely walk through your own house. You didn't choose a father whose first contact with you came eighteen years too late. And you didn't choose me dulling the shine on your acorn moment by making you feel, even for a second, that you were some rebound move."

"None of that."

His teeth scraped across his bottom lip. "Before I—just one question, okay?"

I nodded.

"All the times we've talked about books, you've never said if you read romances. But are you really ready for one? Not a make-believe or pretend one. The real deal."

"I'm ready."

A brilliant smile. "Then write it, Darcy. Write it…edit it however you want."

The notion drugged me, because I knew what he was really doing. What it really meant. Asher was giving me a gift—not a silver bracelet or a ring. Not flowers or a card or even an acorn charm dropped into my penny tray. My first real gift from a boy was a pen to write my own love story, but—

"That's not fair," I said. "If everything's only what I want, the way I want it, I'm just living one more fairy tale."

"Then write me in, and we'll decide stuff together." He moved closer, calloused hands roaming over my bare forearms. His touch, still so impossibly new, but never foreign. The Asher in front of me was as familiar as tea and books and paint-splattered clothes.

"You're already in. You already were." I held up my acorn.

His hand rose, uncovering the thimble, one brow arching high.

Asher might like fast things, but I knew my first honest-to-God kiss would not be one of them. His smile stretched, yawning across his face, dimpling flushed cheeks. Amber eyes opened like skies hungry for flying machines. He pulled me close, into ribbed gray cotton. One arm wound around my back, the other tracing my face from brow to chin, chin to brow. A heart-shaped face.

He rested his forehead against mine, and we breathed like that, gaining air and dizzying altitude. A half second, then his mouth. His lips brushed soft kisses over mine, over and over and achingly perfect. I caught myself up, let him show me the way of him until we sank deeper and climbed higher, all at once.

We didn't, *couldn't* stop. Kissing Asher—twirling my fingers into the dusky brown curls at his neck, over the wood-solid plane of his back—was like years' worth of granted wishes. Stories had only told me half-truths, never fully admitting it could be this good.

I held on, letting him pilot me to a dream-wake place. I glided over the crackling warmth of a stone fireplace, laughter rolling off a creaky porch swing. I saw a plump, golden moon rising behind bedroom window glass. Fuzzy slippers and flannel and running through sprinklers over sun-warmed grass. When the last image flashed, I swore I was there, wiping dusty feet over a woven mat—*Welcome*—through an open door, into a space clear enough to see the beginnings of forever.

Who does your heart tell you he is?

Emotion scarred the back of my throat as I realized the answer. I'd always had a roof over my head, but Asher Fleet was home.

Thirty

Next

"'Second to the right, and straight on till morning.'"

—J. M. BARRIE, *PETER PAN*

Of course, my real home still stood, newly gray on the out-side and shockingly cluttered on the inside. The courtyard in front of 316 Hoover Avenue was finally finished. Flagstone trails snaked around bushes and flowery shrubs. New, gleam-ing mailbox units walled the far side. We had a new table, too. I studied it for a moment. White and modern, paired with gray chairs with stretchy all-weather seats. Not my table, not Marisol's. But the hearts and stars around our necks and inked over twin souls would always be.

"Are you sure?" Asher asked. We stood at the bottom of the staircase with new railing, leading to old horrors.

"No, but I need to show you anyway. No more hiding."

He pulled me closer. Soft lips grazed my forehead. I leaned

into his solid form, his intoxicating warmth, but I still wasn't used to any of it. It had only been a day since we kissed, and everything still felt like a first.

"You know it doesn't matter, right? Whatever's in there won't change anything for me."

Another gift—he was full of them. But I stood as closed as my front door, my shame so tightly shut around me, and his precious gifts only seemed to bounce off my surface. Still, I tipped my head toward my unit, and we climbed up and up. With my key in the lock, I told him, "This is what happens next."

Dust swarmed over metal, fabric, and plastic. Three steps in, I knew Asher smelled it, too, worked to breathe through clouds of itchy motes. I flicked the light switch and flinched as my real world opened in front of the only boy I had ever loved.

"So, this is me." My hand waved through goat tunnels, flourishing over stacked boxes like a caustic game show model.

Asher moved from section to section, pile to pile. While he examined dishes and electronics, housewares and random clothing, I retreated to the wall. I inched as closely as possible to faded drywall, dodging plastic tubs. Head bent, I nibbled the same spot on my lip, over and deeper.

"Darcy."

I turned my head, but didn't meet his eyes.

"Come here."

Dream words, but I felt if I touched him now, I might splinter into pieces. The room was already too full of them.

He sighed and crossed his arms. "Right. Okay. Let me just…" He ducked in and out of the bathroom. "I saw the fixtures you need replacing. Piece of cake. Should take less than twenty minutes."

"Thank you. I really—"

"I want to help." He maneuvered into my scrap of space.

"I want to do stuff for you, so you have more time for the things you're amazing at."

"Asher, it *will* help. A lot." I stared at both our shoes. "I'm sorry I'm being weird." I dropped my mouth into another exhale, risking all the breaking by burrowing into his arms, the soft weave of his shirt against my cheek. "It's just…it's more than not being used to having you here."

"Tell me," he said, circling his hand over my back.

I looked into his face, the sharp, rugged features whittled into oak—strikingly real. Present, too, not a thousand daydreams away. "I've been living out not only high school with my nose in a book, but my whole *life*. While Marisol and other girls were dating and going to dances, I was reading about them." I took a deep breath. "I don't want to do that anymore. I'm here for real life. But even the first day I met you, I was speaking from a story."

"I saw you."

"I still don't get how. I'd made myself invisible."

"I still saw you. And saw you some more. Then…" He pulled me closer. "And then, everything."

My stomach instantly fluttered.

"*You*," he said, "are so pretty. But when we're at Yellow Feather, and I'm staring at you from across the room, and you're bent over some novel, you're beautiful."

A heated exhale was my only available response.

"I watched you almost every day." He smiled. "Watched you tuck hair behind your ear and fall in love with words. And you're more than pretty. You're like all the places I want to fly to."

Oh, I wanted to kiss him senseless, but my head wouldn't stop rattling, spinning. "God, Asher, you…but I'm—"

"You're what?"

"That real me I told you about? It's a mess. I'm a mess." My hand tipped to the hoard. "It's not just me you're getting. I come with added prizes no one wants to win."

"Cool. 'Cause I'm a mess, too." He sank into one of our surprisingly empty dining chairs. He rolled his left pant leg up to his knee, and I sucked in a sharp breath. Toothy gashes tore his flesh from shin to ankle, still pink with new skin clawing its way to the surface. Straight over his knee, a surgeon had left a long incision after rebuilding Asher to walk again. With time, the wounds might heal more, but they would never disappear. I dropped to the carpet and gently traced each scar, swollen with memory and taunting dreams—all courtesy of one spring evening when he should've stayed home.

He took my hand, introducing me to the gash across his forehead, jagged like railroad tracks. "Messy. When I take you to my house, you'll see all my meds. The bottles cover half my nightstand." He squeezed the hand he held tightly. "Then there's migraines and mood swings. I can't run with you on the boardwalk or even share a piece of chocolate cake with you."

"I don't care. You lived."

"I lived, and I'm here. But when I wear shorts and people stare, or we have to stay in or I say something harsh because my head's a wreck—is that too much for you? Is my mess too much?"

"Never."

"Yours isn't too much for me, either."

I rested my cheek on his lap, shutting my eyes.

"I did some thinking the past few days, too," he added. "I'm not gonna blame myself for the accident anymore. For not staying home. I wasn't supposed to go to Annapolis."

"But what about your dream? The Marines and fighter jets?"

"I like to think of it this way now—if I'd been in uniform, in Maryland, I wouldn't have walked into a certain bookstore.

If I was sitting in a classroom in Annapolis, I wouldn't be sitting here with you." There was a short pause before he continued. "You're part of a different dream."

I smiled, nodding over the blue denim.

"That's where I was wrong before. We can't get stuck on one goal and plan it to the letter. Life isn't to-the-letter predictable. It's messy, like us, and it changes. So our dreams can change, too."

His hands bent under my shoulders, lifting. He set me on his unscarred leg and secured his arms around me. "Never forget. I saw you, Darcy Wells," he said, his lips hovering just over my mouth.

"I saw you, too." I erased the infinitesimal distance.

Asher was mine. I took him in, loving him into memory. I explored smooth planes of skin and bone, an atlas full of peninsulas and labor-sculpted valleys and muscle-wrapped hills. The sun-touched bit of chest peeking through his shirt. His sandpaper throat, smelling today of cedar and oranges. I kissed him there, let him trail his lips over the golden chains around my neck. But I didn't speak any words for long minutes. I didn't need any.

"She's home," I told Asher a short time later. We were snacking on microwave popcorn in the kitchen. The counter barely held enough room for the bowl and our two lemon seltzer waters.

My mother stopped cold in the entryway. Still in work clothes—skinny black pants and a pink cardigan—she held two grocery bags in her arms and a dumbfounded look on her face. She eyed Asher, then speared her attention to me. "You have…company."

I swung around the island, passing stacks of plates reaching nearly to my neck, and took the bags I feared she was seconds from dropping. "I do." I set them down and resumed my place next to Asher.

Load lifted, my mother flitted herself—eyes, feet, hands—around pods of mismatched items and began righting them. Nervous fingers pushed CD cases into rows. Papers were gathered into hasty stacks. She even grabbed an extra-large men's sweater, folding it neatly, laying it on top of a random tub. Was she actually trying to tidy up?

I lobbed a quick glance at Asher, my expression split between helplessness and shock. "Mom."

Like an industrious bee, she widened her reach to pick up clocks and cups and frames. She put them down again. Picked up more.

"*Mom.*"

Andrea Wells finally turned, but before I could manufacture any useful words, Asher stepped past me and walked up to her. "Ms. Wells."

Was she trying to place him? Had she noticed him at the play? My mother's face was long and vacant, full of confusion. She took his outstretched hand.

"I'm Asher Fleet."

She looked at me when I joined them. "And he's…"

"Um, Asher went to Jefferson. He's a fr—"

"I'm Darcy's boyfriend." Asher's declaration held enough power to raze the entire building. But I absorbed all the force, suddenly too hot, too piqued, too…*too.*

"I see," my mother said.

Asher flashed an amiable smile. "I really have to get going, though. It was nice meeting you." Then, to me, "Walk me out?" He gently took my arm and steered me out onto the landing, into the rising chill of a November afternoon. "No turning back now, huh?"

I shook my head. "I don't want to." I studied the closed door for a beat. "But that was just the preview."

"Talk about intense. I hate leaving you, but we both know you need to get right with her on your own." He brushed hair from my eyes. "I'll be back later. Our dinner reservation is for seven-thirty, and those hostesses tend to get pissy when you skip out on tables. Especially with prime ocean views."

"We wouldn't want to aggravate any restaurant staff," I said gravely.

"Never. And no doubt Marisol will want to tell you exactly what to wear down to the thread. You're gonna need time for that."

"She already knows, and I'm surprised she hasn't texted me a mood board by now."

Then, silence. Enough for both of us to worry ourselves over and under the reason for it. Enough for him to close the distance and kiss me softly.

"What you said. To my mom."

"Does that term work for you? Now?" he asked.

Boyfriend. "Right now."

His soft chuckle. "Thought that was the part that needed to happen next."

Thirty-One
Real

*"...but truth is best, and I want to tell
you only what really happened."*

—J. M. BARRIE, *PETER PAN*

I watched my mother work and worry around her terrible collection. I actually didn't blame her. Hadn't I brought more than just a boy into our home? "Mom," I said for the second time. Third?

Her eyes landed everywhere but on me. "A boyfriend. How long have you been seeing him? This Asher," she said softly, like she was testing the word on her tongue.

"Not long." But also for days and months, in every thought I'd had.

She held up the yellow legal pad; all my past and current eBay products were listed. "I was just beginning to get used

to the makeup and your little business venture. And now…
Darcy, I can't believe you brought someone inside."

Now or never. "Having friends and family over is what
people do. This is my home, too. And I'm not going to hide
it anymore. I'm going to start inviting people over. Bryn and
Jase and Alyssa and anyone else I want."

She switched to unpacking milk and bread and cereal, toying with her kitchen hoard with hands that couldn't seem to
move fast enough. She spun her own whirlwind, caught herself up in the center and breathed—wild and frantic. "But you
let him see this."

"Because it's my life." I pressed in like the walls. "And I'm
not going to hide it from him."

A low noise hummed in her throat. She dived her hands
into the other bag, grimacing. "I can't believe it." She held
up a plastic jar. "I'm so stupid."

"What?"

"I swore I was picking up creamy peanut butter, but I got
chunky by mistake."

Which she hated, along with grape jelly. Which every female in my family despised. If there was a Wells chunky peanut butter and grape-flavored anything hating gene out there,
we all carried it. "Mom, please."

"It's chunky."

"You can exchange the peanut butter."

She slid the jar across the counter until it banged against
the backsplash. "You let Asher inside."

"Should I have kept him outside forever? My own boyfriend?"

Caught and captured, she had to turn away. "I know. I
know. And I don't want to be this way."

My head throbbed. I pushed fingers into one temple and

thought of Asher. "I don't want you to be this way, either. But if you need to choose buying, I have to make choices, too."

Figurines, cloth napkins, salt and pepper shakers. She put her hands on everything again. "But—"

"I can't live here, with you, and hide my life anymore." I grabbed my tote again. "And that includes books." I pulled out a copy of *Jane Eyre* and managed to find a place on the coffee table for it. "If you felt you could store things in my space, then I should be able to read a book in the living room if I want. *Our* space. Or keep a few in places other than my room." I drew out two more novels, stacking them on the counter. "I'm sorry you don't want to read anymore, but I do." The last one in my tote was *Peter Pan*. I would never just leave it on the counter, but I held it up for emphasis.

The next moment opened like a snarly toothed mouth, so wide it devoured the room, hoard and all. My mother stared at me like I'd winked into a ghost. "Where did you get that?"

A film of damp panic coated my skin as I realized I wasn't the ghost—*Peter Pan* was. I gripped the cover, overwhelmed by memories.

Things I hate: Grape soda. Endings. Beginnings. Peeling nail polish. Beach sand. Grape-flavored anything.

Grape. My mother hated grape everything, and so did I. *Cran-Grape, eww,* I'd said to Marisol and juice boxes with the twins.

My mother's life was a constant wreck, but she never let her pale pink manicure chip. *Peeling nail polish.* The room closed in, ivory walls compacting again.

The beach, seaweed like mermaid hair, sandcastles. My eyes flew to the ocean-themed bracelet on my wrist. They beamed onto the sand dollar charm and then looked backward, over years and years, to when my mother would scrub sand off her feet in the chilly, seaside shower. She wouldn't tolerate even a few grains between her toes before getting in the car.

"Where?" Mom said again. "That cover with the silhouette was a limited edition and only sold in England twenty years ago." She took it from me and flipped open the pages, jerking back when she saw the scribbled ink, like the book had caught fire. "This was a gift. Where did you get it?"

"It's you," I whispered. The thoughts and poems. The truths and hurts and wisdom. "It was in the used books rack at Yellow Feather. You're the one who wrote in it."

Tears leaked from my mother's eyes. She inhaled sharply, hands over her heart. "When I had to get rid of my books—*your* books now—your grandmother helped me pack a few boxes." She pointed with a trembling finger. "But that one was supposed to go in the trash. The *trash*, Darcy. I was done with it." Her next words, so small. "Done with the girl in that book. The one who had loved your father. My own Peter who could never grow up."

"But...how...?"

"Your grandmother must've assumed I'd thrown it out by mistake. She probably took it from the trash and packed it in a donation box. That day, I was so distraught, she had to pick you up from school. I remember like it was yesterday. She stopped by Goodwill on the way with a couple of the boxes."

I remembered, too. The day I came home with my pink backpack and found her still packing up volumes. I'd begged her to keep them, and those books still lined my bedroom walls today.

She stepped forward. "I can't believe, after all these years, my *Peter Pan* somehow got into your hands."

I clutched the volume to my chest. "I needed it. I needed these words so much. They found me."

"Oh, Darcy."

"This girl in here. This girl was you. *Is* you."

My mother nodded.

Then the flames consumed me. "The question isn't where I got this book or how it found me. That's not *my* question."

"What? Darcy—"

"*No.* Where is the poet who wrote about love in a way that taught me some real truths about it?" One finger to her chest. "You taught me how to cover up the hard things. Oh, I learned how to treat people well, how to be loyal, how to work and overcome and survive, but I learned most of that from books. Stories taught me how to be a friend and a student. How to love and how I wanted to be loved back. And I even learned it from *this* book."

Andrea Wells had braced her arms around her body, like she was trying to hold herself together. I'd broken her, sliced her into shards, but I couldn't stop. I flipped through the pages. "Where is this woman, Mom? Where's the woman who hurt and *felt something*, who was honest with herself about the pain? Where's the poet and list-maker I found in here? The one who gave me advice and got me through hard conversations? Where is this mother? Because this mother, this woman, is someone I want to know." I shook now, whimpering. "She's someone I need now. I always have."

Her eyes creaked open.

"Where is she?" I demanded. "The mother in this book?"

"She's gone. The poems and dreams are gone." My mother picked up another useless item. "This is all that's left of her."

"That's not true. You think it is, but it's not." I opened *Peter Pan* to a random page, filled with her scribbles. "The man you wrote about in here—my father—he's not worth your hoard. No one is."

Her hands moved wildly, settling over her ears as her body swayed.

But she was hearing me. I knew I was unlocking doors that had been shut too tightly for too long. The book in my hands had keyed hope and change. "You're still this beautiful writer," I insisted. "You're still the reader who loved stories. Deep down, you're a mother full of words I need to hear."

"No, I'm not. I can't be. I tried and failed."

"You can start again. You can clean up everything. The mess around us, and the mess inside, too."

Rage swept her features. "Impossible."

I no longer believed in that word. "The man you loved is gone, but you're still here. You don't have to shop and collect things and hoard for him. It won't bring him back."

The rage exploded. "I didn't create this to bring him back!" She flung her arms wide. "This is not because your father left me. When David never came home, the grief shattered me. But that's not the reason for the way our home is. The way I am."

I grappled for air. "Then why? Because he left me? His baby?"

"No, Darcy. Because *I* left you."

Thirty-Two
A Long Time Ago

I broke my tooth on a shard of bone
and stepped into a mud puddle
in new, white shoes.
A long time ago I said a thing
and couldn't put it back.
I let the kiss end and the car start,
five seconds too soon, too late.
I unlatched the door of a metal cage
a long time ago.
Too late, too soon to grasp the yellow, battered wing,
the feet, the words, the heart
before they flew out the cracked open window
of you and me.
It was a long time ago—five years or
five months or yesterday.

—ANDREA WELLS, IN THE BLANK SPACE AFTER
CHAPTER 11 IN J. M. BARRIE'S *PETER PAN*

I wasn't certain I'd heard my mom correctly. So hungry for answers, I'd faced her directly and prepared my heart for anything. But her revelation was another kind of anything. "What do you mean, you left me?" My throat burned. "I've lived with you all my life."

Andrea Wells spoke to the carpet. "You were such a beautiful baby, Darcy. So beautiful."

"Mom."

She didn't hear me, and the words continued to spill out of her. "After I first had you, I thought David would eventually come back. He had to see you. But it got harder as you grew and that day never came. I was so devastated, so broken and alone. It took me over, and I started to…*envy* the fact that he was able to scrap all the difficult parts and move on." One hand flipped. "Just move away and forget I had ever happened." She pierced my face with wild eyes. "Forget you had ever happened."

My body squeezed and contracted. Sometimes truth was like this. Sometimes it pruned like a blade through growing things. "When?" I whispered.

Silence.

"When, Mom? Tell me."

"You were nine months old."

Oh. A baby. Just a little baby.

"I—we—were still living at your grandparents' house. One night, I…"

"Say it."

She shook her head.

"Say it. Once and for all." *Saying it makes it real.*

"I decided to run, too," she raced out, as if time and choice had finally caught up to her. "I chose to leave and start again, all on my own. I packed my clothes and left a note. I just *knew* you'd be better off with Grandma and Grandpa. They loved and cared for you, so much. I was such a failure, and you deserved so much more."

Nine months old.

"I got in the car and drove east. I couldn't stop. I wasn't even thinking straight. I slept in the car or stayed with friends, then even friends of friends. I was so stupid, so rash."

"But you—"

"I was gone sixteen weeks. I missed your first birthday." She held up shaking fingers. "After four months, I broke again. I was staying with an old college friend, and her sister brought over her new baby. I realized what I'd done and how unforgivably I'd behaved. I began to see around myself and suffered a terrible hole in my heart for you. For my baby. I called your grandparents and told them I was coming home as fast as I could drive." Step by step, she moved backward, sitting as the blue tweed couch met her legs. "Back to you."

Then, silence.

For the first time in four years, Grandma Wells stood in the doorway to our apartment. Bleary-eyed and disheveled, I moved aside to let her in. She sneezed and drew a handkerchief from her purse.

I knew she would come; some things were bigger than pride and boundaries. When I'd called a half hour ago, my voice taut with emotion, I asked her to do something that was probably the most difficult thing I'd asked in eighteen years: to come here and be a mother again.

Grandma—this woman who had mothered me for four months, and hidden it for eighteen years—stepped through the door. I led her through the walled path of boxes and gestured to the couch. My mother was burrowed there behind too many pillows.

"Andrea." Grandma Wells looked her over, shaking her head on a sigh.

Hearing the voice of her own mother, Andrea Wells lifted her head. "She knows. She knows what I did."

"Eighteen years, you hid this from me," I said, turning to Grandma Wells. "That night you decided to start telling me some truths, you left out the biggest one of all."

Grandma's face wilted, like delicate petals under heat. "I couldn't, Darcy. Your mother was already too fragile and un-stable. And it was her burden to share with you."

Mom stood in a tempest I didn't expect, raking hands through her hair. "Don't blame her. I begged her never to tell, made her promise. When I came back, I had to beg, too. I had to swear to my own parents that I could be a fit, caring mother. That I would never abandon you again."

I tried, but couldn't pull the words from my blood. They flowed on, part of me now.

Grandma Wells moved into my space and set both hands on my shoulders. "We allowed your mother to take you again, but watched her every move. We got her into her own place and urged her to return to work. She needed that. Grandpa and I took care of you during the day, but we noticed when she began collecting things. We tend to do that in our fam-ily, but with her, it was truly a *lot* of things. Still, at that time, it was nothing like what you live in now."

My arms spread wide. "If not because of my father, then why? How did it get to *this*?"

"Darcy, the more you grew, the more extraordinary you became," my mother said.

Extraordinary. I'd heard that word before, from lips I trusted more.

"I read to you every night, but at three years old, you were reading back to me. Not baby books—actual literature, light-years away from usual. You started reciting Jane Austen and Shakespeare in kindergarten and first grade, taking over English lessons at school—your teachers called me, dumbfounded. Then you started memorizing everything."

I nodded. "But what does—"

"I *left* you!" she cried. "I was given this extraordinary creature to love, and I was so selfish, I left her. Every child is a gift. No child deserves to be abandoned. But to me, you were the kind of child I didn't even dare to dream of having. Someone far beyond me. The kind who can change worlds with her brilliant mind and spirit." Her eyes flooded now. "And I came too close to missing out on all of it. Every book I picked up—pages you could read so easily—taunted me."

I pushed out a breath. "You felt guilty. So you rejected books because I was good at them?"

Mom looked through my room to her old collection, then back to me, finally nodding. This idea was so new, I couldn't speak any more around it until Grandma laid her palm on my back.

"Yes, Darcy. Guilt made this hoard, not lost love," she said. "Books reminded your mother of what she left behind."

"I tried," Mom said, her voice low and muffled. "I tried and tried to fill the hole I made. I'm still trying to fill it, fill my home over and over again. I have to pull things into my world, because it helps cover that ugly part who recklessly gave away just one thing. The most extraordinary and precious one. You."

Did she think the constant buying could change her into a keeper instead of an abandoner? I didn't ask—I couldn't, because my past flashed over the rest of my thoughts. "But you lied! When we went to counseling, the psychologist said you could begin to break the hoarding cycle by admitting the reason out loud. By owning it and moving on from there with all the coping techniques he taught us. You stood in that office and talked about my father abandoning you, and leaving this gaping hole you had to fill. But that wasn't the real reason or the whole story. That wasn't the truth."

I saw it now, clear as glass. "And that's why you've never been able to stop. Why all those techniques have only bandaged you, and us, but have never healed anything."

Then, to my grandmother: "And you—you *knew*. You sat there and listened to her half-truths and let them ride. Let us drown." I picked up items, throwing them, destroying them—I didn't care. "Drowning in wood, in plastic. In cloth and porcelain."

I grabbed my tote. It was my turn to leave. My family was good at it. Both women called after me, but I ran out into the dusk. No books came with me. I needed to fit myself into real life.

As the Honda's engine turned, images swarmed my head anyway. They wouldn't stop. Not from *Pride and Prejudice* or *Bone Gap*, or from any title from my bookcase. These scenes came from my own memory—from so many years ago and days ago and months ago.

When I was in the seventh grade, most of us turned thirteen. I got invited to a lot of sleepover birthdays because a couple girls decided that was the best way to celebrate thirteen, and we should all do it. I even went to some of them. October, it would've been my turn.

Spring of junior year, Bryn went rogue for three hours from rice cakes and protein powder. In a group text, she declared she was gonna jump in her car and raid everyone's pantries. *Be ready.* Marisol was waiting in her doorway with homemade plantain chips. People started filming the goofiest, giggliest Bryn ever, and we watched the edited montage of all her snacking videos the next day.

And just last week, Asher texted a last-minute idea to pick me up from my house for dinner at this cool café in La Jolla, before we went to Jase's party.

Two things were true about these events and countless more. First, none of them actually happened all the way. I'd made sure of that—no friends but Marisol ever came through my door.

As for the second truth—as much as I wanted to deny it, that truth wouldn't leave.

I screamed over it behind rolled-up windows. I plugged my ears and blasted metal jams I'd always hated, but I couldn't stop the deafening rush between my ears. Trying to ignore it did nothing.

I finally killed the engine and gripped the wheel. I couldn't escape. All I could do was listen. And when I did, that one truth shrank into three small words.

I knew them well. I'd said them to myself a lot this week. I'd said them to Marisol. But I had never said them to my mother. Did she even deserve them, after basically admitting we'd been living under a sham for years? Yes or no—it didn't matter. In this one way, we were the same. We'd survived and coped in the same way.

That, I understood. And for that, I would say the words.

But to say the words, I had to stay.

I creaked open the car door, my feet instinctively moving through the courtyard. The new table stood empty. I stopped and passed my hand over the slick white surface. No trusted friends sat here today. No mosaic cracks provided hiding places for my spills and secrets. But I didn't need them anymore.

I climbed up to our end-unit apartment, slowly, with quiet steps. I filled my lungs then turned the doorknob. From the doorway, I saw something I hadn't seen in more than four years. My mother and grandmother were embracing in a tight circle. They hadn't heard me; Grandma was brushing one hand over my mother's hair, whispering to her.

"Mom." I started like that.

The part that happened next began with my mother's look—her eyes wider than this room had ever felt, stretched to the skin and bones to hold so much.

I crept forward as Grandma stood aside. "I lied, too." Three words tagged and quoted by myself.

Mom shook her head. "It's not the same. You were just a child. Just a girl forced to deal with all of this."

I was so straight and tall here. My spine was an arrow, like that bracelet I'd shown Asher at Yellow Feather. "I pretended in all sorts of ways. I told school friends they couldn't come over because the place was being tented, or the carpets were being cleaned, or we were painting, or you worked weird hours." I marked lies with my fingers. "I said you had a thing against sleepovers. And before today, I didn't want Asher to pick me up at the door, because he might look inside, so I met him everywhere. See? It was easier to be invisible. People stopped asking, and I got out of situations when they did by lying. I faded away into words and books." I pointed to my bedroom library. "I hoarded them."

Her mouth parted.

"Yeah, let's use that word. Hoard. I *hoarded* them. And I let half-truths ride because I was ashamed."

I thought of Asher, the homespun warmth of his arms, the way his laugh jetted straight to my knees. *Write it however you want*, he'd said.

"I lied, but now I'm going to own who I was and who I am." That's how I wanted to write *me*. That's how the beginning went. And if I could get real about my past, my mom could, too. Then we could both change our future.

Mom pushed fingers into her temple. "What I did was so much more than a lie, and I can't see past it."

"This is what happens when you try to see past it." I waved my arms through the room. "Don't see *past* it. See *it*."

"Every day, I still…" She paused, her words watery and weak. "I still picture myself driving away."

"Leaving me was wrong, and nothing you or I can say or do can go back and make it right. But *we*—you and me—can be right. We can be okay."

"How?" she asked.

"You can be the mom who left me a long time ago, and then came home and never left again. You can be who you really are, too. Even if she's messy."

Her brows jumped.

I exhaled, a rough, caustic sound. "You're messy, and so am I." I pointed. "And so is Grandma. And everyone in my class, and all those ladies you put eye shadow and lipstick on. They're messy underneath. We all are."

Mom opened her mouth, then shut it. Maybe three or four times, turning her head into the hoard. But finally, she stood as steadfast as I'd ever seen her. "I left my baby."

It was enough of a declaration for me. And so true, I cried. She wound her arms around my back and pulled me close, into more home than she had ever made for me in this house. *Welcome.*

Quiet moments passed before her hand rose to my cheek. "How can you forgive me?"

"I think… I think I already did." That surprise opened like a gift, sweeter than birthday cupcakes.

She kissed my forehead and, for the first time in years, picked up a book. Her old *Peter Pan* rested in her hands, the cover butterflied across her palms—familiar, like she'd never truly grown up from it. "I'm ready to clear away some things. Inside and out."

"We need to go back to counseling," I said, her words running around and around my heart.

Grandma Wells stepped up between us. "I would like to go, too." Each of us nodded, making it so. And as we linked arms, with Mom's old novel in the mix, I thought of another story.

It was the one where an invisible girl left her library and found real life. And in the chapter after everything fell apart, a flying boy gave her a pen and a wide-open book as big as a globe. She wrote him into her most thrilling adventure yet, and edited all her *impossibles* into *possibles*. But his gift was so good, the girl passed it on. She gave it to her mother.

Later, I would share an ocean view with Asher and finally answer his question.

This one. *This* was my story, and it was my favorite.

Epilogue
Day Eight

Two Months Later

We hung out at the new courtyard table only on Saturday mornings, and only in one, carefully contrived manner. Marisol and I lay on the tabletop, feet dangling off the side, eyes lifted to a cloudless January sky. Her blueberry smoothie sat next to my large cup of mango, and the white resin surface stayed clean. From now on, all hearts and stars kept to the gold around our necks.

Lately, when I looked up to my end-unit apartment, I saw past the new gray paint and into a home that was transforming, little by little. There was more empty space than ever between the walls. But somehow, my home had never felt so full.

My phone rang, but Marisol was quicker. "Ha! I knew it. Flyboy on line one. I think I'll answer and see—"

"Give me that."

Dramatic sigh as she plunked the phone into my hand.

"Hey, you," I said to Asher. "Sorry it rang forever. Marisol was being... Marisol." I shot my friend a goofy look, which she lobbed back. Goofier.

Asher laughed. After a pause, he said, "It's day eight, Darcy."

"What? You mean...?"

I felt his dazzling smile through the line. "I *do* mean. How about lunch in Santa Barbara today? Will you fly with me?"

"Yes. Yes, I will," I said breathlessly. I glanced at my friend, who somehow already *knew*, her lip poked out and hands crossed over her heart.

"Come to the hangar. I'm already here starting preflight."

"Soon as I change. What does one wear for lunch in Santa Barbara and flying with a hot pilot?"

He chuckled. "Ask Marisol."

An hour later, I was kissing him from the best shotgun seat of all time. Then I let him work. We both wore headsets, and I marveled at his skill. The way he set controls and checked the majestic aircraft into safety, point by point. The way he communicated with the tower in a secret language, then taxied the Piper Meridian to the runway. He wore dark jeans and a thick navy pullover, requisite aviator sunglasses fitting his angled face.

Asher was always beautiful. But today, holding both our lives in his dream element, he was breathtaking.

While we waited our turn, he said, "I don't know when the next time will be. But today, I'm flying." He smiled. "And you're with me."

"Flying or not, I'm always with you."

At the tower's signal, he held up our storybook thimble, now at home on the console. I reached for the gold chain holding his acorn around my neck. Then he pushed the throttle and said, "This is the part that happens next."

★ ★ ★

Ten minutes in the air with him had me addicted. I relished the recklessness of chasing the wind with the boy I loved, riding the comet tail of his dream. I'd flown commercial before, but in the more intimate turboprop, the atmosphere coursed under my body.

"You like this, Darcy Wells?" Asher said into the headset.

I peered at a blue-jean sky and a watercolor horizon. We pushed north along the Pacific coastline, ant-sized life to our right, sapphire ocean waves at our left. "I love this." I looked at him, my heart whirling like the silver prop with all he'd given me—more than love, more than midnights with no spell-breaking clocks. He was the home for all my words, even the ones I hadn't defined yet. He was the home for all my stories, even the ones I hadn't imagined.

Possible. The word took flight, real and true. And right then, I decided to make his day eight, my day one.

"You keep paper in here, right?"

He pointed to a closed compartment near my right knee. "A notepad in there."

I pulled out the small yellow pad. It wasn't blue stationery, but it would do. The beginning *had* to be now. It had to be here. I grabbed a pen from my bag as my eyes filled. I would tell Asher everything later on a Santa Barbara beach. Now I needed to be alone with words again.

I declared them in my head and made them all the way true. Then the real-me started like this:

Dear David Elliot,
I'm your daughter, Darcy…

★ ★ ★ ★ ★

DARCY'S READING LIST

Pride and Prejudice
Jane Austen

The Book Thief
Markus Zusak

Jane Eyre
Charlotte Brontë

We Are Okay
Nina LaCour

The Hate U Give
Angie Thomas

The Sun Is Also a Star
Nicola Yoon

Water for Elephants
Sara Gruen

Caraval
Stephanie Garber

Looking for Alaska
John Green

The Remnant Chronicles
Mary E. Pearson

ACKNOWLEDGMENTS

Writing a book is anything but a solitary endeavor. I am finally able to hold my debut in my hands and share it with readers because of the support and contributions of so many people.

To my agent, Natascha Morris, thank you for being my fiercest advocate, often-editor, steadfast supporter, pep talk orator, guacamole conspirator, and the finest representative of my work.

To my editor, Lauren Smulski, thank you for loving Darcy's tale the way you do. Your vision and guidance have inspired me to be the best storyteller that I can be.

To Allison Bitz and Joan F. Smith, you are so much more than critique partners. Thank you for sharing your talent, time, expertise, friendship, and your lives with me. I am better for being on your team.

To the team at Inkyard Press, special thanks to Natashya Wilson, Laura Gianino, Justine Sha, Linette Kim, Jennifer

Lopes, Lisa Wary, and Connolly Bottum. To Erin Craig and Elita Sidiropoulou for making Darcy's library come alive on my cover. There are so many involved in creating such a beautiful representation of my story, and sharing it across many platforms and across the world. I appreciate all of you.

To Jessica Faust, James McGowan, and the whole team at BookEnds Literary.

To Beth Ellyn Summer, for plucking my book out of your Pitch Wars pile, and being the very first to mentor me and my story.

Dear writing community, I value you and thank you for guiding me through the many aspects of publishing. Special thanks to Elizabeth Van Tassel, Kelly deVos, Heather Cashman, Nikki Roberti, Aimee Salter, Rachel Lynn Solomon, Mara Rutherford, Hannah Capin, Alechia Dow, Eric Smith, Vicky C., Autumn Krause, my Pitch Wars family, Team Nat agency siblings, and #Novel19s debut group.

To my dearest friends, old and new, and my wonderful family. I treasure you.

To the McCauleys, for filling me with music and friendship.

To Ximena Avalos, for being my Marisol.

To my beloved husband, Ed, for your unwavering support, and being my faithful coffee courier and real-estate book source.

To my children, Alec and Kate. I am blessed to be your mother, and you make me so proud.

To my own extraordinary mother, for more things than I have time and space to list.

And finally, but never lastly, to my father, who instilled in me my love of reading. One day, I will get to tell you about my book. And to God, who holds you close until then, and in whom I am never lost.